Praise for *The Elusive Tr...*

"Joanna Davidson Politano brings Edwardian England to life as she matches silent film star Lily Temple with handsome underground investigator Peter Driscoll. Readers will be captivated as they follow Lily and Peter's journey to solve the mystery of the Briarwood Teardrop. Romance, mystery, and clever twists and turns will keep readers turning pages until they reach the very satisfying ending. Well-written and highly recommended!"

Carrie Turansky, bestselling author of *The Legacy of Longdale Manor*

Praise for *The Lost Melody*

"*The Lost Melody* serves a pitch-perfect blend of history, romance, mystery, and faith."

Booklist starred review

"Joanna has masterfully given life to those who had no voice and has captured the essentials of the human soul. You will be inspired, encouraged, and moved to remember that God always has a plan, even when you are in the darkest of places."

Interviews & Reviews

"Joanna Davidson Politano perfectly balances faith amongst the very dark backdrop of an asylum to write a beautiful tale full of struggle and triumph."

Fresh Fiction

Praise for *A Midnight Dance*

"Politano writes beautifully, evoking the magic of ballet and the theater from the opening turns to the final curtain, leaving readers applauding for an encore."

Booklist starred review

"*A Midnight Dance* is a beautiful ballet theatre story with hints of mystery woven in, just one more stunning masterpiece by the talented writer Joanna Davidson Politano."

Life Is Story

"With mysterious fires, legendary figures, and an uncertain future intricately tied to the secrets of the past, Politano deftly weaves together beloved gothic literature tropes and original ideas with a generous sprinkling of luminous story magic."

Christianity Today

THE ELUSIVE TRUTH OF LILY TEMPLE

BOOKS BY JOANNA DAVIDSON POLITANO

Lady Jayne Disappears

A Rumored Fortune

Finding Lady Enderly

The Love Note

A Midnight Dance

The Lost Melody

The Elusive Truth of Lily Temple

THE
ELUSIVE
TRUTH
OF
LILY
TEMPLE

a novel

JOANNA DAVIDSON POLITANO

Revell

a division of Baker Publishing Group
Grand Rapids, Michigan

© 2024 by Joanna Davidson Politano

Published by Revell
a division of Baker Publishing Group
Grand Rapids, Michigan
RevellBooks.com

Printed in the United States of America

Library of Congress Cataloging-in-Publication Data
Names: Politano, Joanna Davidson, 1982– author.
Title: The elusive truth of Lily Temple : a novel / Joanna Davidson Politano.
Description: Grand Rapids, Michigan : Revell, a division of Baker Publishing Group, 2024.
Identifiers: LCCN 2023041225 | ISBN 9780800742973 (paperback) | ISBN 9780800745691 (hardcover) | ISBN 9781493444823 (e-book)
Subjects: LCGFT: Christian fiction. | Romance fiction. | Novels.
Classification: LCC PS3616.O56753 E48 2024 | DDC 813/.6—dc23/eng/20230911
LC record available at https://lccn.loc.gov/2023041225

This is a work of historical reconstruction; the appearances of certain historical figures are therefore inevitable. All other characters, however, are products of the author's imagination, and any resemblance to actual persons, living or dead, is coincidental.

Baker Publishing Group publications use paper produced from sustainable forestry practices and postconsumer waste whenever possible.

24   25   26   27   28   29   30   7   6   5   4   3   2   1

To my children,
the unwitting recipients of a wealth of stories,
fables, and wild imaginings, as well as a great
many adventures. Thank you for humoring me.
You enrich my stories, and my life.

1

Life itself is the most wonderful fairy tale.

~HANS CHRISTIAN ANDERSEN

Whitestone Manor, Hove Seaside, 1903

I hadn't decided if I'd tell the whole truth or not, when the men arrived. Peter would have, because he's *Peter*. I, however, never let facts hinder the power of a good story. Like water, innocuous and common, a good tale rushes forward, carving its own path through rock and hill and sod, sculpting the earth into a bold new landscape before anyone knows what is happening. Where Peter used silence, patience, and unending *goodness*, the best weapon in my quiver was the pointed truth, driven home by the arrow of a well-told tale.

Truth has many facets, anyway.

Such as this place, for example. I sat back against the French provincial sofa, sipping orange blossom tea and appreciating the details of the well-appointed withdrawing room. It did not brag outright but held a subtle air of opulence, lace dripping like icicles off every surface, crystal accents hanging here and there from lamps and curtains. Solid mahogany furniture from the earlier years of Queen Victoria presented a shabby yet comfortable air. A steady Mozart tempo crackled over the gramophone, and a thick blanket spread over my lap kept me quite warm, along with the fire popping in the hearth.

Yet what an unmitigated disaster the place was from the outside. The half-abandoned, old country estate rambled more than Aunt Agatha on a winter's eve, with crooked turrets hanging off jettisoned walls, crumbling facades, and a pile of bricks that had once served as steps. Whole sections of roof were missing in the closed-off wings.

Ah, the deception of it all. That was life, though—the stories you tell yourself, and the stories you present to onlookers. Rarely did the two match. We're all of us a combination of romance novels, humorous tales, and tragedies, depending on what angle we show the world.

Me, I preferred adventure stories. Tolerated a romance now and again.

Another sip, citrus flooding the senses, and the front door clattered open—the men were back. I clutched the cup handle.

It was time.

My scattered brain thought of Peter again, his steady, watchful look that penetrated the fluff and pomp of my stories, my silly misdirections, seeing the truth immediately. I shivered in my damp clothing. In a way, it was to his benefit that he was locked up just now, and he could not interrupt my story or correct it.

It was all for him, anyway. For wretched, foolish, overly principled, utterly irreplaceable Peter Driscoll. Not that he completely deserved it, mind you—this rescue attempt. The man might be guilty of a great many things—petty annoyances and rude infractions and the like. Killing me, however, was not one of them.

The shucking of rain gear sounded, and the growl and tromp of a man in the corridor. I sipped. Waited. The parlor door banged open, and there stood the muddiest uniform I'd ever seen, worn by a giant of a man who looked mad as hops. "What . . . what . . . who *are* you?"

I dropped another sugar into my tea and gave it a good stir. "I'm Lily Temple, Mr. Mutton, and I'm here to help you."

He stood like a wide-eyed fool, dripping mud and rain upon the worn rug. "But you're in *my house!*"

"The most logical place to find you, sir."

In another twist still, the grand old conflicted mansion was, in fact, a prison. A temporary holding place for criminals of the Brighton and Hove areas while they awaited transportation to their own personal miscarriage of justice at London's Old Bailey.

My Peter being one of them.

"I'm not one for trekking over field and farrow to chase a man down, especially in a storm." I straightened on the horsehair sofa, shoving aside the lap blanket and tucking my booted feet beneath the sofa. Anchoring myself. "I've come to speak with you about a prisoner, if you could spare a moment. Maybe two or three, since the weather will keep you inside anyway. Come and sit, I've made a fire."

Still, he stood and dripped. "How in blazes did you get in here?"

"The door." I paused for a sip, and it warmed my insides. "I'd have to break a window otherwise, and I didn't cotton to the idea of shredding a new shirtwaist on the shards."

His gaze swiveled to the window as if to assure himself that rain did indeed patter on the thick glass panes, then back to me. "That door was locked."

"Indeed it was. Oh, how uncouth of me—there now, let me fetch you some too. Have you another cup?" I sprang up and walked to the cabinet where I'd found mine. "Do you take sugar?"

He took four steps in my direction, wood squeaking under his heavy boots, eyes narrowing in a rocky old face as his gravelly voice rumbled in my ear. "Get out, ye fool woman. *Now*."

My hands closed around a cup, and I paused, breathing deeply of stale air. "After you've heard me out."

He wouldn't agree to it, though. I could tell by the look on his face.

He'd live to regret it. Lily Temple did have a few more aces up her sleeve.

The man yanked the empty cup from my hand and hurled it to the floor, stalking away. "Who the dickens do you think you are?"

"I told you. I'm Lily Temple, and it's in your best interest to hear me out."

His eyes went wide at the name that was only now registering. "You're . . . you're . . ."

"Stubborn?" I strode right up to him, the clicks of my boots resounding through the emptiness. "One hundred percent. And there's something you must know about Peter Driscoll. He isn't guilty and it's terribly vile, you holding him here this way."

He stared, pale and wide-eyed, then snapped back to composure. "I'll not be convinced of *nothing*, ye hear? They pay me too well to keep them locked up, and I won't ruin that to release 'em. Not even one. They're a dangerous lot, these prisoners."

I laughed. I couldn't help myself. Perhaps it was everything at stake, my taut nerves . . . or the idea of Peter Driscoll being called *dangerous*. "They pay you in what, lodging?" I glanced about the dusty old manor house–turned-prison.

He scowled over his shoulder. "Driscoll killed a woman—did you know that?"

"Did he, though?"

He looked down, then back up at me, quite obviously confused. Scrambling to understand. Or deciding whether or not to believe the name I'd given him. "Exactly sixteen different witnesses say he did. And he stole a priceless gem from her. The Briarwood Teardrop, no less. No magistrate in London will let him off. Not unless he dies before he reaches the gallows, God guard 'is poor soul. Mark my words, the man'll swing for it."

I dropped my teacup, which shattered on the floor.

Boots pounded by the front door. "What was that?" Then yells, echoing through the empty halls. "Here. It was in here."

Oh good, an audience.

Mutton thrust me toward the door. "Out, out, *out*! I'll not be caught with some little chit on my hands, all kinds of trouble to pay. Go on, out with you."

"But my story. You haven't heard it yet." My voice echoed in the narrow hall. "It's rather a good one."

He lunged with a growl, grabbing for me. He struck a three-foot vase instead.

Crashhhhh.

I froze. He froze. Wings flapped somewhere above in the roof-less towers. Water trickled in distant places.

Voices . . . then stomping. Six or seven men poured through the doorway, including a red-faced Constable Willis, trench coat flapping. "What's this about, Mutton?" The towering bearded giant looked me up and down. "The deal was, *no women*. You're on your last warning, man."

13

And wait—who was that behind him? A rather dukeish-looking gent, with a very familiar golden crest upon the breast of his overcoat. It must be one of the infamous Marlborough House set, the fast-living social circle of no less than King Edward himself. The *king*. I tingled to my fingertips.

Audience, indeed. This would be *perfect*.

Poor Mutton still blubbered behind me. "She ain't—she's . . . she's leaving." He shoved me down the hall, palms rough against my shoulder blades, and I dug in my heels, stumbling as he pushed.

As if sheer force ever derailed the locomotive that was my plans. I ducked and twisted toward the men. "Check his pockets."

He shoved harder. "Out, you fool—"

"Wait a moment. What was that, miss?" The constable stepped toward me, shoving his open palm toward poor Mutton to silence him.

"I said . . . check his pockets." I stood arrow-straight, arms folded.

The guard's face was darker than the storm outside. With a low growl that made my hair stand on end, he kept his eyes on me and reached into his right trouser pocket, then his left. Pulled out the fabric lining of both.

"The other pocket, luv." I pointed at his chest.

He jammed a hand into his frayed waistcoat and lifted a long, dangling necklace by its chain. Upon sight, he flung that thing like a hot coal and stumbled back, colliding with the other men.

There it lay, the setting of that legendary Briarwood Teardrop on the worn carpet, six men hulking in a stunned half circle around the ancient gold piece, the swirls and leaves that were so recognizable now. Only, the large blue stone was prominently missing.

"But . . . where's the sapphire?"

They looked from the delicate gold piece to the man who'd dropped it, and back again as the thing wove its spell in the air. Distant thunder rumbled across the sky and rain torrented against the old walls. The clock ticked forward the awkward silence. Who would make the first move?

After thirteen ticks, I decided it must be me.

Always a woman who did the doing, wasn't it?

"I suppose you'd like to hear about this, since you are about to transport the man who supposedly murdered me and stole it."

"You?" Constable Willis blurted out the word, then slowed his stride toward me, looking me up and down. "You. You are . . ."

I stepped closer, feeling the power shift directly onto me. I quieted my voice, for it did not need to be loud now. I would be heard. "The roads are nigh on impassible just now, especially for a prison wagon. I'm surprised your horses have gotten you here. I should think a good story might pass the time. If Mr. Mutton can spare a few moments to hear it now."

Silence. Then the constable invited me back to the sitting room with a single jerk of his head.

I swept past the men and collected cups from the corner cupboard, kicked aside the broken shards, and poured plenty of tea.

The men filtered in, new arrivals silently boxing in the resident guard who was now tangled up in the gem mess.

Poor man glared. Snarled. "I know what you're about, and I'll not be manipulated. I don't believe you're Lily Temple, and the prisoner will *not* be released." He shifted, leather holster creaking. "There were witnesses. Plenty of witnesses. He had a gun. And a motive. He had a way in, and he knew how to get it. And you don't look a thing like Lily Temple."

"Every story has its layers. You'd do well to remember that. Sugar?" I dropped in two cubes before he could answer and handed it over.

He took it and I settled myself on the edge of a springy old chair, gripping the arms for all I was worth. I was an actress, a professional storyteller, here at the holding cell of a condemned man, armed with naught but a story. And hopefully the wits to use it well.

The dukeish-looking gent downed his drink as one who knew how to do it, then leaned across the table, elbows planted in the middle. "So, Miss . . ."

"Temple."

"Miss Temple. Right, then." He scanned my face as if to confirm or deny my identity. His narrowed eyes indicated he'd aired on the side of doubt. Surely I didn't look that different, did I, without the grease paint and costumes?

Yet he made no move to release Peter of the murder charges. Or even pose a few questions to his supposed victim.

"I'm interested in hearing what you have to say about the sapphire everyone in the world would like to lay hands on. The one that belongs with that necklace." He jerked his head toward the other room. "Where is it now?"

"Well, now. That would be giving away the end of the story." I poured him more tea and moved the sugar toward him. "Shall we have a listen?"

Mutton collapsed back onto an ancient chair. "You'll not listen to a fool *woman*, will you? With no less than sixteen witnesses—"

"And this?" I lifted a large blue stone from my purse, and the room hushed at the sight of it. Again I felt the power of that sapphire.

"Is it—?" the magistrate began, but I let the wondering hang in the air.

They looked back and forth at one another, as if debating whether or not I was actually parading a priceless gem before them. The stone flashed and sparkled with brilliant reflections of light, a deep azure color that looked like it had indeed been ripped from the sky, as the legends claimed.

I smiled at the blustery fellow. "He who has all the answers will never ask questions." I held it up between two fingers. "And he who doesn't ask the questions forfeits a wealth of knowledge." I covered the stone with my other hand, and with a flick of the wrist it was gone. I held out both empty palms. "Because even your eyes deceive you, and the truth is rarely obvious. But stories . . ." With a smile, I leaned forward and plucked the stone from Mutton's collar, holding it out to the watchers. "They tell us the truth our eyes miss."

"You put on a fine show, Miss Temple," said the crested, duke-like man calmly as he accepted the blue stone, inspecting it critically. "But you'll need more proof."

"You keep it." I jerked my head toward the blue stone. "A fine imitation, don't you think? Enough to catch a man's attention for a moment. Worth about two quid. I'll take my prisoner, though, seeing as I'm not dead."

"That isn't possible, Miss Temple. We simply haven't the proper authority to invalidate an arrest once it's made. You'll have to bring your proof to the authorities and let justice take its course."

"But I'm—"

"Nothing you could say will convince us to break the law and release him this moment, to risk our positions and reputations, so you'd best not waste your time."

"Don't be so certain. You haven't heard my story yet." I settled back in the chair, looking over their dubious expressions. "Now, then. The mud will keep us here awhile more, I'm afraid, and you are all curious, even if you're not admitting it. I trust I may proceed."

I took their silence as consent and drew in a breath, settled in, and peeled open the memories. "It began in the spring, when George Smith was setting off hot-air balloons and musical nights at St. Anne's Well Gardens, and Peter Driscoll happened upon me by accident. Or, so I thought."

It was easy to slip back into the story of him—the story of us. In some ways, my life hinged on that moment, and everything that had happened since. Even if I never again saw Peter Driscoll's face, if he was never released and—God forbid, perished in Newgate—I'd never in a million moons be the same woman I had been that night in the well gardens.

2

When we get to the end of the story, you
will know more than you do now.

~HANS CHRISTIAN ANDERSEN, "THE SNOW QUEEN"

t returned to me in film clips, short snippets sliced and pasted
into one heartrending reel. Glittering gowns, flashy smiles,
and the glow of electric lights strung like man-made stars
overhead at St. Anne's Well Gardens. The orchestral music driving our steps in dizzying circles, great throngs of people . . .
and a fabled blue gem.

It had begun as a fairy-tale piece, a prop for one of George
Smith's fantastical cinema films, but whispers had started
among the wealthy visiting Hove's shores. There was talk of
the gem being cursed, and of it being a stolen artifact from
another country.

But for now, for this night, it was my bauble, secreted on a
chain about my neck. I wore it beneath my gown as I'd done
so many times.

Gypsy Lee had predicted that a man would approach me

to ask about the necklace, calling it the Briarwood Teardrop, and that this man would be significant. She didn't say it, but I knew what she'd meant—this was a dangerous turn for me. Someone was onto me.

Yet as the night neared its close, not a single man had questioned me about anything. No one had mentioned the gem. I felt the smug satisfaction of realizing the brightly clothed fortune teller—the great Gypsy Lee—had been wrong. All these months of living at St. Anne's Well Gardens, she in her caravan and I in Grasshopper Cottage, and this had to be a first.

She'd once predicted the unusual pairing of a duke with a lady he had not yet met, and they had crossed paths soon after on a train platform and later wed. Just a few years ago she'd claimed His Highness's coronation would not take place as scheduled, and eerily, Edward had indeed fallen ill, needing to postpone the event. She prided herself especially on that one, and had earned national attention for it.

But this? She'd crossed her tea leaves. Not a soul had bothered about me.

Then, a whisper in my ear. "I say, there's a man asking after you. Has he found you yet?" Bertie, my co-star, sidled up to me. He was a spirited little string bean of a man with a great poof of dark hair that always looked as though it had barely survived a windstorm.

I released my breath and flashed him a smile. "How curious. Who is this man? I know no one in Hove outside of the lot of you."

He elbowed me good-naturedly. "A fine lot we are to know too. Who else do you need?"

"The man, Bertie. Which one was he?" He did veer off the point more often than not, but he was a dear.

"Right, the man. That one, over there. Said his name was Draper."

I donned a mask of amusement, scanning the crowd as if it was all a lark.

And it was, wasn't it? Some jokester. A man angling for an introduction to the newly discovered actress. Our fairy-tale film series with the sapphire had done well, drawing in thrice the crowds of previous shows by the second installment.

Yes, a lark. That's all it was. I wove my gloved hand into the crook of Bertie's arm and let him lead me around. There were gawkers aplenty that night, smartly dressed bankers on holiday, solicitors and business owners, tight clusters of barons and baronesses with sparkling smiles to match their gems . . .

And one lone man who did not belong.

My vision snagged on him. About fifty or so, mild of manner and long of face, a knowing stare that lingered.

He'd found me.

On my free hand, my fingers curled into a fist. My cheeks suddenly hurt from smiling. Why was I so afraid, though? He stood an entire crowd away from me, stirring a drink and idly passing time. I could slip out now. There were so many people here. So many people between us.

I leaned back toward Bertie. "The one in the brown tweed?"

Bertie squinted in Draper's direction. "Yes, that's him. Didn't seem to know your name, as it happens, but he pointed you out specifically. Asked if I knew you well."

"You told him no, I hope?"

"Naturally. Who can even begin to know the multifaceted Lily Temple?"

I breathed out the tension and bumped his arm with a smile.

Bertie fidgeted beside me, tapping his glass until I wanted to knock the thing from his hand. Dratted nerves. "Where's Mae? Haven't you asked her to dance?"

His eyes scanned the crowd and gentled when they settled on the plainly dressed costume modiste with loose curls down her back. She stood near the tables, swaying to the music, stealing glances our way in little sips.

Fingers drove through his poof of hair. "Suppose she'd say yes?"

"The moment she's asked." Men could be so blind.

"To this ordinary bloke, even?"

"And no one else."

He heaved out a breath and straightened. "Very well, I suppose I could give it a go. She could use a turn about the gardens, pale as she is. If you'll excuse me." One arm boldly across his chest like a soldier, he departed, leaving me alone and vaguely smiling.

I turned and there was that shadowed face, closer now. Maybe three paces away. The man, Draper, didn't look my way, but he knew exactly where I was. Whether or not I moved. Something about the way his glance flicked in my direction every so often . . . he was watching me. Pretending not to, but watching.

I turned on my smile the way we switched on the electric lights in the pump house, slipped into the crowd of dancing guests, and spun from partner to partner, laughing merrily.

The Fourth Royal Irish Dragoon Guards played tonight, driving energy into the old place. Into me. It was a grand life, one luxurious in natural beauty and intriguing work, clever amusements and interesting people. It might go on forever.

Lily Temple was invincible.

Another spin and I collided, laughing, with a woman in red silk damask. "Oh, I beg your pardon."

"Oh, not at all, not at all. My, how wonderful to find myself crossing paths with the famous Lily Temple! I've seen you from across the gardens, but never at close range. Oh!" Her eyes rounded. "How well they disguise your nose in films."

I steeled my smile in place. "Well."

"It's quite pretty in the flickers, and I can't imagine how that George Smith carries it off. But then again, he manages so many thrilling illusions with those tools of his."

The woman in scarlet prattled on faster than a stallion's gallop, but my mind strayed to the unsettling form to my left. He was closer now, staring more openly. I snuck glances his way, keeping watch.

Rather unremarkable looking to the outside observer. Wasn't smiling, wasn't dancing. But even as he talked to some foppish man with a too-wide smile, responding to a joke, he was watching. Aware of me.

I'd evaded him a number of times before, in other settings, bearing other names, but his eerie calm as he approached me this time unsettled me. Who was this Draper?

I stared too long, and his gaze found me. Caught my eye. Winked.

I spun away. And then I happened upon what would be the second man of import that night. I laid hold of the nearest unattached guest and pulled him along into my whirl. Dance partner . . . shield . . . utter stranger.

For now.

And that is how I met Peter.

3

The prince, charmed with these words, and much more with the manner in which they were spoken, knew not how to show his joy and gratitude; he assured her that he loved her better than he did himself.

~CHARLES PERRAULT, "THE SLEEPING BEAUTY IN THE WOODS"

Lily swept into Peter Driscoll's life like a storm. Not a driving rain, but a thick, swirling snow delightfully obscuring one's vision from the ordinary world. He was there among the well-dressed crowds at St. Anne's, then suddenly he was twirling with her, caught up in her rhythm, yanked out of his steady reality.

"Get me away from here." Her words were low, direct, breathed close to his ear as they waltzed, and they ignited his protective instincts. He felt his shields go up, his defenses tighten around her. She was shaking. Poised and self-assured, but trembling. Her eyes darted about, landing time and again on some man near the fringes who was most decidedly watching from beneath the brim of his bowler.

A gentle pressure from her hand and they were twirling, twirling away from the crowds, her white gown flaring at the bottom and sweeping leaves and cut grass as she spun them toward the shadowed wood. "Come on then, follow my lead. Don't step on my feet."

And away he twirled.

For twenty-eight years, his life had been far too easy and uncomplicated, and that's why she'd come into it. Of that he was immediately certain. Slight and feminine with an engaging face, she swept one up with surprising pull, a centrifugal force he was disinclined to escape.

So this was Lily Temple.

When he'd seen her on film, she'd blinked across the screen as a charming yet simple, rather silly little fairy-tale character, but to hold her in one's arms and experience her—expressive and potent—was to know she'd merely played a part before the cine-camera. She guided him toward the woods with power no onlooker would notice, but which was impossible for him to ignore.

Just inside the trees a single trail was lit, but she veered into the shadows off the path. He paused and ruffled what he assumed was dirt from his hair, straightened his jacket, brushed flitting critters off his face. She returned and grabbed his arm, pulling him along what he hoped was an actual path winding away from the main one.

Yes. Yes, there was gravel beneath his feet.

He had the odd notion that this lovely creature had come from the forest, sprung from its blue-black foliage, and now she was bringing him along to see the fairy-tale world of her film.

Through the trees they wound, branches and underbrush snagging his suit, until at last they reached a large clearing, a hill where electric lights and a few lanterns on poles beamed over a structure made entirely of glass. For a moment, his mind wandered from the debris likely lining his pockets, and he took in the large walls before him.

She pulled him toward them with two hands holding his, walking backward and inviting him on with a playful smile. "Here we are." The fear had gone and now she glowed, her white-gold embroidered dress shining satin in the starlight. "What a gallant rescue. You don't mind, do you? It has saved me a great deal of unpleasantness."

"Not at all." He pulled a twig from his hair. "Might I escort you somewhere? Make certain you're safe?"

"How thoughtful." Her smile was serene. Controlled. "I couldn't accept, though. Not after I've already stolen you from the gala." The soft lilt of her voice threw a filmy veil over the accent of some distant part of England—London's working class or somewhere northern and rural. The moors, perhaps. "One difficulty a night is the most I'm willing to cost a man."

"Truly, I wouldn't mind. In fact, I'd quite prefer it to leaving you here alone. It's my duty to protect."

She stiffened, looking him up and down. "You're with the police."

A light laugh. "I most certainly am not."

"Then why so protective?"

"Does it bother you?"

Her eyes narrowed. Those lovely, slanted green eyes that snapped and shone. "I suppose not. Only . . ."

"Only?"

"I can't imagine the reason for it."

She was one of those. Being given something for nothing was not part of her world. He should leave rather than remain here alone with her—she'd be more at ease. So would he, come to think of it.

But then a silent impression came, swift and clear, from somewhere deep at the core of him, where God dwelled.

Stay.

Listen.

He clasped his hands behind his back. "At least allow me to keep you company for a few minutes, until I can be certain you're safe. Please."

Her tiny smile, albeit hesitant, was lovely and disarming. "I suppose I could show you about. You seem perfectly harmless. And I'm rather a good judge of character." She lifted a lantern from one of the poles and led him up the hill.

Harmless, was he? Peter pinched back a smile as he strode behind her. Some called him ineffectual and bookish, silent and lacking in might, but only because they didn't know what real strength looked like or from whence it came. He followed her to the little glass house, looking up at the moon streaming through branches.

"I suppose this is what you want to see. Everyone does." Her voice echoed inside the walls. "It's the film set. George Smith's famous glass house. All the magic begins here." She stood in the center, turning about with her arms extended, and her white dress fairly glowed in the lantern light. Her honey-colored hair shone like gold. "Isn't it glorious?"

"Indeed."

"Even more so in the daylight, believe me. You won't likely see it then, though. I've had to sneak you back here, and we have the benefit of darkness to cloak us. No one is allowed here ordinarily, mostly because dear Smithy's afraid something will happen to the place. I suppose that's the risk you take, building something entirely of glass, but the poor man doesn't always think of practical things like that." She shook her head, flashing a white smile. "He's brilliant, but a bit eccentric at the same time, you know. I suppose we all are, in a way. Me, I think I'd build a house of crystal rather than glass, with prisms everywhere." Her smile was wide, eyes bright. "Just imagine the sunrise in such a place!"

My, how she went on. But after a lifetime in his dreary old manor home where even the air seemed heavy, he could listen to her lilting voice for an eternity. It was soft and delicate, which only invited the listener to draw near and hear better. "I'm sure there's a reason he built it the way he did."

"For the light. The natural sunlight." She turned, pointing just outside the front entrance. "He even laid down little tracks so he may rotate his set to follow the sun. It pours in through the glass, and with it he can create anything his mind has dreamed up. None of the rules apply to George Albert Smith, you know—not of physics or of man. He can pull off any illusion and make his films tell whatever story he wishes. Unbelievable illusions and tricks of the lens."

"Sounds rather a dishonest business."

She bristled, those high cheeks standing out against her piquant features. "No more than any form of art. He simply creates the story he wishes to tell, much like any writer crafting a sentence or painter putting oils to canvas."

"Only the stories he creates are quite sensational. Men flying into the face of the moon, a disappearing woman, him taking off his head and placing it on the table beside himself . . ."

"Four times."

Peter ran his hands along one wall, rapping on the thick glass with one finger. "I beg your pardon?"

"Four heads removed four times and placed on the tables beside him. Carried on a conversation with himself, he did. Isn't that clever?"

"It's deception."

"It's innovation." She eyed him. "Before you go and judge—"

A scuffle of leaves. She spun into his chest, hiding her face like a hunted fox as some creature skirted through the woods.

He took the lantern from her hands, set it on the table and let his arms hover about her, boxing her in, yet loose enough for her to break free. Enjoying her soft hair tickling the underside of his chin. There was something infinitely valuable about this one. Something rare and shining that was worth guarding. "I told you I'd protect you," he said. "Did you not believe me?" She reminded him of a delicate bit of sea glass glistening alone on a dark beach. The sort that had been weathered and polished in the water, tossed and smoothed, but was liable to shatter upon the rocks.

Her fingertips danced against the lapel of his jacket, then she stepped back, looking up at him. If she was ruffled by the indecency of it, she hid her embarrassment well. Or perhaps she was bold enough not to be bothered in the least. For all his skill, he couldn't read her. Not yet, anyway.

Tipping her head just so, she moved farther away and beckoned him. "Come. I've decided I like you well enough to show you one more thing." She picked up the lantern she'd fumbled as if nothing had happened. She left the glass house and ran ahead through the undergrowth and weeds along a narrow wooded path, again giving the impression of a sprite who lived among the trees.

The woods opened onto a slope looking down over a great dewy field alight with flickering green orbs. She lay on her stomach and propped her chin on two fists, looking down over the meadow. How many times had he seen glowworms? Yet never like this.

He knelt beside her on the grass, hands anchoring him, and gazed down at the shimmering field. Tension melted into the ground beneath him, and silence reigned.

"Magical, isn't it?" she breathed.

"Indeed." And it was—every bit of it. The cool carpet of grass he hadn't felt since boyhood. The light breeze scented with wildflowers. The very ridiculousness of crouching here, alone, beside this neatly dressed sprite so full of charm and warmth.

He had a sense of breath returning to his body, as if he'd been holding it for years without realizing it. A nightingale cooed, and the woods echoed with its song.

This was the gift, wasn't it? The reason for the prompting he'd felt to protect this woman. It wasn't *her* who'd needed rescuing. God wished to grant him this glimpse of serenity, of perfect beauty. To remind him, perhaps, of how far he'd strayed from this and what he might attempt to find again.

Her soft voice floated into his thoughts. "Such a mirage, isn't it?"

"Hm?"

"In broad daylight, they are bugs. Wretched little beetles without the sense to do more than attract a mate and make more of themselves before they die. Yet at night when they put on a show for us . . ." She spun onto her back and looked up at him with those blazing green slits of eyes. "Can you imagine anything more romantic?"

"I . . . I . . . no."

"I once heard it said that they fall in love, these glowworms."

Her voice softened. "The passion in their hearts is what lights their little bodies, to help their beloved find them."

"A delightful fairy tale."

"You do not believe in fairy tales?" Doubt colored her face, as if his hesitation toward the more fanciful pieces of fiction was a flaw in his character.

"I read books—many of them. Novels, even. But I lean toward tales that have something to say about life. About God. Dickens on the horrors of the poorhouse. Elliot on the plight of women. Fairy tales are quite removed from our reality."

"Are they, though?" Her head tilted to the right. "Love and violence . . . twisted family secrets . . . great, epic love stories that climb to a climactic, ironic tragedy and end often without happiness. They may not be real, but they are true."

He took her in as a whole then, white and nearly glowing in the moonlight, subtle sparkles on every edge and fold of her gown, warm golden hair tucked up under a glittering headpiece.

She brushed her fingertips over the cool blades of grass. "Insects *cannot* fall in love, of course. But it is true that passion is bright. Contagious. It attracts as a glowworm's tail does and at times it's useful for lighting someone's way. I never forgot that."

"I see."

She set her truth by fanciful tales. She was an actress with an accent not quite from here or from there. She had remarkable poise, yet trembled at the sight of one nondescript man watching her from the shadows, and never, ever seemed to lower her façade.

"So, Miss Temple. What's your story?"

She rolled to her side and propped her head with one hand, catching her smiling lower lip between her teeth. "I've had a hundred of them. A star blinking out of reach, a foolish house-wife whose stove explodes, an elf stealing gems from a bride."

"Not the flickers. Your true story."

"They were all true. At least for a fortnight or so."

He leveled a look her way.

"Oh, you spoilsport. You wouldn't believe the truth, any-way."

"Probably not. But try me."

She sat up and leaned back on her hands. "You've heard of the chalybeate springs, of course. The miracle water that draws every desperate hurting person to this very garden for healing. Well, years ago I took a larger sip than normal, you see, and it has changed me. For the better."

"Has it, now?"

"I should say so. Can you keep a secret? I'm actually eighty-seven years of age, with eighteen children and three homes, and I've outlived no less than seven husbands. I could be a walk-ing advertisement for the springs, but I won't let poor Smithy make sport of my good fortune. That's the sure way to have it all reversed, you know, flinging your good luck about. And I'm not much for bragging, of course. It never adds to a woman's beauty. Especially at the age of eighty-seven."

Peter felt a smile overtaking his face. "That is the most dar-ling 'never you mind' I've ever heard." She was a tonic, and he was quickly becoming addicted to little sips of her. He wished for more—for gulps of her story, told in that lovely singsong voice. Her *true* story. He had the sense it would be memorable.

He looked out over the field of glowworms and felt suddenly that he too existed within a fairy tale just now. Despite the questions surrounding this woman, the warnings nagging at his mind, everything seemed right in the world. His soul alive.

Then her voice came again, a story emerging in the style of old ballads. "There once was a most noble and heroic pair living in the darkest days of France. A pair of matched souls destined to form a bond in the midst of chaos, two lights of righteousness in a wicked world. It was their very goodness that made them equals, for they both suffered horrible injustice and stood up against it."

Peter sank back onto the grass from his knees. "And it was through this pursuit of justice that they came together."

"Indeed. It all began with the girl's father, a kind, aged doctor, innocent as the wool of lambs, who'd seen naught but the inside of a prison for eighteen years. He'd done nothing to earn it, save angering the men in power—those with pound notes in their vision and lead in their chests.

"Then one day he saw the most beautiful sight—the sweet face of his daughter, Lucie, all grown and lovely and there to smuggle him back into the world again. Lucie Manette was lovely of nature and of face, and a delight to everyone who knew her. Yet she'd had a hard life, believing herself orphaned—until she discovered her father lived, and rescued him.

"They escaped together, sneaking out of France aboard a boat in the dark of night. They were nearly caught, but they happened upon the very noble man of the story—the deeply troubled, strong, and well-intentioned Charles Darnay. He aided their escape. And thus, their love story began."

It was Dickens. She was telling him a Dickens serial novel, but he held his tongue, afraid to puncture the moment. Somehow it was a different story altogether, spoken in her voice, and she told it with a guarded caution, as if she were sharing something important. Personal.

"The noble stranger guarded Lucie and her father from the

soldiers and ushered them to safer shores, with no thought to his own safety. He had deeply troubling secrets of his own, but he threw in to rescue the pair and see them to England.

"Of course the family grew to consider this Darnay a friend, knowing little about him but his kindness. And in time, as you'd expect—"

A bell clanged. Two, three times. It echoed through the sparse woods, jarring him from the enchantment of the moment.

4

"Just living is not enough," said the butterfly,
"one must have sunshine, freedom, and a little flower."

~HANS CHRISTIAN ANDERSEN, *THE COMPLETE FAIRY TALES*

jerked fully upright. "The film. They're about to start it."
Scrambling, I stood and grabbed his hand.

"We'll never make it back down the hill in time."

"You're right." I tensed, mind racing. "Come, this way. We can still see it." I ran through the trees, off the path, and deeper into the woods, weaving through the way I knew so well.

My poor companion was not as adept. "Wait. Miss Temple, wait." He ducked and dodged as he climbed through the bramble. He'd miss it. Did he realize how brief these films were? Five minutes at most.

He huffed the rest of the way up and stood beside me, looking down over the octagon-shaped bandstand, and the suspended white sheet rippling slightly in the evening breeze. The trees were sparse up here, and the view clear.

"We have the best seats in the whole place," I whispered,

lowering myself to the grass and wildflowers. I patted the space beside me. "Come, watch with me."

The violins began with one long, somber note, then the clarinets and cellos joined, setting the ambiance for the images that would soon flicker on the screen. Lights flashed against the sheet as the film projection began, clear images of myself and the others, and the audience applauded.

The Enchanted Garden and the Gem, in six parts

"I'm afraid I've missed the other parts," he said. "You'll have to tell me the story."

Eyes focused on the screen, ready for the first glimpse of the fairy tale, I whispered the parts he had missed. "It's about a beautiful garden—an *enchanted* garden. That man there, he's the gardener. He planted a great many flowers, and they were beautiful, but they did not speak with him, keep him company. He tried to coax them to, but all they did was nod and bow, like so."

The lovely tulips and hyacinths bowed in the gentle breeze on the screen.

"So he planted more seeds, and he read to them. Sang to them. Fed them with flower petals and other beautiful things. And this time, he grew a little fairy."

"How magical."

"Don't ruin it." I swiped at the grass near him. "Now look, see the fairy waking in the grass?"

It was me. Lily Temple, but not Lily Temple. My flower petal gown, hair done up with ivy and sprinkled with something glistening. I watched his face, pleased to see he was already enchanted. Engrossed.

"She has found a looking glass that shows her another world, and she wishes to go to it. She's restless and wants to see more than the gardens. To fall in love." I paused as the fairy on the screen approached the gilded looking glass hanging in the branches and placed her hand on its surface. A large city—London or Paris, perhaps—showed within the looking glass. Tall buildings, cobbled streets, smartly appointed carriages and horses. The fairy reached up and touched the glass's surface, head tipped tenderly to the side as the music swelled to emphasize the importance of this discovery.

The garden had been colorized through long, painstaking hours of hand-painting each frame. I myself had tinted the flowers, and how vibrant they appeared in this projected version. How thrilling. It made me catch my breath. Yet the world beyond the looking glass remained in a dull sepia wash.

"That's brilliant. The two worlds on one screen—how has he done it?"

I smiled, pleased the images playing out silently on the screen had managed to captivate him in spite of himself. "I cannot reveal that secret. It's a trick of the film." I leaned back against a tree.

"Ah. So what about the gem? How does that figure into the story?"

"It's the only way to pass between the two worlds. The fairy watched the gardener do it once, and now she wants to try. But he doesn't want her to do it."

"Of course. Is it a rock from the garden?"

"In a way. In the first film, the gardener stretched his hand up into the clouds, broke off a piece of the sky, and pulled it down. He used it to help the seeds grow. And once, to visit the world through the looking glass."

"All that from a mere rock?"

I shushed him. "There's more to it than that. Watch."

The sounds of the distant orchestra fell over us as the silent story tugged at my heart, inviting me into the moving pictures.

◆

The fairy, her wings wilted behind her, motions toward the looking glass. The gardener shakes his head no, and firmly leads her away. She repeats the request, gesturing pleadingly, and again he says no, then he leaves her. He conceals the blue stone in a chest and locks it, placing it up on a high shelf in his potting shed.

The fairy returns to the looking glass, perched on a stump before it. She touches it with her fingertips. The glass ripples and her fingers slip through, into the other world, but remain colored. She reaches out and touches several things in the bleak world, and she colorizes what she touches. A soft glow of green lights a patch of grass, and a bicycle floods with a lovely red at her hand.

A noise, and she pulls back. A white rabbit in a neat little green jacket comes to stand at her feet in the garden. The fairy pets the rabbit but remains dejected. Then the white rabbit stands on his hind legs, and gestures toward the shed.

"Look there, on the shelf!"

She straightens, face alight. She spins in the grass, then runs off toward the potting shed.

But wait—a creature stirs in the shadows. A dwarf steps over his floor-length beard and approaches, raising his arm, palm out, motioning her to stop. He shakes his head as he points to the shed. The fairy gestures with her hands, indicating the shed, and then the looking glass, trying to make him understand her need for the gem.

Again, the dwarf shakes his head and points her out toward the garden.

> **"Stay away from that gem, and the looking glass!"**

Tossing back her head, the fairy twirls into the garden behind the shrubs. But as soon as the dwarf is out of sight, the fairy slips out. She sneaks back to the shed, pries open a window, and emerges moments later, holding the gem and the key to the chest. Her face is victorious.

She stops, she looks. Someone is coming! The fairy slips both items into the folds of her flower petal skirt and greets the gardener with a smile, swaying back and forth as they talk. She takes one step back—then two. She waves goodbye with her free hand and slips through the trees, toward the looking glass that awaits her, a flash of blue in her hand. The fairy swirls her skirts, the orchestral music swells, and with a cymbal clash and a chorus of violins, the picture fades as sun glints on the looking glass.

"A dwarf. And a human-like rabbit. How did he manage all that?"

I smiled. "The dwarf he hired as a bit actor. The rabbit is a marionette with very thin strings. It's all for effect, of course."

"Hello? I say, is anyone in there?" An unfamiliar masculine voice sounded in the distance.

I stiffened, poised and alert. "They've seen us." I scrambled to stand. "We should go. They'll worry. Or be cross that I've brought you here, one of the two."

"Of course." He rose and offered his arm, helping me down the hill.

At the woods' entrance, we found the voice. A man stepped into view and straightened, brushing off his suit coat with a frown. "There you are, Pete. I was half mad with—" His gaze latched onto me, and not with pleasure. Sleek gray hair topped a well-groomed yet aged face that registered every judgment he was too well-bred to speak. "I do beg your pardon, madam. I didn't realize Mr. Driscoll had a companion."

"Ah, it's you, is it?" My rescuing stranger cleared his throat. "Miss Temple, this is my valet and good friend, Roderick Heath. Roddy, I'd like to introduce Miss Lily Temple of St. Anne's Well Gardens. She lives here on the grounds and performs in George Smith's flickers."

I blinked at Driscoll, this man who had collected small droplets of facts about me and put them together rather well. And me, not even knowing the man's name until now.

A quick flare of the intruder's nostrils was the man's only acknowledgment as he scanned me again. "I hope you aren't forgetting your work, sir."

"Actually, I'm doing it." His nod indicated me.

His eyebrows, arched and silver, shot up. "I beg your pardon. Is there a threat about these gardens? I hadn't realized."

I folded my gloved arms. "The likes of you. The world is full of your sort, all righteous and seated on your high horse as you prance by us poor unfortunates and turn up your nose at those you believe beneath you."

Another flare of the nostrils, and he turned to his master. "She has rather a lot of opinions, hasn't she?"

"Rather." I frowned.

Amusement turned my companion's mouth up at the corners as he slid between us. "Let's not spoil a perfectly fine evening."

"It isn't as if you're here to play at heroics, sir. You've a matter to handle, I'm afraid."

Driscoll froze the man's words with a stare, willing him to bite his tongue. "Have I mentioned that Miss Temple," he began, "happens to be one of the finest actresses outside the theaters? She's known as the queen of the flickers."

"Beg pardon, Highness." Roddy bowed at the waist. "I shan't mistake you for a common stage actress again." He straightened and shot his master a raised-brow look. I wondered what he was saying.

Driscoll pressed his lips together and gave a single nod.

Then Roddy tipped his hat. "Well"—he stepped back— "I'm never one to be the third wheel. I'll ready the driver and wait for you by the carriage, milord. I trust you can find your way without encountering too much trouble?" His gaze slid back to me.

Driscoll clapped the man on the shoulder. "I'll be along, Roddy."

"Very good, sir." With a crunch of leaves, the man moved stiffly away, leaving us to the quiet of the enchanted woods once again, and my companion turned to me, expression brimming with thoughts.

"My apologies, Miss Temple. He hasn't much diplomacy to go with those opinions, but he is a most worthy valet."

"Valet . . . or chaperone? He's worse than an old biddy with a fresh charge." Lily was upset. She stood with arms folded and stared at him.

"His distaste for women—all women—is unparalleled, as is his protectiveness of me." Peter sighed, shaking his head. "I tell you, all it took was one bride leaving me on one set of church steps, and suddenly all women are evil."

She sobered, her lips pressing into a little rosebud. "I'm terribly sorry."

"Don't be." He waved it off, hand going to the back of his too-warm neck. "It was a long time ago, and it taught me caution." Which he didn't seem to be using this night.

They started back on the path, the electric lights coming into view in the distance. Comfortable silence settled between them.

Then, "I do appreciate the rescue, Mr. Driscoll, despite the trouble your valet seems to think I've caused you."

"Think nothing of it."

She glanced his way as if he were a riddle too complex to solve. She wished to ask something—he could see the question waiting to emerge. Why? Why put his valet in his place on her account? Why go to any lengths to protect a woman who was nothing to him? *Because I'm a gentleman* would not ring true to her ears, so he did not state it.

Yet a great stillness swelled inside him even now—a cool, quiet knowing that spread rapidly through him. *Stay. Watch her*, it seemed to say, as it had all night, and he knew that voice. That prompting. "Say, I wonder if you might do me a favor. I'm in need of an assistant of just your coloring and disposition. Suppose you accompany me on an assignment, and in exchange I'll pose as your suitor for the rest of the night. No man you find offensive will come near you."

She perked. How vulnerable and hopeful she looked, standing straight as a swan on that path, with her eyes and cheeks shining in the lantern light. Did she even realize it? Strength and frailty danced together beautifully, and he wanted to safeguard her. If only she'd let him.

But she looked away, toward the clearing where the military band continued to play. She crossed her arms, a wall between them. Her vibrant independence had once again arisen, a buoy bobbing between her and any man who might offer rescue. "I have work already. I love it here, and dear Smithy would be lost without me. I will not desert him. Not for anything in the world."

"You needn't leave your work here. I only ask a few hours of your time."

Still, she eyed him. "Why should I spend my spare time on you, of all people? No harm intended, but you look rather an ordinary sort. I would guess your work is the same. I don't believe I'd enjoy it."

"What if you did?"

One dainty eyebrow rose. "What is it you do?"

He tipped his head, studying the woman who might flit away with one wrong word and, with a deep breath, let the truth fall out between them. "I am, Miss Temple, the finder of lost things, pursuer of truth, restorer of what's been broken."

She watched him for another moment, sizing him up in a quick flicker of green eyes.

Quiet. Wait. Listen.

"Not everything bears restoring. It goes against the natural order of things."

"On the contrary, Miss Temple." His steps slowed. "God designed this world to undergo constant restoration. That *is* the natural order. You see it over and over again in Scripture."

Her folded arms tightened. He'd angered her. Offended her. "You don't believe in God."

"He is to me what fairy tales are to you. I simply don't see the point in pretending."

He moved closer, looking down over the moonlit planes of her face. "You, lovely storyteller, are missing out on the greatest narrative in history."

"The one where the world is wicked and everyone dies? Where every story eventually turns into a tragedy and he doesn't do a thing about it?"

"I've heard writers say that their characters jump up and take on a life of their own. They deviate from the story their author has plotted out. Mightn't God face the same problem? But either way, he uses people at times to set things right. I hope to be that sort of person."

She turned away, seeming not to hear him. But she suddenly lifted her face again. "I shall call you Jack."

"My name is Peter."

"Jack, because you remind me of a little flicker called *The House That Jack Built*. Oh, it's interesting enough, seeing a tower of blocks knocked down, then watching it magically rebuild itself, but it isn't exactly the way of things in the real world." She paused, fully invested in the conversation now.

"You see, we film the tower being knocked over. Then we stop the camera and feed the film through in reverse so that it looks like the topple is reversed and the tower rebuilds itself."

"An illusion."

"What else could it be?" She shrugged. "Once a thing is destroyed, there's nothing for it but to leave it alone or make something new. Either way, the old one is finished."

He watched her face. Peered below the layers, willing his mind to perceive whatever it was she was trying to hide. To rationalize, perhaps. "My offer stands. My help for yours, and you can see the sort of restoration I do."

She turned from his challenge, a smile lighting across her face. "I believe I can take care of myself for the rest of this evening, but you are a dear to offer."

He gave a small bow and stepped back. "Very well then, I shall melt into the crowds and never bother you again." He had the fleeting sense as he watched her that her life was a stick bridge made for delicate trodding, and a wrong step would cause the whole of it to crash into the rapids below. And the waters surrounding her life, he guessed, were treacherous.

He reached the edge of the woods alone and she emerged into the large clearing beside him, then shrank back at the sight of something. She turned and clung to his arm with both hands. "Well, don't just disappear on me."

The man was back. The one in the brown suit who stood at the fringes and watched. Peter's arm slid naturally around her, and he laid his hand over her clinging ones. "Shall we say nine of the morning tomorrow?"

She pressed her lips together and cemented her hold on his arm. "Half past, and not a moment before. I'm not ordinarily on speaking terms with early morning."

With a nod, he led her out into the open. "There is one other matter I'd like to inquire about. Your necklace, actually—the one you wear beneath your gown. Have you ever heard of the Briarwood Teardrop?"

She stiffened.

He'd brought it up too soon, obviously. He'd expected surprise, perhaps denial, but not the utter horror that flashed over her features. Soon the mask was back in place, she was smiling, and he was left wondering if he'd imagined it.

"My necklace?" Her smile froze in place as her fingers flitted around the slender chain. "Oh, it's nothing. Just an old bauble I can't bear to part with."

"A sapphire you call a mere bauble?"

She stilled. Lifted the necklace from beneath her gown. Eyes focused on him, she dropped the gem into her hand and held it up, moonlight blinking off every smooth facet in a way that was nearly blinding. "See? A bauble."

"It's . . . enchanting."

She smiled, pleased at his answer.

"It's the one from the fairy tales, yes?"

She nodded.

"Where did that gem come from?"

She held it up toward the sky, as if fitting a piece back into a puzzle. "See where that darkness is? That little hole? That's where it once belonged. It was pulled down from the sky in an enchanted garden, a small piece of the place to take with you when you leave . . . and to bring you back. That's what I was told as a child, and somehow I cannot unbelieve it." She sighed. "It's of another world."

"I've seen the fairy tale, Miss Temple. I'm wondering how *you* came by it just now."

She shrugged. "At times I like to borrow it. No sense it sitting in a box by its lonesome, which is where it's usually kept."

"And how did you manage to go about getting it out?"

Her grin rivalled the twinkling stars overhead. "I don't give up my secrets that easily."

But she would. One day soon, he would hear them.

5

I am under no obligation to make sense to you.

~MAD HATTER, IN LEWIS CARROLL,
ALICE'S ADVENTURES IN WONDERLAND

A pregnant thundercloud shielded the moon from his view as Peter ran out to the carriage. He pulled open the lacquered door before the driver even noticed him, and climbed up, bouncing the leather seat as he settled.

Roderick's look was grim in the shadowed carriage. "Bad news, Pete."

"You don't care for the woman."

"Worse, I'm afraid. Someone's after her."

Peter sighed and settled in the seat. "Tall, cheap, hiding under a bowler hat?"

"Tried to pay me to keep watch on her. He wanted to know everything I knew about her."

"It's a good job you haven't anything to tell him, then."

"Oh, Roddy had plenty to tell him." His white smile shone in the darkness. "None of it true, mind you, but I told it all anyway."

Peter exhaled and flashed him a smile too. "Well done."

"He offered me ten pounds to inform on you, Pete. He wants to know when you're with her, when you're not. What you speak of."

"Is that all I'm worth these days? Well. In any case, we won't be helping him."

He sighed. "I expected as much. But . . ." He flipped a metal object, and Peter caught a shiny pocket watch. "He gave me collateral."

"Roddy, how could you—?"

"Don't tangle yourself in knots, Pete. I'll give it back. I had to let him assume what he wanted to assume. In the meantime, see what you can find out from it."

Peter lifted his eyebrows in appreciation, then turned his attention to the watch, flipping it over. *S. Draper* was etched on the back, with a special swirl to the *S*. "Draper . . . Draper . . . I know that name. How do I know that name?"

"You're forgetting yourself, Pete." He shook his head. "Your case? You said you had some matter to see to."

"That I did." He reached into his pocket and pulled out a few folded pages and handed them to Roderick. "Lady Claire Mansfield, Dowager Countess of Wiltshire, has hired me to make discreet inquiries into the gem she saw in the film. She believes it's her stolen sapphire, the—"

"The Teardrop? You don't mean to say . . . after all this time, the Briarwood Teardrop has been located?"

"It has been nearly twenty years, but she's positive she can identify it, if it is her gem. She sent me to get a look at it. Discreetly, of course."

"And you thought spending the evening with one of the fairy-tale actresses a good way to accomplish this?"

He smiled in the dark. "I did. Especially since she's the one currently in possession of it. For the evening, at least. I was standing at her elbow, ready to ask a few polite questions, when she actually spun directly into me. Pulled me into a dance and asked me to hide her. Then we walked and talked. She showed it to me."

His eyebrows shot up, mouth slightly aghast. "Just like that. A legendary gem that's been missing for decades and she simply . . . shows it to you?"

Peter sighed. "She claimed it was a piece of the sky, taken from the garden of another world."

"So she has no idea."

He shook his head. "She hadn't any notion that I'm an inquiry agent either, for most of the evening, which is all the better for me. I have to find out who she is. What her connection is to this stone."

"I've seen the gem on display at the gardens. Assumed it was the property of the theater. The producer, perhaps."

Peter shook his head. "He's happened upon it, quite some time ago, but there's some connection to Lily Temple. She mentioned stories she heard about it in her childhood, so she's known of it for years. But George Smith, the film producer . . . he's only happened upon it at the gardens within the last year. Dug it up in a box, he said, along with a book of fairy tales. One of which is the current film."

"So they don't know what it is either, do they?"

"They all think it a lark, this fascinating blue rock that's too large and perfect to actually be a real gem. It's merely another sideshow for Smith. Miss Temple . . . well, she believes what she believes about it being enchanted."

"So what did you find out? Is it—"

Peter stiffened. "My coin purse." He patted his chest, every pocket. Down to his trouser pockets. "It's gone." There was no feel of soft leather, no familiar bulge, and he rapped the carriage roof with his fist. "Driver, hold to the right, please."

They'd barely made it a block with all the congestion around the garden, so Peter leaped out onto the walk, having some idea where his purse had got to. He walked quickly through the gates and up the path to the olive green caravan with faded curtains and scrolling designs painted on the sides. After a hard rap, he stood back, waiting for the fortune teller to appear. The door opened and a large feather protruded first, then long brown curls over thick shoulders.

"Yes, luv?" Gypsy Lee, St. Anne's resident fortune teller, was colorful and comfortable, a person who had settled into her widening frame without concern. "Ah, it's you."

"Shouldn't you have known it would be?"

She came onto the steps with one hand on the rear wheel, which was overgrown with weeds and grass, not having moved in at least a decade. "Well, then. Did you find her?"

He nodded. "I did, and I am grateful for the information. I'd also be grateful for the return of my coin purse." He held out a hand.

She shoved it away and put hands on hips. "None of that, now. What would I want with your coin purse? I take visits from the king of England, I do."

He stood back, studying the woman's rounded face, then admitted with some surprise, "You're telling the truth."

"And why wouldn't I?"

"I just can't imagine where else it could be. I hardly came near anyone all night."

She crossed her arms. "There was *one* other."

51

"Scarcely anyone besides Miss Temple, actually. I—"

Her lips thinned.

"You cannot mean that *she* . . ." His eyebrows rose. Now *that* he hadn't expected.

"Things have a way of disappearing around that one."

She'd evaded his every question into the details of her life, but these weren't the conclusions he'd drawn. "You're saying . . . you're suggesting she's a common thief."

Her mouth curled into a knowing smile, highlighting the apples of her cheeks. "Oh no, sir. Nothing common about that one."

6

"I can't explain MYSELF, I'm afraid, sir," said Alice,
"because, I'm not myself, you see."

~LEWIS CARROLL,
ALICE'S ADVENTURES IN WONDERLAND

I stared down at the lovely daguerreotype, touching the pictured woman's serene smile, her rosy cheeks. It had arrived this morning by way of a little messenger boy, along with a gown, hat, and gloves and a note asking me to come near as I could to resembling the woman. I'd done a first-rate job of it too, by my estimation. Yes, Lily Temple could play any part.

What story would I tell this time? I spun in the frothy chiffon gown with a pointed peach-colored sash that seemed a bit much for day wear, but I felt lovely. Princess-like. Nothing resembling my usual blue serge skirt and shirtwaist.

I adjusted the chiffon so it hung gracefully over my shoulders and stared at the woman I had become. My own father wouldn't recognize me.

How that fact ached at times, in these quiet moments. With

no camera lens on me, no filmstrip before me to cut and color, reality caught me in a chilly embrace.

My childhood had been lovely. Incredible, in some ways. But the camera had panned in a slow circle until the landscape now, years later, was changed entirely, and the familiar cast had fallen away. Only strangers remained. Not a single person in this garden even knew my real name.

But the necklace. The sapphire bridged the two worlds— then and now.

Chest tight, I yanked open the little drawer beside me, and my fingers spidered through linen handkerchiefs and head wraps until it felt the familiar cool surface of the necklace. I held it up to the sun-filled window, watching the large blue gem glitter in its own unique way, just like a star. I tried out the name on my tongue—the Briarwood Teardrop—and wondered idly if that's what it was.

A piece of the sky. It looked every inch that description. Taken from the heavens above the enchanted garden, the one where my childish self—had that truly been me?—had been utterly happy and complete. I slipped it back into the drawer and remembered in an instant when it had belonged to me. Not rightfully, but it had.

And then I had given it up.

I regretted the fateful moment I'd chosen to bury it, tucking it into that little metal box and placing it in the hole way up on the hill where the glass film set now stood. Safekeeping, I'd thought at the time, and that had been the case for some years. But then someone had found it when they'd begun construction, and true to all of George Smith's art, the charming little gem had entered into his films.

And thus it had drawn me back here.

Yet . . . how different things were. There was no larger-than-life man tending the rose gardens, and the necklace technically belonged to Smith now, since he was the leaseholder of the gardens. Or perhaps to the Goldsmid family, who were the land's deeded owners. I hadn't considered that when I'd left it behind.

Regret was a poison that never left the bloodstream.

The ache tightening in my middle did not release until I stepped out into the garden, and once again the atmosphere of the place rolled over my senses—dewy blossoms, bright bursts of color, and butterflies exploring the wonder of each quiet garden in turn.

Just like the sapphire, the garden might never belong to me, but I belonged to it. And it was still possessed of the same magic that had drawn me and filled me with life every day of my childhood. No matter what happened outside these gardens, the busy streets and crowded blocks, this garden was largely untouchable. A haven for the soul.

Just behind the yew tree, a little pale face peered out at me. There was a broken place in the metal fence, near the tennis courts in the rear. I'd found it by accident on a walk and so, it seemed, had this urchin. More than once.

I smiled and hummed, pretending not to notice the girl. I had become, much to my delight, the fairy tale spinner of the gardens, and many local children hung about to hear them during the day. I poured into them the delight I'd breathed in as a child, here in these same gardens.

But this girl had never let me approach. She had an uncanny ability of disappearing, and I'd always let her. Once I'd been able to tell her an entire story while she hid in the hedgerow near my bench, but otherwise she ran like a hunted fox when I approached.

Yet somehow, this girl with the wide eyes and long dark braids reminded me of my younger self. There was a lost quality about her expression—a longing. And her haven, clearly, was the same as mine had been.

By the time I'd passed her, my spirits had buoyed, and the ache had left completely. There was something about this place, about the stories that seemed to roll through the green grass and rain down from the flowering trees, that was healing. No matter what. Clearly, I wasn't the only one who thought so.

As I neared the end of the garden path, it came upon me that I was about to reenter the world. That I'd agreed to leave my garden and its muffled safety.

The man—the one in the bowler hat, who had watched me through the crowds—was out there somewhere, and so were all the people I'd known in the past. People who knew who I was.

Perhaps leaving the gardens was a mistake. A terrible, no-good mistake.

I'd be with Peter Driscoll, though . . . but somehow even that brought a vague worry. I couldn't lay my finger on it. Wasn't he the most moral and utterly ordinary person that ever was? Surely no harm would come to me from him.

I stayed tucked into the shadows as I approached the gate, scanning the empty street.

"Fine morning, isn't it?"

I jumped, heart exploding, and clung to that gate. I turned toward the round, smiling face of Urania Boswell Lee, known about the gardens as Gypsy Lee, and blew out a breath. "What a wretched tease you are. It's far too early in the morning for such frights."

The old Gypsy woman laughed, curls bouncing. "I never seen

the before-high-noon Lily Temple. Dancing-in-the-moonlight Lily a time or two, and late-for-tea Lily all the time, but this is a surprise. To what do we owe the pleasure?"

"I'm meeting someone."

Her face lit, lips spreading across slightly crooked teeth. "Ah, the story continues. It is *him*, yes? The one I told you would come?"

Panic cinched like a belt around my middle, my vague fear clarifying in an instant. It hadn't been the odd man in the shadows who'd asked about the gem, had it? It had been him. Peter Driscoll. There had been such an ominous tone to her prediction. And now I was going who knew where with him.

"He is coming for you, is he not?"

"You needn't seem so pleased."

"Ah, it isn't anything Lily Temple cannot handle. Go and tempt the danger." Her eyes sparkled, earbobs jangling. "Then dodge its blow, the way you always do."

I sighed, leaning my shoulder against the bars. I was one for poor decisions, it seemed. I simply kept making them.

Well, I could unmake this one.

"If you'll excuse me, I believe my bed is beckoning me after all." I turned on my heel to face my garden, but the thrumming chug of a small locomotive pulled my attention. A flash of black and red appeared around the corner. There he came, sailing down Terrace Road in a cherry red contraption puffing steam like a train closing in on Charing Cross Station.

Peter Driscoll sat with leather driving cap and goggles behind the wheel, tall and elegant, a scarf flung over one shoulder. That sleek machine slowed, a real horseless carriage coming to rest at the side of the road, waiting for me. For *me*. A flutter of excitement propelled me on, and I was clambering onto the black leather seat, inspecting every lever and latch, before he could offer me a hand up.

He came around to assist me, tucking the edges of my borrowed skirt into the vehicle. A blanket was laid over my lap to protect the gown from the road. "Ready for your assignment? It isn't a long drive. Just over to Brighton, actually."

I ran one hand over the arched leather seat beneath me. "You can take me anywhere you like in this thing. What is it?"

He gave a sideways smile as he crossed back to his side of the vehicle. "A Stanley steam car. Of sorts, anyway. An American invention. I pieced it together from a few prototypes discarded by friends of mine."

I bit my lip, trying to hide my awe.

He walked around the front of the contraption and motioned back to me. "Hold down that lever, won't you?"

He threw open the little trapdoor on the front and grabbed the hand crank, forcing it into motion and picking up speed as I did as he said. He gave it a few more hard cranks, then slammed the bonnet back down over the engine with a wide grin. "That's it. Well done."

He climbed in and I clung to the seat and braced myself, watching him shift two smaller levers, tap one of the many round gauges until the arrow spun, and settle in. "How fast does this thing go?"

"It runs on steam, like the steam engine train. It can get us from here to the coast in about five minutes."

I gasped.

"Not to worry, we won't move that fast through Brighton. That's only for the long country roads." He yanked down on another lever, leaned forward, and the steam car jerked ahead, rumbling down the road at the pace of an old nag, but with a great deal more noise. Steam puffed and swelled behind us and before, and I imagined for a moment we were flying through clouds. The air was like a curtain as we drove—a soft, cool one lying against my face.

I drank it in for a moment, the thrill of it. Then I turned to him and shouted over the rumbling engine. "So what exactly is this favor? You never said."

"Didn't I?" His gold spectacles winked in the sunlight.

What a cad. Well, I could clam up too. He'd gotten very little out of me last night concerning the necklace, and for that I was infinitely grateful. Or perhaps he was punishing me for that very thing now.

I clung to the seat. "This woman in the photograph. Perhaps you ought to tell me who she is."

"Her name is Adelaide Walker," he said over the rush of steam. "She's the daughter of Charles Wallace Walker III, one of Bristol's most wealthy shipping merchants. She was engaged to a soldier, but her fiancé was reported dead at the front nearly a month ago."

"How dreadful!"

"Well, perhaps not." He wove the car neatly around the throngs of carriages and pedestrians on busy Warwick Road, slowing the pace to a disappointing minimum. But then his voice came more clearly. "There's a wounded soldier in hospital now, who claims to be this man. You, dressed as Adelaide, will go in to meet him."

"What, she cannot be bothered to meet her betrothed herself?"

"She isn't aware he's here. Indeed, as far as she knows, he's still dead. Her father had word of this newly arrived soldier, and he hired me to find out for certain if it's him before he breaks the news. He's afraid it'll shatter her heart beyond repair if the man turns out to be a fraud."

My hand flew to my chest, naturally picking up the threads of this story. "She's very much in love with him?"

"According to her father, it nearly destroyed her when he was reported dead, and he isn't certain she'd survive a second disappointment."

"I should think not," I murmured.

"However, Walker is a very wealthy man, and his daughter's husband would inherit a great deal of holdings throughout Sussex as well as cash investments. Any of the men in her fiancé's regiment might have heard of the match and seen an opportunity when the true Captain Pelletier perished."

"That's absurd. He must know that the family would recognize straightaway that he was a different man."

"Hence the injuries. Most of his face is wrapped in bandages."

We rounded a corner, and I clamped the hat to my head with one hand. "Clever." How wild it felt, riding in this thing without horses to traipse the path before you and alert you to the coming turns and curves.

"Whoever he is has been badly burned by steam. I hate to imagine he's done it to himself to carry out a deception, but Miss Walker's father suspects that's precisely what has happened."

Another yank on the lever, and the car sputtered and slowed before the gates of the Brighton Borough Convalescent Home, a tall stone structure rising before a dark wood. The car idled in front of the iron gate.

"And you believe I can determine if he's the right man?" My story-loving heart flared, desperate to know at once if this was Miss Walker's soldier or not.

"He'll let you know easily enough. All you need to do is walk into that hospital looking something akin to the portrait he would have seen, but not exactly her, and see if he calls out *your* deception."

"Becoming a fraud to catch a fraud."

"Precisely. The real fiancé would know Adelaide Walker in an instant—or rather, know you are not her." He dug about between the seats and extracted a narrow box, handing it to me. "The jewelry I promised. Charles Walker's daughter wouldn't go about unadorned."

I opened the box, and there lay a long string of pearls, a sparkling bracelet, and a garnet broach. "You might have just sent these along with the gown and hat, you know. It would have been easier to arrange the entire ensemble before my looking glass."

"I didn't want them to go the way of my coin purse."

I looked into those clear eyes framed by spectacles. "I haven't got your coin purse."

"I can't think why else it would be missing."

"Is it, though? Is it missing?"

"I'm afraid so."

"Perhaps you simply placed it in a different pocket. People do that, you know."

Eyebrows up, gaze on me, he slipped his free hand into his coat first at the left, then the right, and brought forth the leather coin purse. "How peculiar. I'm right-handed and always put my coin purse on the left. Always."

I stiffened beneath his stare. My, but the man was impossible. "Your precious pound notes are still there. I only wanted to see who you were. I've never heard of an inquiry agent who wasn't in league with the police. That's what you are, isn't it? A private detective?"

He shrugged, replacing the coin purse. "Of sorts." He threw

one arm over the back of his seat, looking up at the hospital as he patted the restored coin purse in its pocket. "Find what you were looking for in it?"

"You're someone important. A high-ranking official."

"Only a solicitor."

"Ah." I relaxed after clasping the pearls on. "I dislike you a great deal less than I expected to."

His smile deepened, steady brown eyes alight.

"Writing briefs, smoothing ruffled feathers, drafting contracts —you couldn't ever convince me to do that sort of work."

"Couldn't I?" His eyebrows rose. "I haven't told you about my hidden talent yet. The one that allows for my more interesting work."

I eyed the man. "What, can you see through walls? Read a person's mind? See the future?"

"Yes. Well, not the last one." He leaned back against the seat. "My talent—which you must reveal to no one, even upon pain of death—is *listening.*"

I blinked, then burst out laughing. "I suppose we all must invent ways to feel heroic."

"You mock me." But his expression hinted at amusement rather than anger.

"Indeed I do." He jested. Surely he did.

He turned to me then, that steady look only hinting at what was about to come. "It's incredible, you know, the power it holds. Close your mouth long enough and people will confide in you what they wouldn't reveal to their mother. Things such as a powerful distaste for rules, both in art and in life, which points to betrayal by an authority figure. A rather public one." He adjusted his spectacles. "You distrust them all, including God, who you view in parallel to whatever authority figure once let you down. It would have been someone important—a police officer isn't high enough. A judge perhaps?" He eyed her. "No . . . a magistrate. Am I close?"

I clung to that leather seat. "That's enough. I won't—"

"You used to attend church when it suited, but you feel no qualms about slicing that small matter out of your life. It's a worthy price to pay for complete freedom, you tell yourself, yet you feel anything but free. And how could you? This authority figure has cost you your family—I'm only assuming this is the case since you speak of them all in present tense, yet they are not here to protect you from this man who has lately been following you.

"You had a sibling once—a sister. The confiding way you have with people tells me that's how you used to be with her. You love the color yellow as long as it's not too brown, and hate loud noises, strong tea, and losing at anything, unless it's to your sister." His head tipped to the right, gaze burrowing deeper. "There's a lingering sadness in your eyes, and a pinch of bitterness at the corners of your mouth over whatever has happened. A slight. A wrong. An injustice that you cannot let go."

I dared not speak.

He rested his arm on the seat back and leaned toward me, as if to see even better what I did not wish to say. "You have so much to tell," he said, his voice low. "So much you know about the whole sorry mess, whatever has happened, but no one will listen to you. So that knowledge sits, bottled up, hardening into bitter resentment."

I swallowed. Swallowed again, and looked away. How loud that idling engine seemed. Deafening, almost.

"I'm only guessing, mind." His voice was quiet.

Breathe. Slowly, steadily, deeply. That was the fail-safe acting trick. Control the breath, control one's self. Yet I couldn't look away from that gaze. That challenging, steady gaze laser-focused through gold-framed lenses.

"Oh, and that little bauble you carry around? The one you feel is a little bit yours? It's the missing Briarwood Teardrop. A gem of incalculable value."

I frowned. "Perhaps it is you I should fear. You, who shadow me for unknown reasons and know more than he ought about everything." Silly prediction. Gypsy Lee didn't know anything. Not *anything*.

His eyes sought mine. "I only want you to know you needn't lie to me. About anything. Even the gem."

I inhaled slowly, steadying my nerves. "Why do you want to know about it so badly anyway?"

"Why do you carry it about outside the film set?"

"You only ask the questions, I see. Never answer them."

We stared at one another, gazes challenging and probing. "I have discovered more about the mysterious Lily Temple than most anyone else has. All I did was listen to you."

"Well done, then. Your hidden talent has indeed led you to me, and provided you with a host of useless details. Nothing relating to any of your actual cases."

A flicker of a smile. "I wouldn't say that."

The air had left. Not just from the car, but all of Brighton. There was none left to breathe.

A guard approached the vehicle, eyes roving over the noisy curiosity. "Name, please?"

"Peter Driscoll." With a quick grin, Peter turned and the tension evaporated, string cut.

I sucked in a dizzying breath.

The man checked a list on his clipboard. "Very good, Mr. Driscoll. The director is waiting for you."

After walking to the gate, he cranked a lever and the metal doors ground open. Peter once again pumped a lever, flipped two switches, and steered us forward. The guard watched us go, openly inspecting every inch of the horseless carriage with interest.

I faced forward, folding my arms. Why so stiff? Lily Temple didn't suffer from nerves.

Change the topic.

"So. You're meeting with the director?"

"A ruse to get us in. You'll have to go up there alone." Another jerk of a lever, press of a foot pedal, and the car rolled up the unadorned lane.

"And you? Where will you be?" *Far away from me, hopefully.* I couldn't work when he was around. Could barely *think.*

"Well, I *will* meet with the director, for a brief moment. After I deliver a package to him, I'll be waiting in the car while you meet with your soldier—a Captain Amos Pelletier." He threw a glance my way. "Miss Temple, it isn't about what you say, but what you get *him* to say. That's where the gold lies in any conversation—remember that."

"I believe I know how to hold a conversation."

We rode silently past the overgrown hedges and too-tall flowers that drooped into the lane.

I fidgeted in the seat. "Do *you* think he's who he claims to be? This soldier?"

"Neither answer would surprise me, I don't think. What's your vote?"

I inhaled deeply. "True. I say he's true. At least, I *wish* him to be." My voice grew quiet at the end.

"But something deep inside you says he's a fraud, does it not?"

"That fairy tale of the glowworms." I faced him. "My grown-up view on that story is that everything that seems beautiful is actually an insect in the light of day. Everyone is creating an illusion. Acting. All of us project some conjured-up façade to the world, whether we mean to or not."

"Which is why it's even more important to listen. Be patient and wait for the truth to surface." Wind ruffled Peter's dark blond hair. "There always is one, you know. A story, that is. Always more to the truth than mere facts."

I dared another glance his way, a spark of recognition registering in my heart. The gentle curve of his jaw, the keenly perceptive eyes shielded behind the metal frames of his spectacles . . . all at once I felt an odd kinship with him.

"You were right, back on that hill. Beauty can turn out to be an insect, but that means that so too can an insect hold surprising beauty."

My soul flooded with a sense of validity. Of unexpected happiness.

"You see? I do listen. Even to fairy tale spinners." A quick smile, then his attention was back on the hospital building. "Mr. Walker tells me he's on the third floor, ward 5. Civilians aren't allowed up with the soldiers before they've been briefed and vetted. You never know who's a thief, a spy, or . . . French." He smiled good-naturedly. "Well, then. How about it? You'll have to pull off a little acting to get past the nurses, if you can manage it."

I smiled, back in control. "Come now, give me a little credit."

This part would be easy.

7

Who in the world am I? Ah, that's the great puzzle.

~LEWIS CARROLL, *ALICE'S ADVENTURES IN WONDERLAND*

Three flights of steps had a way of working away the tension. It refocused me, and now I felt only the need to prove myself.

And I would.

I'd snuck easily through the main floor of the hospital simply by keeping my head down and walking with purpose. Then I'd slipped down a few quiet corridors and up the rear service stairs. Now on the third floor, I moved down the narrow hallway with flickering lights and glanced into each room. Rows of cots lined each one, all filled with soldiers. Ward 5—which one was that? Nothing was labeled. How did anyone manage in this place?

"I'm sorry, but you can't be here, miss—"

"You must be Thelma." I whipped out a smile as I approached the drably uniformed matron and held out a gloved hand. Luckily her name had been displayed on the desk. "How fortunate that I have a chance to thank you directly. I consider it a personal favor to me, the way you care for our soldiers, and I cannot thank you enough for the work you do here."

"See here, miss. You can't—"

"Oh, I know those men aren't easy to care for, with their rotting uniforms and gaping wounds, and I'm sure the odor is nothing to delight the senses. They put up a fight at times, don't they? It's what they're used to, of course, fighting in the field. Struggling against everyone."

Her gaze darted about.

"Yet you're only trying to help, and they hardly seem to realize it. And there's not a single thank-you from the lot of them, is there? They're wild with pain and delirium, and perhaps some distress of the mind as well."

Her mouth twitched. She looked over my shoulder. "Jus' doin' my duty."

I lowered my voice. "You've had to tie a few of them down, just to dress their wounds, haven't you?"

She eyed me, wavering. Drinking in my words with guarded longing.

I touched her arm. "Your work here is remarkable, and don't think it has gone unnoticed. You're doing a hard task quite well." I lifted a tender smile. "On behalf of all these soldiers, and the families who love them dearly, you are owed a debt of gratitude, dear Thelma. Most people would see these men as a vast sea of faceless brutes, but you know them all, don't you? You know what they're about, and what sort of men they are. What they need at any given time." I paused. Glanced behind her. "And of course you're aware that Captain Amos Pelletier is trying to escape this very minute."

Her eyes flicked—almost imperceptibly—toward a room

across the corridor, but then her defenses were back in place. She straightened. "You'll have to leave."

"Oh, I mean no harm—"

"I'm not breaking regulations, miss. Not for you or anyone else." She put a firm arm around me.

I blew out a breath and touched my coiffed hair. "Very well, then. But I haven't any idea which direction I came from, or where I should go." I giggled. "I have the most dreadful bearings, you see. Deplorable, really. Couldn't find my way out of a one-room cell. You'll lead me out, won't you?"

"I suppose." She frowned, estimating my intentions with a single look up and down. "This way, miss."

She turned and I made as if to follow, but I slipped into that room across the corridor as we passed it and walked quickly down the row of men. "Amos? Captain Amos Pelletier?"

Men shifted and groaned, heads turning my direction. I pulled out a handkerchief and pretended to dab at my face, especially around my nose. The odor of dried blood and earth rotted the senses.

At last one man looked directly at me, summing me up with a frown through heavy bandages. This must be him. Oh how my heart pounded beneath that peach-colored gown. I came around to the left side of his bed and looked over his face, tucking the handkerchief away. Only one large bandage wrapped around his forehead, and he was older than I'd expected. At least forty. And bitter enough to be twice that age.

"Addy."

I froze. The raspy voice came from the bed behind me, which sagged under the weight of a much younger soldier. I turned slowly, holding my breath.

"Addy," rasped the wretched figure. He was focused solely

on me, eyes glazed with pain and body limp. "Addy . . . *Addy.*"
Over and over. Worn, mud-spattered boots wilted beside his
bed, and a metal identification tag bearing the name *Pelletier*
lay on the crooked bed table beside him.

The man was darker than I'd expected, tanned by the Boer
sun with wild, windblown hair tufting out above the bandages
that swathed most of his head and face. Not the type I'd imagine being matched with the finely dressed woman in the picture,
but then there's much to be said for a good bath and clean
clothes. He must have been quite dashing once.

The poor wretch groaned as he clutched at the sheet and
writhed, mumbling guttural nonsense. "Addy," he breathed out
again, and I clung to the little silk bag in my hands.

No. No, don't call me that. I held steady, watching. Analyz-
ing. *Take a good, long look. Call out my fraud. Tell me I'm not
her. Come now, do it!*

He breathed heavily, eyes fixed, drinking in the sight of me.
Relaxing.

Wretchedness clutched at me. Tightened my chest. No one
deserved to endure flesh as raw as this. Limbs as skeletal and
weak. One could see in a glance every last thing the man had lived
through, yet I was about to yank away his last remaining hope.

Unless he proved himself.

I cleared my throat and crouched near the cot, smoothing
the dark tufts of hair off the bandage. "There now, you'll be all
right. They'll fix you up, won't they? They've done a fine job
of it already." I patted his good arm and pulled the thin sheet
up to his shoulders. "Get some food in you and a little rest and
you'll soon be ready to leave."

He glanced around at the soldiers watching us, then back at
my face. "Take . . . me . . . *home.*"

I took a deep breath and laid a hand on his heaving chest. "After all you've seen, my love, I wouldn't dream of moving you until you're healed. I couldn't bear to see you suffer any more." A tear squeezed out from my eyelid, sliding warm down my cheek. "Just rest. Rest and grow strong, then all shall be made right . . . my dear Pelly-pell."

This was it. The final test. Surely the awful moniker I'd just now coined would trigger something, some calling of bluffs. I watched his agonized face for any awareness of my slip, any flicker of doubt.

His wild eyes searched mine. "Addy," he said, as if willing himself upright. "Please . . . out. Me . . . out." Every breath cost him. Ragged breath rolled around in splintered lungs. "Addy."

Stop. Stop saying that! I blinked back more tears. "Can you see my face, dear Pelly? Are your eyes clear?"

Another glance at the men who all stared openly at the little drama unfolding in their ward. "We must . . . must get out. I . . . need . . ." Eyes wide, he again willed his broken body to respond. Was he actually trying to rise? To walk out of the ward?

No one wanted to remain in hospital. Stuffy, filthy death traps, they were, and patients seldom fared well once inside. But this man seemed desperate. Perhaps a little too desperate.

My heart clenched around the sudden awareness that he was likely delusional. "Stay here." I kept a gentle hand on his chest. "You'll be all right, I promise. Only . . . don't get up."

"I must. You . . . Please. Help. Help me. Help . . . your Pelly-pell." He shuddered with pain and fell back again with short grunts and gasps.

My heart stretched the limits of my ribs, aching. Shattering.

I rose, but he clung to my hand, my clammy fingers protected by a glove. It was a weak grip, calloused, dirt-crusted hands in need of a good wash, but I did not pull away. Couldn't.

"Out, *out!*" The nurse Thelma descended upon me waving her arms, and I leaped away from the bed.

"Forgive me." I offered an unsteady smile. "I did warn you, my sense of direction is quite poor, and I tend to wander." A light laugh. "There's much to see here, and in a hospital of this size, one cannot be expected to—"

She lunged with a guttural noise. "I'll call the police!"

I darted out of reach and hurried down the stairs, clinging to the railing as I sailed around each bend. I reached the bottom breathless and tingling, heart racing, and paused in a small alcove to compose myself. One deep breath. Two. The tingles thinned out.

Then I continued to the main floor. Yet as I stood in the quietly bustling foyer, my pounding heart refused to be steadied. I had escaped, hadn't I? They would do nothing but eject me. I was out.

But he was not.

I blinked back tears. Held my suddenly weak stomach. Why did it matter? Why in the world did it even matter? This wasn't *my* fiancé, my story. Why should I care if their betrothal disintegrated into a million pieces? What did it matter if they had to live out their lives without one another? Whatever I reported back to Peter Driscoll, and whatever came of this case, mattered little to me.

Yet I wore their pain. The silent woman in the photograph, poised with her attempt at bravery as her future shattered. The man locked up and writhing in hopeless pain. I couldn't bear it. "Addy . . . *Addy!*" His raspy voice, those desperate eyes, haunted my senses as I made my way past the nurses, through the tiled corridors.

Head back, chin up, I sailed out the front doors without attracting further attention and followed the porch around two corners to find the steam car in the side drive. There he waited, one arm slung over the back of the seat, red scarf draped over his shoulder, watching me through puffs of steam. He came around to hand me up into the seat, cranked something under the lid, then when it rumbled harder, forcing out giant puffs of steam, he jumped in without a word. He yanked a lever down, the automobile leaped forward, and we were chugging back down the lane. We rode in silence until we'd reached a quieter, narrow road with few pedestrians and fewer carriages.

"Aren't you going to ask me?" I unhooked the gems and dropped them into his hand, then stared straight ahead. The clatter of horses and buggies around us faded into the distant scream of gulls as we neared the shore.

"I can see the answer on your face."

A know-it-all, that's what he was. I stared at my hands lying weakly in my lap. "So you'll tell her father?"

"That's the logical next step."

But it hardly seemed like a fitting ending to this story. The mystery had simply . . . stopped. The wind cooled my hot face as we chugged back to St. Anne's, the trees waving sadly to us as we passed. That's what became of one who breathed in enchantment and exhaled fairy tales. One expected life to unfold in the same way, but it never did. Even tragedies came full circle—they had closure and made sense. "How I hate endings like this." It came out a whisper.

But he heard it. "Maybe the point isn't the ending. Maybe it's the story."

Yet my mind couldn't let go. Couldn't simply accept this as an ending.

We neared the garden and immediately, something seemed off. Something . . . no! I shrank back against the seat as a man in brown tweed, bowler hat angled to the right, faced the garden entrance with a casual stance.

"Why not try the back gate, if you please."

His gaze shot toward the man, and he gave a grim nod. As he pulled the car alongside the curb on the narrower side street at the rear of the gardens, I forced my heart to stop pounding. Made it settle in my chest.

"You've been a great help to me today, Miss Temple. I'm deeply grateful."

This jolted my recently settled heart again. When we slowed, he pushed a pedal down to the floor and came around to help me.

I laid my hand on his arm when we were both out. I shouldn't linger, in case the man had seen us and followed. But it needed to be said. "What if there's some other explanation? For the soldier, that is."

"Such as?" He paused and searched my face, as if it truly mattered what I said next.

I let out a breath. "Oh, I don't know, just . . . wondering."

He leaned in toward me, a scientist spotting something of interest. "What is it? What crossed your mind just now? Something made you say that."

I shook my head. "Nothing. He failed the test. Called me Adelaide. Addy, actually, but it's all the same. He isn't the missing captain." How did one face these sorts of outcomes every day? Driscoll's work wasn't boring as I'd imagined . . . but neither could I bear it.

"I see. Well . . . thank you for your assistance." He watched me for another moment. His look was solemn behind those gold spectacles. "This needn't be the end of the case, you know. I'm still waiting for whatever else you have to say, and I promise, I'll believe you. Even if it's a mere hunch."

I ran my hand over the strap of my bag where it lay on my arm. "I've heard it said that every tale, every story that ever existed, returns to its beginning. Comes full circle. The hero returns to the location, faces the same monster that marked the beginning of his journey, but since he himself is changed, the results are different this time. That's how we know a story is finished. Whether it's tragic or surprising or utterly happy, those echoes from the beginning mark the perfect closing."

"Spoken from the lips of the finest fairy-tale spinner."

"Well, this story . . . it hasn't come full circle. It simply stopped."

"It has, hasn't it?" His eyes shone. My, how they shone. As if I'd understood something he hadn't even said, and he was pleased.

"I don't even know what I mean to say."

"We will ask more questions—dig deeper. As I said, it needn't be the end."

"Of *course* it's the end." I willed myself to swallow those words. "That's why I stopped myself from saying it. This is no fairy tale. Countless soldiers go missing every year, and many families go to their graves without answers."

"There *is* an answer, which means it's possible to discover it. And I will." His jaw was set, my face reflected in his lenses. Behind them, his eyes were clear. Sure. "Even more quickly if you agree to help."

"Are you always so confident?"

"No, just determined." He walked around the thing and

knelt to inspect a little flame inside the vehicle, blowing it until it glowed brighter.

"You are used to succeeding in your cases, aren't you?"

"I am."

"You've found every single one, have you? Every lost person, every hidden secret you were hired to uncover?"

The engine chugged again and he stood, arms folded over his chest and eyes squinting into pleasant crinkles. "I cannot bear to part with a novel—even a bad one—before I've discovered its ending. Real life holds no less appeal."

Every one. Every lost person. Even the ones others had failed to find. Quite an anomaly, he was. I toyed with the sash at my waist. "And you take cases from anyone?"

"Any person who knows where to find me may avail himself . . . or *herself* . . . of my services." He dusted off his hands and waited. Watching. Time passed. Still, he delayed, no hurry in his posture.

Seconds stretched. Wrapped themselves around us.

"Well, then." I exhaled and offered a parting smile. "Good day, then."

He touched my arm as if in farewell, but did not leave. "Who is he to you? The man who follows you?"

I frowned. "You really do need to know everything, don't you?"

"I can't protect you from an enemy you won't name. Tell me who he is."

I fidgeted. Debated. Silence strained between us as I brushed at my gown, twisted my fingers together. I stared at the gates, feeling hemmed in by his gentle presence. Did that make me safe . . . or trapped? "I . . . I don't really know who he is, actually."

"I see." A light squeeze to my hand. "Send for me if your

shadow ever shows his face again. It would be my honor to protect you." He offered a quick bow and turned. "Oh, and . . . check your pocket, Miss Temple," he called over his shoulder. "A bit of a *thank-you*. And you may keep the gown as well."

I shivered. I wanted to tell him that my foe was bigger than the man in tweed. That if I had to send for help, it'd already be too late. But a spitting drizzle began and Driscoll was running to the car, shielding his face. He fit his leather cap and goggles on and saluted as he shifted the lever, and the vehicle leaped forward, away toward the coast. I stood alone in the cloud of its exhaust.

My pocket. Check my pocket? I smoothed my hand over the filmy gown, but it had none. I hurried back to Grasshopper Cottage and shut the door behind me, tossing my hat down and running a hand over my hair.

It was all right. I would be all right. No one had bested me yet. I was still here, on my feet, with a future of my own making before me. I put a hand to my abdomen, which had twisted and contorted now that aloneness was closing in on me.

Then I saw it. A book protruding from the wide pocket of my coat, which hung on the hook near the door. He'd been in here—or sent someone. It unsettled me, that he had that sort of access, and I couldn't decide if I felt invaded or protected.

I turned the key in the door for the first time since arriving, and I pulled the book from my pocket—Thomas Hardy's *Far from the Madding Crowd*. A novel of slow but powerful romance, in which the hero hung about, rescuing the independent Bathsheba Everdine in small, consistent ways whenever a problem arose.

Inside, a note:

Just call me Gabriel.

Bathsheba had always been wonderfully clever and resourceful, but Gabriel always seemed to know when he was needed too. Always. I put my fingertips to my mouth, a deep hunger yawning wide within. Would that this could be my story, instead of the one I had to live. For once, I wished someone truly could save me.

8

One feather is of no use to me,
I must have the whole bird.

~JACOB GRIMM,
THE COMPLETE BROTHERS GRIMM FAIRY TALES

The Dowager Countess of Wiltshire kept Peter waiting. He glanced about her receiving room, the plush red sofa and candelabra on every tabletop and mantel. The lovely blue gem he'd seen in the gardens should fit among this splendor, but somehow it didn't. It belonged to another world—an enchanted one, full of natural beauty and God's creation.

"Mr. Driscoll." The dowager countess joined him through the rear double doors, and her butler closed them behind her. She walked to him and held out her gloved hand in greeting. "You've brought news of my gem, I hope." Her voice was soft, as one who expected to be heard and obeyed.

He took her hand and bowed over it. "I have, my lady." He waved away her offer of refreshments and seated himself in the narrow wingback near the hearth.

She perched on the edge of the opposite chair, back straight. "Well, then . . . is it?"

A single nod. "I believe so. The Briarwood Teardrop has been found."

With a sigh, she wilted back against the chair, hand to her chest. "Bless my soul, it's found."

He frowned. In the midst of all this opulence, what was one more gem?

"You're certain? There's no mistake about it?"

"No one at the film studio seems to realize what it is. A prop, they call it, and toss it about like a bauble. Put it on display at times, the same way they do the monkeys in the monkey house. I was able to look upon it in person, up close. And I'm fairly certain"—Peter reached into his suit coat and drew out the folded gem mapping she'd given him, smoothing it out between them—"it was this. A star sapphire, with five inclusions radiating out from the center. And another small inclusion . . . here." He laid his little finger along the line. "It was as positive an identification as a man could make, without being a gemologist."

"Very nicely done, Mr. Driscoll." Her smile didn't reach her eyes. "Now, I would appreciate if you would deliver it to me."

His chest tightened. "That wasn't part of our agreement."

"Neither was your laying hold of it. But since you evidently have . . . I'd like it returned to me directly."

The blood left his face. "I don't have it, Lady Claire."

Her eyebrows rose. "Haven't you? Well, if not you, then someone else who knows its value. Which, according to you, is no one, correct?"

Breath caught in his throat. "It's missing?" He pictured her easily—Lily Temple, holding out the gem on her bare palm.

Refusing to explain how she'd come by it. Slipping the gem, as a fairy on-screen, into the folds of her skirt, all while keeping that cherubic look on her face. Pasting a smile over the theft in such an effortless way, even as the gardener approached her.

Lily, with her eyes going wide as he told her, in his automobile, that the gem was real. That it was, in fact, the legendary Briarwood Teardrop worth a fortune. He knew the exact moment she'd been convinced. "Has the current owner reported a theft?"

"No, of course not. But it has been in the display box every day since the fairy tale began filming. I had a report from my housekeeper this afternoon. It's not there. You told no one, I assume, what you discovered about it?"

He grimaced. Then forced out the truth. "Two people, but you'd be wasting your time chasing them down."

"And they are?"

"One, my valet, Roderick Heath. He's my assistant, and utterly trustworthy. The other . . . Lily Temple."

"The actress?"

"As it happens, Lady Claire, I might know who has it. And it isn't missing, as you suspect. But frequently . . . borrowed. I'm guessing your housekeeper will see it back on display on her next visit."

"Good. And now, I shall need you to retrieve that sapphire."

"I'm sorry, my lady, but that's a matter for the civil authorities. I'd be happy to submit my findings on the gem's authenticity to the—"

"No!" Her eyes flashed wide. "No, there will be no police. I've hired you for a reason. Twenty years ago when the Briarwood Teardrop first went missing, they refused to do anything about it, and I see no reason to trust them now."

"I'm sure they did what they could, but sometimes the leads on a case fizzle out."

She raised her eyebrows, took a sip from a crystal chalice. "Then tell me why they closed the investigation after a mere two hours. Why they asked me no questions and did not even look over my documents identifying the gem. They cannot possibly have followed any leads, no matter how slim. No, Mr. Driscoll, I'm afraid the police haven't any interest in assisting a wealthy woman in retrieving one of her many jewels."

"Begging your pardon, my lady, but why *is* this particular gem so important to you? Has it sentimental value?"

"Not exactly." She leaned closer, evaluating him before divulging more. "The sapphire has healing properties, Mr. Driscoll. Healing properties of which I find myself greatly in need. My grandson, you see . . ." Her face softened for the first time. "Little Henry. His body is weak, and no one has been able to help him. It's a blood disease, and he's only seven years of age. Laugh at an old woman if you like, but I must try. At least I'm not subjecting him to that beastly letting and the like."

"Of course. But I never took you for a superstitious woman, Lady Claire."

"I am not in the least. But the Briarwood Teardrop . . . it brings strength and life to the person holding it. Emboldens and empowers. It's something no one can explain, but nor can they deny it, once they've held it for themselves."

He pressed his lips together, remembering the way Lily Temple had held it in both of her hands. Cradled it and looked upon it with awe. There *was* something unusual about it. Something otherworldly, as if it had come from the heavens above an enchanted garden.

Then of course, there was that star. That glittering display of flaws. He'd never seen anything quite like it.

"Now then, your fee. I assume one hundred pounds will be sufficient?"

Peter coughed. Blinked. One hundred pounds? The amount was astronomical. "I thought we'd agreed on an alternative payment for this case."

"Yes, that, of course." Her smile was mild. "It has already been paid, in gratitude for the first part of your mission." She walked to her desk and retrieved some papers. "A copy of the register for my steamer, the *Queen Anne*, en route even now to America." She ran her fingertip down the scribbled signatures until she reached one that looked so familiar it made his chest squeeze. *Esther Driscoll Hayes and child.*

Child? Well, babies did grow up, of course. His sister's infant must be nearly ten by now. He hated that she had to bear this alone. That her husband had disappeared, that she'd broken ties with her family, and now she was about to be alone in a foreign country. But at least she would be safe now. Have a new life.

He mentally cursed himself again for letting this happen. Elopement was seldom a grand idea, and he should have known better when she'd approached him for help. Yet he'd assisted her in sneaking out and almost immediately come to regret it. The house had shattered into a million pieces in her absence. Mother blamed Father for being too harsh and chasing her away. Father blamed Esther for being wicked and foolish. Peter's older brother, Thomas, had found out about the midnight escape and blamed Peter entirely.

He'd wanted to make it up to her himself—support, a home, a fresh start, but aside from his painful lack of funds, Esther had already refused Peter's help numerous times. She'd run deeper into hiding every time he'd located her. Eventually, he'd had to stop looking.

Until, for better or worse, the dowager countess had approached him for help. And he had, in turn, asked for hers. Her missing gem case wasn't one of reunion and restoration . . . at least, not directly. But it would do for his family what he hadn't been able to accomplish in many years of trying.

His sister's escape to America wasn't what he'd hoped for, but it was the closest thing to healing that could ever come to their family, and he had to accept it.

"So you will retrieve it for me?" Said as smoothly as a request for more soup.

"I appreciate your help for my sister, but I'd much prefer to pass along the rest of this case to the authorities, Lady Claire. Now that the sapphire has been located, it shouldn't be difficult to persuade them to fetch it from Mr. Smith. Very few resources expended."

"One hundred pounds for this second stage. On top of helping poor Esther. And that's a generous offer."

"Indeed it is." He cleared his throat, shoving aside the image of himself handing the pound notes to his mother. Folding her worn hand around them and instructing her to pick out a respectable cottage for them. A home. The moment his elder brother married in a few short weeks, he and his mother would be without one. "I will escort you to the gardens if you like, and—"

"It's no good. It'll only alert the nosy public and a treasure hunt will ensue. Everyone will know the rumors are true—that it *is* my missing sapphire, and it will disappear. I cannot risk it. No, you will finish the task. Discreetly. Simply discuss the matter privately with the man operating the gardens, and I'm certain he'll return it to you to save himself the legal trouble. If not, you will of course know another way to fetch it back."

She paused. Her voice grew softer. "It is my ship carrying Esther Hayes, remember. Her life is, just now, in my hands. And when she reaches America, it'll be my connections finding her work . . . or leaving her without." She leaned forward, placing a gloved hand on his arm. "You're in too far now, Mr. Driscoll. No sense in backing out now."

It was wretchedly miserable, this job. From start to finish. He shouldn't have taken it, and wouldn't have, if Lady Claire hadn't offered to help him in the one way he desired most— rescuing his sister.

Few were the well-heeled private inquiry agents connected enough to walk among the ton, the titled nobility, without raising alarm. And few were the agents who'd proven themselves as effective and discreet as he. For a priceless gem, there were few others she could trust—and sometimes that honor became a burden.

When he reached home, a slender, cloaked figure waited for him. "She insisted on waiting for you, sir," said Frederick, the butler. "She's here on a matter of private business. I didn't think you'd mind."

"Of course not."

A poised, anxious, but elegant young woman turned in the shadows of his parlor when he made known his presence. "Mr. Driscoll?"

He nodded, offered the guest a chair as the butler departed. She remained standing, though, clutching her reticule. "I am

Adelaide Walker, and I know my father hired you concerning Captain Pelletier, my fiancé."

Peter observed her narrow face in the jumping shadows. So this was the woman whose soldier had been declared dead . . . then appeared at Brighton Hospital. She looked sad and tired, but also wise. Aged beyond her years. "How may I be of service to you, Miss Walker?"

"I'd like you to pursue the case a little further."

"You were not meant to know about the matter."

"I know, but I do." She stepped forward, her boots clicking on the wood floor until they reached the rug. "I've heard you have an uncanny way of finding people when no one else can. That's why I've come. And also because no one else will listen to me. They all think grief has addled me, and that I simply cannot let go of him. Call it foolish hope, call it a woman's sense, but I truly believe this man may be my Amos, and I simply cannot let the matter rest until I know."

He leaned one hip against his desk and observed the slender woman. "Not to worry, Miss Walker. I have a few more ideas to try."

She straightened, drawing her gloved hands close. "So you'll investigate the matter?"

"I will." Another glance, taking her in. Sensible and of good breeding. "I cannot promise what news of him I will find, only that I will find it. You must brace yourself for the possibility of a bad report."

Her warm gray eyes were steady. "I can do that."

He rounded his desk and sank into the chair. "Very well then, come and sit. Tell me the reason for this sense you have."

"You believe me, then?" She perched on the offered chair, leaning forward.

Peter smiled as he leaned back. "In my experience, a woman's intuition is seldom wrong and never unfounded."

She rewarded him with a smile and pulled a letter from her reticule. "I wasn't sure I'd show you this, but I think I shall." She handed it over, her look easing. "I cannot offer you more money, but—"

He waved this off as he skimmed her letter.

"I'm sure you'll notice the date—and the postmark."

Further down, he raised his eyebrows. It was a rather lengthy goodbye. Posted just after the battle where he'd gone missing, and likely written just before it. As if he knew more than he let on. "Rather a compelling reason to doubt." When he'd finished, he put the letter on his desk and looked up to the petite woman opposite him. "I'll hold on to this for now, if I may. I'll be in contact soon, Miss Walker. The moment I have news."

She sat forward in her chair. "I know he's alive, Mr. Driscoll. Life is only beginning for us." Her long, slender fingers lay over a barely perceptible swell at her abdomen. "And I need him. Desperately." A single tear escaped and trailed down her porcelain skin, even as her eyes remained wide and steady. Her nostrils flared and desperation pinched her features. "Please. Whatever it takes." Her voice was soft. "I don't know how to do this without him."

Peter swallowed. "I promise to find the truth, Miss Walker. You have my word."

Roderick Heath emerged from the shadows as the woman departed. "At least it wasn't Lily Temple come to call. I was concerned when I heard a young lady was waiting for you. What did Miss Walker want?"

"You should know," Peter said, pouring himself a drink. "You've been eavesdropping, have you not?"

"I'm above such things, sir." He straightened. "Actually, I was coming to bring you my findings on the other matter." He strode into the room and helped himself to a cup of tea. "Lily Temple is actually a runaway governess from Surrey. Her real name is Flora Cross."

"I rather prefer the other name."

He sighed. "She's a pretty face, Pete. Nothing more. Keep that in mind."

"Don't trouble yourself over it, Roddy. I have plenty to occupy my time just now." He caught Roderick up on both Miss Walker's visit and the call on the dowager countess.

"So which will it be first, Pete? The missing soldier or the missing gem?"

"Both, perhaps. At the same time."

Roddy blinked, eyebrows forming a *V* between them. "You aren't seriously considering bringing her into the case again, are you?"

"What better way to approach her again without raising alarm? It's quite simple, really."

But in the end, nothing involving Lily Temple was ever simple.

9

"Do you know," Peter asked, "why swallows build in
the eaves of houses? It is to listen to the stories."

~J. M. BARRIE, *PETER PAN*

t's still gone." Peter scanned the dusky gardens, grim. "And
so is she."

Lily Temple was a blizzard of delightful snowflakes that
fell on one's face . . . then melted away. It was evening at St.
Anne's Well Gardens, and George Smith had arranged an open-
air bioscope show under the stars, welcoming the public for
sixpence apiece, which meant a chance to speak with her about
the gem. To look into her face when she told him she hadn't
taken it.

Yet she proved elusive.

Peter's man Roderick trailed him, as he often did when the
trusted servant believed his master was about to do something
foolish. "I'm not sure what else you expected from her, Pete."

It was now two minutes to seven, nearly time for the bioscope show, and Peter had seen no sign of the girl with the

warm golden hair and snapping wit. "You think me foolish for involving her in the case. For not reporting her to the police."

"She's an actress. It's a bit dodgy involving yourself with her at all."

"That's rather narrow-minded."

"You're forgetting who she is."

"She's not a stage actress. It's different."

"So I've heard." Peter could all but feel Roderick's eye roll. "And a great deal more on the subject."

"You've barely met the woman."

"A man can have opinions, can't he?"

Peter eyed him—a clean-shaven yet stiff upper lip, silver hair tamed to one side, tailored suit worn like a perfectly turned-out uniform. "Not without good reason."

"You do it all the time. You call it a hunch."

He paused, attention turning again to scan for the one who would always stand out. "My hunches are *always* grounded in logic."

Including his interactions with Lily Temple. He'd seen it. A glimmer of authenticity. Bottled up behind that animated, charming face with the long, dark lashes lay a diamond— glittering, hard, and after the application of immense pressure, impossible to break. Beautiful, rare . . . valuable. Despite her penchant for acting, there was something authentic and real in Lily Temple that resonated with his solid nature.

Roderick eyed his master. "Your compassion is both your strength and your downfall, sir. Would that you had a little less of it."

"The compassion I offer her comes from the same well as that which I dole out to others." He leveled a pointed look at his man.

Roderick grimaced, clasping hands behind his back. "Point taken, sir. I simply don't want her taking advantage of your good nature. When it comes to love, you deserve better than that."

"I've said nothing of love." He rocked back on his heels. "I promised myself long ago that I'd never involve myself in that again unless I was certain of a favorable ending."

"But no one can possibly be certain—"

"Precisely."

The men stood silently, soaking in the sounds of organ music, of light, happy voices awaiting the descent of dusk and the show.

"I cannot help but think about the story she was telling me, Roddy. It was that Dickens tale of the French Revolution."

"*A Tale of Two Cities*, sir."

"Yes. That's the one. She told it as if it were her story. As if she were Lucie, living with injustice and poverty and . . ."

"And her poor father, the innocent prisoner? Her husband, wrongfully locked up because of his family?"

"They're puzzle pieces. Symbols. I'm just not certain yet what she means to say." Peter scanned the crowds again. His gaze stopped on a man to their left. "Roddy, he's here. He's here." It was the man who'd been shadowing her, he was certain. He stood on the fringes of the crowd, hands in pockets, the only one not in a cluster of talking guests. "S. Draper. S . . . Samuel! Roddy, it's Samuel Draper. *That's* how I know the name."

"Ah. And who exactly is Samuel Draper?"

Peter swallowed. "The Yard. He's with—"

"Scotland Yard? He's with the *police*?" Roderick blinked, then clasped his hands before him and shut his mouth. He looked down, then back up at his master with a signature sparkle of *told-you-so* in his eyes.

"I suppose it hardly matters now, does it? She has vanished."

"Not quite," said Roddy. He pointed up toward the white screen, where the image of Lily Temple twirled in glowing color among the flowers.

The Enchanted Garden and the Gem, in six parts

A dusky hue signals nightfall in the garden, and the fairy holds up the gem, which flashes in the moonlight. She flits away with it and comes to stand before the looking glass. Then she places her hand upon the surface of the glass. When it ripples, admitting her hand, she steps through.

The film blinks and jerks. We are now in the looking glass world.

A quick puff of smoke, and the fairy appears in the busy world on the other side of the looking glass. Carriages, houses, people, all rush around her. She looks about, hands framing her delighted face. The lens pans out, buildings growing smaller, and we see how small this fairy is in the great world.

Hand shielding her eyes, she makes as if to look for something. The image of the man in the looking glass appears toward the top corner of the screen, as if in her thoughts. She holds her arms out in question, then spins about.

"How ever will I find him?"

Night falls, and the fairy is weary, her wings sagging. She uses the sapphire to find the looking glass and gazes upon the garden beyond. Then she holds up the radiant blue gem, which glows in stark contrast to the world around her, and her skin—her color has drained.

She touches the gem to the looking glass, and the glass ripples like a pond. The fairy steps through.

The film flickers and shudders.

Her image fades in, slowly solidifying. She's standing in the garden, one hand against the surface of the looking glass, one at her side. She looks at the mirror and the man in that other world whom she has not yet found. She touches his reflection longingly.

The gardener is stomping through the dewy grass, calling for her.

"Where are you?"

She turns. The fairy holds the gem aloft, twirls, then slips it behind her back. She looks to the approaching gardener, then to the looking glass. The gardener draws near and the orchestral music swells. The fairy smiles sweetly at him. He points at her hands. She holds them up, showing both are empty. The gem is gone.

Another spin in her petal gown. Cymbals clash, the music takes over, and the picture fades.

Applause rippled through the garden, and the crowds rose, milled about.

"But where did she hide it?" Roderick Heath watched with folded arms. "That's what I'd like to know."

"I'm not convinced she ever stole it. She just likes to borrow it from time to time."

"Let me remind you, Pete, how little you know her."

He wasn't wrong. Most people were readable, but Lily Temple presented more of a challenge. Her acting skills were superb, and he wasn't entirely sure what to make of her. "I suppose we give her the benefit of the doubt and simply ask her."

The audience applauded as a juggler approached the stage and bowed, and Peter moved through the crowds.

"But she isn't here." Roderick trotted to keep up with his master's long strides.

She wasn't. Fear tightened in Peter's chest. An urgency. The tweed-coated Draper moved through the throngs as well. Peter slowed, wandering idly among the guests before the bandstand, where a small knot of people worked over the cumbersome metal box of a bioscope. "People don't simply vanish, though."

"People in your circles, perhaps. But she is of a different ilk—if I may be bold enough to point it out once again."

At last, Peter spotted a bit of hope just beyond the monkey house. "Gypsy Lee." He hurried over and approached the woman's table, took her hand in his as he greeted her. "How fortunate to find you here."

"And where else would I be? 'Tis my home, don't you know."

"I thought it was Miss Temple's as well, yet I don't see her."

The woman's wide, lashed eyes watched Peter. "If you know my lass well enough, you'll know where to find her."

His glance darted about the park. Toward the woods.

"Not there." She took his chin in her beringed hand and turned it toward the greatest mass of guests, and the thing around which they had gathered after the show. It was an old cave on the edge of the woods, and at the mouth, some spectacle. Some person holding captive everyone's attention.

An old man. The bearded, crooked old man who, according to legend, lived in the haunted cave. He'd become a regular attraction for the children. The vagabond lunged and growled, and the front row of young audience members shrank back, several cries piercing the tranquility. Parents laughed.

"Of course," Roderick mumbled. "Wherever the crowds are gathered, there she will be at the center of them. Like a viper reeling in prey."

Like a light drawing insects.

Gypsy Lee shook her head. "Poor Carl has been ill for a week. Home in bed, I hear."

"And Miss Temple was the obvious replacement."

"She can play any part. Quite remarkable, that one."

The edges of Peter's mouth flicked up. "So it would seem." Warning bells sounded inside, likely because of all Roddy had said, but it was easy to shove aside. He smiled as he watched Lily Temple jumping about in oversized rags, animating a story for the half-terrified children. And all he could think was . . .

she's still here. *She's still here.* Light swelled in his chest like a field of glowworms at night.

He turned to his valet. "Keep a look out for that man, Roddy. Make certain he doesn't cause trouble. I'll meet you at the carriage in an hour or so."

The faithful valet gripped his bowler in his hands. "Don't forget what you're about, Pete. You've a job to do. Don't come back without that sapphire."

When the music started again and the crowd flitted back toward it, Peter slipped away and approached the cave, hands still in his pockets. Shuffling echoed just inside, and he ducked his head to enter, pausing for his eyes to adjust. She stood with her back to him, picking twigs out of a long white beard and wig. A wilted hat lay on the ground nearby. The key tonight would be to approach this carefully. To entice her to trust him.

He stood just behind her. "Good evening."

She spun with a cry, then broke into a full-bodied laugh at the sight of him. "What a cad you are, Peter Driscoll, spooking the spook."

He pressed back a smile, but lightness still filled the hollows of his chest. "Do I call you Carl? Or Miss Temple? Or perhaps the venerable old man of the cave."

"Lily will do." She shook out the dirty old rags she wore and scratched her chin under the beard. Music swelled behind them.

He focused on her slender neck, looking for the gold chain that dropped below her costume. But it was not there. "I see you're not wearing the necklace this evening."

"What brings you into my cave? Another favor to ask, I assume?"

"A dance, perhaps? That would do nicely."

Her hand stilled on the beard tied around her face with ribbon. "Now?"

He shrugged, hands still in his pockets.

Her garb was hastily donned—long, limp burlap costume, dirt smears covering smooth arms, and bushy eyebrows applied a bit crooked on her keen little face.

The effect was rather engaging.

"Very well, then." She held out her hand and he took it, guiding her into a dance with the distant organ music, and he couldn't help but notice how much she did not look like an old vagrant in a cave, even with the costume. She was charming and feminine but also light and quick in his arms, perceptive of his every intention. And even in burlap she was more than a little lovely to look upon.

They spun out of the cave and into the orange sunset that reached its fingers down through ancient pines, a hazy spotlight on their waltz. He never *chose* to waltz, though he did it reasonably well. Yet around this woman, he couldn't help but be swept up in her spins, her music, allowing the rest of the world to blur. There was an air of mystery about her—a sense of fairy tales come to life. He wished to keep spinning with her so he could watch her sparkle from every angle, a prism hanging in the sunshine.

They drew apart, hands still connected, then back together, side to side and around. "I'm never sure what's true of you. I cannot trust what I see with my own eyes."

"There isn't much a body can hide from you, Peter Driscoll."

"Let's play a game, shall we? True or false. We'll start with your name."

She swept in close, then back. "False."

A spin, arm over and along her back. "Hair color."

Her eyes shone. "False."

He caught the rhythm, his feet carrying him back and forth with ease. "You're marrying your co-star, Bertie Riggs. I saw it in the rags."

She threw back her head and laughed as they spun. "Also false."

"You're purposely lying low, dressing in costume. To avoid that man in brown tweed."

Her smile faded, arm stiffening as they stepped apart, then back together. "True."

He sighed, tapping his chin. "Your life can be likened to a certain Dickens character."

Her chin edged up, shoulders tight, and she said nothing.

True.

Intrigue flared in his chest. She was like a riddle, this woman. And he was solving it. He must tread carefully, though. Much as he wanted to rush to the finish line, to push her about the sapphire, that would be sure to get him exactly nowhere. Which meant keeping her at ease with him. He flashed a smile. "By the by, I saw the flicker today. The fourth installment, is it? Quite lovely."

Her face relaxed.

"Moving between the worlds—it was brilliantly done. A film trick I expect, yes?"

"A simple stop-action shot, with a small splice as I move through the looking glass. One world transitioning into another. And the close-up, that was Smithy placing his cine-camera on a wheeled chair and pulling it closer with a rope. But it makes the picture seem believable, does it not?"

"Indeed." He extended his arm, twirling her away from him, then pulling her back in. "I take it you helped with the splicing?"

"I pieced the two strips together. I've an eye for matching them precisely. And I rather enjoy illusions."

He spun her again and pulled her close, lowering his voice. "How did you do it? How did you make the sapphire disappear?"

She froze. His next step landed on her toes. She stumbled back, laughing a full, bubbling laugh. What manner of woman was this? He watched her, soaked in the atmosphere she radiated. Another turn and again his foot found her toes. She pulled away, tripping over her costume and laughing into her hand. "It seems the old man in the cave isn't one for social graces. Imagine that."

"I'm afraid it was my missteps, Miss Temple. Not yours." He couldn't keep himself from smiling as he righted her. It really was easy to be around her. To observe her myriad expressions, to cast out some joke and set off her hair-trigger laugh. He wouldn't let himself imagine how it would feel to watch her be apprehended if she *had* stolen the sapphire.

"Come, I must prepare for the next show. I'm in two more, you know, but this time I get to dress nearly as myself."

"And who might that be?"

One eyebrow arched. "Always swimming deep, are you?" She turned and marched across the clearing. "No one cares a fig who I am outside of the cine-camera lens."

"On the contrary—"

"The sapphire. Quite a trick, wasn't it? It's called a substitution splice. Smithy stops the film and all the action freezes. Mae runs up and takes the sapphire from my hand, then the cine-camera is cranked into motion again, and the action continues. With some careful editing, we make it a seamless transition, and as long as the framing remains the same, the audience would never know."

"What an odd sleight of hand."

"It was an accidental discovery, you know. A Frenchman named Méliès was out filming a train tunnel when his film jammed in the cine-camera. He banged and hit and cursed until the film came untangled, and he started filming again. Then when he returned to his studio for editing, he noticed the film played as one continuous shot—only, there was quite a transformation. A bus drove into the tunnel and came out as a hearse. Men became women and children vanished entirely. It was brilliance by mistake, I suppose. Which all genius must be, don't you think?"

How many words she had. Always brimming with words. Yet there was much she avoided saying, especially about the deeper, more personal matters. Hollow words cluttered up the emptiness in those parts of her being.

"It's special to you, isn't it? The gardens. That gem. Almost as if the fairy tale were closer to real life than anyone knew."

A tic. A barely noticeable jerk of the muscle between neck and shoulder. Her gait livened, took on a slightly staccato tempo. "Mind you, don't snag on those tree roots."

Something like the game of hot and cold from his childhood—and her expression told him he was quite warm. "How much of the film relates to truth? The stealing of the gem, for example."

"I thought you didn't believe in fairy tales."

"With this one, it's rather hard not to."

She turned away so he couldn't read her face. "I've not stolen it. I took it out of the box because Smithy doesn't guard it well enough. Doesn't realize how much people want it . . . and how easily they can have it."

"You believe you'd be a better owner of it."

She pressed her lips together, then spoke quietly. "I believe few can appreciate it as I do."

He narrowed his eyes, reading between the lines. Not entirely sure what was being said.

She paused, frowning. "I'll show it to you, if you'd like. I haven't made off with it and pawned it, if that's what you're curious about. Stay for the next show and then I'll run back and fetch it for you."

His skin tingled. "I should very much like to see it again. But then, I'd also be delighted to see your show."

"I've got to replace it before anyone notices it's missing. I only keep it with me during the shows, when the path to its display is closed anyway, and also when things tend to go missing from the gardens. Smithy isn't one for precaution and security."

"You're sort of a guardian for the stone, aren't you? Protecting it and watching out for it whenever you can."

"Someone must take it on."

They came into another clearing and paused before a two-story Grecian-looking structure with a heavy wooden door behind three columns. It was a miniature London townhouse, there out in the woods, with the words St. Anne's Well, Natural Chalybeate Water inscribed over the entrance. "This used to be the well, you know. The main attraction of the entire park—healing and refreshment and the purest water one might find anywhere about. It's rather a charming place to work."

Her muscles had bunched into knots everywhere they were visible—jaw, neck, hands—and now released once she was out of the public's sight. She was being shadowed—hunted. Odd, that she continued living and working at the gardens, despite this.

He took this in. Her nearly dancing posture as she moved

about the old pump house. "It's more than that. More than work."

"What does that mean?"

"You're drawn here. Irresistibly and undeniably. You cannot help yourself. Like the fairy who has not yet realized it's her source of life." He turned to her. "But what I don't know . . . is why. What tender memory do you have of this park? What happened here that you came back to remember?"

She looked up, memories flickering frame by frame across her countenance. Happy, heartrending, tender. She braved his gaze and their closeness disarmed her. A truth slipped out. "This is the last place I was happy." Her eyes swam with the trueness of it.

"It's your garden of Eden. The only place on earth where everything is as it should be. And it draws you back. Its irresistible pull. You want very much to be here, in this specific garden, don't you?"

"I suppose." Then she lit up with a forced glow, the mask in place again. "Now, don't go and change the subject. You owe me the end of the story."

10

She generally gave herself very good advice,
(though she very seldom followed it).

~LEWIS CARROLL, *ALICE'S ADVENTURES IN WONDERLAND*

The man was insufferably nosy. And his presence had me slightly on edge—why *had* he returned?

He smiled. "Which story?"

"Adelaide Walker and her soldier." I turned toward the little house, fitting a key into the door and kicking it past the ivy that had grown over its edges. "I've witnessed the middle chapters, heard the beginning ones, now I need the ending. Like you, I'm a sucker for a story." I sobered, holding the door for him to follow me in. "I do hope you were able to offer the poor woman reassurance. You have such a soothing nature, and if anyone could calm her, it would be you."

He hesitated, seeming to want to steer the conversation elsewhere. I tensed. He had an agenda, this man. Yet he turned a gentle curve into my question instead. "I haven't given Mr. Walker my report yet, actually. I find there's quite a bit more work to do yet." He watched me. "Truth comes in layers, after all."

"It's a wonder you don't see the value in fairy tales, the way you speak."

The room was dark and moist, off-putting and eerie until I flicked on a single electric bulb overhead with the yank of a string. It was the pump house, once the access point to the chalybeate springs, now done up in trampled papers, makeshift workspaces, tinting trays, and scraps of glossy film clippings littering the floor. I saw it for the first time through the eyes of a visitor. Three mismatched chandeliers hung unlit from the low ceiling, and all manner of handmade gadgets covered the surfaces, and really it looked like a perfect jumble.

But it felt like home. Like the birthplace of a million stories.

"Actually I came to give you more than an update. I was hoping to have your help again. If you're willing, that is."

I pulled off the hot beard and wig, tossing them on the desk. "I thought you were hired to investigate the man currently in hospital. Prove him honest or false. You've already done that."

"My work is about more than what I'm paid for. I've told you what I do."

"Yes, dear Jack of the rebuilt towers, you have. It isn't sensible, though." I wiped at the dirt smudges on my face, staring at my broken reflection in a chipped looking glass. "And you're nothing if not sensible, Peter Driscoll."

"You know me that well, do you?"

I paused, lifting a smile of kept secrets. "You're easy to know." I leaned toward the looking glass again, scrubbing my face in earnest. Then I carefully pinned a flowing, feminine wig of black hair in place. "What cause could you have for delaying it? Adelaide Walker's fiancé is still dead, and the man currently in hospital is a fraud. What could you possibly hope to restore to them?"

"The ending. You were right—it hasn't come full circle yet." He explained his visit from Adelaide Walker, the doubts he had of what conclusions they'd drawn. "His last letter . . . it was posted after his supposed death. From England, not Africa. And it sounded like a farewell. As if he knew the fatal battle, which had been a surprise attack, was about to take place . . . or wrote it after the fact."

"Implying he survived."

"You don't find that telling?"

"Telling of what, though? That someone laid hold of that letter and posted it from our shores after returning? Or that someone stamped it with the wrong date? Or perhaps that he knew it likely that he, a man in the midst of battles and war, might be about to be killed? Any of those sound more likely than what you're suggesting." I unwrapped the ragged burlap I'd tied around myself to play the part of the old man, revealing a pale pink beaded gown underneath. Then I slipped out the door, locking it behind us. In the distance, metal clanks and groans could be heard from the bioscope as it started up for a show.

He shifted. "You'd think his belongings would have been blown to bits along with the man himself. Including this letter. It wasn't as if he had a steamer trunk to hold everything while he fought."

We wove through the thick darkness until I found the perfect spot on a grassy hill overlooking the show. I stopped and curled my knees to my chest, and Peter sat beside me.

"Truth is available, Miss Temple, and Adelaide Walker deserves to have it. There's little peace to be had in limbo. And looking just a little bit closer, working just a little harder, will bring her the truth."

I in turn told him, after a pause, about the extra test I'd slipped in during my visit. "Pelly is a terrible nickname, which I made up on the spot and he accepted it. Not only that, he *used* it. I'm quite certain the true Adelaide Walker is a self-respecting woman of at least mild intelligence who is not given to odious pet names like *Pelly-pell*. So now, at least, do you believe me? The man is a fraud, and the story's over."

His voice dropped to a whisper as the bandstand lit with music. "Then why does this man in hospital have the captain's identification? Would that also have been lost in the blast that supposedly killed the man? I cannot ignore that detail."

I tipped my head and pointed at the banner hanging on a post near the bandstand. "Look, look at that." It was an advertisement for the fairy tale, showing the world inside the looking glass, with Bertie in sepia tones. "Can you tell which true-life street that might be?"

Peter squinted. "It . . . it appears to be Paris. Yes, there's the Louvre in the background."

"The man in this picture is Bertie, who I know for a fact has never been brave enough nor rich enough to leave England. The scene pictured there was filmed in the glass house." I framed the image with my fingers. "We cover up the lens with a small cardboard frame with the center cut out so we only expose that part of the film. Then Smithy brilliantly used the cut-out part to cover the center and expose only the background when he traveled to France for a meeting with the Lumière brothers. When he came home, he mixed the subject with an entirely different backdrop. You see? Bertie goes to Paris without ever leaving home."

I dropped my hand. "Your soldier stole a captain's backdrop, but that doesn't make him the captain. The truth may come in layers, but layers can be manipulated. And in the end, everyone is a manipulator." I leveled a gaze at him. "Including you. In fact, I've changed my mind on showing you the sapphire again. Whatever you're here for, it isn't my help. I haven't any talent for your sort of work, and we both know I'm not terribly clever."

"False modesty."

"Admitting one's ignorance is the first step in acquiring knowledge." I smoothed my gown at every angle. "You've seen the bits I play in film. I make people laugh, not think. You need someone truly clever to help with your investigations. Go on then, I must be ready, and you're not doing your reputation any favors, being here alone with me."

He looked me up and down, measuring something. "Very well, I'll leave you to it." He stood and offered a slight bow from the waist. "But, Miss Temple, if you hope to convince someone of your ignorance, you'd best not go and quote obscure lines from Plato."

"Socrates."

"Ah." He smiled. "Right you are."

11

For, you see, so many out-of-the-way things had
happened lately, that Alice had begun to think that
very few things indeed were really impossible.

~LEWIS CARROLL, *ALICE'S ADVENTURES IN WONDERLAND*

The man in brown tweed watched the show from beneath a tree. Alone, hands in his pockets, he watched the stage as I peered out from beneath it.

It was tempting to flee with Peter, to leave the gardens for a time and escape the shadow of this man whose presence lurked in my thoughts as much as my garden. Yet . . . perhaps Peter was *not* my rescuer but the one I should be hiding from. Something about him, about his offers of help and his requests for assistance, didn't add up.

The music interrupted my thoughts. I clasped my gloved hands before me, peering out from my hiding place under the stage at the sea of hats and glittering headbands.

Once I'd told stories from behind a hay bale, a makeshift stage, with my moving hands wrapped in doll's clothes as the characters. It was limiting. I couldn't gauge my audience's reaction, couldn't build upon it.

And now it was nearly the same, hiding out beneath the stage with the heat of the spotlight on my back, the looking glass before me to cast my ghostly image upon the stage.

Yet the story I would now spin had seeped into my very bones long ago. I took a breath and leaned into the microphone, gripping the round instrument with both hands, and spoke. "My beloved Wolnoth left me on July the twenty-second, when the roses were in bloom and he had never looked more stunning in his uniform." St. Anne's legend poured out over the audience, word by word, as if it were truly mine, just as much as her gardens belonged to me and I to them. "We did not linger, for I never doubted I'd be reunited with my soldier." I paused, sobering as the audience fell silent, thoughts narrowing into one question: *Will she?*

Most of the children had left the garden when night fell, leaving the lawn filled with fashionably dressed adults ready to hear the tale as old as St. Anne's itself. Ready to be stirred by a well-told tragedy.

"I clung faithfully to the memory of my soldier, to the hope of my beloved Wolnoth returning to me, and I wouldn't hear of another suitor. Not ever. What man could measure up to him? Then one day, word came that my beloved—my dearest Wolnoth—was on his way. He was expected home in a fortnight!"

Gasps. Whispers.

I looked through the warped boards of the stage at the faces, the glasses motionless in people's hands as the gardens held a collective breath. I felt again the heady power of storytelling, the slippery line between real and make-believe these listeners were only too eager to blur. I may not have been clever, may have tried to put on my chemise over my dressing gown that very morning, but I held the power of story in my hand and pushed and pulled their hearts like a rudder.

"Up I climbed to watch for him from Furz Hill, every day until the sun went down. The day of his expected arrival came and passed, and still he did not come. 'Twas a terrible time, hoping and waiting . . . all in vain. If I had only known . . . if I had sensed . . . he was just a mile over the hill, down in the valley, yet he would never return to me."

I shuddered and felt the dull stab of loss. The blade fit neatly into an old wound.

But then, a strange thing. A more recent man's face flashed through my mind—that bandaged soldier with the tortured countenance. Looking up at me. At his "Adelaide." Not an ounce of guile had shadowed his features. Only pain . . . and desperate hope.

But that man wasn't Captain Pelletier. *Wasn't.*

And I didn't do tragedies. Recite them to a charmed audience, yes certainly. But witness them in the flesh . . .

Life was too short.

I continued in a low voice. "So it is, that on that day my love story became a heartbreak." Warm air brushed my skin, threading through the knotted boards. "Less than a mile from home, Wolnoth perished by the hand of a jealous man. One we'd known all our lives." I went on, lowering my voice. "My beloved had survived the war and come home to die at the hand of a supposed friend.

"Oh, how I wish someone had warned me. Warned Wolnoth." Chills climbed my skin. "If only I had noticed something before it was too late. If only I had wandered out that way. If only someone had bothered to look . . . a little closer . . ."

110

I paused. Caught Peter Driscoll's gaze in the crowd and swallowed. Swallowed again.

Adelaide Walker deserves the truth. And if we look a little closer, work just a little harder . . .

Oh, stop.

But an echoey sense of *what-if* haunted the chambers of my head, my heart, as I thought of the tiny pieces that didn't lie flat. The lack of closure. I shook them away like cobwebs and fought my way through the end of the story, of Annfrieda's tears of grief becoming the well garden's spring that went on to heal thousands, and of how restoration and hope eventually came from tragedy.

But they didn't. They couldn't. Tragedy was wretched, and I couldn't bear to spend another minute thinking about it, much less pursuing it. Facing it head-on.

No.

It flashed again—the agonized face of that soldier in hospital. The hopeful face of that lovely Walker woman. I willed my mind back to the distant Annfrieda, her tragic Wolnoth, and their great love story that I'd spun like a silken web across the audience.

My final words hung in the air for a savory moment, then I twirled with a graceful raise of my arms and the spotlight behind me was cut, the apparition vanishing. All was quiet across the park, then a ripple of applause, stirring and noisy. It faded, and conversation gently closed over it. The orchestra, muffled by the stage I still hid under, swept in with background music for their chatter. A few breaths to restore myself to reality, then I snuck back out of the stage to the fresh air and moonlit night.

It would be a tragedy, this case of the missing solider. It would. A runaway carriage headed straight for the cliffs.

Unless . . .

My pulse skittered. Why did Peter leave me with the sense that I could stop it? Grab the reins and steer the carriage in a different direction?

A sudden urgency seized me and I scanned the field, but Peter Driscoll had absented himself. No, there he was, a shadow on the fringes, pausing just before the exit to look back over his shoulder. He'd never hear me yell, and it was too late.

Relief. That's all that plummeting feeling was—*relief*. It had all been in my own head. My overactive conscience. I moved back under the stage and located the little wooden box in the dimness, drawing out the necklace and clasping it in place. The star inside it caught the light and flashed, making me smile again. Showing it to Peter Driscoll was tempting. So fulfilling it was to share it with someone who felt as much awe over it as I, and Peter was one of those people.

It wasn't as if he'd take it from me. Gentle, chivalrous Peter who had never hesitated to pave the road before my steps. To make the way easier for me. He wasn't capable of snatching this dearest treasure from me. I dropped it out of sight beneath my gown.

Head down as I moved around the crowd, I made for the cottage, but poor Smithy, the painfully undervalued genius of the moving picture industry, stood alone with his ruddy cheeks and curly hair in a great sea of guests.

"Oh, there you are!" I hurried to where he stood blinking as if in shock at all the people. I absorbed his tension, his self-awareness and insecurities, wishing I could untangle him from it. Could I convey to him in a single look how much of a success he'd been these past weeks? How wildly brilliant he truly was?

I straightened the crooked little rose in his lapel and brushed grass clippings from his jacket sleeves. He was very nearly a father to me, but in his awkwardness he held back from lavishing upon me any sort of true affection.

It mattered not. To act as a daughter . . . that was all my heart needed.

"Miss Temple, finely done. Very finely done." His bush of a mustache lifted at the corners, framed by the long dimples of an aging man.

"Thank you, Smithy." I checked the hem of his jacket sleeve—it was fraying. We'd have to mend it. "I've given some thought to that next film. Why not do Annfrieda's legend? You saw how captivated they were just now. It has its own sort of magic, don't you think?"

He sipped his punch, leaving a rim of fuzz on his abundant mustache. "Haven't we spun that tale to death, though? We tell it at least four times every summer."

I handed him a linen handkerchief, pointed at my upper lip, and he blotted the fizz. "Yes, but perhaps we give the story a different take for the cine-camera. Why must everything be a wretched tragedy? Give it a bit of comedy, or perhaps make it a romance. An adventure story. Or add a twist—have Black Harry perish from guilt and shame, rather than the hero. Or someone warns Wolnoth, and he hides." The fact that Wolnoth had died so close to home, in a way entirely avoidable, was the worst part of the story. The *worst*. It left me tied up in knots. Perhaps in film I could give them the ending they had deserved.

He blinked. "Yes, but then there would be no well of tears. No healing springs. And then it wouldn't be the legend of St. Anne's Well anymore. The power of Annfrieda's story lies in its tragedy."

But if only they'd known before he was killed. Had the choice of a different story. I put a hand to my head as Adelaide's sweetly smiling face surfaced in my memory.

No, Annfrieda. *Annfrieda.*

She had deserved to know. Deserved the truth. Annfrieda, that was. *Before* it was too late.

I settled my gaze upon George Smith, willing him to hear the feeling behind my words. "You, Smithy, are a genius who can make anything you want of any story. Tell a tale worth hearing. There's already too much tragedy in the world. Go and make a better story with your magic, turning everything—"

"Yes, yes, yes." He sliced through my flow of ideas. The story so rich I could *see* it. "Far too much film reel. Something that's about sixty feet and no more. I haven't a fortune, mind. A short story is all I can manage."

"Or . . ." I tapped a finger to my chin as my imagination spun uncontrollably. "What if Wolnoth survived the attack and they didn't know until later? Or she falls in love with the soldier who brought her the news? There has to be good in there somewhere."

He blinked. "And the chalybeate well? Is it not enough that her tears brought healing to thousands? That's quite a fine ending, in my view of things."

I blew out a breath, my voice soft and small. "Not for her. Give the poor woman a decent ending."

"How you carry on." He shifted, idly watching the crowds of people.

I blew out another breath, cooling my face, but it was point-less to argue. I no longer held his flitting attention.

"Put out some more bread, would you?" He waved vaguely toward the empty table. "The guests are hungry tonight."

"Of course." I threw him a smile he did not see and fetched another basket from the tent.

Yet possibilities pounded through my veins. Perhaps it was this place, where legends perched on every shrub, hanging from branches and leaping from fountains, darting between the flowers. Many simply fell away, light and fluffy little things enjoyed for merely a moment. But some tales, like Annfrieda's, sparkled with timeless charm, an unseen element that ran parallel to something in our modern life so that we could not let it go. Not until we'd explored and understood every corner of the story, seen the whole of it, and thus seen and understood our own.

I was laying sliced bread across the table when the leaves rustled. My fingers jumped protectively to the hidden necklace.

Small bare feet protruded from the brush and the rough, uneven hem of a child's frock. I let out a slow breath of relief. What a scared kitten I'd become. Another reason not to involve myself with Driscoll and his investigations.

I hid my smile as a familiar smudged face peered out, much less hidden than its owner imagined. Humming the lively strains of "Early One Morning" cheered my heart, hastened my fingers. She always seemed bolder, drew nearer, when I hummed. So long as I pretended not to notice her.

A look of such fear had always flitted over her face, so I hadn't pressed . . . only welcomed. From a distance. And as someone had once done for me, I opened up the world of fairy tales to the young girl who was only too eager to eat them up. I sang them in songs, I spoke them aloud, whenever she was within hearing. I fancied us friends, this waif and I, even if she wouldn't allow me to speak to her. It offered me a small taste of the past, as if stepping through the looking glass to speak with my childhood self. To comfort her and smooth away the lost look upon her face.

I glanced to the right, still humming. George Smith remained, watching his gathered guests with a detached smile. Something in him delighted in—no, *needed*—polished beauty at every angle, and ragamuffins intruded on his paradise. If he spotted her, she'd be thrown out posthaste. She had been before.

Humming all the louder, I left the heels of bread at the far edge of the table and danced a bit to my song.

> Oh, don't deceive me,
> Oh, never leave me,
> How could you use
> A poor maiden so?

What a shame they always went to waste, these ends of the bread. Shame, shame. I turned with a grand sweep of my arm—a crying shame if they happened to hit the ground.

They did.

I felt him draw near—George Smith and his eye for flaws. I spun, blocking his vision of the lost bread heels. Of the little girl. "Oh Smithy, come meet your guests for once." I tugged his arm, throwing him a winsome smile. "Be agreeable and let them know you aren't the hermit in a cave yourself."

"*Meet* them? Whatever for?"

Another tug, and he stumbled along. "More ticket sales, yes? People pay more for the handiwork of a man they know and enjoy."

"People . . . *enjoying* me?" He shoved a hand under his hat, into his curly hair, and mumbled something about the cost of art.

The moment he turned toward a clump of guests, a rail-thin arm snaked out from the bush and snatched the fallen bread. I urged the man along. Smith glided into the crowds with an awkward bend to his limbs, and my prompting in his ear. "That's the way, dear Smithy. Go on and meet them all."

Finally with a smile on my lips, I turned alone into the muffled quiet of the rose gardens and felt again the magic of the place. It had been easy to believe they were enchanted, these gardens, especially when the man who had once seemed to own the place had told me so. It looked the same as it had that day, so long ago. Velvet shadows lying over the muted colors, life blooming everywhere, tugging me out of deeper thoughts into the pure beauty.

I had been crying that evening, and I couldn't recall the reason—only that the garden had seemed to absorb my sadness rather quickly. I had paused at the flowerless hedges along the path, running a hand along the back of the bench there. Remembering with tightness in my chest.

It had been a smaller rose garden then, and its resident gardener had been working over the short plants. He had paused, leaning over his spade, and eyed me. He was dirty, calloused, and a little stiff looking from the work . . . but his familiar face-creasing grin welcomed me as surely as the scent of lilacs had, and frost-like blue eyes made him seem as if he carried the sky within his soul.

He cocked his head. "You're watering my garden," he said. "Are you perhaps an enchantress? Those are exactly the sort of tears I need."

"I'm not watering anything," I grumbled. I sensed what he was doing, and I hated to be made light of.

He turned and watched me, head cocked. "Have you heard about the swan's tears that made Loch Barburry?"

I frowned. "There is no Loch Barburry."

"Well, of course not. She's stopped crying now." He wiped

his brow, looking up at the sun. "But look at the beautiful flowers her tears have left us. Nothing quite like them, is there? The tears of the wicked can drown a person. But those of the good and righteous . . . they make things grow."

My gaze flicked over the cascade of color over hills, climbing stone fences, regally lining the paths. Then back to his face. My tears would probably do nothing but rust this lovely white bench.

He turned back to his work and I pulled my knees up to my chest. I didn't wish to stay, but neither did I wish to leave. I had a special fascination with swans . . . and with enchanted gardens. And I needed to know *how* this garden was enchanted.

But he did not tell me. Instead, he climbed that hill with the aid of his spade and lowered himself to the bench beside me. By this time, I didn't mind the company.

"Traveling terribly light, aren't we?" He indicated the little bag at my feet.

"I'm lost."

"I see. Well then, where are you trying to go?"

I settled my chin on my knees and shrugged. "I don't have any place I'm trying to go. Just . . . away."

"Ah, then there isn't a wrong way. You simply have to pick one."

"There is *one* wrong way, and that is back."

"And it's no use going back, because you were a different person yesterday."

I sat up straight, blinking at this man, in this place of elastic reality where sharp edges were muffled and adults spoke in fairy tales. "You've read *Alice's Adventures in Wonderland*."

"Only six or seven times."

I grinned then. I couldn't help myself. I should have known

that's what had always animated his features—a wealth of stories. "How old *are* you, anyway?"

He regarded me. "One hundred and eighty-two. How old are you?"

I laughed out loud. "I'm forty-seven stories old."

His grin was wide. "Ah-ha! I like that answer even better."

A grin cracked my face as well. How did he always do it? Somehow a few words, and I felt settled. At home. He saw my peculiarities and valued me more for them.

There wasn't another soul alive like Gordon Makepiece. Stories had spilled out of him for hours, wrapping themselves around me, muffling the hard edges of the world, enlivening my creativity.

I ran often to help him in the gardens so he could deflate terrifying stories when they gave me nightmares. Sand off the rough edges and rebuild something different in their place. Tragic finales he turned into endings of unexpected beauty—true identities revealed, minds magically changed, enemies miraculously defeated. The world appeared rosy and shiny at every angle, soft as a petal to the touch.

The world had been gentle and plush then, God very real and nearly tangible, and everything dear to me permanent as foundation stone. I allowed myself a moment of suspended reality and imagined everything was still the same. I could smell the fresh earth, and vividly picture the welcome in his weathered face.

The rasp of his voice through whiskers.

The rustle of his heavy coat.

It was all still so clear, when I closed my eyes.

In time, after years of fairy tales and walks and mind-stretching talks, I told him about the gem. The lovely blue stone that caught the sun in the most fascinating splendor, and he began the story of the flower fairy and the enchanted gardens.

We took turns telling it, but his additions were always the best. A piece of the sky, he'd called the gem, wrenched out of the heavens by the gardener who grew enchanted flowers and lovely fairies. But, he promised, the gem was as enchanted as the garden from whence it came. It was a place where everything was as it should be, and the gem a piece of that place. It healed and set things to rights again—and it would also draw the bearer back to the enchanted gardens . . . at the right moment.

And it had. For here I was. Sixteen years later, and the gem had, through an odd turn of events, drawn me back to the place of shimmering beauty, of endless possibilities, and of fairy stories.

I sighed. When I opened my eyes, I spotted something—a white rabbit watching me from the hedges, twitching its nose. Delightfully odd, for there weren't many white rabbits about these gardens. Even the one we'd used for the fairy tale had been a marionette on strings.

I wandered over and smiled down at it. "Hello, little one. Have you—"

I stopped short. Stretched over the creature's shoulders, nearly blending in with the foliage around it, was a tiny green jacket.

Also like the fairy tale.

My heart popped. Flipped over and pounded. I moved closer—I must be mad. Or going mad. I blinked, and the rabbit was gone. An illusion. The momentary illusion of a fanciful girl. There was no shortage of green about this garden, and that's surely what I'd seen. Not a jacket. I'd prove it to myself. I hurried over and searched the bushes. Looked on the other side. Where had the thing gone? I glanced around, but saw no one.

Curious.

A rustle sounded in the bushes, and I pushed through to inspect. "Here, rabbit. Here! Where are you?" I peeked under the leaves, along the woods. I came around a corner, and spun, nearly running into a man. One in brown tweed. With a cry, I stumbled back.

A grin flickered over his shadowed face. "There you are."

I pedaled backward, hands feeling for bushes. A garden wall.

"What? What do you want with me?" Was it his rabbit? His trick on me? "Why are you following me?"

"It matters little who I am. What's more interesting by far is . . . who *you* are. And there are many answers for that, no?"

I blinked, mind racing back. Back through memories, former lives, forgotten faces. I couldn't place him.

He paused, hands up with a sad smile. "You needn't fear me. I want nothing from you, and I have no desire to harm you."

I spun, looking for help. My mind registered the sight of the white rabbit. The odd little girl from the bread table emerging from the hedgerow mere yards away, scooping him up. I wasn't going mad, then. I wasn't. I hadn't stepped into a fairy tale.

But he was wearing a jacket.

And the girl was there. The one who suddenly seemed a giant mystery herself.

The man's voice lowered. "I will, however, need you to come with me."

My heart lurched. I spun and ran, sprinting through the rows of flowers and leaping over tiny new hedges. Back to the safety of the crowds, the well-lit bandstand.

But chaos swelled there too. Something was happening. The crowds had knotted into one area in the far corner, and the murmuring was slight panic rather than gaiety. It was the stand with the sapphire in it, and Smith was standing before it, frowning.

"There!" one woman shouted, pointing my way. "There she is. It's her!"

I stopped on the fringes of the crowd, and they turned to me. "What's this about?"

Then the man in tweed was behind me, his voice low in my ear. "The sapphire in the glass case—that *was* in the glass case. It's missing. And as it turns out, the last person seen with it . . . is you."

No! I'd forgotten. I was too late. They'd think—

My fingertips found their way up my warm neck, to the thin gold chain hiding there—but found only bare skin. I sucked in a breath, felt frantically about. Cold prickles began in my face and swept down my body as I patted the top of my gown, whipped my fingertips all about the neckline. It was gone—really and truly gone. "I don't have it," I said with wonder. Then again, louder.

I spun. Faced him head-on and whispered loudly. "How did you— What did you do with it? Who *are* you?"

The crowds came closer, looking from me to him.

"I've not stolen anything," he said, holding up his palms. He removed a leather fold from his suit coat pocket and flipped it open, revealing his warrant card. "I hate to show my hand this early, but I suppose circumstances call for it. I'm Samuel Draper with Scotland Yard. I'm investigating your Miss Temple on another matter."

12

Alice: "This is impossible."

The Mad Hatter: "Only if you believe it is."

~LEWIS CARROLL, *ALICE'S ADVENTURES IN WONDERLAND*

Play!" came George Smith's frantic voice in the distance. "Play the music!"

With an awkward tangle of strings and flutes, the orchestra began again. The guests looked about, uncertain, it seemed, what they were meant to be doing. Should they chase down the thieving actress? She wasn't running. Turn and watch the musicians? Leave the park?

"Begging your pardon." A man slid between Draper and me, his tailored suit brushing my face. Peter Driscoll held out his hand to me, his smile diffusing the tension. It was instant. And very welcome. "May I, Miss Temple?"

Dancing. That's what should happen next—*dancing.*

"Delighted, Mr. Driscoll." I stepped into his embrace and he spun me away, waltzing toward the lively crowds, and only then did I begin to tremble. Vibrate, almost. I could scarcely keep my footing. I was always that way—a rock to withstand the high tides washing over me, a shaking mess when they finally receded for the moment.

I shivered and poured all my nerves into a most passionate hiss, protecting my rawness. "What are you still doing here?"

"Leading with a simple 'thank you' wouldn't be wholly inappropriate."

I puffed out a breath. "Very well then, *thank you*."

I was strong. Impenetrable. Yet how secretly wonderful it felt to be swept up in someone else's strength, held close, all of me—the charm and the prickle, all in one tightly wrapped package.

Peter's arm framed me in, palms anchored against my back. Then his fingers settled on the back of my neck, and the knots there loosened at his touch, infused with his calm.

Peter's ever-tranquil eyes watched me. "Are you ready to tell me about it yet?"

I shuddered. "Not just now." I still wasn't entirely certain what had just happened. Or what might happen next.

"Fair enough." His chin lifted, casual glance taking in the dancers beyond us. "You are well, I trust?"

I closed my eyes and let the answer sink into my core, disturbing the flutter of emotion with a sigh. "Yes. I'm well." It could have been worse. Far worse. "Now, pray, why are you still here?"

"Like anyone else, enjoying the music. And . . . the sight of a small child lifting bread from the table."

He was distracting me. "It was on the ground."

"Was it?"

"Well, eventually."

"I believe it had a little help." His face bore no accusation.

"The poor child's starving. We don't serve the ends anyway."

His look was warm and playful. Disarming. "I said I enjoyed

it, did I not? You needn't defend yourself." His smile deepened, and it was impossible to feign anger with the man. So easily did he melt a person's defenses.

How wretched of him. I rather enjoyed my defenses.

He was staring at me now, head tilted. "You've changed your mind, haven't you? About the soldier case. You wouldn't mind leaving the gardens now, would you?"

"I, uh . . ."

He leaned close, glancing over my shoulder at the crowds. "I could sneak you out of here this moment."

The breeze whipped stray hairs across my forehead, tickling my bare neck, and I looked past the reflective glass to his eyes. "You don't want me working with you."

"Why not?"

Only a hundred reasons.

I turned, lest he see exactly how *much* I wanted to say yes in that moment. To escape everything that didn't make sense around me. To attempt to set someone else free with the truth. To work on something positive and good and just. Anything, if I was honest, to stay in Peter Driscoll's calming presence. Not that I needed the man—I didn't *need* anyone.

But life was different with him nearby. Better than it ought to be. And I could use that just now. "Even if you've fooled yourself into thinking I'm clever, surely you realize my moral compass points an entirely different direction than yours."

Those velvety brown eyes remained steady. Amused, even. A smile played on the edge of his mouth. "We're not as different as you'd think."

I eyed him. Was he a better actor than me? I couldn't fathom his angle. His purpose. "You'll only be disappointed."

"In you? Not likely."

"In him. The soldier," I hurried to add. Yet his honest admission continued to wash over me. "He doesn't say much."

"Then I must teach you how to ask questions."

I stiffened in the frame of his arms, the lovely mirage evaporating. "You praise my intelligence one minute, insult it the next. I may not be an expert investigator, but I believe I'm capable of speaking with another human."

"Do you always mask your insecurities with anger?"

I glared at him. "You're about to feel the toe of my boot in your shin." When it came to men, the power usually rested in my hands. Not that I used it often, but I instinctively knew I could push or pull and they would follow.

Not this one. A tug-of-war is what we had, with equally matched teams.

If that didn't make me want to pull all the harder.

We twirled to a stop, my beaded skirt gently whipping his legs as the music ceased and a smattering of applause sounded around the yard. I waved a gracious thanks, dipped a few curtsies, and turned back to my problem at hand. The tall, good-humored problem who had an uncanny way of knowing more than he ought. More than I'd ever wish to show him. "I'm not certain I should be involved in this, Mr. Driscoll. I find myself in a bit of trouble." I jerked my head toward the crowds, which had only now begun dispersing and dancing. Toward the Scotland Yard inspector nipping at my heels lately.

"What you're saying is that you're in need of a solicitor." He grinned.

His one raised eyebrow made me laugh. Despite everything.

"Admit it. You're no more ready to let this case go than I am. Deep down, you want to see it through. Because the story isn't letting go of you, is it? Something in you knows that poor woman needs the truth, and there's a good chance we can get it for her. It's like a riddle you can't quite solve, a puzzle with only a few missing pieces. And as a storyteller, you despise not having the entire story. Especially when you want *out* of your own story for a bit."

"Count yourself a mind reader, do you?"

He tipped his head the slightest bit, remaining idly focused on me, waiting. How infuriating he could be, even when he said nothing at all. *Especially* then. "You've thought of something," he said. "A plan, perhaps. I can see it in your face. Come now, what is it? At least tell me. I don't for one minute believe you've not thought about it a little."

I glanced behind me. Nearby dancers were watching me, in tiny sips as they spun. Watching . . .

I turned back to Peter. This was a terrible idea. Rotten, no-good catastrophe of a path to trod, linking arms with him. Leaving with him. Yet my feet found their way there. "You'd have to bend your compass needle a little in my direction."

"Getting me into trouble too, are you?"

His smile. Everything else about him was perfect and symmetrical, but somehow his smile reached his eyes to different degrees, crinkling one more deeply than the other, especially when he was amused. That delighted me to no end. "Supposing I'm under arrest tonight. What then?"

He shook his head. "If they haven't already, it's because they can't do it yet. You're under what's called provisional liberty, due to lack of evidence. You may move about freely as they investigate the case. All they have now, I believe, is a few guests claiming they saw you tampering with the box. Until they have substantial proof . . ."

"Such as?"

"Well . . . finding the sapphire in your possession. Which would be terribly hard to do, if you're gallivanting off with me on a case." He raised his eyebrows again, an invitation.

"I suppose I must." I let a sigh escape. "A rescue for me, a case for you. Isn't that our deal?"

"I would have stepped in anyway."

"Oh, stop being so wretchedly *good*."

To this, he smiled. "Tomorrow evening, then. Shall we say seven?"

I nodded.

He turned and left me with a rather unsettled—but not unpleasant—feeling coursing through me. How quiet and steady he was, yet how easily he rattled a person, stirring up the contents of a body's heart, without any apparent effort. In fact it was the very *lack* of effort—his constant calm—that did it.

It made me want to tell him. Tell him absolutely everything. A cascading story that, once started, could not be stopped until it was spent.

He would try to help, I was certain of that. But did I dare risk it? Then there was the matter of his conscience. His goodness. If I laid the entire matter before him, everything concerning the gem . . . what would he do with it?

Wretched gem. Wretched Father.

13

Tink was not all bad: or, rather, she was all bad just now,
but, on the other hand, sometimes she was all good.

~J. M. BARRIE, *PETER PAN*

Peter's mind was deep in the mire of Miss Temple's plight that night, arranging and rearranging the pieces she'd revealed, as he rested his elbows on the rough countertop in the Dragon of Fire Inn. So many possible pictures emerged from her stories.

She wouldn't have stolen the gem. Not her.

But she *could* have. He pictured the easy way she'd brandished it that night in the woods. The way she'd spoken of it, looked upon it . . .

No, she wouldn't simply vanish with it. Not permanently.

But . . . she seemed to believe it hers. Act with a sort of possessive guardianship, despite what the legal paperwork claimed.

He took a long swig of cider.

"Driscoll?" The voice was barely audible through the din of the pub, but Peter had trained himself to stay attuned to such quiet summons. Especially here. His brain struggled to surface through his chaotic thoughts.

Yet not without tendrils of her curious story still tickling his mind.

Peter turned on the stool to face a liveried servant, black hair slick with pomade, countenance strained and cautious. "Yes, I'm Driscoll."

The man leaned close, head down. "Number 34 Terrace Place, Brighton. It's urgent."

"Understood." Peter slid his half-empty mug across the counter toward the publican and rose, straightening his suit jacket. That was another inn of sorts, if he wasn't mistaken. A rather middle-of-the-road collection of townhouses for let, actually, on the outskirts of Brighton. It wouldn't be a local patron summoning him, then, which made little sense. He worked purely by word of mouth. No one from outside this little seashore area even knew to call on him.

With a few parting nods toward familiar faces, Peter made for the door and summoned a hansom, wishing he'd thought to bring his motor car out tonight. He'd lent it to Roderick so the faithful servant might track down records on the sapphire and on Lily Temple. With a long exhale, he mentally shelved the investigation that had captured his mind and imagination, shifting his focus to whoever had cast out an urgent summons for him.

Within the hour, Peter was being hurried through a well-appointed hall by a nervous housemaid and toward a sweeping staircase. Only a few old oil lamps lit the house, and most rooms were shut up as if not in use. A draft chilled through his cotton shirt, a hint of the resident specters that must belong to this house. It felt abandoned—dust laced the surfaces and a stale mustiness hung in the air.

"This way," the maid whispered, and Peter tried to keep his breath shallow. They paused before a beautifully framed door and the woman rapped lightly. "It's me. He's come."

The man from the pub opened the door to them, standing guard over a dimly lit chamber with a fire warming the hearth, despite the season, and a great man huddled in a wheeled chair.

"Good evening, Mr. Driscoll," said the valet. "Thank you for coming. Forgive my earlier lack of introduction. I'm John Skinner."

Peter gave a nod of greeting, idly imagining the man skinning foxes and rabbits in the cellar. He had the appearance of one who might prove menacing in the light of day, but it was impossible to tell for certain from his solemn expression.

"Go on, then," Mr. Skinner urged Peter. "You will be discreet, won't you, with everything he tells you?"

He gave a nod. It never grew easier, this job. It was rather like a priest giving last rites or hearing confessions. He was privy to all of Brighton's most ugly secrets, and at times he felt heavy with them. Peter strode to the side of the man in the fire's leaping shadows, and remained with arms clasped before him as he gave a slight bow. "Peter Driscoll at your service, sir."

"Sit," a low voice commanded, and Peter took the high-backed winged chair beside the wheeled one.

Peter looked into the haggard, bitter-looking face of a man as old as the north-facing cliffs. But no, he shifted out of the shadows and some of the lines vanished. He must be nearly sixty, but he wore a lifetime of cares and grievances upon his face. The weight of riches and success lay upon him. "Do you know who I am, Peter Driscoll?"

"I'm afraid I've not had the honor of an introduction, sir."

The man studied Peter openly but didn't offer his name. "You are in search of the Briarwood Teardrop, are you not?"

Peter hesitated. "I'm not at liberty to give information about my other clients."

"It hardly matters," the man snapped. "I already know the answer. The Dowager Countess of Wiltshire has hired you to retrieve it for her, and you've not yet succeeded. In fact, it has surfaced only to go missing again. Well, I want to hire you as well."

Peter frowned. "I beg your pardon?"

"Bring her the gem, and bring me the girl who stole it. I shall reward you handsomely."

"I'm not interested in throwing anyone to the wolves, sir. No offense to yourself. That isn't what I do."

Mirth played at the edges of his mouth. "A wolf, am I?" He reached into his suit coat and extracted a white vellum card. "My name is Josiah Fairchild, magistrate of the Marlborough Street court district. I'm sure you will investigate my identity, and I invite you to do so. In the meantime, I need your help in setting things aright. You have, it seems, been able to do what no other detective or officer of the law has been able to do in nearly three years—gain the trust of Lily Temple. I hear you've even spent time with her, walking and talking."

"Actually, sir, Scotland Yard is already involved. Samuel Draper has been seen about the gardens, investigating the matter."

His smile was playful. "How do you think I know so much already? I'm the one who tasked him with the search to begin with, but it's not good enough. Believe me, my boy, I've been in this business a great many years, and the Yard fails more often than they succeed. Especially when it comes to this particular woman. How well do you know this . . . Lily Temple?"

"I know that isn't her real name. I know she is actually a governess from Surrey named Flora Cross."

This only made Fairchild laugh. It was a rich baritone sound, gruff and serious with edges of hidden mirth. "Is that the only identity you've uncovered? You must not be very far along in your investigation. Before she was a governess, she was known as Marigold Fontaine, visiting cousin of a wealthy family. Before that, Astrid Carmichael, esteemed companion to a marchioness, and before that, a stable boy named Thorndike Clay. All these names. Who do you say she is?"

"I'd say her current role is a pretty accurate one."

"Indeed." He clutched the arms of his chair, obviously pleased with Peter's answer. "And you are one of the few who *might* prove clever enough to see through her act. She's fooled many. Escaped more times than I can count. But she must be brought back to London."

Peter forced a swallow. "What will you do with her?"

The man leaned back in his chair, patted the arms with his giant palms, and his face softened. "I will set everything right. As any man of the law would."

Peter frowned, looked over the wilted giant's body in that chair. "You came all the way here from London . . . just to locate one thief?"

His gaze leveled upon Peter. "She is a unique case. And I have reasons for going about it this way."

"Her past escapes."

He nodded. "She would know me. Take off like a shot fired from a cannon. Explode in who knows which direction, only to become lost again."

"So you want me to apprehend her. Turn her over to you."

In answer, the man again reached into his suit coat and pulled out his coin purse. After extracting a roll of pound notes, he peeled them off one by one and laid them on the little table between them. One hundred, two hundred. "You bring her to me"—three hundred, four—"and this will be here waiting for you." One more unfurled and joined the others. Five. Five hundred pounds, ready and available for him. A cottage for his mother. A large gift for Esther and her child. A fine office space and flat for himself and Roderick. A life that wasn't so hard. So futile. So dangerously close to the workhouse for himself and those he loved most in the world.

"Take your time, think it over. Look into what I've said, if you like. Prove to yourself that it's all true. And when you do"—he patted the bills—"I'll have this waiting for you."

But Lily. Bright, effervescent Lily Temple, locked up. "You're that certain she's guilty of something?"

"Aren't we all?" Then the laughter faded from his eyes, and a solemn look weighted his features. "I know exactly who she is. Far more than you do, Mr. Driscoll. I'm one of the few who knows the truth." He smoothed his suit coat against his chest. "This isn't any ordinary task, I know. And I'm paying accordingly."

The old Gypsy woman's words rang through Peter's memory like a prophetic declaration. *"Oh no, sir. Nothing common about that one."* "If I may ask, sir, what exactly *is* Lily Temple's real story?"

He shook his head. "You're not ready for that, Driscoll."

14

Perhaps the greatest risk any of us will ever
take is to be seen as we really are.

~CHARLES PERRAULT, *CINDERELLA*

warned you, luv." Gypsy Lee's low voice tickled my shoulder from behind. It was soft and melodic, as if every word
she spoke was laced with foreshadowing. With significance.
"Warned you about the man who would ask about the necklace." She dabbed my skin with the cool cloth and stepped
back again.

We'd been filming for three very hot hours already today,
and George Smith's famous glass house was beginning to swim
in my vision. I'd even imagined I'd seen the little girl who'd
taken the bread. But the mirage of her disappeared so quickly,
I couldn't be certain.

"Yes, and then you encouraged me to go off with him."

"Ahhh, but did I also tell you to be careful? To dodge the
blow?"

Heat poured over my skin, a nervous energy pulling at my

heart and mind. I'd heard hundreds of Gypsy Lee's predictions. Never before had I been on the receiving end of one.

She stepped around to the front of me and cooled my forehead. Those curls framed her shrewd face as she calculated my thoughts and my mood in a glance. "He's asked for you again. Wanted me to give you a message about the matter you're handling . . . together."

I shook off the chronic nerves and threw her an actress's smile. "Peter Driscoll is harmless—truly. I'm only helping him for a little while." My fingers flitted instinctually up to my neck, and again felt only bare skin.

But it couldn't have been Peter who'd taken it. Was that what she was suggesting? He still wanted me working with him. Planned to rope me into yet another job this very night. So he wouldn't have it.

Unless he'd never planned on meeting tonight.

No, I hadn't even worn the necklace around Peter that night. I'd fetched it after leaving him . . . then realized it was gone before his rescue. It was Draper. Or perhaps George Smith. Those were the only two I'd spoken with that night after clasping on the necklace. The only two I'd gone near.

"There's trouble in your brow."

"Not from him."

"They came at the same time, yes?"

I rubbed my temples and Gypsy Lee frowned, lips pinched and eyebrows rising.

"Let's loosen that hair of yours. Sure and enough your mind needs to breathe." She sank gnarled fingers into my coiffed tresses and loosened an hour's worth of work, then plaited it into a loose braid that hung over my left shoulder, tugging it looser still with strong fingers. I turned to the looking glass on the set. The effect was feminine and soft, just what audiences would love. "Such *beauuuuty*," she crooned, pouring her voice into every syllable of the last word. "What a charmed life, with nary a teardrop falling on those lovely cheeks."

I tensed. She knew, of course. Knew about the Briarwood Teardrop. The great Gypsy Lee. She'd heard of it like everyone else. But . . . it had been part of her prediction. Before anyone but Peter had connected the two.

I smiled through a convulsion of chills as her fingers traced the path of a tear down my cheek and across to the bare spot on my neck. "Too pretty to listen to old Urania." She chuckled and tapped her head. "You walk into the trappiest trap of all traps."

Then I saw the little vanishing girl, most certainly, digging about in the dirt with her toe. Just inside the woods, leaning against a fir tree. Wait . . . *she* had been there that night. She'd observed my conversation with George Smith. She'd seen me alone with Draper, watched me dancing with Peter Driscoll. Every encounter I'd had between fingering the gem around my neck and realizing it was gone . . . *she had witnessed.*

Sheer relief, panic, desperation, flickered through every inch of me. Answers were within reach.

The sprite was looking up at the branches, then she looked toward me. Our gazes locked. Then she ran. "Urania." I touched the woman's blousy sleeve. "There's a girl who hangs about the gardens. Small, quiet, never speaks . . ."

"Ah, the lost girl of the enchanted woods." Her words carried high and low in a whimsical manner, a storyteller in her own rite. "Such a terrible tale, that one."

"You know her?"

"Much as I know the king of France, luv."

Which was to say, not at all. Not personally, anyway. But,

like the king of France, Gypsy Lee knew *about* the girl. "Who is she?"

With a deep sigh, the old Gypsy woman closed her eyes, tilted back her head, and spoke. "She finds herself in a different world, far from where she belongs, and she's lost her way. Going back is not as easy as holding up a gem and stepping through a looking glass. Her mother . . . *perished at sea*. Her father . . . *missing*. She is alone, and quite afraid, with no way back to where she belongs. No way of knowing *if* she belongs, even if she returns."

I stared at the spot where the girl had crouched behind the tree, her bare feet among the fallen needles, and my heart deflated a little. "Why must everything be a tragedy?" The world outside this garden was harsh. The beauty had all been shored up in this place, leaving the rest of the world in gray tones. Stone houses, bleak faces, man-made structures crowding out natural creation.

It almost wasn't worth leaving this place.

"It has tragic pieces, her tale. But she will be found. She must!" She twirled her ringed hands. "Her name means 'little miracle.' Little *Mila*."

"How do you know—"

"Come now, in the shot, Miss Temple." Smithy clapped. "Come, come."

Gypsy Lee pinched her lips into a secret-keeping smile. I sighed and turned away.

The director beckoned me from just inside the glass house, pivoting this way and that as if his brain was sending him in five directions at once. Smithy was always like this when filming, electrified and on edge, frustrated and deliriously happy all at once.

This was a whimsical piece requiring loads of creativity and a fair bit of film manipulation—all of which made dear Smithy the happiest film producer alive. Without the gem, we'd been forced to break from production of the fairy tale and instead work on a short reel Smith would take to the festival in Paris in the fall. He needed something that would show off his unique sleight of hand with the cine-camera, and this used many of his tricks.

Mae, there as the modiste, darted up and threw a shawl over my shoulders, trapping in even more heat. I inched to the right in the overwarm studio, a glass box exposed to the hot sun from every angle.

Sweat. All the sweat. *"The trappiest trap of all traps."* The notion haunted me, pestering me with doubts I couldn't quite identify.

I despised traps. Feared them above all else. No matter what name I wore, what story cloaked me, I always felt on the verge of stepping directly into one. Always about to be found out. I forced my gaze onto the looking glass and stood straight, but movement caught my eye. A deer moved in the trees just behind us. A deer . . . wearing a crown of flowers.

I blinked. Couldn't be certain. But yes—it was what I thought. As if the woods behind us were the enchanted forest come to life, and the deer had stepped out of one of Gordon Makepiece's stories. One very few people would have read.

I looked deeper into the trees and tasted the girl's name on my lips. *Mila.* But she was not there.

"Now, stand over there. No, that way. Yes, just like that. Forward, just a bit more." He hopped about behind his black box on a stand, adjusting gold knobs and lenses, shifting the camera on the chair and tightening the thick strap holding it there. "To the left, just an inch."

I held my position, and Smithy cranked the wheel, film whirring through the machine. "A look of shock. Of horror."

I slipped my hands up onto my cheeks, mouth open, and froze. The deer, I noticed in the looking glass, had vanished. Either back into the depths of my imagination . . . or back to whomever had adorned her with that crown of blooms.

Could it be? Was Gordon Makepiece here? Impossible.

Focus. Focus!

The excitable director grabbed hold of the rope and pulled that chair on casters closer and closer, focusing the moving cine-camera on my look of shock.

Later, he'd pull the rope the other direction to widen the lens while he filmed his wife, dark-haired actress Laura Bayley, staring back at me from the looking glass as if she was my reflection, because nothing was as it seemed. Not in dear Smithy's hands. Not in this pleasure garden. Not in life.

And clever, educated Laura Bayley would play the fool again, making ridiculous, wild-eyed faces like a court jester. Yet another farce. I kept my back to the camera so I could speak without the camera capturing my moving lips. "Sometimes I think Laura should play the beauty," I told Mae, who had positioned herself just out of the camera's scope to my left. "She has more talent than anyone here, and she always plays the fool."

"It takes more talent, I think, to play the fool than any other part."

"She's highly underestimated, is all. Even off the stage. I saw her one night in the pump house, cutting and piecing together that seventy-five-foot filmstrip about the x-ray machine and mixing the tints. Sometimes I don't wonder if she's the one with the ingenious ideas and Smithy merely carries them out. Then he acts as though she only uses her head to keep her ears apart."

Mae giggled.

"Ready! Ready, everyone." Smithy's voice rattled the whole place, and everyone scrambled while I struck a pose like a Grecian statue, one hand overhead. A thunk, then the familiar clack and clatter of film winding through the cine-camera, exposed and then wrapped onto another reel as Smith cranked the machine, calling out orders.

Everything was the same. The same. Even without the necklace, everything was the way it had always been. The world was not about to fall in on itself, I was not about to fall over and die.

Smithy pointed at me. "Lily, you're stunned. You glimpse your appearance in the looking glass, and you cannot believe what you see."

I turned to the looking glass, swept both hands up to my cheeks, and exaggerated my shock for the camera.

Mae's gentle voice came from the left. "So this man. This Mr. Driscoll. He is nice to look at?"

"Depends on who's looking." I swept up a hairbrush and posed before my reflection. I spun around, hands in the air, miming my shock, then approached the glass again and touched it.

"Aaaand *stop.*"

I held my breath as the clacking slowed to a stop. Smith capped the lens and his wife, Laura, hurried to stand before the looking glass as if she'd just come out of it. I locked eyes with her in greeting but didn't dare smile. One inch off when he restarted the film, and the picture would jump unnaturally, reminding the audience that the story was only pretend.

When Laura dropped the smoke tablet, a puff of smoke billowing around her, Smith lifted the cap, cranked the lever, and the familiar *clack-clack* of rolling film freed me to move again.

"You're frightened, Lily," he called out. "This older version of you, an old crone, has just stepped out of the looking glass to stand before you."

A tiny twitch of the eyelid was the only reaction poor Laura gave to the words *old crone* from her husband.

"Good. Laura, stand . . . yes, right there. Now *smile*."

She did, actress that she was. She waved her arms and danced about, frizzy gray wig framing the frenzied expressions on her face. She fell back, arms pinwheeling, and landed in a heap of petticoats, skinny legs popping up in the air. She shot back up to standing in one acrobatic arc of her body, and a laugh bubbled up inside me.

She truly was a talent.

"Stop! Stop, stop, stop. Break the scene."

My pose melted and I strode out of the box of heat, fanning my face and brushing away stray hairs.

Mae came to hand me a glass of lemonade, offering her usual gentle smile. "How ever did you manage to fall in with an inquiry agent, anyway?"

I followed her and blotted my forehead, wishing I could splash the lemonade over my face. "He shielded me from a rather bothersome man." Pine needles crunched under my boots, and the fresh air blissfully saturated my senses. "He requested my help in exchange, so I'm giving it."

"And?"

I stopped. "And what?"

Mae smiled, pale freckles stretching across her cheeks. "You're Lily Temple. There's always an 'and.'"

Again my fingers climbed to my bare neck. "Perhaps a small one. But it's tiny, mind." I told her quickly about Gypsy Lee's oddly accurate prediction and the necklace he never could have known I had.

Her lips pressed into her signature smile as she stood behind me and fitted tiny flowers into my braid. "I suppose the romantic in me hoped the 'and' was something else."

"Not a bit of it." I waved her comment off. "It's beastly of me to say it, but . . . well, he's rather dull. A rule follower who reads books and even wears spectacles. He belongs in a schoolroom, shushing unruly children."

"And you would be the ringleader of those children." She smiled and bumped my shoulder. "So why on earth do you agree to go about with him?"

"I suppose part of me is still intensely curious how he knew about the necklace. And what he wants with it. He also seems to want to protect me. To help me. Although I cannot think the reason, and that makes me even more curious. There's something odd about the man. No . . . unexpected."

But he didn't steal it. *Couldn't* have.

She sidled up with the smile of a secret. "Well, the prediction isn't any mystery. That Driscoll man came to St. Anne's asking about the necklace and spoke to Gypsy Lee. It was she who told him you had it and sent him your way."

I frowned. "Did she? You're quite certain?"

She curved her lips into a frail smile. "I heard him speaking to her in her caravan before the event a week ago. Then he turned your direction and never looked away."

"That little minx." I grabbed another lemonade and drank it down. "Fortune teller, indeed." Although still, I wondered how she'd known about the little girl. Perhaps she had actually won the child over and gotten her talking.

I turned back to watch poor Smithy growl and bang on the cine-camera. It tended to receive the brunt of his artistic frustration. The director waved his hands. Let out a yell. "Go and luncheon, all of you. The dratted film is jammed. *Again*."

Arm in arm, Mae and I hurried away from the excitement and down the path to the cottage we shared. She tossed her hat onto the bureau and turned to me. "Was he from the police, then? Investigating the sapphire? It *is* the Briarwood Teardrop, isn't it?"

I collapsed back on my bed with a sigh. "I haven't any idea. I suppose it is."

"Shame you don't have it anymore." She watched my face, as if waiting for me to reveal something to her. "You didn't answer his questions about it that night, did you?"

"I did. Just not very thoroughly." I twirled a strand of hair around my finger. "I suppose I do enjoy my secrets. Better to be silent than vulnerable. Especially to a stranger like Peter Driscoll. And especially now, with everyone looking at me. Suspecting. Gossiping. Accusing."

"Then perhaps you should turn the tables on him." She gave a warm, playful smile. "Ask *him* the questions. Find out how he's involved with the sapphire, and why he is so certain it's the Briarwood Teardrop."

I frowned. "What makes you think I didn't ask such obvious questions already?"

"Have you?" She smiled in that way that implied she knew me better than I knew myself.

I stared at my reflection in the looking glass. This was absurd. I asked questions. Of *course* I did. All the time, actually. What sane human didn't?

See? Question.

She came to sit behind me on the bed, perching her chin on my shoulder and watching me in the looking glass. "If I were you—and I often wish I was—I'd stop talking and start digging."

I sighed out the ache that tightened in me. One never forgot how to have a sister, even after years of separation. It was an entire piece missing out of one's life, not having someone in that sacred position when there once had been. I smiled at Mae, imagining for a flash that she was Leonora. "Very well, then."

"Just bring up the subject and let him talk—you might find out more than you'd expect."

If the subject arose, it would likely be him doing the finding out. That was the way of things around that man.

"When do you go to help him?"

"Tonight. After filming is done for the day."

She laid a gentle hand on my arm, eyes glowing. "Well then, Lily Temple. Here's to your digging." Then she disappeared behind the ragged curtain to her little corner of the cottage.

15

A good friend doesn't let you do
stupid things . . . alone.

~JACOB GRIMM

My idea for sneaking us back to see that patient proved a worthy one. "Lucky for you, I remembered about the vines." I grabbed hold of the rough bark clinging to the hospital wall and pulled myself farther up.

Somewhere below me, Peter grunted. "Yes. Fortunate." The vine shook as he threw his weight onto it and struggled to pull up.

They were solid, heavy-built vines that had been climbing the sides of this stone building longer than I'd been alive. Nearly as good as a ladder. That no one else had even attempted this method utterly shocked me. "At least you haven't a tangle of heavy skirts to weigh you down. You'd never last." I bunched up the fabric of my nurse's uniform and flung it over my arm for the umpteenth time. "Come now, hurry it up before a guard spots you dangling there and decides to round up his men."

I clambered up onto the slate roof beside the dormer, arms

burning, and leaned back against the small, circular window. If my guess proved correct, this would lead to a closet or a small office—hopefully one that was unoccupied. We didn't need witnesses as we slithered through and dropped onto the floor.

Leaves shook on the vines I'd just climbed, then the top of Peter's head came into view. More huffing, then he climbed up beside me and fell back against the brick wall, one leg extended across the shingles. "When the door is closed, find a window, I've always heard," he said between heavy breaths. "Much less appealing when it's on the second floor."

"It's only sensible to lock all the windows on the first floor. You cannot fault them for that." I brushed stray leaves from his shoulders and hair. "At least I didn't make you climb to the third. That's where our patient is, you know."

"Believe me, I've thought of little else since we started." He swiped a hand through his hair, then removed his spectacles and pinched the bridge of his nose.

I looked the man over with a critical eye, flicking another leaf from his waistcoat and cuffing his linen sleeves. Funny. He wasn't a surgeon—not by any stretch—yet he wore this borrowed clothing I'd snitched from the costume box as if he lived in it every day. The bands around his upper arms, dirty apron tied around the waist, even the cheap costume boots fit him as if he'd always worn such things and worked hard in them.

Breath steadying, he turned to look at me. "They will kick us out if they catch on."

I shrugged. "Then we'll move on to another plan."

"Which is?"

I shrugged again, turning toward the window and shoving my fingertips under the sash. "No sense making a plan before we need it."

"Heaven forbid."

I put a finger to my lips and tipped the window out toward me, propping it up as I slid my body and the skirts beneath the sash and into the room.

A chemist's cupboard. Tiny and cramped, but vacant.

With a few grunts and a little struggle, Peter inched his torso through the window. His waist caught and he dangled there, grunting and huffing, legs hanging outside.

"Come, give me your arms. Quiet, now." I braced my knees against the wall, grabbed his arms, and pulled. Pulled again. On the third, he tumbled through the little opening, rattling glass jars on shelves as we landed in an awkward pile on the floor. His spectacles clattered to the wood planks, and I blinked up into gold-flecked brown eyes, now hitting me in full force without their artificial barriers. They stared down at me, dousing me with their liquid goodness. He was like a glowing hearth, this man, surprisingly warm when one neared it.

He pushed up and knelt, pulling me up to sitting with his arm behind my back. How near we were, his breath puffing out across my face, his parted lips just before my nose. He frowned and patted about the floor in the dark, so I reached for the metal spectacles and slid them onto his face, surprised at the silky feel of his hair—like corn tufts.

He smiled his thanks and kept his gaze on me. It was as if the rest of the world had disappeared, simply because we couldn't see it, and none of the usual rules applied. He might say anything, do anything.

His head tipped very slightly to the right. "Something's happened. Is it good or bad? It's telling, isn't it? Something to do with the sapphire. You have some notion of where to find it.

A lead, perhaps, but you're not certain what to think about it. You're confused, and ah! You also wonder if *I've* taken it."

"Why do I feel as though I'm not even involved in this conversation?"

"By all means, add whatever you wish."

Finger to my lips, I helped him rise and motioned for him to follow into the main room—a surgical recovery ward, from the looks of it, with trays of dirtied bandages and men wilted onto cots. We slipped from the closet, and the patient with tufts of overgrown hair at every angle stirred to look at us, but the other four lay limp on their beds.

I pushed Peter out ahead of me before the blinking man could voice a question. How long until he told someone what he'd seen? What *had* he seen?

I buttoned my leg o' mutton cuffs more firmly onto my forearms and pushed forward with all the efficiency of a nurse on duty. "Head down, pretend you know where you're going. Stairs are in the rear, left of the nurse's station."

"Nurse. *Nurse!*" The man's weak cry sounded as we passed into the hall.

Two women in white aprons and caps hurried around us into the room we'd just quitted, and Peter widened his stride. Up the steps and through the next corridor, I pinched his arm when we'd reached the room I remembered and nudged him into it. "We haven't much time."

The convalescing men hardly noticed us as we entered. I pointed out a soldier against the far wall, sprawled under tangled blankets, and Peter gave a nod. We approached, and Peter looked the man over while pulling a rickety wooden chair to the side of his cot and lowering into it as if we had all the time in the world. "Captain Pelletier, how are you feeling?"

The man struggled to turn, then blinked up at Peter with a weak noise in his throat. I moved back into the shadows, lest he recognize my face.

Peter Driscoll's affable bearing, the welcoming way he sat forward in the chair, gave him the look of a true surgeon even more than his clothing. "I need to get a clearer picture of your condition and the background of your case to ensure you are receiving all the treatment necessary. Will you indulge me?"

"Of—of course." His voice was weak. Breathy.

I leaned forward. Was he a little worse? He seemed it.

Peter's voice remained low and even. "Very good. Now, can you tell me where you were taken captive?"

"Somewhere on the sea. After we left the Boer region." The patient was undeniably weak. He barely moved on his cot.

"And how was your health? Were you struck with any illness there?"

"I . . . no. But my memory . . . it isn't so clear."

"You've endured a great deal. And they took you where, when you landed?"

He shook his head. "No idea. We were piled in a train car. It was dark."

"I do hope they at least fed you."

"Sour milk and slimy . . . slimy salad." His breathing was heavy. "I barely ate until I escaped."

Peter leaned back with a frown. "So they restricted your food."

"Talked of . . . spiritual food. Fed us on prayers. Hymns. Confession."

"The rest of your unit—are any of them yet with you?"

"Dead. Lost. Captured. All but me."

"What medicines were you given?"

"Something . . . strong. For pain."

"Right. Good. And now, what is your real name, sir?"

Pain shot through my clenched hand. I didn't even realize I'd been gripping a metal bed frame until I flexed my fingers.

The man's eyelashes fluttered between bandages. "Addy. Fetch Addy." Moaning, he writhed to the side. "Addy! *Adelaide!*"

Footsteps pounded. I leaped forward to quiet him, but he grabbed my hand when he spotted me, those eyes blazing into mine and his grip surprisingly strong. "He's alive, Addy." Sweat coated his face and he spoke rapidly. "Don't know where. We were captured. Did you get the letter? I made them post it, because he saved my life, helped me escape. I vowed I'd find you, however I could. He saved me. And now, he . . . he needs . . ."

"What?" Peter urged. "What's happened to him?"

"I didn't know how else to get to you, Addy. I didn't know." He squeezed my arm with a trembling hand. "He didn't want you finding out he's alive. It's dangerous. Especially if they find out he's a captain. That's why he gave me his tags, told me not to tell you, but you can save him. He's—"

Three nurses in tall white caps rushed into the room and made a half circle about his bed, shielding him from us. One turned to us with a skeptical eye, and it occurred to me that my uniform was all wrong. It was gray, and theirs a solid navy-blue serge. Now I stood out. Probably we both did. "Who you be?"

Peter gave a slight head bow. "We're just departing. My apologies for the upset."

"*Guards!*" Her voice barreled through the wards and footsteps pounded down the corridor, boots thudding on tile.

Peter shoved me past them and out the door as uniformed men charged into the room. Chaos broke loose behind us as we flew down the staircase. I heard their voices—loud and angry. They were coming, yells echoing.

"Wish . . . I could . . . wear trousers." I huffed out my words as we flew down. "No, I wish . . . we'd heard his answer. You were close—infuriatingly close." I grabbed the rail and spun onto the next set of stairs. "Will we go back?"

We. When had that come about?

"No. He'll be moved. I've seen it happen before." His breath came heavy until we lunged out the side door and hopped the porch rail. He pulled me after him to the grass. There he let out a giant exhale and pinched the bridge of his nose, displacing his spectacles for a moment.

The door banged open behind us, and uniformed men poured through it.

I grabbed him and we ran. "What now?"

"There." His red steam car rumbled just around the bend, driven by his valet. We nearly threw ourselves into it, and the thing took off as we clung to slick leather. It leapt forward and bounced down the drive, us barely holding on.

A sharp turn, and I was flailing to hold myself in. "What sort of—"

"Beg pardon, Highness, that my automobile handling doesn't meet your standards."

Peter clapped his valet on the shoulder. "Easy, Roderick."

"You warned me to make a mad dash once you came out," the man yelled over the engine's rumble. "So here's your mad dash, Pete."

I clung to the bar beside the seat, eternally grateful for its lifesaving presence as we raced at a reckless speed over gravel and small shrubs toward the gate. "Any faster and the car will leave us behind in the road." A horse might be swifter, but somehow it felt, without a creature drawing the vehicle forward, as if we were careening toward certain death. It was terrifying.

Exhilaratingly so.

The car seemed to lean out over the ocean as it swept around a curve, and I threw my arms around Peter with a cry and a pounding heart that turned into giggles.

Peter cast me that bright smile of his, one eye crinkling nearly shut with merriment. "Still think me harmless, do you?"

I tossed back a smile. A laugh. Thrilling, it was, every encounter with this man. "You really should let me drive," I shouted. "I'd make us a marvelous getaway."

He pulled me close as we cleared a small hill, bouncing a bit on the landing, and I laughed again. How it tickled my insides.

It might be exciting, working with Peter Driscoll—and unlike film, these stories were real. So was the danger.

Even better.

My heart pounded all the way through town even as we slowed, and the steam car neatly dodged carriages and strolling people, creeping through the crowded streets. When we at last came in view of the ragged cliffs and bumped over a quieter rock-strewn road, Roderick slowed the vehicle again, and we all shifted in our seats, sitting straight for the first time since our grand exit.

I peeled myself off Peter's chest and looked past him to the lush shoreline. "This isn't the way back to the gardens."

"I thought perhaps you could do with a little time away from them. Some tea perhaps, and a little time to talk things over. To tell me your theories." He turned and doused me in an affectionately playful look that warmed me through.

I should not have encouraged what I saw blossoming behind his sparkling gaze. I should have turned away, but his amusement was contagious. So was his obvious affection for me. It bubbled up and ended in a broad smile that stretched my cheeks. That was the point in which I should have undone what had been set in motion with four pivotal words: *Take me home, please.*

But I did not. It's a pity and a blessing that we cannot see the future until it is the present.

16

"But it's no use now," thought poor Alice, "to pretend to be two people! Why, there's hardly enough of me left to make one respectable person!"

~LEWIS CARROLL, *ALICE'S ADVENTURES IN WONDERLAND*

A wide, sweeping turn and we were driving up a road with pines lined up like liveried servants awaiting our entrance, which only set the tone for Peter Driscoll's home. A great hall loomed just ahead, with a checkerboard hedgerow and rounded windows like gaping eyes watching our approach. Towers framed the main structure at odd intervals, as if added one by one as afterthoughts. There could be no other estate like it.

Peter smiled as his hair flipped about his forehead. "Well done, Roderick. I believe we managed to elude them."

"So, then," said Roderick, "was it successful, sir?"

I cringed, turning away. I wasn't used to failing at a thing and didn't much care to admit defeat to Roderick Heath. But it couldn't be helped.

Peter handed me down when the car stopped at the great house, then turned to Roderick with a string of words I never could have predicted. "Check into French hospitals along the southern coast, Roddy. Something that was once a consumption sanatorium. See if they have any soldiers in them who might pass as Pelletier. Anyone unidentified or perhaps . . . misidentified. Anyone whose file raises questions."

"Right on, Captain." He saluted and charged inside.

I looked over the bespectacled solicitor who had somehow drawn me into his game that continued unfolding. That was the nature of our relationship, Peter and I. He was so predictable and ordinary that I always knew what he was about—then he went and proved me wrong. "How did you—"

"The slimy salad, the hospital run in the religious order . . . it's quite obvious, isn't it?" He tossed the surgeon's apron into the car and led me up the steps into a nearly unlit house.

"How, exactly?"

A swish as he shrugged out of his suit jacket and hung it on some unseen hook. "Well, he's being held in France, a place where the hospitals are still run by the church, eating 'slimy salad' kelp and 'sour' goat's milk, which puts him in a rural yet coastal area. We know from the man in hospital that he's alive, or was when the man last saw him, so by my estimation he's been captured by a Boer-sympathizing French fleet and he has allowed his fiancé to believe him dead either due to disinterest in her, which seems unlikely, or out of love for her, believing his current condition—physical or mental—would be a detriment to her. Either way, the man's lost."

I blinked at him in the dim entry, glad he could not see the shock coloring my face.

"We won't let him *stay* lost, though, don't you worry. It's all very end-of-Jayne-Eyre." He lit an old oil lamp on a table and a soft glow swelled in the entryway.

"So, what, we simply drag Miss Walker to some equivalent of a burned-up manor and let her convince this blind—or otherwise injured—fiancé to return to her? That he should cast aside all hesitations and go on to marry her as if nothing had happened?"

He blinked at me. "Why . . . yes." Lamp in hand, he led me then into the great hall of his home—the polished wood, gleaming tile, the ceiling so high it seemed there should be celestial, winged beings singing in a floating mass above our heads.

I stood in the center, straining to see exactly how high this dome was and whether or not it was blue paint at the top or simply sky. Filmy curtains fluttered at the drafty old windows, and the lamp softened every hard edge of the house, giving it a fairy-tale-castle quality I found irresistible. Surely there were specters and secrets slipping in and out of the stone rooms and all manner of tales, true and embellished, waiting for me to reach out in any direction and find them.

I could scarcely take it all in. I turned to my companion to share a look of astonishment and found him watching not the house—it was *his home*, after all—but me, with tender delight at my silly, open-mouthed wonder. I snapped my jaw shut and straightened, reigning in the last of my dignity. "I assume this is all meant to impress."

"It fails on me, if that's the aim." Peter's footfall echoed across the great hall, then through the corridors. "May I assume you're accepting the challenge, then?"

"The soldier?" I shifted quickly back to the case. "But what if he won't come back? What if he *can't*?" I still hadn't convinced myself he wasn't dead as reported.

"He will. Eventually." He strode with me down a blue-trimmed corridor with gaslit sconces turned up toward the ceiling, leaving the rest of the wall in deep shadow.

He paused. "Come, have a seat." Then he threw open double walnut doors to a veritable wonderland of leather spines, gold-embossed titles, and the scent of a thousand stories between pages.

I gasped. My inner child burst forth from the depths where I ordinarily kept her hidden, overwhelmed at the beauty within arms' reach. Books filled every square inch of wall up to a walnut balcony, then continued right on up to a cathedral-style ceiling. Ladders lay invitingly against several shelves and candles stood at the ready on several tables. Light poured through arched windows and fell upon a blue-and-gold Oriental rug spread over the floor.

I knew Peter expected us to talk here, but I couldn't keep my gaze from crawling over every inch of this place, touching and experiencing every nuance two and three times, just to take it all in. I half expected a gnome to wriggle out from between two chairs or a twinkling fairy to perch on a golden chandelier, looking down upon us.

And in the corner, a tall, covered object—it had to be a harp—loomed like a specter idly observing the room, waiting to be noticed.

I noticed.

And I ached to run over and pull that sheet off, glorying in the sight of the instrument that matched this elaborate room. It would be gold with perfect strings, a swan's neck arch to the frame, and the face of an angel at the helm. It would smell of polish and sound like heavenly voices.

But it was not my home, not my study, not my harp.

"Oh." A woman's voice. Then a poised figure emerged from the shadows—deep purple skirt in a bell shape, with a lacy white shirtwaist for its handle. "Harrison didn't mention I had a caller."

Peter stepped forward, hand on his chest. "Iris, this is Miss Lily Temple. She's my guest. Miss Temple, my brother's future bride, Miss Iris Stanhope. She makes her home here at the country estate and my brother is in town while they await the impending nuptials."

Her eyebrows arched. "Miss . . . *Temple*, is it? How interesting."

"What a glorious place to bide your time, Miss Stanhope. You must count yourself most blessed among women."

My host only glared. How stiff she was. How disapproving of everything unfortunate enough to come within a yard of her. Especially me.

"Forgive me, I am in such awe of this lovely room. You must spend simply *days* at a time in here."

She leveled an unblinking gaze my way. "I imagine it does seem quite grand to you." Her smile was prim.

I unsettled her. Like tiny pricks from sewing needles. But why? Did she believe I was insulting her home in some backhanded fashion?

"It isn't just its magnificence, Miss Stanhope, but its uniqueness. Uniform and symmetrical houses are plentiful, but this one . . . Mismatched towers, odd corridors that don't seem to lead anywhere, unexpected rooms here and there just begging for exploration, and shadows—lovely, irresistible shadows at every turn. Who knows what might turn up?"

"An errant milkmaid, for example. Or a daisy."

I stiffened. Feigned a smile. "What an odd thing to say." It was never pleasant, this crossing over of invented lives. I couldn't even recall where I'd met her as milkmaid Daisy Fink—the market, perhaps? Yes . . . yes. The more I stared, her angular features clarified into a memory. A specific moment. A red feathered riding hat, a gray dappled stallion. Had she been the one to nearly run over my milk cart with her horse?

I dared not glance Peter's way. His eyes were upon my back—I could feel them. He was clever enough to pick up on her hints—read my thoughts, perhaps—if he had a mind to. I pressed my lips shut, lest I say anything amiss. My position was tenuous at best every moment, even here.

I turned away and my eyes landed on the sheeted object, that ghostly harp, and soon my feet were carrying me toward it, closing the distance. My hand was reaching up and pulling. With a dusty *whoosh* the cover was off and a magnificent golden harp stood, inclined toward me.

I caressed the frame, leaned my head against the polished wood, and trailed my fingertips over the strings. A soft melody wafted over us, loosening the tension, warming the room as it was meant to be. I plucked and strummed, noting the vibration of each string and moving to the next and the next.

A story seeped out of my imagination, and I voiced it along with the harp. Sure and clear in the style of ballads, about a garden and all the creatures who found a home among its beauty. The notes, the words—everything wove into a song that had never before been heard.

It was the story of an enchantress who disguised herself as a lowly street vendor, selling her handfuls of daisies in the market square. A brazen woman came tearing through on her horse, whip cracking over and over. The pair had careened directly toward several small children, but the brave maiden yanked them out of harm's way.

I dared not turn and look at her face. The maiden, I continued, resolved to spend her life bringing justice against the reckless horsewoman in a most unexpected way. The law was worthless against the wealthy, but the maiden, the disguised enchantress, didn't need it. She would be ready when the time was right. She would bring about justice and teach the wild woman what her actions might have cost. When she least expected it . . . there it would befall her, and the world would be set to rights.

As it came to a natural conclusion, I looked up at the woman who had been stunned into silence—either by the beauty of my playing or, more likely, her shock at my forwardness. I deflected her stare with a smile.

She was less attractive with that look of horror upon her features, but infinitely more familiar. Yes . . . yes, my memories had been correct.

A laugh sounded behind us, hearty and rich and full-bodied. Peter.

The Iris woman's head snapped to the left, staring Peter into silence, but it did nothing to quiet the twinkle in his eyes. "I must beg private use of the study for a few more moments, Iris. We've business to discuss, then Miss Temple will be on her way. We won't be long, I promise."

Her mouth pinched. Nostrils flared. And her ears—the poor woman's exposed ears turned beet red. She excused herself and departed, leaving me alone with Peter and all the hints she'd dropped to the room at large. All the unanswered questions. And me, running low on excuses and evasions.

17

We are all very anxious to be understood, and it is very hard
not to be. But there is one thing much more necessary.
. . . To understand other people.

~GEORGE MACDONALD, *THE PRINCESS AND THE GOBLIN*

Peter approached me with a host of thoughts visible just
below the surface. He took my hand, lifted it to his lips,
and brushed my knuckles with a kiss. "Might I hire you
to do that again sometime?"

"Don't be ridiculous. Nothing I did was worth a farthing."
I shook off the silken cobwebs of the story.

He stood before me, beaming in that glowing ember way of
his. "Do you know how many people can ruffle Iris Stanhope's
feathers—"

"Anyone who lived and breathed, I'd imagine."

"—and come out on top?"

I cleared my throat. "Well."

He sighed. "She's the one who insisted the harp be covered. It
belonged to my sister, and she hates to be reminded of Esther."

"Was Esther worth despising?"

"Everyone loved Esther. Simply everyone. She was absolutely beautiful in every way. Inside and out, with hair as black as night and a fair complexion."

"Well, no wonder she loathes the woman."

That laugh again. Rich and whole, like a baritone. "Shall we sit in peace now?" My host indicated a little pink brocade chair and brought tea service closer, pouring two cups. Something about the grandness of the place matched his quiet dignity. Peter looked at home there. Of course, he looked at home nearly everywhere.

Well, except high up on the side of a hospital building. He'd been rather awkward about that.

We spoke of unimportant things, of the train station rebuild in Brighton, the bright crocuses this year, and the absurdity of a horse named Flotsam—*Flotsam*—taking third in the June Derby that year. It was all so much circling around the important matters while our thoughts settled. No mention was made of Daisy Fink the milkmaid.

Then he fell silent, his eyes magnified by clear lenses watching me. It struck me again that he had a way of looking at you as if he heard your thoughts, understood what you couldn't put into words, and it was all of the utmost importance. I was certain then that he couldn't have missed what had gone on below the surface a moment ago, and I waited for him to ask.

He did not. "How long since you've seen your father, Miss Temple?"

"Seven years." It was out before I could think. I swallowed. He was coming too close to the truth. Had likely already figured out some of it. I broke the gaze. Seven years without Papa's baritone voice vibrating through my chest. Without Papa's bold look of pride cast my way, his flood of devotion that had carried me along the rapids of everyday life.

"And you're wishing you could see him again."

"It isn't likely. Not in this life."

"Yet a part of you is holding on to the hope that you will. That all things will be restored, the way they are in happy stories."

I moved closer, looking into that face that was becoming so familiar. "How do you do that? How do you know exactly what I'm thinking? It's rather unsettling, you know."

"You have a tell." He reached up and touched his chest, and I suddenly realized I'd been fingering the place where the sapphire had once lain hidden. "You always do that when your thoughts stray to your father. They're connected somehow, aren't they? Your father and that missing sapphire."

"I'd rather not say."

"Fair enough." He poured us both tea and handed me a cup.

I fiddled with mine. "So when you meet a stranger, and you don't know her tell, how do you find your information?"

He shrugged, wiping the pot with a rag and setting it down again. "I go about in certain circles and hear certain things. I get to know most everyone."

"People just . . . *tell* you things?" There had to be more.

"I ask good questions." He took a sip. "But mostly, I let them talk. You never know what someone might say with a posture of interest and a little patience. And most people make the same assumption about me that you did—that I'm harmless." This he followed with a wink that I felt all the way to my toes and back up again.

"How ever did you find this sort of work? You don't seem to have an office with a sign."

"No, and that's half of my appeal. I've always made a habit

of collecting details, holding information, the way some collect cuff links or bottles of bordeaux. People began to think of me as a resource, ask me favors, to find runaway sons or illegitimate heirs, and it grew into what it is now. An accidental business that very nearly supports me." He took a sip. "What of your position? How did you take up acting?"

"I've loved stories forever. I used to sneak storybooks up to the attic to read. I told tales over and over to my father while we walked home from the garden late at night." My heart slipped and choked at the memories of warm summer nights, of singing grasshoppers and a sky of stars . . . and a dear face right beside me. "Yes, I've . . . always loved stories. They made life bearable when things didn't go aright. When they fell apart."

Stop. Why had I said that? My neck heated.

His gaze continued to burrow, releasing a passel of butterflies inside me. I waited. Stiffened until every muscle ached. Answers and evasions for every possible question about who I was flew through my brain as I waited for him to ask one.

Instead, he held out a plate of bread. "Well now, how about it? Will you see this soldier case to the end? Or will you shut the book early?" And in that simple question, the conversation about my secrets had come to a close. It was a relief, yet I remained on edge. It wasn't what he said, but what he *didn't* say that made the man so unsettling. So hard to dodge. One never knew which way he was about to turn. What he actually knew.

I took a hunk and studied the crusty edge. "How will this work? There must be hundreds of hospitals in France. You can't possibly visit them all."

"Two, actually." Roderick emerged through the doors and held out a slip of paper to his master. "I've made some calls. There are two hospitals in France that meet all the criteria."

"Ah. Well, that sounds quite a feasible trip. Especially for a woman in love. Do you suppose she'll refuse to trouble herself to come with us, once she learns her beloved might be alive?"

I stared down at the rug, that plush, ornamental rug from some far-flung Eastern nation. "No. I don't suppose she will." She was Annfrieda—only her Wolnoth still lived.

Probably.

"Thank you, Roderick." Peter sat and scribbled something on the back of the paper Roderick handed him. "Make some inquiries in the morning, use these names to bend a few arms if necessary. See if our missing soldier might be hiding out at one of them. He'll be under another name or listed as unidentified."

I looked at the well-dressed man, sitting amicably in the midst of his books, who dealt more surprises than an illusionist. "You truly meant what you said about your cases. You never fail at them."

He sipped and looked over the top of his teacup at me. "Not if I can help it. And I usually can." There was no presumption, no arrogance, in his statement. Only honesty.

"So . . . *any* lost person. A crumb of information, and you can find them? As simply as that?"

"Who is it you wish me to find, Miss Temple?"

I fiddled with the strap of my little handbag, the braided rope that slipped through my fingertips. "His name is Gordon Makepiece. And I simply want to know that he fares well."

"A friend of yours?"

I sat straighter. "I don't have a mountain of banknotes to pay you."

"I didn't ask for any." His gaze was steady but not unkind.

I took a deep breath. "Very well, then. As payment, I might . . . *might* . . . be persuaded to tell you more about the sapphire, since you seem to want to know so much about it. But you must trust everything I say, no matter how odd it sounds."

That easy smile reached his eyes, one almost disappearing in the pleasant crinkles. He rose, lifting the pot. "More tea, my lady?"

I held out my cup, gaze steadily searching his. "Can I trust you, Peter Driscoll?"

He poured the tea and set down the kettle, then reached out his hand to mine. "I will find your Mr. Gordon Makepiece, Lily Temple. I vow it."

"Very well then, one question. You may ask me one question, and I will answer honestly and thoroughly. Anything you like. And I'll pay your fee when I'm able."

He narrowed his eyes, wiping up tea drips. "Three questions, and no fee. Ever."

"I can't argue with that price." Yet as I considered this, suddenly his request seemed more costly than the small fortune I didn't have. I hesitated, ready to draw back.

"Done."

But it was too late. I braced myself.

"Let's begin with talking about Mr. Makepiece. Who was this man?"

"A gardener at St. Anne's, working among the roses specifically, and he wrote fairy tales. He's always had a certain knack for storytelling. I owe my fascination with stories to him."

"How amusing he must have been. A fine distraction."

"He was far, far more than that." I took in a deep breath, resisting the urge to tell everything.

"Some people reshape the world for a person—change reality. Or one's view of it, perhaps."

"Yes. He did that for me all my life. Most adults never waste time on fantastical novels—literary nonsense, that sort are called. But as a man of mature years, he read all of them—studied them, even. Made up his own too. He told me stories all the time about little girls and trolls, fairies and goblins that all stood for something. Symbolism.

"His stories . . . they were an escape from life at first, a boon for a rather out-of-place girl. But then, they helped me untangle my thoughts too. See life clearly." I clutched my hands in my lap. "If he'd tried to explain the difficult people in my life, or the heartache of losing my mother, it would have fallen flat. But in stories . . . truth took shape in my mind. Somehow, I reached conclusions on my own. Gleaned wisdom. So to your question . . . Gordon Makepiece. He is the one who wrote the fairy tale we're filming now, and he did it for me. About me. It was his final gift to me."

"How terrible it must have been for you to lose him."

"You have no idea." I sighed, pain bunched in my chest. I'd taken a gigantic risk, suggesting the use of his fairy tale in the films, but I'd had to. It was a summons, a subtle signal to him that, if he still roamed the earth, I was looking for him, and I was in the gardens. If he one day saw it, the risk would be well worth it. "That welcoming smile was rolled out for me like red carpet any time I came near him. Not many adults are like that with children. He filled my life. And then one day, he simply vanished. He never came back."

"And you always wondered."

"To this day." I shook my head. Blew out a breath. "There, that wasn't terrible."

"Good. Because that was only the first question."

I straightened, grasping the chair. "That was at least six!"

"I only asked you one question, Miss Temple. The rest you

volunteered yourself, with a few remarks from me to prod you on. No other questions, mind."

I clutched the upholstery, uncertain if I should be incensed or impressed. I was both.

"And now, my second question." He set down his teacup and sank into the brocade sofa adjacent to my chair. "What did your storyteller's tales teach you about God?"

What a curious use of a question. No real secrets buried in that answer. Nothing about the sapphire. I bit my lip, sank back deeper into the memories, digging for what Gordon's earnest eyes had held concerning faith and God as he'd spun his tales. "He never directly spoke of God, actually. My grandfather had been a cleric, so I had plenty of teaching in that direction . . . but not from him. Are you certain you wish to use a question on this?"

"I am. Please continue."

I took a long, slow sip and closed my eyes. Recalled his weathered face. His eyes flickering with restrained amusement. The way his wiry gray-peppered hair tufted out as the wind teased it, and he, so wrapped up in a tale, never noticed. "He taught me about nature. The created world. All his stories had to do with that, and how everything in the garden was created to work alongside everything else. He loved it there, and he said he could feel the Creator. The place was steeped in him, he said.

"And then there was this one story . . . A girl approaching the king, asking for a favor. She was afraid to ask, but she was desperate and she did it. The king was very kind and granted her the small field she'd requested for her family. If that king was meant to represent God, which I always thought was the case, that lesson was lost on me. All I took from that story was that the king knew nothing about her life, cared little for her, and granted a tiny request only because it was as easy for him as nodding his head and cost him nothing."

"That, I suppose, is your understanding of God."

I shrugged, shoulders tight with the direction of this conversation. I stopped short of telling him of all the times I'd cried out to God, begged for him, and felt nothing. "Good and bad fall on everyone in equal measure, with no logic to any of it. I cannot convince myself that God is an active part of anyone's story. Obeying him, praying to him . . . none of it seems to shift reality in any way."

"How disappointed with him you seem."

"He's never given me reason to feel otherwise." My words took on a bitter nip—more than I'd intended. "God belongs to people like you, who have an easy, straightforward life and a simple connection to him. I grew weary long ago of crying out for him, waiting for something to change, for someone to come save me." I blinked rapidly. "No one ever did. *He* never did. The only rescue I ever got was the one I worked out for myself. No, I don't suppose I'm putting much stock in that fairy tale."

"I see."

I dashed away tears. Straightened. "And now, your third question, Mr. Driscoll."

He tipped his head. Watched me. "I believe I'll save that for a rainy day. I will, however, implore you on one count." He scooted to the edge of his sofa, taking my hands in his. "Do not mistake people's betrayals for God's. Their shortcomings are their own, and he is on a far different plane."

He could think what he needed to think. "I have a question for you too, Mr. Driscoll, and you must answer honestly. And *not* with more questions."

"Very well, what is it you'd like to know?"

"Why are you interested in the gem? Why did you ask me about it in the first place?"

He smiled. "That's an easy answer. Because I was hired to do so."

I blinked. I should have known.

"The legal owner of the gem has hired me to find out if the one in the exciting new moving pictures is her lost sapphire. And now she wishes me to fetch the sapphire for her, which of course, became more complicated when it disappeared."

I withdrew my hands, tucking them onto my lap. An odd sense of betrayal snaked through me as I realized the actual reason for the interest he'd taken in me. "So you were going to take it. To hand it over to Lady Claire."

"You knew who'd owned it?"

"Of course I did. The Briarwood Teardrop is legendary, and everyone's heard of it. I just didn't realize—" I drummed my fingertips. I'd never imagined the sapphire I'd known for so long . . . was *that* sapphire. Or even that it was genuine. Not until he'd suggested it. "Do you know how many gems that woman has? She collects baubles, fancy jewel-encrusted trinkets, anything unusual. Her husband purchased the Briarwood for her at a Christie's auction, and it is one of hundreds of pieces she owns . . . and never wears. It sat unused in a little box on her trinket table, and then in some safe. Owned for the simple sake of owning it. Until it was stolen, of course."

"It seems you are making a case for the thief."

"Why would I do that?"

He shrugged one shoulder. "You tell me."

I steeled myself. Steeled against the unfolding situation. Against the man so carefully peeling back the layers.

"You're afraid." He spoke quietly. "Afraid of being found out, of all the running being for naught. You're thinking, what if someone pulls the string? Unravels my entire costume? What will I do then?"

He thought me a thief. He, who saw everything.

Horsefeathers. He wasn't God.

"Right now you're thinking of your father, aren't you? You have mixed feelings for him . . . loyalty. Frustration. Hope. Despair. And you wonder what he'd think of you now, if he could see where you are. If he'd care."

This was impossible. Simply impossible. "No one truly knows me."

"Then, Lily . . . I'm no one."

I clutched my knees, bunching the fabric of my skirt. I couldn't stop the heat from coursing through me. The heat of embarrassment, of being exposed.

The warmth of being *known*.

No.

I was Lily Temple, and my life was whatever I made of it. Whichever side I faced toward the camera. Yet I was overcome with foreboding.

"And, Lily . . ."

"Hm?"

"This 'no one' also suspects you didn't steal it." His gaze was direct. "We'll work together. Find that sapphire, return it to the countess, and clear your name. Lily, will you trust me?"

My heart beat staccato. I let the question linger, then I held out my hand, placing it in his. The smile he offered in return warmed right through my nerves to the very core of me, where this man always seemed to reach.

And yet . . . I was drowning in the sense that I had stepped out into foreign territory, and there was no going back. No undoing what I'd just done.

And no getting the sapphire back.

He drove me home in the closed carriage, not his motorcar. He saw me to the cottage and gave a quick nod, but I stopped him as he turned to go. "Peter, that girl. The one who . . ."

"The bread."

I nodded. "Her name is Mila. I think. She may have seen who stole the sapphire. Everyone else was at the bandstand, but she was there. And she was watching. There is something else odd about her too." I told him, in quick, halting statements, about the white rabbit from the fairy tales. The little green jacket. And that the little girl had scooped him up. How my face heated in the telling!

It all tumbled out, even what Gypsy Lee had told me about her being stuck in this world, losing her mother at sea and her father to who knew where. "But, of course, none of that may be true. It probably is, because Gypsy Lee is seldom wrong, but I just . . . I can't think why she'd know it. So . . . maybe she doesn't. Perhaps it's all a fairy tale. Except for the part about her seeing the thief. That is real. And the white rabbit . . . I think." I puffed out a breath at the end. "She always wears her hair plaited with ribbons, and I've never seen the like around here. She's from . . . somewhere else. This long dark hair, white face . . ."

"Thank you." He watched me for a moment more, gave a nod, then left me at the door. "Good day, Miss Temple."

His reaction—or lack of it—left me wondering if I should

have kept silent on the matter. Now I felt a fool. And he likely thought me one.

I slipped inside. And there, leaning against my crooked mirror, was an exquisite drawing of a woodland maiden in a weeping willow gown of green, with honey-gold hair and daring green eyes. Clipped to the side was a brief note of thanks for my assistance in the case. Beside it, a scripted, embellished title card, such as one seen in the flickers to add narrative to the story.

> **Our heroine does not yet realize**
> **she's a heroine.**

And in the drawing, she held a lily.

I looked at that clever-seeming creature meeting the artist's eye with a half smile, a glow of sweetness and energy radiating from her. And suddenly I didn't know who I was anymore.

18

He rode home, but the singing had so deeply
touched his heart, that every day he went
out into the forest and listened to it.

~GRIMM BROTHERS, "RAPUNZEL"

P eter Driscoll returned sore and scraped from a hasty trip
to the cliffs four nights later. It had started as a walk to
clear his head, to ponder Lily Temple and the two cases,
but then the storm had caught him.

He tossed his hat onto the table, stretching to alleviate the
usual tightening of his chest when he entered this dungeon
of a house. Yet when he closed himself into the study, where
hundreds of tightly packed books muffled the outside world,
a new peace insulated him.

She'd left her magic in the room that day, her glowing presence that throbbed with life, drawing forth more of it like vines
twisting up the walls and flowering spontaneously right there in
the study. Four days it had been since her visit, yet something of
her remained. He inhaled deeply of the quiet, the understated

delight, and approached the cold hearth, rubbing his hands together. Would that it was cold enough to light a fire—it certainly was wet enough. Or at least, *he* was.

Almost immediately, the sight of a new file on his desk caught his attention and he crossed to it. Roddy had been in London and in Hove, gathering files Peter had requested. Three people, he'd said. Three names to investigate and see what could be found. Gordon Makepiece, the gardener-storyteller; Josiah Fairchild, the magistrate; and a girl named Mila. An unknown, skittish waif who had wandered into the gardens and possibly been the only witness to the theft of the gem.

Dropping his suit jacket on the chair, Peter checked his pocket watch—half past six—then settled in to look over the documents. He closed his eyes, thoughts of Lily Temple shimmering in the air. Opening his eyes, he let the memory of her harp music wind through his mind as he delved into the files that would hopefully unlock another piece of her story.

He leafed through Magistrate Fairchild's records, every court case he'd heard, and skimmed the familiar legal jargon on each page, looking for keywords and phrases, anything that contained a shred of connection to Lily. He kept the names he'd heard in the forefront of his mind—Daisy Fink, Astrid Carmichael, Thorndike . . . something. None of them appeared in the court records.

Then he skimmed the files again, stopping at every female of approximately the right age, seeing if any stood out. It was impossible to tell—laundress, heiress, parlor maid, tutor . . . any of them could be her. This was an impossible task.

He shivered. Then, a whisper of taffeta on wood, followed by a feminine voice. "Difficult case, is it?"

He inclined his head toward the lovely swan of a woman

standing in the doorway, garbed in widow's weeds that did not diminish her loveliness. "Mother." Peter rose and held out his hands. "You could be an inquiry agent too, the way you slip about so quietly."

She entered and perched on a striped damask chair to the right of his desk. "It's most helpful in evading certain daughters-in-law. That is, *future* daughters-in-law."

Peter closed his eyes and puffed out a breath. "She's at it again, is she?" He rued the day his moldable older brother had laid eyes on Miss Iris Stanhope. "You shouldn't have to sneak about in your own home. How are you doing, Mother? Truly?"

"I bear what I must." She quoted Iris with an elegant flair of her nostrils. "It simply makes life less complicated to slip into the shadows of an evening. And we'll soon be free of this place, won't we, son?" She laid a hand on his arm. "I cannot wait for the day we have our own humble cottage. It shall be simple and yet marked with peace and calm. And your lovely music."

He blinked.

"You were humming. Just now."

"Was I?" He glanced at the harp, now ghostly quiet again with its sheet in place, but he could still hear her music, picture her flushed face as her fingertips found their way among the notes, collecting them into her own little melody. Her ballad. It must have leaked from his mind to his lips.

"A place where you can hum all the time, where your eyes glow the way they do now . . . that is more beautiful to me than all the estates in England." She squeezed his hand with shaky fingers. Her tremor had grown worse. Nerves? Or more?

"That day is coming, Mother. *Soon.*" He laid his own hand over hers.

Much sooner, in fact, if Lily Temple proved to be a criminal.

One he felt needed to be brought in to Magistrate Fairchild. Once he delivered her to the man, if he chose to, the problems of this family would come to an immediate end. Life would turn a corner for all of them. Which was long overdue.

Yet it wasn't likely to come about this way. He wasn't setting out to investigate and capture her as a criminal . . . but he would observe and learn. Then he'd do what he must to uphold the law. She hadn't stolen the sapphire, of that he was certain, but huge shadows loomed in her past. In all her unspoken stories. Those dim corridors might contain anything.

Peter would see justice done, where it was necessary, no matter the personal cost to himself. And then, one way or another he would provide a soft place to land for the woman who had raised him.

His mother was clever and independent, but not built to endure the constant strain of sharing her roof with a quarrelsome woman. Lavinia Driscoll had breathed peace and strength into their home all his life, but Thomas had chosen a wife so opposite in nature—exacting, bitter, and prideful. It was taking a toll on Mother rapidly, living in this dungeon. "I shall get you everything you need as soon as I can."

Mother's smile was weak, but kind. "Oh Peter, I've had a letter. It's from Esther." She breathed out the name, with all the emotion surrounding its bearer. "That's what I came here to tell you. She writes that she's leaving England. Starting fresh with Mabel, and she's found a most accommodating position aboard a ship. Nearly free passage for the both of them, with the security of a position when she reaches new shores." She paused, raising her eyebrows. "I don't suppose you had anything to do with this stroke of good fortune, did you?"

He dropped his gaze.

She took his hand in her lace-gloved ones and squeezed. "You are a good man, Peter Driscoll. A very remarkably, wonderfully good man." She blinked back tears. Took in a breath.

He squeezed her hand back with gentle affection.

"Now. What's this case about?" She sat forward, peered over his arm, and frowned. "A criminal case? It isn't like you to investigate such matters. Especially ones several years in the past. But . . . you know what you're about, I'm certain of that."

He met her warm smile with his own. "You're a boon, Mother." He straightened the papers and flipped back to the beginning, feeling energy surge through his muscles. Peter felt a sense of harmony as he moved about the world, setting one of its troubles to rights. It was his place in humanity, his role in the story of the world. Perhaps he should have been named *Jack* after all. "It's an old case, but one worth revisiting. You see, there's a very clever, beautiful woman with enemies—"

"Mmmmm." She gave a slow, deliberate smile that brought sparkle to her eyes.

"Well, she's facing all manner of trouble, and she's wanted by the law." He patted the file.

"Is she?"

"That is, unless I uncover the true story and set things right."

"Which I've no doubt you'll do."

He told her then about Lily Temple the actress, who'd lived so many lives, and the clues that he had. "Problem is, she won't tell me much of anything, and I don't even know her real name. She could be any number of women in here."

He scanned the pages, praying that he'd notice some detail, some telling bit, that would point him in the right direction.

"You're forgetting what she *has* told you, dear one. Her story."

He paused. "The Dickens tale. Yes! Lucie Manette was not

wrongfully thrown into prison—it was her father. That's whose case I should be searching for. Mother, you're brilliant. Simply brilliant!" He flipped madly through the pages, whipping them one after the other, scanning for the name he should have searched out in the beginning. Finally he struck gold in the 1896 cases—*Makepiece*. Trial date set for February the twenty-fourth over the theft of five hundred pounds and several gems valuing over seven hundred pounds. He had attacked and robbed an unnamed man in the man's own house before raiding the place, but was later apprehended just outside St. Anne's Well Gardens, covered in twigs and petals, presumably from his climb down the trellis.

He blew out a breath, blinking at the immensity of his find. "Hello there, Miss Lucie Manette. I believe I've uncovered your story."

Magistrate Josiah Fairchild had sentenced Mr. G. Makepiece to twenty years in Newgate, just like Lucie Manette's father imprisoned in the Bastille. Gordon Makepiece was not *missing* as she'd implied . . . but imprisoned. He pushed back, blew out a breath, and closed his eyes, picturing her. Hearing her voice. The memory of her music intensified. Crescendoed in tragedy. For all these years, she'd been chasing something that wasn't likely to happen. A reunion she wouldn't be able to have. Yet, she'd seemed to know that already.

It isn't likely I'll see him again. Not in this life.

"Her father. He's in prison. In fact, I'm surprised he's not been hung for the crimes against him. I'm afraid all is lost. *He* is lost to her."

"In prison, you say?" Her voice was velvety. "Taken from her, yes, but not lost. Besides, she believes his imprisonment was an injustice, if we're to believe her tale. Just like Lucie's father."

"Right you are. I . . . I believe I can solve this, Mother." He couldn't stop his smile from spreading over his face. "I have his name. The records. The truth is somewhere right here, in front of me."

"This case matters to you a great deal."

Peter sighed and leaned back in his chair. "Because it's several cases, actually, and it's imperative I find the truth. The damage if I don't could be irreversible."

He told her then about the meeting with the magistrate, and his bid for Peter to find Lily Temple. Then of the dowager countess, and her desire to find the gem that Lily had possessed . . . and now stood accused of stealing. "I know there's more to her story. Whether or not she should be in prison, whether her *father* should . . . I have yet to determine."

His mother smiled. "It seems to me you've already decided about her. You're merely trying to prove it."

He smoothed back his hair, massaged his temples. "I'm drawn to her, Mother. It's as if . . . as if God is inviting me to protect her. To untangle her story and set her free from it." How mad it sounded out loud. "Someone needs to find out the truth and prove it—about the gem and whatever Fairchild believes she's done, as well as her father's theft—and that'll be no small task, the lot of it. It'll take someone with knowledge of the court system, and a tireless spirit."

She raised her eyebrows, the light of approval in her lovely eyes. "Which sounds precisely like my son."

Peter heaved a sigh and read the case report over, then again one more time. Then his gaze snagged on a name, and he paused, frowning. "Skinner. Mr. John Skinner is the key witness. The one who saw the break-in, saw Gordon flee, and reported it."

"An unfortunate name, to be sure."

"Yes, and a memorable one. I thought it when I met the man . . . at the magistrate's rooms. Skinner was the man who summoned me to meet with Fairchild and he worked as his right hand. His valet, I believe."

"Hm." Her eyebrows arched.

"In all of England, there isn't a magistrate that would hear a case with his own valet as lead witness. It's highly unethical."

"Not to mention coincidental."

He sighed, leaning back in his seat. "She's right. Lucie Manette is right. Her father *has* to be innocent. It's simply not the way things are done. The whole matter is a fishy mess."

He swept through the report again, then dug about through the other papers on the desk.

"More research?" His mother leaned forward, peering down at the paper.

"I've had Roderick investigating three different people of late. Makepiece, Fairchild, and a little girl. Just a waif who happened to be around when the necklace was stolen. They hadn't even a name for her. Nothing is known about her but conjecture from an odd woman in a caravan." He told her about the girl's white rabbit which had come, as it seemed, from Gordon Makepiece's fairy tale, wearing a tiny green jacket. The way she hung about . . . but regularly vanished when approached.

"It's believed that she lost her mother at sea and her father is nowhere to be found. So I had Roddy dig around for shipwrecks anywhere near here, and it seems there have been a few in the last several years. Most notably, some right around the shores of Hove. That little inlet there. I'm not certain, but I'm guessing this girl survived the shipwreck that took her mother, and she's washed ashore here, in a land foreign to her. That explains her skittish nature . . . and her refusal to speak with anyone. Perhaps she can't. It also fits with the information we have of her being displaced. She certainly acts as though she is."

"Poor child!"

"I'll go through these logs when I can and try to narrow down who she might be."

"Where does she stay? Has she anyone to care for her?"

"I don't know. Maybe." He ran his hands through his hair. "That's the other reason I've been tracking her. She may need help."

"Do you even know where to find her?"

"I've a hunch. The one thing I noticed about her was the reddish stain around the hem of her gown."

"Chobald Caves."

He nodded. The caves—rocks and sand that contained an abundance of iron oxide—left a rust-colored residue on clothing that was nearly impossible to remove. And that red coloring had edged the bottom of her gown. He'd noticed idly, but now it stood out to him, that small detail pointing to the place she stayed—or at least where she visited. It was odd because hardly anyone risked being trapped in those caves. Especially in high tide. "Unfortunately, that's all I have on her."

"Oh, Peter."

"And this . . ." He paged through the folder of papers. "Information about Gordon Makepiece." A more thorough history lay on top, in Roderick's neat handwriting. At the time of his arrest, Gordon Makepiece served as a gardener at St. Anne's Well Gardens. He had no assets to speak of, save a tiny cottage near the grounds. He had a wife and children—Emily, Rose, Margaret, and Simon. Then there were more papers—a copy of his rental agreement and a census record.

It wasn't until the third page that Peter paused, staring in shock. Why hadn't Roddy told him this himself? Why hadn't he *run* to him waving this paper overhead?

Gordon Makepiece's case remained open. It was ongoing . . . because the defendant had vanished from the prison. "He's missing." Peter spoke the words slowly, trying to absorb this turn in the story.

"That makes the sudden appearance of the white rabbit from his fairy tales a bit more interesting, I'd say," came his mother's soft voice.

"Indeed." He tapped his chin with the pen. "Indeed it does."

19

The thing that is important usually
is the thing that is not seen.

~ANTOINE DE SAINT-EXUPÉRY, *THE LITTLE PRINCE*

George Albert Smith flitted like a bird about the bandstand, accomplishing little as the rest of us worked on pinning the banners and readying the stage for the night's bioscope show. It would be the fifth installment of the fairy tale, and ticket sales, he had told us, were nearly triple what they had been any other night. The gardens would be chaos, with eager throngs of people all here to see his film.

His body could not contain his excitement.

But as soon as dusk began and the throngs arrived, it was clear they weren't here for the show. At least, not that alone. They spilled in through the entrance gates and fanned out over the grounds, poking under bushes and benches.

They were looking for the sapphire.

Reporters arrived and followed me about, nearly tripping

over the hem of my gown in an effort to pepper me with questions. I waved them all away. I soon hurried back to the cottage and peered out from the window, waiting for night to fall. Donning a black wig, a beaded headband, and a gown of green sable, I slipped back out to watch the bioscope show from a hill way in the back.

The images flickered, then solidified on the screen, and there was my face—and the sapphire. The audience gasped, pointing at the gem on-screen.

It had been my inspired suggestion to take the gem from the previous filmstrips and splice it into this installment so the tale might go on. I smiled now at the reaction it received.

I sat against a tree, knees curled to my chest, and watched the story play out. I never had imagined my grown-up self playing the fairy, but the gardens—the colorization—brought the story to life just as I'd pictured it when I'd heard it aloud as a child. Laura Bayley, Smith's wife, had brilliantly dipped the filmstrips in amber and marigold tones before toning, giving the garden an enchanted glow that made it seem as magical as my childhood memories.

I'd been lying flat out on the grass when I'd first heard the story, with the aroma of lilacs coloring the images his voice had painted. I watched now as the gardener, played by dear Bertie, approached the fairy in one of my favorite scenes. He came, head bowed, and handed her the most beautiful rose in the garden.

But the moment he left, she dropped the rose as she ran to the looking glass. She held out the gem and, without a backward glance, slipped through once again.

Yet on the fringes of the garden, we see the gardener watching. Watching with such abject sorrow that one could not help but weep with him. It was not just loss but rejection, and his body sagged under the weight of it.

Why would the fairy ever wish to leave the garden? What sort of man-made world might even entice her to do so? I'd always wanted to live in those gardens as a girl, sleeping beneath the magnolia trees and waking with the freshness of dew on my skin. I'd yearn for it when I lay in my own uncomfortable bed. Then I'd sit up, look at the blue gem that hung around my neck—that piece of sky—and think how fortunate I was to have a bit of the garden to carry with me. To tempt me back. It did not magically transport me, of course, but it drew me. Reminded me at a glance what I was missing by not being at St. Anne's.

Peter was absolutely right, I realized with sudden clarity. It was a small haven, an Eden in the midst of a chaotic holiday town, and my pull toward it was soul deep. It always had been.

It wasn't an escape from reality as much as it seemed part of another world. One more real than the ordinary one outside its walls. Naught but a few trees dotted most of Hove, so full of buildings and storefronts it was. Man's intrusion on the world sprung up on the seashore to serve the many holiday-goers, but here . . . this garden . . . A small bit of Eden persevered. Things were as they should be.

So many other places had been my home in recent years, and I'd left them all when it became necessary without a thought. But here . . . I would always come back. Even if it might give me away when I needed to hide—I would come back.

And hopefully . . . one day, he would too.

I watched the screen again, seeing the story and hearing it in his deep, resonating voice. The gardener had risked everything, left his beautiful garden, to wander into the colorless world after the fairy. I watched, holding my breath as the man sadly scooped up a handful of petals he'd brought in a satchel from the garden and held them up on his palm.

The wind swept them up and scattered their color around the world. Lovely, sparkling petals floated down around the busy chaos, most being trampled underfoot or swept into rubbish bins. A few landed on a person's face and each of them would pause, pluck it off, and look at it in wonder. Color bled from the petal into whatever it touched, a bit of the flower's loveliness seeping into it. I felt the truth of this image to my core.

I startled when someone sat beside me. "A bit lonely out here?"

"Mae." I smiled at her. "Just enjoying the show . . . without the interrogations."

I couldn't tear my eyes away from the bright petals, falling silently among the busy streets.

"Right good job you did on those petals. It was brilliant, the way you made it seem like the color leaked into the people."

"I always saw it that way in my imagination."

"Where did you come up with such a story, Lil?"

I shook my head. "I didn't, actually. It came from a brilliant man named Gordon Makepiece. This is his work. I made certain Smithy credited him at the start of the film."

"G. A. Makepiece. I always thought that was a nom de plume of sorts . . . for you."

"I couldn't write a thing worth filming. All I can do is bring to life what someone else has created." And pray, ceaselessly, that he saw it.

"What do you think he meant, with the spreading of color and the petals going everywhere?"

"I always thought it was about the garden, and about drawing people. Look, see? Those people are pausing to glance about when the petal touches them, as if realizing there's something else beyond their world. Something infinitely richer and more lovely. But mostly . . . it's about his fairy. About drawing her back. Petals dropped like little breadcrumbs to lead her back. There, she found one. She's staring now, missing the garden. Remembering its beauty."

"Why didn't the gardener simply smash the looking glass? Or the blue stone?"

"Because he won't force her to stay. He only wants her to."

"But she's his creation. He can make her do whatever he wishes."

I shook my head. "It wouldn't be the same if she longs to be somewhere else. Removing the 'somewhere else' wouldn't make her any happier at the gardens."

She sighed. "I always thought you were a little like that fairy, Lil."

"Oh?" I twirled grass around my finger.

"Restless. Never able to stay in one spot. Eager to see and do more."

"But I'm here." I whispered the words. "I'm here in the garden, and I've never wished to leave it." I watched that sad gardener on the screen, forgetting it was Bertie in a beard. Instead, I saw him. I saw that dear familiar face with the slight stoop of hard work, the hazy glow to his blue eyes, the endless welcome radiating from his face.

I'm here. I've come back to the garden. But where are you?

Somewhere along the line, my childhood self had fashioned him into a symbol of God. An earthly representation. While I was crammed full of the Scriptures for years from my grandfather, made to memorize Proverbs and live them out, this one particular man had at the same time opened my heart to a new concept of the deity above. One of warm welcome, of amusement, of looking at people and the world with utter appreciation and even a touch of wonder. His kindness knew no bounds. His welcome never ceased.

He'd seldom even spoken to me of God, but his stories brimmed with real, accessible truth, and I'd soaked up more wisdom with him than I did in the cramped little stone church we had attended in town. He exuded a special quality, as if he ushered in the presence of God wherever he went. Whatever he did. Hoeing gardens, trimming roses . . . where Gordon Makepiece was, there also was God.

But he had vanished from my life. And with him, the nearness of God. The silence of both had been deafening.

I ached for it.

I'd left letters in the garden, I'd called out to God . . . but neither of them had responded. That magnificent storyteller had simply disappeared. And in time I had hardened myself against hope. Especially when I was told, while sitting on a bench near the tennis courts, that he had actually been arrested. That he wouldn't be coming back for me. It was only later that I fully understood the reason for his arrest, and what it all meant.

Then, I had run. I left the name and home I'd always known as a child and made my way into the world, dragging my broken heart with me. For the entire mess . . . it was wrong. All wrong. And only I knew the truth.

But who would ever listen to me? I hardened myself and moved on, trying to forget everything that had happened.

Until the gem had reappeared. Dug up in the construction of the glass house on the hill, along with a most special book of fairy tales I'd hidden with it. Smith had discovered the gem, tucked in the metal box that had once been mine, and cleaned it up, placed it on display in the gardens, an attraction like the monkey house or the hot-air balloon.

And very soon it had worked its magic. It had drawn me back to the garden, reminding me in a moment of this colorful taste of heaven. The only thing missing was its rose gardener. I decided I would find him. I would splash his beautiful stories all over the screen, show off the sapphire that our stories had often revolved around, and wait for it to work its magic. I'd wait for it to draw him back.

No one in my life had ever meant so much to me. And I had a lot to make up for. It was because of me that he'd been arrested, and I had to make things right. Had to make certain *he* was all right.

And I longed to see him again. To sit at his feet and hear his stories spun like climbing ivy, winding this way and that on his rich baritone voice. He was the only person who could make sense of my life, who could tell me what I needed to do now, with everything I knew.

So I sat beside Mae in my enchanted garden, glittering with moonlight and the sparkle of lovely gowns and gems, and prayed he would appear. Prayed that Gordon Makepiece, and God, would step back into my life and make sense of what it had become.

As the end of the filmstrip flapped on the reel and the audience applauded, Mae jostled me, stunning me out of my memories. "Lil. Hey, Lil, look at that."

It was a little elf boy. Green belted suit, curled hat on his mop of a head. To casual observers he looked like one of the attractions, but we both knew he was not.

I had told Mae about the little white rabbit, hadn't I? The

one taken directly from the fairy tale. *That* had seemed a co-incidence. An odd one, but an isolated incident.

"Isn't he from the fairy tale too?"

"No," I breathed, heart trembling. Thoughts racing. Was it possible? "Actually, he's from another one."

A different fairy tale spun on Gordon Makepiece's voice, wild and fanciful, but never on the public screen. Never read by anyone, I'd always believed, except me. Breathless, I shot up and ran down the hill, pulling my hood over my face and running toward the guests.

But the boy had gone.

Samuel Draper stood, feet apart and shoulders tense, before the mighty magistrate Josiah Fairchild the following morning. "I have a plan in place." He inhaled courage. "I'm happy to report that I've found evidence tying the actress Lily Temple to her original identity. A certain link she cannot dispute. I will be able to bring her to you without delay." It wasn't so much the size of the magistrate that intimidated but the presence of him. The power he held.

"Good." He stabbed his pen into its holder. "But you're too late. I've already hired an inquiry agent to handle it."

He stiffened. "That was highly unnecessary, sir. I've been the lead on this case for—"

"Seven and a half years. And you only managed this advance because she's loosened her cloak. Been less careful. Anyone might have found her. She's all but broadcasting her location."

Draper stiffened. His knees locked. "I never let a task go unfinished, sir."

"Especially when it means a rather large promotion, yes? And a substantial reward."

He grimaced. "Have you even told this inquiry agent who she really is?"

"Of course not. It wasn't necessary."

"He hasn't any of the history. The knowledge. Please, sir, I beg of you to let me carry out the mission you first tasked me with. I *will* bring the girl back. Tomorrow night."

The man across the desk lifted thick eyebrows. "Very well then, do what you will. But I won't call off the inquiry agent. You've disappointed me before. Too many times. You and the Yard."

He clenched and freed his fingers. "She's rather a difficult one to lay hold of."

"You've been granted another chance, Draper. Take it or leave it."

"I'll take it, sir. There's to be a balloon launch tomorrow, and I've discovered the gardens are open the night before—that is tonight—to allow for the setup . . . but no guests will be present. I can simply walk in and approach her without hindrance. She'll be forced to come with me."

A rumbling laughter. "Forced? After all this time, I'm afraid you don't know her very well."

"Won't you consider calling him off the case? I tell you, I can handle it!"

He smiled, playing with the pen. "May the best detective win."

20

Seeing is not believing—it is only seeing.

~GEORGE MACDONALD,
THE PRINCESS AND THE GOBLIN

P eter squinted, looking over the cliffs, the water, the shadowed palm of the caves, for any sign of the girl. The more
he thought of it, the more he felt like the disappearing
waif with the rabbit held the key to so much.

He'd been out multiple times now, scanning the shoreline,
scaling the rocky caves. In the evenings, the shore around the
caves was empty. During the day, it was filled with families on
holiday—especially today, with the gardens closed to guests.
Preparations were underway for a balloon launch at St. Anne's,
and he had half a mind to invite Lily Temple out to help him
search, since she wouldn't be needed at the gardens.

But the thought was interrupted. A flash of movement, that
wisp of something white standing out against the darkness, had
driven him to return. It always appeared in the distance near
Chobald Caves, right around a quarter of eight, but whoever
it was eluded him every time.

He'd asked after the girl in the little fishing village near the caves, and people knew of her—but were of no help. The *ghost girl* they called her, and no one knew her name, or where she'd come from. A superstitious lot, they avoided her whenever she was about at the caves, and she continued to look for shells in peace.

After tying his horse to a tree jutting out from the rocks, he scrambled up the cliff, sending a tumble of small pebbles down with every step. Water rushed between the rocks just below, coursing into the caves with echoing rushes. He clung to the rock, slipping on the mossy outcroppings.

He paused as a clatter sounded behind him. Huffing and scrambling, then a shadow. Peter tensed.

"Dratted child obviously doesn't want to be found."

He released his breath. Straightened. "Roddy."

"Had a beast of a time finding you." He clambered over the last rocks, huffing. "We've had a lead—the missing soldier. I thought you'd want to know. A hospital in France is unofficially holding several foreign officers, some of whom are confirmed to be British. It's a start, though, and worth a second look. Especially since the other hospital on our list had no foreign patients."

"I'm in the middle of something, Roddy." He lowered his voice, staring at the spot where he'd seen the flash. Straining to see in the darkness.

Roddy sighed, bowed his neat gray head. "I don't know why you do this to yourself, Pete. You won't find the sapphire. It's long gone now, wherever it is, and the dowager countess will simply have to look elsewhere for her magical cure."

But the sapphire *was* somewhere, and one person had witnessed its theft. Knew exactly who had taken it, and what had happened.

"Come along, I've brought the carriage. You can hitch Gray to the back." He motioned toward a narrow path winding back down to the shore where his mount waited.

Peter eyed the small rivulet of water between him and the next cave, the green rocks waiting to receive him. He gauged the leap, lunged, and fell, sloshing into a shallow pool of chilly water.

Well, now he'd done it.

He struck the water with his palm, and Roddy leaped back, flicking water off the front of his suit jacket. "A fine mess, Pete. A fine mess." Bracing himself on the rock wall, he held out a hand and pulled Peter out of the mucky water.

"I just have to catch up with the girl. Once—just once. She can answer everything in a few sentences." Peter peeled off his jacket and looked over the water. Sometimes it felt as if half the world was adrift at sea, about to be lost or drowned, and it was up to him to save them all. To help them to shore and make certain they still breathed, then see them home to their families.

Roddy brushed flecks of sand off his sleeve. "You know, Pete, for all the times you claim to have seen this child, I have not seen hide nor hair of her. Perhaps there is no girl. Not a live one, anyway. You've not seen her up close yet, have you?"

"She exists." Peter hunkered down, one knee braced on the rocks, gaze scanning the landscape . . . and waited. Wind whipped hair against his moist forehead. His knee stiffened. Roddy heaved a sigh, but Peter's mind tunneled in on a single flicker in the distance. A quarter of eight, and there it was again—the flash of white. The shadow. It was there and gone so fast he couldn't be sure, but he braced himself, focused his attention on that spot.

"Do what you like, Pete, but I'm going for your horse. You

should be home and in dry clothes. And I wouldn't mind a warm-up either." The man disappeared, his voice trailing after him, little whips of sand at each footfall. "People die of cold, you know, and wetness only makes it worse. You're no good to anyone dead."

Silence settled over the vast shore.

Then, a fluttering whiteness again—closer. More distinct. He blinked against the duskiness rolling in, willing his eyes to focus.

No, was it?

Yes. Someone was across the watery inlet, on the little space of beach not yet reached by the tide, a nightdress flipping against her slender legs. A small-ish someone. The figure stopped, dug about in the rocks, and pocketed something before walking a little farther and repeating the process. The dusk was so thick that he saw little more than the white of her clothing and quick flashes of what looked like pale skin, and at times she disappeared completely—likely behind a rock or around the bend. Perhaps he'd approach and find nothing but a stray sheet caught on the cliffs.

He edged closer, rock by rock, chest tight at what he saw. Just glimpses in the moonlight as the clouds released its glow, but it was enough. Her frame was willowy and somewhat angular. She looked slightly familiar. But it was the hair that made him certain—pink satin ribbon was plaited into long, dark tresses.

Found you.

Peter gripped the mossy rock and launched himself over the low spot, tucking and rolling onto the sandy shore where she collected shells. Gasping for breath, he balanced himself and stilled, thinking.

But she heard him. Her head shot up like a swan catching a hunter's scent.

"Hello, you there!" Wind whipped his words, but her gaze flitted over the rocks, looking for him.

She turned her white face, big dark eyes trained on him. The gown hung in rags about her, nearly worn through in patches.

He braced himself against the wind and water splashing against rocks. "Come, let's get you out of here. I want to help you."

Her eyes flashed as if he'd threatened her. Then she turned and scaled the rocks with shocking speed and vanished over top. Darkness and quiet closed about him like a vacuum, and even as he climbed to where she'd disappeared, there was no sign of her.

He blew out a breath, smoothing tense fingers over his hair. It was chilly. Eerie, and almost ghostly, this girl. Especially the way she managed to disappear.

Why did it bring Lily Temple to mind? Flitting here and there, appearing and vanishing, seemingly born of the woods, coming from nowhere. They both tickled the hollowed-out place in his chest that needed to right the wrongs . . . to protect where he'd once failed to do so.

Settling in, Peter focused on the place she'd disappeared and waited. Breathing, staring, expecting.

Then, a noise. *Clop . . . clop . . .* It echoed just out of sight ahead, and Peter stood, gaze honed in on the spot. A large dark shape . . . Peter's breath caught. Then a figure just over the swell. A voice splintering the eerie quiet.

"It's well past the hour that anyone should be out on this beach. You cannot expect to find a child out this late, and neither should you be. Sir." Roderick Heath crested the rise and stood, hands on hips, leading Gray by the reins.

He hadn't seen her. She'd flown directly toward him, but he

hadn't seen her. And Roddy saw everything there was to see. Especially at night.

Peter massaged his neck that was moist with sea air, then shook his head and climbed up to Roddy and Gray. "She needs help, Roddy. It's not just about questioning her. I believe she's survived a shipwreck. She's been separated from her family, which, to a foreign child living with strangers, is insurmountable. Very few people in the village would even be able to help her or know how or where to search for her family. But finding people is what I do. Just a few words exchanged . . . she can clear up a very important matter for me, and I can find her family. She could go home."

"You cannot save everyone. There's no harm in walking away from some, you know. Especially the ones who don't wish for your help."

Peter took his gelding's reins and turned the animal toward the road. "That's just the trouble, Roderick. People have already done that to her, and that's why she is where she is. Everything she's facing . . . it's all so very fixable, and I can fix it. Even if she pushes people away, she desperately needs someone who won't simply step over her and keep going."

"You're speaking of the little girl? Or of *her*?"

Peter looked out across the dark gray water, silent for a moment, thinking of Lily. "Both, I suppose. I never give up on anyone." He shoved his blowing hair back, trying not to breathe too deeply the aroma of stagnant water puddled in the rocks, and turned his mount. They walked over the beach together, leading the horse, until they'd climbed to the Driscoll carriage.

Peter handed the reins to his man and helped hitch Gray to the back. "They've been wronged, you know. She and her father, and now they're separated. She has no one."

Roderick's eyes flicked heavenward with long-suffering as he helped Peter into the carriage and climbed in behind him. "And let us have a guess. You plan to set them all free and arrange a reunion, this supposedly innocent father of hers." A call from the driver, and the carriage rattled up the road, harness clinking against the matched pair.

"This isn't a novel, Roddy. People are not divided into heroes and villains. All people are a little bit good and a little bit bad, and all worth helping. Even her."

"*Especially* her, isn't that what you mean? You're asking for trouble, Pete. She isn't what she seems." He banged on the roof, and the carriage slowed and turned east. "Best have a bite before going home and see about some dry clothes. The witch is in residence."

"She's my brother's wife, Roddy. Well, very nearly."

With another roll of his eyes, Roderick leaned back.

"I've uncovered a few things concerning her father—Gordon Makepiece, if you didn't know."

"I put it together."

"I'm almost positive he is innocent—just like Lily's Dickens story."

Roddy huffed. "He may not have a record, but doesn't it strike you that he disappeared? Evaded the law?"

"I believe I might do the same, if I were being set up. There are other details too—the case was mishandled, at the least. Now to find out the truth—if he was set up . . . and why?" He looked toward his man, who frowned in earnest. "What? What is it?"

Roderick shook his head and turned from the window. "This isn't like you, sir. Spying on ladies, prying into their past."

"This is a case I've taken on, just like any other. She's asked me to help her. And I never stop until we've reached restoration."

"And did she happen to ask you to investigate Fairchild's ruling on him as well?"

"Of course not. But that's the only way to free him for her, isn't it?"

"By bringing out the possible misruling of a powerful magistrate who will make your life a misery?"

"By bringing the truth to light."

Roddy sighed. "And when were you going to tell her how far you're taking this case?"

"What makes you think I haven't?"

"Because she's still speaking to you." Roddy sighed again, then for a moment silence prevailed. "That reward money almost isn't worth all this trouble. She'd better pay you extra."

"She isn't paying me. Not in pound notes."

Roderick's face paled. "She *what*?"

"She doesn't have the money to give, Roddy." Peter leaned out the window and signaled for the driver to stop in front of a busy inn with a sign swinging in the wind.

"And how exactly is she paying you, if I may ask?"

"In answers. I get the answers to three questions of my choosing. I've already asked two."

Roderick sighed, hand to forehead, and leaned back against the squeaky carriage seat. "This gets better and better every minute." The carriage slowed and Roddy jumped out.

Peter followed, glancing about the sodden streets of Brighton that had apparently suffered a brief rainstorm and still had mist rolling off the cobblestones.

"By the by, Roddy. I believe I've located her family. The girl from the shipwreck. Not that it matters, if she won't speak with me. Anyway, if I'm right, her father is a captain from Portugal, and his wife, the girl's mother, was British. Mother and daughter were sailing here for a visit when the ship went down. Their little girl, Milagros, was listed among the fatalities."

Roddy's eyebrows lifted. "So her father believes her dead."

"I've wired him, but I'm still perusing the ship logs. Nothing else is quite as certain of a match, though."

Roddy went oddly still beside him, and Peter stopped, alert and watching. Then he saw him too—hat tipped forward, shadowing his face, tall frame hovering inside a darkened doorway just up the street. It was Samuel Draper, of all people, lingering in the shadows of a brick storefront.

Roddy turned away, voice low. "You'd best go warm two seats for us, Pete. See about a change of clothes at the inn. I'll be along."

Peter forced his steps toward the noisy pub and pushed his way in. Liquid splashed on the floor behind him, and laughter erupted in the corner, voices filling the air. He requested and paid for a spare shirt, then idly observed the knots of locals about.

"Driscoll." A sharp voice sounded behind him. "Glad I've come upon you."

Peter turned. The man was tall and broad with wild sandy-colored hair. "Colonel Powell. I hardly recognized you out of uniform."

"I've entered civilian life. Well, mostly." He lifted a hand-carved walking cane. "I serve in Lord Balfour's office, which keeps me out of trouble."

"I'm sorry to hear of your injury, Colonel."

A nod. "I have worthwhile work." Pain stretched over his features as he eased onto a seat and rested his cane on the wooden bar. "Word has it that you've entered military matters yourself, Driscoll. Is that true?"

"Not a bit of it, sir. My work is as far from militaristic as a body can be."

Those worn features creased, thick eyebrows moving up and down. "Why the interest in a French military hospital, then? Something about some unnamed British prisoner, wasn't it?"

Every muscle in Peter's neck fired up. He finished his sip and replaced the drink, keeping a steady gaze on the interloper. "Where did you hear that?"

"It seemed odd when I overheard the request on the exchange, but even more when your name entered into it." He leaned forward on the chair, onto his cane. "How ever did you track those British soldiers all the way to Calais?"

Peter rose, greeting the publican who brought him a neatly pressed white linen shirt. "Thank you," he said, and flipped two shillings into his hand. Then he pivoted for a moment back to the former colonel. "I assure you I have no interest in His Majesty's military or any defense operations. I'm merely investigating private matters for a civilian client of mine."

The man shoved himself onto his feet and briefly touched Peter's arm to stop him. "Peter, tell me how you knew about that place."

"My sources are as private as an illusionist's playbook." He held up the folded shirt in a brief salute. "Good day, Colonel, and best of luck in your new work." He could change into the dry clothing later. Roddy was speaking this minute with Samuel Draper and saying who knew what.

Before the colonel could fire off another question, Peter tipped his hat and pushed through the side door, slipping along the foggy alley and keeping out of sight, quietly climbing into his carriage and leaving the door open for his companion. Keeping to the shadows, he strained to hear Roddy's familiar voice, and kept his gaze on the two forms standing close together.

Low voices. The clink of metal and the scuff of leather soles on cobble. Peter ducked and peered out the window. Then a *click-click* of footsteps and Roddy was sailing around the side of the carriage, face a hard mask as he climbed in and slammed the door. "What a load of rot this is, Pete. I don't like it." He looked Peter up and down. "You ought to change, you know, and you should have stayed inside the inn. You'll catch your death. All on account of eavesdropping on me."

"I was merely being cautious. Making certain you were safe."

Roddy considered Peter's expression with a knowing frown as the carriage jerked into motion. "Who bested you in there? Have some bad news?"

"A man from the PM's office. They've heard mention of our search for a missing British soldier. And the hospital in Calais where we suspect the real captain may be."

Carriages rattled down the road amid shouts from pedestrians. Children scurried.

They didn't have to say it—both men knew what this meant. The home office had been alerted about the hospital in Calais, and any soldiers they could hope to find would be hidden quickly. French intelligence would no doubt get wind of the search, if the British officials already knew, and their only lead on Captain Pelletier's whereabouts would be cut. "What of Draper? Did you follow him?"

A nod. "He wanted to see about hiring a barouche for two days from now, for a long trip. No driver, just him. On business with the Yard, he said."

"Did he see you?"

"Of course he did. I called over to him myself and passed the time."

"Did he tell you anything of use?"

"Not a thing." Roddy dug about in the folded overcoat he carried. "But I did find this in the trinket shop." He tossed a well-worn hand-bound volume to Peter.

"What's this?" Peter opened the crinkling pages, warped and curled at the edges, and found a wealth of color inside, as if St. Anne's Well Gardens had spilled itself over the page. How elaborate, how mesmerizing, the illustrations on each page. And on the left-facing side, a fairy tale penned in swirling strokes of pen. He blinked. Flipped back to the handmade cover. "'G. A. Makepiece.' This is . . . it's his stories. His fairy tales. You lifted it?"

"Purchased it. A mere pittance—you owe me a half a sovereign, by the by. Apparently Smith claimed he found it on the grounds of the garden a year ago—*with* the sapphire. Peddled it lately as the original fairy tale of the sapphire, on which his films are based. Needed some coin for supplies."

"Brilliant, Roddy." Peter grinned in the dark, turning the thing over and over, paging through.

"By the by, this shop owner is the only trinket peddler in town, and he said someone tried to sell him a gold setting with no stone in it. Gold swirls and a long chain."

"The Briarwood's setting." Peter sat forward anxiously. "Who sold it to him? We're so close. So close."

He shook his head. "Couldn't remember. Turned 'em down, so he didn't pay it any mind. He thinks it was a woman, though."

Peter was still grinning like a fool at the enchanting little book. "I should pay the gardens a visit. She'll be so pleased."

"The gardens are closed tonight, as it happens. A big setup

for some hot-air balloon launch. In fact, you'll be busy too, from the sounds of it—traveling to Calais."

"Now?"

"Or never, it's your decision. They're onto us, and those soldiers will be moved, likely by first light. If they're not already."

Peter considered it. The very idea of an about-face, of moving away from England's tangled messes and toward a place he was truly needed, brought calm to his spirit.

Roddy's face gentled. "She'll be fine for the night, Pete. The gardens are closed to the public, and nothing will happen in a few hours. Two short months before your brother's wedding, before you and your mother will be without a home . . . you ought to carry on with your other work—your *paying* work."

As the carriage swayed them back and forth, Peter studied his man, his most faithful servant. His dearest friend. He gave a nod. "Very well. Turn this carriage about. Let's slip down to the docks and see who we can bribe to sail us across the channel." He whipped off his spectacles and rubbed them clean with the coarse white shirt, then banged on the carriage roof. The driver stopped. "Roddy, go and inform Miss Walker, if you would. She'll want to know what we're about. Take this book back home too. Meet me down at the shanties just off the docks. No more than an hour."

Roderick nodded. "Nicely done, Pete. I don't suppose we need to stop anywhere else. You've everything you need?"

Peter crossed his arms, bit his lip. "Nearly everything."

21

She was close behind it when she turned the corner,
but the rabbit was no longer to be seen.

~LEWIS CARROLL,
ALICE'S ADVENTURES IN WONDERLAND

Someone walked the far garden—even in the dark, I had a sense about these things. The crowds of workmen had clustered by the bandstand, watching the balloon sway as the others drove stakes into the ground to secure it.

Darkness lay upon the gardens with cool stillness, but one person had wandered along the path to where I had hidden myself on a bench behind the hedge. It was one of those odd nights, when the gates lay open but the gardens were closed to the public. Anyone might wander in and secret themselves in the shadows.

That's why the footfall alarmed me. There was a scrambling sound of someone running off. I rose and followed around the perfectly shaped hedges to where the gardens met the woods. I stopped short as the swinging lantern light fell upon the most curious sight—a tiny green jacket. I stopped and picked it up, marveling at the neat little stitches, the buttons sewn in place.

It was real. My hand shook. But how . . . ?

I looked up—there. There in the woods. A girl darted into the north end of the gardens, behind the hedgerow. Dropping the little jacket, I ran after her, lifting my skirts out of the way. My heart pounded. I strained for any sign of the small child from the bread table. Careening around the corner, nearly falling over a bench, I stumbled to a stop before a different little waif with familiar blue eyes turned pleadingly up at me. "Oh Miss Temple. It's you!"

The little girl flung herself at me, warm forehead pressing into my abdomen. She had been crying.

"Thea. Thea, what are you doing here?"

It was Mae's little niece, who often hung about the gardens when she could. We'd talked several times, and though I hadn't much experience with children, I clearly recalled my years living as one. And I remembered the desire to be heard.

Little jacket forgotten, I knelt before her blotchy face, my hands on her shoulders, and invited a dam of words and emotions. Her stepbrothers were picking on her. She didn't wish to be at home. She was an ugly duckling, they'd said, and taunted her for the freckles on her face, and the burns up and down her arms. Deep red and purple stained her skin, and though she normally wore long sleeves to conceal it, today had been hot and she had given in to cap sleeves.

"I don't know why I'm even here at times, Miss Temple."

More footsteps sounded on the padded dirt path, but I watched and no one came.

"Call me Lily." I settled on the grass and pulled her into my lap. She tucked her leather-shod feet up close and leaned on me, and suddenly, with the precious weight of her head against my chest, the world slowed. Time stood still and ticked silently back . . . back to another time in this same garden when a young girl had run, tormented, into a welcoming embrace.

I'd forgotten my book beneath a tree that afternoon, and the clouds had been rolling in ever since supper. A dry storm, they called it, when lightning crackled and thunder groaned across the sky. If I had waited until morning and the rains *did* come, the book would be lost and Mother would never allow it to be replaced. *Natural consequences*, she called them, but I was not one for allowing matters to take their course.

So I slipped out and ran back to the garden for my book. By the time I crossed Aberdeen, the storm had begun flashing and the lamplighter had extinguished the last streetlight. A wide-open emptiness enveloped me, chilling me to the core. I realized my aloneness. My smallness. In the garden, trees shivered around me, alive, as if they'd slip their roots up from the ground and begin creeping after me. The field seemed suddenly foreign—unknowable, with endless possibilities for danger.

More thunder. A pop and a groan as the electric charge struck and felled some large thing. Chills tore up my spine.

With a crying sob, I sprinted blindly into the hay shed and hid, breathing in the moist scent of the bales, the warmth of the rolling moist air, and prayed. Prayed.

Tried not to cry.

That was back when I believed God answered—and maybe he did this time, for then someone was there, thumping up the path and settling into the bench with a groan as if it had been a lovely wingback chair. He sat in easy silence, then his deep, familiar voice had rolled right over the darkness, sweeping through the moment and displacing my fear. "An uncommonly fine night, isn't it?"

Silence. Another shiver.

"Calm and peaceful, and yet . . . with a lot of noise. What might it be?"

I blinked, shivering still.

"Rather a misunderstood rumbling, isn't it? But it wasn't always so. Not for those who know the real story."

"A story?"

"The one of thunder and how it splits the clouds."

I closed my eyes as his fairy tale settled upon me, a thick woolen blanket, safe and warm. Slowly my fear of the storm was muffled by the picture he painted, reality softened and transformed by mythical sight.

It was always that way—whether you were doing the telling or the hearing, stories could change your mind. Soften the edges, refocus the view. That's what it did for me, and years afterward, I still enjoyed thunderstorms.

Now I sat among the garden's beauty as a grown woman, pouring the deep truths of life into another little urchin leaning warm and weighty in my lap.

". . . So into the world came a long, slim tallow candle, white like his mother, a sheep, and drawn to the flame like his father, a cauldron." How it healed something elemental, having a small girl's head resting against my chest, her body curled into me as a fresh story wrapped around us. My fingers combed her tangled locks as the tale spilled from that place in my heart that had stored up every last word picture that had once been painted for me. "They were a wonderfully happy family."

"A sheep and a cauldron would never be married."

"Well, in this story they are. Anyway, this lovely white candle wondered where he belonged—giving fleece like the sheep, or holding meals like his father. He could do neither, so he wandered through life, begging for purpose and meaning. No one knew quite what to make of his waxy self—"

"But *I'm* not like that. Not tall, or pure and beautiful, or even snowy white." She ran a fingertip over the mottled red that bloomed on her right arm. "I don't see how this will make me feel any better."

"Perhaps you'd better listen, then. It's not over, is it? So this candle struck out to travel the world, over lush grassy fields and stone-crusted meadows, over beaches and water and forested glens. What ever was he good for, he wondered for years—till he met a match that glowed with fire.

"'Ah-ha!' said the candle, and drew near the flame. His purpose had something to do with this glow, for it livened something in him and he longed to be near it, to taste it and see for himself what he could do with such a thing.

"Ever so slowly the matchstick bent near, for never would anyone let him close—but this candle seemed accepting, even eager to try. Then the flint touched his wick and a glow sprang to life. And as the sun slowly curled under his puffy white quilt for the night, the candle glowed, and the children out playing could still see the path. The hunter and his hound could return through the woods, and the birds and the frogs had the way lit for—"

A stick snapped. I stilled, but the child puffed the most giant sigh and twisted in my lap to look up at me. "I don't think I'd care to be a candle, standing about waiting for someone to come along and light me."

I hovered protectively over her, straining to hear.

"And I'm not lovely, leastwise, and I hate when people pretend I am."

"You're the match." The low voice came from behind us in the dark.

I jumped. The girl rolled from my lap, and I spun to see lamplight from the path glinting off gold spectacles and a white smile as Peter Driscoll emerged from the hedgerow. "You are the match, not the candle, and you light the wicks around you. The stick needn't be fancy, so long as the flint is good and the glow steady. And you aren't limited to lighting only a single room like the candle. Who knows how far your spark will spread?"

I gathered the girl back into my lap. "Heavens! Of all the ways to approach a lady."

"Begging your pardon."

"Not me. Mr. Driscoll, you are in the presence of Lady Althea of Dorset Lane."

He swept his hat from his head and bowed. "My lady."

The girl observed him, and a smile appeared on her narrow face.

I sighed. "Very well then, off you go. They'll be wondering where you've got to."

She sniffed, smiled her thanks, and scampered away. Peter drew near, those dancing eyes focused down on me.

"How did you get in here? They've closed the gardens."

"But not the gate." Another step toward me in the darkness. "The story ends tonight, Miss Temple, one way or another. The missing soldier and his lady. We can grab the rudder and steer it ourselves or let the wheel go where it may."

I hesitated, twisting the fabric of my gown around one finger.

He held out a hand. "Care for another adventure?"

I eyed the man, taking his hand and rising to face him. "Do I owe you another favor?"

"Probably."

22

Would you like an adventure now, or
would like to have your tea first?

~J. M. BARRIE, *PETER PAN*

I lay on the floor of the roughly built trawler, looking up at the rhythmic puffs of steam blooming from the stack as it carried us across the English Channel. The cool quiet seeped into my very muscles, and in that moment at least, I was glad I'd agreed to come. Peace seemed to follow Peter Driscoll everywhere. Peace . . . and ironically, a bit of danger. Who could resist that?

I was to play the part of chaperone, as it turned out, for Miss Walker had insisted on coming to find her soldier but could not travel alone in the company of two unattached men. Yet I'd done little chaperoning on this trip, for the slender, resolute young woman had remained belowdecks in a cramped and smelly hold, so that seasickness did not overcome her. Plucky thing she was, but rather a weak constitution.

So it was that I found myself bobbing out in the middle of

the English Channel in the company of two men—one who liked me for unknown reasons and one who decidedly did not. Also for unknown reasons.

Thankfully, the latter mostly ignored me.

Peter's voice rumbled in the dimness to my left. "That tale about the tallow candle. Did you make it up? You're quite a storyteller."

A dramatic huff came from the shadows across the boat. Roddy's bent legs extended from the darkness, a pile of coats covering his head as he feigned sleep.

"It's an old tale from that Andersen fellow of Denmark." I sat up, propping my back against the creaking mast. "It's been told for more years than I've been alive. A fine tale, don't you think?"

He smiled in the flicker of lantern light as he leaned back against a broken fishing crate, hands clasped behind his head. "You bring a sort of magic to the telling. You almost make me appreciate fairy tales and other fanciful literature. If I were ever of a mind to be deceived . . ."

I sighed. "When did people come to see stories as mere fancy? As indulgence? All our own flaws and questions dressed up in other people's clothing, strolling about in front of us so we may more clearly see what's true about our own selves. Truths deeper and more meaningful than mere facts, told in a way that our minds can uniquely understand. Yet we relegate stories to the fringes of our lives, those elusive 'spare hours' where we permit ourselves to indulge in the frivolous which we believe has no real practical value."

"If you feel that strongly about it, perhaps you should share another. We've quite a long passage, you know. It'll help keep us entertained."

That face. The subdued smile. Was he silently making fun? "What sort of story?"

His eyebrows lifted. "Actually, you've already started one. Have you forgotten? Lucie and her father, and the stranger who rescued them. You were going to tell me about this noble gentleman, and I wish to hear it. They were soon to wed, I believe. Go on, you know how I feel about unfinished stories."

I paused and luxuriated in a long exhale, feeling the gentle bob of the boat, clearing my mind. "Yes. Lucie Manette and her hero. Well, it just so happens that this noble stranger had little to his name, for he was naught but a poor tutor. Rich in character, poor in purse. But when another suitor appeared, the brilliant but foppish barrister, Sydney Carton, who even resembled Darnay to a remarkable degree, she did not even hesitate to choose the poor, noble tutor over Carton and his wealth."

"Brava! Good for Lucie. A fine choice."

"Oh, but it's not over."

"I should hope not. No story ends without fanfare. What became of the lookalike she didn't choose? I don't suppose he killed off her poor husband and took his place, did he?"

"He did, rather. Well, not the killing part." I toyed with the frayed end of a rope nearby. "As it turns out, Charles Darnay was actually born Charles Evrémonde, nephew and heir to a wealthy but wicked aristocrat. The Evrémondes were responsible for the destruction of many innocent families—including Lucie's, for they'd been the ones to have her father thrown in prison. Before meeting Lucie, Charles realized his relations behaved deplorably and he wouldn't stand for it. He had renounced his inheritance and his name, and had left France to live in poverty."

"Perhaps Darnay should have kept the fortune—for the sake of his future wife and her relations."

"Oh, but he couldn't. On principal. How could a man such as Darnay possibly remain a part of that family? Money isn't worth the cost."

"I suppose it was good he escaped it, then."

"But he didn't, as it turns out. That's what I was coming to. The French revolutionaries went about beheading the landed gents for years of persecuting the people beneath them in society. Everyone of rank was an oppressor, in their eyes, and must be executed. Even one who had renounced the name."

"No!" He moved closer, as if pulled by the strings of my tale.

"Oh yes. To them, he was a wicked Evrémonde, even if he'd never acted as they had. He was guilty by association. He and Lucie would be made to pay for wrongs his father and uncle had committed. And they would have, except for that blessed lookalike. Poor Sydney Carton . . . he traded places with Darnay. Slipped into his jail cell and switched them out just before the execution. It was his one act of selflessness. So Evrémonde escaped with his life . . . but only because Sydney Carton gave his own."

"Poor Lucie. Her father, and then her husband. And Carton! The moment he finally becomes a good human being, he loses his life. The most decent characters in the whole lot see the worst of fates, it seems."

"It almost doesn't pay to live a moral and upright life, does it?" I studied his eyes, his countenance. Did he know? Did he sense the story I was telling? It wasn't *precisely* my story, of course, but there was a dangerous amount of truth in it.

His head tipped just a hair to the right. "There's a certain beauty to it, no matter the outcome." How bright his eyes were, how alert and lively as he took in the tale. And that gently smiling mouth . . . nothing had ever looked more inviting.

In the rawest depths of my heart, I wanted a taste. I wanted to kiss the mouth that had spoken such things to me. I wasn't used to it—this kindness that had no limits. I leaned closer, imagining the feel of his warm embrace, of resting in him and delighting in his presence. Of belonging there.

I stared at his chin, his mouth, not daring to look in his eyes. His smile deepened, that masculine chin growing even more defined. My fingertips itched to touch its smoothness. How easy it would be—we were that close. Then I couldn't bear any longer, the not knowing. My eyes flicked up to his to read what I might.

And they shone out at me with affection. Swelling passion. He smiled at me.

"Are you quite done?" Roddy's voice cut through the quiet.

My heart pounded triple, then slowed, a heavy rock beating against my ribs with the sudden return to reality. The one in which I would never allow myself to fall in love with anyone, and Peter, elegant, loyal, rule-following Peter, would find his equal and bestow a wealth of devotion upon her lovely head.

Peter sighed. "For what it's worth, that Dr. Manette and Charles Darnay . . . they were quite fortunate, both finding the love of an exemplary woman. One made all the more beautiful because of her struggles in her father's long absence. I cannot help but think that when either of those men looked upon her face, they were keenly aware that some beauty and goodness *did* exist in the world. And that beauty might make all the hardship and lost time worthwhile."

I stole a glance up at his face, hoping he did not see the longing that swelled there. With every well-placed word he spoke, every thought of mine to which he gave voice, I became even more his. The loneliness of years faded, and my hunger, my deepest desires, pivoted by knowing him. For being exposed to the sort of man I'd never even known existed. The one who proved there was goodness in the world. In *my* world. And that perhaps it might stay.

Again I had the sense that a gentle meeting of our lips was the next step.

"If I may point out, sir," broke in Roderick. "It is past midnight already. And if we're to sleep a wink tonight, this is the only chance we'll have."

Peter flashed a smile. Gave my arm a swift pat. "I suppose we ought to give it a go then, eh?" He settled down into the fishing nets, heaving a sigh and closing his eyes.

Right, then.

I did the same, curling into the bottom of the boat and closing my eyes against the open sea breeze, against a vague feeling of rejection, determined to rest. Instead I saw the story against my eyelids, Lucie and Charles and Dr. Manette and the rest, and the terrible ending toward which they were all hurtling. All because of their goodness.

I opened my eyes and squinted at Peter Driscoll. Mere minutes it had been, and already the man was asleep, lashes laid against flushed cheeks, breath deep and even.

"Always been a sound sleeper, that one." A voice came from just beyond Peter.

I startled, gripping the nets. Roderick Heath had been staring at me across the piles of fishing nets, elbow resting upon knee as those dark pockets of eyes remained trained on me. Were Driscoll not between us, the man would have dropped me over the side of the boat, sure as I'm lying here.

"Sleeps the sleep of the innocent. No guilt to trouble his rest."

"He seems a decent sort." My casual words felt pinched and false.

His gaze evaluated me, adding up the parts and finding that the sum fell short. "Fancy yourself a good and moral creature, I expect. England's own Lucie Manette, is it? It's a Charles Dickens story you're telling, you know."

"He merely asked for a story. I never said—"

"One in which Lucie is written as a supremely good and moral creature. A worthy woman." His face remained placid, gaze steady. "I've watched him break once before because of a woman. Shattered him, she did, nigh onto a million pieces. All the lovely butterflies of the world, they flit from flower to flower with no intention of landing. Ought to keep to themselves. But no, they need to be admired, drinking it in like nectar from this flower and that, giving nothing in return."

He looked at me again, and I recognized bitterness in him. A certain jaded quality that only beset the innocent who had been deeply disappointed by the dishonest people of the world.

"What was her name? The woman who left him?"

"Sarah. Sarah Margaret Swan, and he was completely gone over her. Would have given her the world ten times over and lassoed the stars just to pull them closer if he could. Wasn't enough, of course. Never is, for that sort. She wanted more."

"'Tis a shame." My voice was low. Almost unrecognizable.

"Isn't it?" The rocking boat didn't dislodge his stare, so intense it was. "I won't see him dashed upon the rocks again."

"Then you'd best keep your eyes closed." I settled back and shut my eyes tight, making it clear I intended to sleep rather than talk. The world was gentle with no one. Even the likes of Peter Driscoll.

Dickens would have swept up a character like this Roddy Heath and stuck him right into a novel. All judgment and foppishness he was, especially for a man in service. Neatly combed hair contrasting with his riotous opinions . . . and a whole lot of nerve.

It spoke volumes about Peter that his man felt such confidence in his presence, the boldness to speak his opinions. Peter Driscoll was not a man to feel threatened, to enforce his authority over anyone—even those in his employ. Instead, he had the wherewithal to recognize a person's unique value and encourage it—to draw it out from hiding and let it breathe. And then naturally command the respect of nearly everyone he encountered, without demanding it.

Which only made me appreciate him more.

My thoughts went wild, dipping in and out of drowsiness, half-formed thoughts and scattered images, then before I knew it, I was waking, damp and chilled and assaulted by an especially bright orange sun in the east. I blinked at the offending orb, then covered my eyes.

"Well, good morning, sunshine," Peter's low voice rumbled.

I stretched my aching neck and shoulders and grimaced his way, adjusting my hat and stabbing it with its pin. "Remember what I said about mornings."

His grin widened. "This'll be a good one, though. Can't you feel it?" He inhaled deeply and leaned back as if drinking in refreshment from the air.

I shot a glance at Roderick, who was sleeping in a position that would give him a terrible crick in his neck when he woke. A stream of drool glistened on the side of his mouth, and I couldn't help but feel a certain satisfaction at the sight.

"Look, just over the water. We're approaching Calais."

I stared at the blurry horizon, the empty poles of fishing boats leaning back and forth. "That soon?"

"Only an entire night of traveling." He shifted against the nets and directed that smile once again at me. "Time for another adventure with your dull solicitor."

I brushed a stray clump of hair off my face and tried to force the gears of my brain into working order. Orange glow highlighted terra-cotta roofs lining the shore. A cramped fishing village.

I puffed out a breath. "How is it that he's come to France again?"

"My suspicion is that the French plundered our troops in a battle, killing nearly everyone. The few who lived were taken as prisoners, held in the hope that they could provide useful information on our movements in the Boer region. We've all been fighting like dogs over the same scrap of land, and they'll take a foothold where they can."

"So why was he listed as killed at first?"

"Because anyone happening upon the aftermath of that battle would have assumed the entire battalion lost. However, Pelletier's captain rank would make him a valuable source of information."

"But not worth returning to England."

"Certainly not."

Our boat moved intentionally away from the busy port toward the bare coastline that lay between Calais and another town several miles up.

"There. That must be it. Go rouse Miss Walker."

But she emerged from belowdecks, gown rumpled and hair frizzed around yesterday's chignon. She climbed up the ladder and stood at the rail, studying along with us the place that Peter pointed out. Past all the inviting whitewashed homes bunched up near the water was a large stone manor that resembled a gargoyle, held up high above them by a bald cliff and set off by itself as if it did not get on well with others. I shivered.

"How will we ever get him out of that place?" Miss Walker hugged herself, looking as though she'd spent a month rather than a night at sea.

"If he's there," Peter said, "we'll get him out. We must find his records and see what the situation is, to make certain he won't be trailed back to England. If I can gain access to their records room, I know what to look for."

"And if we discover they *will* trail us?"

"Down," Roddy whispered, crouching into the boat. "Stay down."

We huddled together among the fishing nets and the lingering aroma of a month's catch, as a broader, more commanding boat sliced through the water. Only the weathered old fisherman steering the boat remained at the helm, visible across the waves. He lifted a hand in greeting toward whoever manned the other boat.

I turned with a whisper. "Peter Driscoll, are you breaking the law?"

His grip on my hand tightened as the boat passed by. "Not exactly. But it's best if we're not spotted. Explanations might be messy."

When it was clear, we rose again and looked over our destination, the dark stone manse atop that rugged hill. "I don't suppose they welcome visitors in such a place."

"Of course not. But we have our very own secret weapon to get us in." A wink.

Secret weapon. What was it this time, kindness? Rule following? Then I blinked and noticed his gaze . . . which was steadied on my face with a disarming smile.

I groaned. Of course.

Me.

23

You are mine, and I am yours, and no
one in the world can alter that.

~JACOB GRIMM, *THE TWELVE HUNTSMEN*

The climb was silent other than the desperate pants of those not accustomed to scaling a craggy rock. The narrow stairs that cut into the northern face were almost vertical, with rickety railings that ought not to be trusted with so much as the weight of a lady's handkerchief, but they were better than trying to scrabble up the rock face.

Once my boot touched the moss-covered stone at the top, I turned to look at the beach behind us. The little whitewashed houses with terra-cotta roofs, rows of wood beams driven into the sand along the shoreline like a fence. And the double-masted, steel-bowed trawler—our means of travel—was pulling away from shore. Apprehension rippled over my skin with each bob and weave on the water.

Yanking my gown free of my feet, I pushed ahead through the tangled overgrowth. A door slammed ahead. Peter herded us all into shrubbery on the east side of the building, tucking us into the shadows and holding one finger to his lips. He motioned toward a side door, and we moved in one huddle toward it. Peter rattled the knob, but it was locked. Settling his shoulder against the wood, he gave several quick shoves, but it didn't budge.

I tried not to roll my eyes.

Shooing him away, I pulled out my hatpin, gave it a quick bend with my teeth, and inserted it into the old mechanism. A flick and a pull and the door creaked open.

Peter cast that look of admiration my way. "I've been meaning to ask. How ever did you learn to do that? You're a regular fingersmith."

"Fingersmithing is filching. I don't steal."

"But what you did with a lock. Where did you learn—?"

"I said, *I don't steal.*"

"Right, then."

I pinched my lips and pushed the door open, ushering us into the dim interior that smelled of yeast and wood and something sharply medicinal. We crouched under the stair landing as a nurse sailed by in long black robes and a hat that might have doubled as a white winged boat. Across the way, barred by a heavy wooden door, stood what must be the office. A record room of sorts. That's where Peter needed to be.

So did a guard, apparently. Rough and burly, twice the weight of any of us, the armed man patrolled between the office and the front doors opposite it.

"Guess we won't see the inside of that record room now, will we?" Roderick Heath's whisper shot around the shadows.

I glanced about, then pointed to a hanging lantern behind us. "When I stop walking, flash that light upon me. And stay back. Stay in the shadows." Drawing my shawl over my head, I stepped out into the arched entryway, my momentary stage. Positioning myself at just the right angle, I faced a tall, dust-covered looking glass and stopped. One . . . two . . . *flash.* The light struck from behind and hit the looking glass, neatly casting my reflection into the empty, shadowed corridor. "Bon soir," I said, and the guard spun toward my ghostly projection.

Startled.

Stumbled back in sheer panic and darted away. Any less of an actress and I'd have laughed out loud.

Now, for Peter and his man. I grabbed both their arms and urged them toward the office.

"You speak French?" Peter whispered over his shoulder. "Where did you—"

"Get into that office. Find whatever you need. You haven't all day. Night." I shook my head. "Day."

Peter laid a hand on Adelaide Walker's shoulder. "You three stay together. Roddy, you keep watch over them. Miss Temple will see you into any part of this hospital you need to go."

I crossed my arms. "I don't know this—"

"You'll find she's rather resourceful." His wink silenced me. "If all goes wrong, call out as loud as you can and I'll come running."

"And you, sir?"

"I'll be waiting for you out back. In the walled garden." A quick smile and he was gone, and I was somehow in charge.

"Come." I pointed up, toward where the wards must be.

Together we skimmed the steps, trodding lightly when they creaked, and came to a narrow corridor with low-beamed ceilings and doors that opened into tiny, airless wards.

Straining forward, almost willing us to go faster, Miss Walker grabbed my hand with her trembling one and pulled us on. She was frantic and jittery. How neatly she'd managed to repair her hair, without benefit of a looking glass.

"Easy, easy. We're almost there—the last leg of the search."

She spun on me. "That's the hardest." Her eyes were wide, her voice high and tight. "He was dead, and now he might not be. Might be mere steps away from me. My entire future and heart are at stake, and I cannot bear to wait." She surged on, peering into every room.

A sick feeling suddenly filled me at the thought that we wouldn't find him. She'd make us search until we did—closets and attics included.

Down an east-facing hallway and three more wards, then she stopped, still as stone. I knew at a glance which one her soldier was—limp form sinking into a gray cot, dark hair falling over a wretchedly scarred, nearly disfigured, face. He did resemble the unnamed soldier in Hove. The way he lay, however, I wondered if he had actually died—only here, rather than on a battlefield.

With a rustle of fabric, Adelaide Walker brushed past us and fell upon her intended, lavishing affection upon his ravaged face with quick kisses, fingers smoothing hair away, gentle words only he could hear. Something in me twisted. Twisted and knotted and stayed uncomfortably tight, although I couldn't say why.

His eyes fluttered open. His gaze met hers. And every feature in his face glowed with relief. He lifted a hand as if to touch her face, but he only lifted it inches off the sheet. She grabbed it and brought it to her cheek, laying her face into his palm.

I stepped closer. Then wished I hadn't. Their words . . . I won't ever be able to unhear them.

He was dying. His injuries were severe, and infection had set in. A few days at most, depending on when his strength gave out. The thing inside that had twisted up suddenly double-twisted and squeezed.

"I couldn't let you see this face," his raspy voice managed. One long, tender kiss upon his forehead, then quick brushes of affection upon the ugly gashes of his cheek. Her fingertips trailed in the path of her kisses. "But I love this face. It is so dear." The look of pleasure, of calm, that engulfed his countenance cannot be properly explained. It made me weak and giddy and impossibly weepy all at once. I dabbed furiously at my eyes with my shawl. How could she bear it? How could her perfect little lips curve into that lovely smile, knowing and seeing all that was before her?

"It matches the one in here." She took his hand, threading her fingers through his, and laid them on her abdomen.

Baby. There was a baby. Shock rolled over me. Suddenly her illness on the ship, her weak constitution, made infinitely more sense. And I was filled with an even deeper respect for the woman who had held up so admirably.

The wounded soldier turned his head to where their unborn child grew, and wept.

She smiled through sparkling tears. "This means I shall always have a small piece of you. I'll be able to lavish kisses and love upon his little face when I cannot see yours."

This wasn't how it was supposed to be. Restoration didn't look like this. I'd take a flicker any day over real life. That sort could be clipped, colorized, and patched together to form the story that needed to be told. None of these ragged-edge, messy endings full of despair and what-ifs, regret, and grief. Hot tears budded in the corners of my eyes at the look of her curled over his broken body. The intensity in the small space between them as they both cradled their growing babe.

"You let me think you were dead. You knew what they'd do—and you still let me think it."

His head rolled side to side on his pillow. "Had to. Dangerous for you to be here. In France. And . . ." He made a weak gesture toward his deep gashes and scars. "I'm not the same."

She leaned near, speaking softly and punctuating her words with gentle brushes of her lips across his face. His scarred, war-torn face. "You're sorry I came, then?"

He shook his dark head slowly back and forth on the pillow, and he strained to speak. "Worth it." His fingers curled against her cheek. "Now . . . I know."

He knew. About the babe . . . and about the depth of her love.

Then I looked up and saw the set look in Roderick Heath's face. I wasn't a mind reader, but I could see every thought scrawled over his face. *This is the sort of woman Peter needs. The sort he deserves.*

And that knot twisted harder as I found myself in agreement. Despite his spectacles, his quiet demeanor, his infuriating habit of rule following, he was not an ordinary, everyday sort of man. Not at all.

A sob from the bed drew my attention. Adelaide Walker had climbed up beside her soldier, curling beside him and laying her head on his chest. His thin cotton shirt absorbed her tears, and I turned away. My heart, my heart was swelling past the size of my rib cage and my chest ached. I wrapped my arms around myself and left them to each other, this pair who had found each other again . . . but too late.

I felt her grief, and it welled up inside me in shockingly powerful waves, curling from the inside and engulfing me. Swaying me on my feet. My body remembered how to walk the dark path of grief mingled with regret, and it returned there quickly. Uncontrollably.

Roderick stepped forward and took the paper pinned to the end of the soldier's bed, scanning it with a frown. I stared at his face, willing it to lighten, to signify relief that the man's actual condition wasn't as bad as he had stated. Roddy caught me looking, though, and gave a quick shake of his head.

No. No, he would not be going home. No, they did not have a future together.

I clung to the back of a chair, suffocating under the darkness. It fell in familiar waves over my head, instantly drawing me back to the dark prison cell. The battered hands I had once loved reaching through the bars, grasping mine. Begging. Squeezing. Hoping.

Then releasing.

Oh Silas.

Breathe. Just breathe.

Then, there were voices. Low and urgent, speaking in French. I hardly heard them. But the air shifted and my mind registered the danger.

"They've heard us." Roderick lunged, herding me through the tall windows onto a terrace barely wide enough to hold us in one narrow row against the slate roof.

He turned back and pulled Adelaide off the captain, forcing her through the long, curtained window. Flailing, she gave one loud sob before clapping a hand to her mouth, and footsteps pounded our way. Shouting followed. One more shove, and Roderick had her out on the balcony and he swept the curtain closed.

I leaned against the steep roof, heart pounding, and listened to the sudden burst of people in the ward. Women with pinched, panicked voices speaking in French. Men with angry growls and thudding boots.

Roderick grabbed the rusted rail and leaned over, looking down at the rocks. "We'll have to go down."

"We can't make that sort of climb," I whispered. "Look how steep it is."

"Would you rather jump? They've heard voices. They know which ward. It'll be a matter of minutes before they find us."

A few more voices had joined the cluster just inside.

This was it. How I'd die. They'd shoot us or lock us up. All this running, planning, working . . . all these years . . . only to wind up here. To end my story in this foreign place, all but alone.

Miss Walker approached the window, clutching at the curtain. "Don't move from this balcony," she whispered in a steady voice. "Not one little noise, until they're gone. Then you must hurry out and make your escape."

What was she doing? I couldn't quite grasp it.

Roderick grabbed her arm. "I can't let you do this, Miss Walker. I—"

Miss Walker's soulful glance stopped him. A look passed between them, high and tight. A nod from him, then from her, and he released her. Stepped back. In a breath, the slender young woman swept one curtain aside and slipped away from us into the room.

I lunged for her, but Roderick yanked me back with an arm about my waist, hissing in my ear, "Do you want to get us killed?"

I narrowed my eyes at Roderick. "You coward! You let her sacrifice herself for us! She is—"

"Choosing this. She's *choosing* it. Don't you see?"

My breath came in frantic gasps as the chaos just beyond the curtain swelled, then moved toward the door and faded. "Whatever for?"

His eyes bored into me, demanding that I realize what I'd just witnessed. What it meant. "She chose to stay—*with him*."

I closed my eyes, fingertips massaging my forehead. No. No, no, no!

Roderick leaned close, dropping his voice. "This is how her story must end. Surely you see that. It's only right that they remain together now. They haven't much time."

"And then what? After he . . ."

Roderick sighed, looking out over the vast fields below us. "We'll fetch her father when we get home. He'll arrive on the fastest clipper and carry her away back to England. He's a powerful man with ample wealth to back his demands. All will be well."

"But Peter . . . he won't let this happen. He won't leave her here." The idea of making our escape while she remained among enemies, witnessing the death of her beloved . . . it was too much.

"You don't know him, Miss Temple. Peter was once part of a most passionate love story—only he was not the hero of it. When his Sarah realized, on the day of their wedding, that she desperately loved her art tutor, he—"

"Valiantly did the honorable thing and released her from their engagement. Even at the last moment."

"And delivered her to the man in question, rushing to catch him before he sailed for the continent to be away from her." Roderick sighed. "Peter has a sense about how stories should go, and he allows them to unfold as they ought. Especially in his cases."

I looked out over the water, the calm, heavy tide that so resembled the man in question. "That makes for a frightful amount of sad stories. Tragic ones." Pain still stretched across my chest. "How does he manage?"

"It destroys him a little bit each time. He feels it all. But then, it somehow holds him together too. All the broken pieces of him."

Peter. Dear Peter. Real life had no place for such a man—he was far too good for it. Broken by the world, yet trying desperately to restore every little corner of it he could reach.

Restoring everyone but himself.

Then he appeared below us, a figure tall and steady in a white linen shirt and clutching a file as he strode away from the building toward the rocky hills beyond. He spent himself on Miss Walker, on me, on everyone who had need of his clever mind. His surprising strength.

And in that second, suspended as we were on a French hillside, I was assaulted with feelings I did not wish to possess. Ones I'd sooner push away than touch even with a gloved fingertip. But it was an avalanche, and I couldn't move out of the way.

My deep affection for the man was undeniable.

There was a rarity to Peter Driscoll, one my battered soul sensed immediately and wished to cling to. And for as much as the man knew me, read every word of my soul, heard every note, I knew him too. Knew what he'd do if faced with choosing his life or another's. If a wayward acquaintance came to him for help. If a person of any sort wandered away from the fold and couldn't find his way home.

If a bitter and scarred actress came into his path, caused him trouble, and tried to send him on his way.

There was simply no one else in the entire world like Peter Driscoll. Suddenly I understood Adelaide Walker. Our hearts had reached the same rhythm, and her angst, her longing to fly to France in the middle of the night to find her beloved, became all too clear.

"Come," snapped Roderick. "They've gone." Placing fingertips against my upper back, he urged me through the window where Miss Walker had gone.

The captain lay deflated on the cot, breathing more labored than when we'd arrived. Miss Walker was gone. Where? What did they do to ladies who infiltrated military hospitals?

Out into the hush of the room, into the now-empty corridor and down the twisting, narrow steps, Roderick hovered beside me as if shielding himself with me—or shielding me, I couldn't tell which.

With each step I wanted to cry. "We can't leave her with *them*."

"It seems we are."

"It isn't right!" I couldn't stop seeing her hand resting protectively on her abdomen. That flicker of youthful hope in her photograph. I wanted to jump into the fray and grab her, whisking her away from danger. Coming on this journey to France in search of her lost love, then delivering her back home, or even leaving her with her dying soldier, was one thing. But leaving her to face this alone, abandoning her into the hands of the French military, was quite another. I wouldn't do it.

"*Life* isn't right, Miss Temple."

He hustled me through the corridors, then I twisted away. Enough of Roderick Heath taking charge. "Adelaide!" Head down, I rushed down a C-shaped corridor that bent along the backside of the building, following the vague sound of that familiar, high-pitched voice. It was her. She was demanding something. Throwing out words they likely didn't even understand.

She'd get herself killed.

Roderick caught up to me and steered me left. Again, I twisted away. "She needs our help."

"Handing down orders now, are we?"

I tore through the corridor, and surprisingly, he sprinted after me. Her voice was louder—she was ahead.

If she insisted on staying behind, she had to at least make her position clear to her captors. For all they knew, she was a madwoman flinging threats their way, and they'd simply lock her up. "This way. I hear her." We sailed down the steps, which led to a door to the outside on the left, and another corridor to the right. A scream split the air, echoing through the halls just beyond a door. I threw myself at it.

But another problem stood between us and Adelaide Walker. "It's locked!"

I banged it, poked at the keyhole, inspecting from every angle. An ancient lock, which meant it was heavier and more immune to my persuasion. I fished about the keyhole with my bent hatpin but couldn't catch the heavy mechanism. "Not to worry. There isn't a lock in England that has stopped me yet."

"Wonderful. We aren't *in* England, Your Highness."

I found the resistance and twisted hard, fueled by irritation. Pride.

Thunk. I felt the pins move, then the hatpin snapped. A few panicked moments, and footsteps sounded behind us on the stairs, voices echoing down.

"Je les ai entendus."

"Là, en bas des escaliers."

Then, a flurry of footfall.

"Let's go, you're coming with me." He tugged me toward the other door. The one that led outside, to freedom. "Whether you agree or not."

Away from Miss Walker.

"No!" I shoved him off. "Once we leave, we're never getting back in. See? That door will lock behind us."

"Splendid, let's use it."

I launched myself at the other door, the one between us and Adelaide Walker, ramming it with my shoulder. Kicking. Pounding. No sense in silence now. "Adelaide!"

Roderick threw himself at the outer door and yanked, over and over. It was stuck shut.

"What are you doing? You accept failure? Accept the loss of your master's client? Come help me, you louse. You were meant to protect her!"

His glare rivaled a thunderstorm. "You! It is *you* I'm resolved to protect, you foolish crow. Endangering you is the pinnacle of failure for me, don't you see that?"

The men came pounding around the bend of the stairs.

I stopped, and Roddy grabbed me, shoved me back against the door to the outside. "But you hate me." I was dizzy. Breathless.

"Well, yes. *I* do." His nostrils flared.

In a moment of clarity, everything slowed. Muffled. My mind only breathed, *Peter.*

Then the door fell away behind me, I tumbled back, and there he was.

24

Death walks faster than the wind and
never returns what he has taken.

~HANS CHRISTIAN ANDERSEN,
"THE STORY OF A MOTHER"

Lily fell into Peter's arms. Angry and desperate and all fiery passion, fighting against his hold.

"Roddy, the door! Shut it!"

It slammed, then they were running, stumbling through the overgrown courtyard and under the arches that led to freedom.

Men clambered out the door, voices raised, and Peter stopped to grab a weighty rock and launch it toward the east, away from them. As the pursuers veered toward the clatter, the escapees cleared a hedgerow, with Peter hauling Lily over, and ducked.

Peter was rattled. "Why did you stay? You could have been thrown in prison—had us *all* locked up!"

"I would have broken us out."

He eyed her. "The day you break me out of a prison is the day I let you drive my automobile, Miss Temple."

Roddy frowned. "Be careful what you promise, sir."

"I'm afraid she overestimates her lock-picking abilities. And underestimates French military prisons and their cast-iron locks."

Roddy huffed. "Let's just avoid French prisons, shall we?"

The yard had quieted.

"Enough talk. Grab hold," Peter whispered. "And run!"

Hand in hand they sprinted over grassy fields and overgrown gardens, wind whipping at Peter's loose shirt and cooling his skin.

Lily's breathless voice tangled with the wind. "Is it always like this with you, Peter Driscoll?"

"Afraid so."

She frowned. "How did you know where—"

"I'm always listening. And your voice is hard to miss."

They ran through a narrow wood and slowed atop sandy dunes that led down toward the beach. Which was swarming with men. Lily bent forward, hand at her chest, trying to catch her breath.

Peter took a quick glance over the group. "Where is Miss Walker?"

"There." Lily straightened and snapped out the word full of her opinions on the matter, her face flashing anger for just a moment.

"Of her own choosing," Roderick added quietly.

Peter looked to Roderick, then to Miss Temple, gathering the truth of Miss Walker's situation. A nod from Roddy confirmed his suspicions. He took a breath, steadied himself. "She is well, I assume?"

Roderick shrugged. "She's safe, and she's where she wants to be."

"Peter, she's in danger. We *must* get back in there and—"

"Not this time, Miss Temple. I'm with Roddy on this matter."

She spun on him, the full color of her emotion displayed on her flushed face. "You're agreeing to this? To leaving her here?" Her words dropped as jagged stones between them.

All humor disintegrated. His smile wilted and he shifted his shoulder blades, stretching sore muscles. "Miss Temple . . . Lily . . . Captain Pelletier won't be leaving the hospital. I've seen his records. I'll not separate them now. Not when they have so little time left." Peter hated each word as it came from his lips, but he couldn't be less than honest with her.

It was internal bleeding, the records stated. They couldn't find the source, and life was quickly ebbing from his body. Exploratory surgery had netted no results, and the bleed had only worsened, and an infection set in. Another few days was all he was expected to live.

Lily's lips pressed together and a solemnity stole over the little hillside. "You have failed her. Broken your word."

"I've found the truth. That is precisely what I promised to do."

Her eyebrows lowered, two slashes of judgment. "What sort of ending is this? Where is your all-important restoration?"

"You were witness to it, Miss Temple. Restoration did occur. We cannot burden the ending of any story with our expectations."

She stood rooted to the hillside, looking out over the channel as the wind tangled her hair, whipped her torn gown about her legs. A pillar of sorrow, but he could not do as he wished and wrap his arms about her. Or shortcut the grief. She'd have to walk through sadness to reach the other side, and all he could do was journey it with her. He grasped her hand and she clung to it, even as she looked away from him. How deeply she felt. How exquisite was her empathy, as if she wore the pain of those near her, shared the burden of it.

No wonder she ran from tragedies. They wrecked her.

Peter shucked his suit jacket, wrapped it about her, and led them toward a deep crevice in the rocks. It turned out to be a narrow slit into a rather generously sized cave. "The boat will be here in another couple of hours. We'd best keep hidden until then."

"Brilliant," Lily snapped, folding her arms under the oversized coat. "I want nothing more than to be home in my own bed." She turned back to look at the hospital just beyond the ragged cliff and drank in the sight of it. Of the place where Adelaide Walker's love story would end. Then she looked upon him, and under her scrutiny he felt every inch a failure.

"Best get some rest," he said, and motioned toward the small opening. The beach lay just beyond, water splashing and hissing over the shore. Fewer soldiers were there now, and the sand was mostly empty.

The three slithered into the narrow opening and followed it to a small grassy knoll completely hidden on the south side of the rock face. Roderick quickly nodded off in the cover of the rocks with his legs sprawled out. Lily, with her pristine features and bright, snapping eyes, stared endlessly out over the water, Peter's suit coat draped over her narrow shoulders.

The sun rose higher in the sky, warming the dry land, but she did not move. After a time he rose and went to her, lying on the grass nearby, and crossed his arms behind his head.

This isn't how I'd planned for things to go. I hope you know that, Lily Temple.

"What are you thinking about?" he asked. Peter looked her over, noted the drawn lips and flushed skin. The eye movement to the left—dipping into memory. "This reminds you of something, doesn't it? You're thinking of . . . a sweeter time. Something to do with the seashore and . . . family. Am I close?"

She was harder to read than most, more of an actress, but he was getting better. Just below that filmy façade was something solid and true and deeply authentic that called out to him to be explored.

"Long, relaxing days by the water, chattering away with someone you loved. Someone who let you talk endlessly, drawing words out rather than trying to stem the flow. Perhaps your mother? A dear friend? No, not quite. It's that sister. You're thinking of her."

Her head tipped a bit more to the right, gaze catching on his. "Actually I was thinking of my father. We used to lie beneath the stars when I was small, in an old hothouse. Foolish, of course—we might have caught our death, but what a lark. We used to stay out there telling secrets, trying to shock one another with things we'd heard." She lay on her side, facing him, pillowing her head in her arms. "But there weren't any sad things. Never any sad things." She said this last part quietly.

She was wearing Adelaide Walker's pain, wasn't she? Lily grieved along with her, and she could not tolerate pain, it seemed. Feared it, perhaps.

She'd faced her fair share of it. A sudden longing to share a certain secret with her bloomed in his chest, nearly overwhelming him. It wasn't wise, but the solemn tilt of her face, the sorrow coloring her eyes . . . it could all be wiped out. Could be lit up with joy instead. With hope.

He's escaped. Likely innocent, and I can clear him. I believe he's near. And that he's looking for you.

But he'd already let early hope cause her pain. Best to keep still for now. "You must miss him a great deal. Your father, that is."

She closed her eyes. "More than is reasonable sometimes."

"Hmm." His heart pounded. The words gathered on the edge of his tongue. *Help is coming.*

Roddy's snores had ceased, Peter suddenly realized. Was he listening? Waiting for Peter to tell her? Perhaps he should. *You'll have your father back. After years apart, you'll be embracing him by the end of the month. I'm nearly certain of it.*

"He was often busy, often working, but sharing secrets with him felt like the finest thing in the world. Because I had him all to myself."

Then she turned her bright-eyed gaze upon him, lips parted and waves of hair blowing. It felt oddly intimate, lying almost nose to nose beside her in the vastness of this place. He marveled that this very woman appeared on screens for anyone to see, yet here she was, rumpled clothes and loose hair about her shoulders, that eager face staring back at him in this private moment on a French shore.

"Perhaps I can stand in for him." Peter rolled onto his side, keeping his voice low. "I rather like the notion of sharing secrets beneath the stars. Or . . ." He looked up at the barely lit sky. "A cloudy day, at least."

How steady her look was. How sharply intelligent. He had the sense, watching her wide eyes, her gently angled face, that she longed to tell him everything. That the stories she hid from everyone lay just beneath the surface, and they fought to emerge. Maybe she'd let them.

Instead, she lifted her gaze and said, "You start."

"My life holds no secrets worth knowing, Miss Temple. I have an older brother and sister, a mother both wise and poised, a father I adored until his death. My childhood—"

"Not that sort of secret. Tell me how you do it. How do you

read people the way you do? The way you just did to me? Is it something like the fortune tellers? I know most of their secrets, and you don't do any of the same things."

"I told you. I listen." Heavy breathing sounded from Roddy again, so he lowered his voice. "I listen with intention, I should say. I watch reactions more than I listen to answers. People often tell you more than they intend to."

"That's all?"

"Well, you must ask the right questions, and in the right way. They must believe that you are like them, that their truth will also ring true with you and thus they are safe in revealing it."

She picked at the grass. "And you say the flickers are manipulative."

"I never use this skill to manipulate. Asking questions, especially when you already suspect the answers, is strategic. Clever. Purposeful. I can help so many of them, but only when I'm armed with the truth. And that is rarely the first thing anyone offers me." He burrowed into her gaze, inviting—begging—her to open up. To tell him about her life. About her father and his innocence.

He *was* innocent, wasn't he?

"So you ferret out their darkest secrets. But only for their good, of course."

"Nothing like a ferret. The strongest technique I have is—"

"Silence. It's silence." She centered her green-eyed gaze on his face. "You fall quiet whenever there's something you especially want to know."

"Silence unsettles people. It demands to be filled. You wouldn't believe the gems that have fallen into the ditch of silence, when it's opened up." He flashed a smile. "All right, your turn. What are your secrets?"

"Never." Her chin edged up, face toward the sky.

"Just one. Remember, you still owe me one answer. Any question I like, and I choose this one—a single secret of yours."

She slanted a gaze at him. "*Which* one?"

"Tell me who you are." His voice fell low and calm upon the great open space, the distant hiss of waves, the cool, moist air that tickled their skin.

She let it sink into the emptiness between them, the great chasm that had never seemed larger. "I don't know." A breath of wind. "There. A sad excuse of an answer, but . . ."

"But an honest one."

With everyone else, it was merely a matter of finding the key and inserting it into the lock. Opening a door. But Lily Temple was a stone wall, and he had the task of dismantling the fortress, stone by stone, and getting small trickles here and there. Until he happened upon the one that held up the whole wall, the one that would release a flood of words, he had merely to hold on for the ride. He'd swim in it. Take it all in and float there as long as he was allowed.

She turned, propping herself on one arm. "For years I've been a professional actress, working to become each part I play. I have become flavored by each of those roles until I'm a combination of everything I've seen and been. Only now it's hard to find the line between what's real and what isn't anymore."

"Especially when you don't want to."

Her eyes met his, her mouth a delicate frown.

"According to a rather clever cat in a story about Wonderland, imagination is the only weapon we hold in the war against reality. I suppose that's especially true for you."

She shrugged. "How am I to help it, if real life is intolerable?" Her head tipped to one side as she bent to examine a blade of grass most thoroughly. "I used to love play-acting. Even as a child, I made up elaborate plots and told them to whoever would listen. And when there was no one, I told them to myself, and lived out all the most wonderful fantasies my heart could create. Anything I wished would actually happen—I made it so. It was a marvelous time. Then I grew up and hid behind them. Preferred them to the path my life actually took. And now . . . well, I've played so many parts and hidden for so very long that I'm rather like that projection."

"Which?"

She fluttered her hand. "Oh, that theatrical ghost effect I did at the gardens. And in the hospital. The mirage of a woman, a faint and ghostly outline of something that doesn't actually exist. She's out there on display, but come close and put out your hand to touch her, and it'll go right through." She sliced the air with her hand.

"You're right, she is an illusion. But here's the truth—there can't be a reflection without a real woman to reflect."

Long, slanted eyes blinked at him. "It was Smithy, by the way. The lock picking. The sleight of hand. There you are, a free question."

"He taught you those things?"

"When I first met him, he was an illusionist. I was his assistant."

He smiled. "Another petal unfolds."

She lay back again. Her cheeks were flushed from the drowsiness, or maybe the depth of their conversation. She absorbed his response silently, her lips drawn into a neat little rosebud. "Peter, why are you content with this ending for her?"

"I trust her story's author."

She stared straight ahead, eyes dry and unblinking. "Why would you, when he writes stories such as this?"

And mine? He could almost hear this question whispering out from her mind.

He remained silent, letting the large questions settle between them before he answered. "It's easy to believe our stories need rewriting. That it's too risky, too important, not to take control, to ensure the right outcome. To cast yourself in the role you're meant to play. But here's the problem with that, Miss Lily Temple. The further we get from the story's author, the more we lose sight of our actual story. We long for our stories to come full circle, but that's the only one that will."

"I'm not holding out for some magical ending. Not for her or . . . anyone. I used to trust, but I grew weary long ago of crying out for it, waiting for something to change, for someone to come save me." She blinked rapidly. "No one ever did. *He* never did. No, I don't suppose I'm putting much stock in that author. But my story is far better now, with the pen in my own hand."

He reached out. Touched her shoulder.

She flinched but did not pull away.

Peter Driscoll was a master at keeping still, but sometimes—such as now—it didn't come easily. Rescue work had proved most complicated, for like the poor lost girl on the shore, one had to convince the lost heart it needed a rescue. One's entrapment became comfortable and familiar, and it was hard to conceive of anything better—safer—than what was known.

"You *are* looking for him—God, that is. I can see it in your eyes, hear it in your voice. It's the echo of everything you believe you want . . . whether you know it or not. Your longing to be reunited with your father. For intimacy to be restored. A return to the gardens, where things are what they were always meant to be. For a sense of home and deep-seated peace and rightness. For justice to be fulfilled and wrongs to be vanquished.

It's bottled up in your heart, Lily Temple. Only, you're focusing on the ghostly reflection, rather than the real story. The small here-and-now story instead of the larger. The eternal. The magnificent."

"You're right." She hugged herself. Turned away. "I should keep my head in the fairy tales. That's where real beauty can be found—because it can be written. By me."

"But he *is* your story. Lily, can't you feel it? Can't you feel him calling out to you from every story that wraps itself around your heart? Every tale that draws you in? The hero on a quest, the hardship, the crisis and rescue . . . They're all just a reflection. A shadow. That's why you love them so much—because they awaken what is buried within. What you're *supposed* to long for. What you've lost sight of, but never lost. Because it's yours." He leaned forward. "God has placed eternity in the heart of man. In the heart of *you*."

She stared at him, that bright face still and eager. Saying nothing.

In the end, she sighed, turned her back on him, and lay silent.

25

I have many beautiful flowers, but the children
are the most beautiful flowers of all.

~OSCAR WILDE, "THE SELFISH GIANT"

The sun was preparing to sink for the evening when England's shores came into view, a bright orange glow stretching from east to west with the colorful ball in the center. An entire day had passed, with several of those hours spent on the water.

We'd hungrily eaten the cold ham sandwiches and grapes from a hamper belowdecks, but not many words passed between the three of us. Much as the men stood by their decision to leave Miss Walker, that unsettled feeling had crept over us all. The sooner I could return to my cottage at St. Anne's, the better. Driscoll could have his cases—I'd make my shillings on the stage.

As we approached the shoreline, the men behind me scrambled to the edge of the boat. Leaned over to stare at something on the shore.

Roderick snatched a pair of binoculars from the owner and leaned perilously far over the rail. "Pete. Pete, look at this. It's *her*."

Peter took the glasses and pointed them toward the shore, straining to see whatever Roderick had pointed out. For the life of me, I couldn't see a thing, aside from the tide and the flutter of a few stray items on the beach. Or was that perhaps . . . a person? I blinked again.

He lowered the glasses. "Miss Temple, I'm going to need your help again."

I laughed, incredulous. "Are you, now?"

Roderick huffed. "What'll you have her do, *charm* the girl out of hiding?"

Peter set down the binoculars and turned, that direct gaze settling upon me. Breeze feathered his hair. "It's a special case. One you are uniquely qualified to do."

"As they all seem to be."

He smiled through my quip. "You've read Dickens's Christmas story, haven't you?"

"The one with the miserly old master and the specters who light his way? Frightfully vulgar in some ways, yet somehow amusing."

"Then you'll understand the delicacy of this case."

The wind tugged at my straw hat. "You wish me to what, speak to a spirit?"

"It's an eerie matter, but no. It's a girl—one who's in dire straits, like Tiny Tim. Several times in the odd hours, early morning and late at night, I have come upon this child on the shore. She's hungry. Lonely. Something is wrong, but she won't let me come close to her. Won't let me help."

He handed me the spyglasses and I stared hard at that ghost-figure—a child. I had hated that part of the book, that Tiny Tim character. The small boy had enchanted me, and I had burned through several candle stubs one winter as if his happy ending was on hold until I, the reader, reached it.

But I never did. Once my mind had absorbed the image of the boy's death during the vision of the third specter, I'd shut that book and hurled it into the hearth. The only time I'd ever ruined an entire book, but I couldn't see the sense in twisting up my heart ever again.

Still feeling like shattered china, I hugged the borrowed coat around myself, knowing I should agree, that I should want to, but I could not. I lowered the glasses, shaking my head. "What can I possibly do for her? I have no money. I cannot care for her. She doesn't wish anyone to help either, from the sounds of it."

He took me by the shoulders, turning me back to face him. The intensity in his warm brown eyes shocked me. "You're icing over, Lily. We live in a world of broken shards and nettles, and you're freezing yourself over to protect yourself from them. To guard that lovely, tender heart of yours from pain and disappointment."

"Don't be foolish." I tossed my head flippantly and crouched in the damp hull, leaning over to trail my finger through the silver water.

"I'm going to make you do this." He knelt before me and refused to grant me a moment to peacefully nurse my selfishness. "I refuse to let you completely ice over. The loss to this world would be too great."

A shudder. I pulled my arm back in. "I'm no saint, Mr. Driscoll. Don't believe me something better than I am."

He cocked one eyebrow.

"I haven't any idea what's true about me anymore. But what *is* true . . . well, I rather wish it wasn't."

"I know one true thing, Lily Temple." His thumbs slid up my forearms, warming away the goose bumps through the shawl. "In your personal little rule book, children outrank adults. They are to be treasured. Enjoyed. *Protected*." Then he faced the shore, where the nearing flutter of white had taken on the clear form of a child. A girl. Long dark hair framed a serious little face. "Especially the ones who have no one. They draw you like no other, because you are willing to help when so few are. You know it's true."

I shuddered, but melted under that gentle brown gaze, feeling every inch of it along the depths of my being. For years I'd paraded before a camera, danced and sang and performed before hundreds. My face was known about Hove.

But my soul was known to Peter Driscoll.

I braced myself as the boat moved quickly toward the shore, toward that girl, for yet another tragedy playing out.

26

In another moment down went Alice after [the white rabbit], never once considering how in the world she was to get out again.

~LEWIS CARROLL,
ALICE'S ADVENTURES IN WONDERLAND

stared at her distant form bobbing to collect shells. Stray hairs tickled my cheeks, my nose. "You're certain it's the right girl?"

"Nothing is certain. Nothing, except the need is great and the time short." He held on to the mast as the little boat swung in the direction of the beach. "If you would, Mack, please shore up by the little inlet there."

The balding man threw his weight into the wheel, and the boat pitched to the east, away from the bright orange sun preparing to set.

The first thing Peter did when we reached the shore was to help me out and then send his hovering valet away. Then he offered me his hand, invitation glowing from his countenance.

I pulled my hand in close, looking around at the empty seashore. How was I to go about helping a child who didn't want it? Possibly didn't even need it? I looked at those narrow shoulders, the back of her bowed head, and suddenly I saw myself. My younger self for whom a "rescue" would have meant doom. "Not everything is meant to be restored."

"Another thing that's true of you, Lily Temple. You're intensely loyal. Especially toward your father." He lowered his hand. "No matter what the world thinks of him, or how many years pass, you've not given up on him. Not truly. It isn't in you."

I shrugged, heart hammering. Guilt and urgency coupled in my chest, a familiar dull ache of unrest. A lot of good that loyalty had done me. Or him.

"I've made progress on your case. The one you asked me to help with."

My gaze snapped to his.

"I believe I can help you. That is still what you want, isn't it?" His eyes searched mine, his breath short and quick. "To find Gordon Makepiece?"

I trembled. The moist air, the breeze coming off the sea . . . my heart's goal being dangled before me. He didn't mean it, did he? He couldn't. I'd worked toward this for years, chasing down that man, filming his fairy tale and showing it to the world . . . and Peter Driscoll simply steps in and does the impossible in less than a fortnight? My heart pounded beneath my wrinkled gown, eager and unsettled and anxious all at once.

"In exchange, all I want is for you to help me. To keep your lovely heart supple and warm. To keep that passion glowing in a dim, sad little world." He offered his hand again. "The only way to keep it strong is to use it, Lily love."

I stared at that hand. The endearment should have jarred me, but somehow it fit this moment and this man. How oddly celestial he seemed, with the pink-and-orange glow of early sunset behind him, softening his features and giving them a heaven-touched look. It was hard not to trust him . . . not to agree to everything he asked of me. Especially when he was offering so much in return.

I could do it. I could. Lily Temple, merely playing a part.

I turned to him, chin up, and didn't even need to speak my acceptance.

He gave a nod and took my offered hand, squeezing then releasing it. A slow smile spread over his face. "You're quite a woman, Lily Temple."

I took a breath and let it out. A child. Simply talking to a child.

"She comes here of an evening to collect seashells and carries them off in her apron, and so far she will not speak a word or even look at me. I came close to her, but she managed to evade me. I've given chase, but she simply vanished. It's all rather . . . eerie."

I crossed my arms, heart sinking. "So she *is* a specter. And you've brought me up here because you cannot face her alone."

"She isn't. At least, I hope she's not." He stood, casting his gaze up the rugged coastline toward the caves. "It merely occurs to me that a woman will have better success than a man. And *this* woman in particular. I daresay she could charm a rock."

A smile flickered over my lips. "If rocks were worth charming." I shivered as night struggled to overcome day, casting warm sunlight over the beach, and shadows inside the caves. I had to blink to see into them at all. Even in daylight, *eerie* was precisely the right word for those caves. And anything that might emerge from them. Another shiver. How chilly it was—how oddly *lonely*. "She must be gone. How long—"

"Look." His voice was the barest whisper, and it made the hairs on my neck stand up. "Over there." He crouched into the rocks, and I did the same.

A figure strode out from the darkness, gray garment glowing almost white as it whipped about her slender legs. Long dark braids hung like ropes over her shoulders, and she was barefoot. The girl picked her way across the rocks as if she didn't feel them, holding her gown up from each hiss of water. Then she stood in the open, looking out to sea with an air of tragedy as if she were watching for a ship's return. She continued on, bending now and again to pick up a smooth stone or shell and drop it in her upturned apron.

"Go on, then. See if she'll warm to you." Peter nudged my arm.

Cold panic stiffened me. Terror mixed with enchantment at the prospect of approaching her. I forced myself forward. My bare feet—I'd shed my boots on the boat—felt every stone and pebble, but I continued on, drawn now by this girl who seemed to live in her own world—which existed right inside ours.

Then she froze, chin up, the fox sensing the hunter. Her gaze landed on me and held. She stared back over her shoulder at me with bright, fearful eyes, and I glimpsed her face at last. The ribbons plaited into her hair. It was her. *Her.* Then she turned and bolted.

After a moment of shock, I ran toward her, dodging the largest rocks. *Mila, Mila, Mila.* She dropped her apron hem, shells clinking across the ground as she leaped and scrambled over rocks like a mountain goat.

Scooping up a few of her shells, I sprinted after the girl.

"Wait! Please wait!" Wind whipped my words away. I scrambled after her, heart thudding. Mind racing. One big leap across a dip in the rocks and I was near. Almost to her. She was struggling against a nearly sheer rock face, clawing her way up it. Heart pounding, I reached out, halfway expecting to feel cold mist on my hand.

But she was warm. Real. She jumped at my touch.

"Please, wait." I panted out the plea and leaned against a rock to catch my breath.

She spun on me then, dark eyes fearful, back against the rock. For a brief second, I stared into a reflection of myself. In her face I saw every wild emotion I'd once felt, glowing through her countenance. That deeply lost look.

I softened. "I believe these are yours." I pressed the shells into her hand and watched her unchanging face. "Now please. I only want to ask you something. It's about—"

"Don't care for being followed." She flung open her palm, scattering the shells, and melted between the very rocks with only a hiss of fabric.

Before I could gather my wits, I was standing alone on the sea-swept beach, breathing in moist evening air and staring after the girl whose face had haunted me since that terrible night.

But she had vanished yet again. Seashells scattered over rocks were the only evidence that she'd been there at all. Shells, and the chill wrapping itself around me.

I climbed back to Peter on shaky legs, yanking the loose straw hat from my head. I'd composed myself when I reached him, and I towered over him on a rounded rock near his hiding spot. "You might have told me. It's *her*."

"And have you go charging in? No, this was better, I think." He stood, eyes alight, and smiled. "Well? Was it successful?"

"She refused to answer anything—quite definitively, at that— just before she disappeared into the rocks and vanished. We *must* find her, Peter."

"Come. Show me which rocks."

I pointed, and he grabbed my hand and pulled me along to the spot. He felt around, brushing sand off the rocks, then around the corner.

I felt around the place where I'd seen her go, and my hand found a cool crevice. "Here. Here we are." I peered around the rock for a better look at what turned out to be an opening tucked almost behind it. "The beauty of magic is that every trick has an explanation." I slipped my entire arm into it, then slid my body into the cool darkness. "Are you coming, Peter Driscoll?" My voice echoed just a little.

His footfall came just behind me. I felt along the walls of a cave, hoping desperately for a quick exit. A light somewhere to guide us through. I turned back and ran into Peter's solid chest.

He laid an arm around my shoulders. "Let's keep going. Just a little farther, and we'll find some sign of her."

"Why are you doing this?" I whispered.

"Because only she knows what truly happened. What's still happening. And besides . . . I may be able to locate her family."

I allowed myself a full perusal of the man with my hand— his tailored suit against his lithe frame in neat tucks and folds, thick, soft hair now wind-ruffled and sandy . . . "Why do you do this sort of work, anyway? Why help me? And her?" It wasn't as if either of us had given him money, or ever would.

He turned away and continued moving through the cave before he answered. "I'm a second son. Raised in wealthy circles, often privy to their secrets, but heir to nothing. I must make a way for myself, and this is where my abilities have taken me."

We maneuvered around a corner and there was light. We emerged into a sandy outcropping, barren and windblown with stray grasses here and there.

"Not detective work. The other thing—reuniting and restoring. What makes you want it so passionately, even when you're not paid for it?"

He dropped his gaze, then lifted it out over the vast shore, its rolling hills holding his attention.

"Ah. That's right. You only ask the questions—never answer them."

More silence. Then, he did answer. "Because once it was too late. I never want that to be the case again. Not if I can help it."

There it was. The crack in his shield. Yet I couldn't fathom the reason. Or whether or not I should trust the man. Common sense told me I shouldn't. Yet . . .

Facing away from the shore, he pointed down at a collection of debris on the sand. A worn path. "Come." He said it gently. An invitation more than a command. It was always that way with him.

And I came.

That's what would bust through my sturdiest wall in the end, wasn't it? Not all the battering or force another man might use, but the supreme patience and kindness of this rare man and his lovely, passionate heart.

"Come, we'll find the girl together." He put an arm around me and steadied me with the other, helping me over the jagged rocks.

Together we scaled the embankment, dried grass waving from atop the sandy hills, then we climbed down the other side toward the debris—which turned out to be the remnants of abandoned buildings tucked in between the rocky hills. Breeze sent up a spray of sand, and I brushed it from my face.

"Esther. My sister. She ran away with a sailor years ago, and I helped her. Hid her secret, hoisted her out the window. She loved him, but our parents would not allow the match. Esther was right, they *were* against it. But it was only because my mother—my very wise mother—saw through the man to a very dark temper within. I was only a lad, so I missed it."

"You were trying to help her."

"Of course, and I did. Right into a life of misery and abandonment. He died in a drunken brawl in Liverpool years ago. They've a babe, a child by now." He stared down at the decrepit little collection of houses. "Her leaving ruined my very close family. Father died of apoplexy within the month she left, my brother won't forgive me, and my mother is a vapor of what she was before. I cannot undo the twist I put in our story, but I can help untwist the stories of others."

"So that's your reason."

He gave a nod and began climbing down toward the little town.

I followed close behind, shielding my face from blowing sand whenever the wind spilled over the cliff.

When I blinked my eyes, we stood on a plateau of rocks and sand, looking across a dilapidated collection of old fishing shacks, splintered and worn as if they'd tumbled all the way down the hills to lie in an abandoned heap before us. "What is this place?" I yelled over the wind.

Besides a derelict ruin. Clearly, no one lived there still.

"An abandoned fishing town, I believe. The tides must have changed the landscape."

We walked a few paces to the east, the sun nearing the horizon behind us. He pointed out a little house whose yellow paint had almost completely chipped away. Splintered windows and doors lay on the ground, oilskin cloth flapping in their place. "This is where she stays, I would guess."

A crooked shutter banged against the house. Sand had piled around the foundation in artistic mounds.

"How can you be certain *anyone* lives here?"

He pointed to the rear of the house, where a sheet could barely be seen flapping on a clothesline. I started 'round the corner, but movement flashed within. We both saw it and halted, staring at the window where the oilskin lifted in the wind. Peter moved toward the house in long, agile strides.

I blew out a breath, flipping salty stray hair off my face, and charged after him.

He ducked as a pot sailed out the window, then a pewter bowl. I stood to the left of the window and strained to see who was launching the attack.

"If you please," I called out. "I'm harmless, I promise." I waved Peter out of sight and smiled at the wild-eyed woman framed in the window. "I'm wondering if you might help me." I brushed sand off my skirts, fluffed my gritty hair. Her face disappeared. "Could I trouble you for a cup of tea? I've been on a boat, you see, and I'm afraid I'll drop right here in the sand." I grabbed the window frame, wobbling on my legs that did, in fact, feel quite weak. "Please, miss. You're a kind soul, you are. I can see it. I'm . . . I'm lost."

Silence.

After a beat, the oilskin cloth over the doorway moved aside. Peter ducked out of sight. A worn and frazzled face peered out, wiry hair roughly coiffed at the nape of her neck. She studied me, every inch. Judging my poise and weighing it against my bedraggled frock. Looking past me for intruders. Then she jerked her head. "Come on."

I entered the shanty and blinked to adjust my eyes. There in the dimness, more than half a dozen pairs of eyes stared up at me. The dirty faces of children. The woman who'd admitted me hunched over a tiny hearth preparing tea, and I turned to the wide stares and smiled. "Hello. Who might you be?"

No one answered. Not the boys in too-short trousers or the girls with neatly smoothed hair. There was a story here—an odd one. While the woman eyed me over her shoulder, I squatted on the floor before them with a cheery smile. "Well, then. Do you all play games? I've a fine one I used to play as a girl. I must guess your name, and you tell me if I've guessed any letters right. Are you ready? You there—" I pointed to a boy with protruding front teeth. "You must be Zerubbabel."

They laughed, just a little, and I felt as if I'd won a prize. The silent woman brought me a dented metal mug, and I thanked her with warmth to match the wonderful tea in my hands.

Tea always was a boon.

She didn't return the greeting, so I turned back to my game. "Hmmmm. Jehoshaphat?"

Another laugh. "*J*! You've got *J*!" said one of the boys.

"Jared!"

"It's John," one of the little girls piped up.

Quickly I learned all their names and drank my tea while the woman looked on, wary as a mother cat with newborn kittens.

But the girl from the shore was not there. Nor was her green-jacketed rabbit. My lead had narrowed to a dead end.

But not quite. "Say, I don't suppose anyone can guess who I am, can they?"

Laughter followed, along with several guesses. Finally, one said Francine.

"Yes! The *F* is right."

A few more guesses.

"You'll never guess. What if I told you I was . . . a fairy?" They giggled. "I'm a fairy, come from an enchanted garden. My name is Greta Makepiece." I dropped the name that lingered in my heart and searched their reactions quickly. Did they know the name? Somehow . . . Somehow that girl on the beach was connected to him. "That's right, a fairy, and I've lost my way, and I'm searching for the looking glass that will—"

A nudge from behind. "Time to get on with you, miss." The woman snatched my mug and hurried me toward the door, lifting the flap. "You've had your tea, now leave us in peace."

I stammered out my thanks and backed out the door, waving to the children and gathering my wits. Outside, I straightened and looked back at the house, thoughts and puzzle pieces bouncing about the walls of my mind.

Peter appeared immediately.

"She isn't there. But there are other children." I stood amid the lightly blowing sand, looking over the world below. "It reminds me of an old schoolroom, with all different sorts of children holed up together. They're not related. But . . . it is a dead end."

"And?" He folded his arms across his chest. "There's more, isn't there? You've a hunch."

I threw up my arms. "Why should it matter one fig if I have a *hunch*? Lots of people have lots of hunches, and they're wrong more times than they're right."

"You saw something. Or heard something, perhaps." He tapped his lips with one finger.

I shrugged, looking out to the sea. "Just a sense I had. Not worth hanging your hat on."

He removed his bowler and perched it lightly on my head.

"Hanging my hat on your thoughts. Now tell me what they are."

I laced my gloved fingers together. "I think we're on the right path. We're close. To the girl, *and* to Gordon Makepiece." Unless I'd been imagining it, the mention of his name had shifted something in the house . . . and earned me a hasty exit. "The girl *does* stay here and she *did* bring the white rabbit to the gardens, and the flower crown, but I can't imagine why. It's almost as if . . ."

"As if what?" he asked softly.

"As if she's a character from one of Gordon Makepiece's fairy tales come to life." I shook my head. "There it is, my hunch. Worth exactly what you paid for it."

"Lost, are you?"

I jumped at the low voice behind me. The woman from the shanty stepped out and let the oilskin door fall back in place.

She stood, arms folded, guarding her charges inside. "What exactly are you doing here? *No one* comes here. Not ever."

"I'm looking for a little girl we saw on the beach. I've seen her about, and again on the seashore just now. But she won't let me near her."

"Maybe you should be minding your own business."

"She may have witnessed a crime. I wanted to ask her about what she saw, and . . . well, I wished to help her too."

"No one here needs your help, miss."

"Temple. It's Lily Temple."

The woman stared, her angular jaw working, lips twitching.

"These children here, they're not even yours, are they?" Peter was eyeing her in that knowing way he had, dissecting her thoughts, laying bare the truth.

"Of course they are."

"You're the guardian angel of the Chobald Caves, aren't you?" His voice was gentle. "Waiting here for someone to wash up on shore and return to you, but he hasn't. Plenty of others have, though, haven't they? And you've rescued them all. Given them a home. Kept them alive."

She blinked, not agreeing, not denying. "My life's been shipwrecked enough times. I know what it is to be alone." She frowned. "They don't need to."

"I'm working to bring that little girl home. To her family."

She went stony. "They *are* home. All of 'em. Now *stay away*." Then she whipped the cloth back and disappeared inside.

"Well." I brushed back loose hair and dusted off my skirt. "She certainly doesn't want us locating this girl."

"Then we must keep looking for her. Shall we?" He offered his arm.

"Now? After stealing me away to France and back again? And on a dreadfully rickety boat, might I add. You do realize I haven't slept in my own bed yet. I'm frightfully tired and I look a sight."

"Very well then, a small respite." He strode over the sand. "But only because I know you'll join me on the search this evening. You can't let her story drop now. We've come so close. Then we'll take the motorcar back to the gardens. Roddy should have brought it."

"And you'll let me drive?"

"Not a chance."

We'd made it nearly back down to the shore again when I saw the little flip of white. It stood out against the dark, mossy rocks, and I bolted. Without even thinking, I scrambled after her, desperate to close the distance. Peter yelled after me. Another hint of cloth, and I changed directions. She had gone into the cave. The tide was rising, though. With each hiss of waves over sand, the water stretched farther into the mouth of the cave.

I saw her climbing and called out. "Wait! I need to ask you something. Please . . . I need to know."

But she climbed out of sight.

I looked back—Peter was even farther now, his voice calling out for me, but I was driven. I reached the top of the mouth and jumped down to the sand. There she was, hovering just inside the cave, fear paling her face. "Please, Mila. I just want to talk to you."

She backed away as if struck, water sloshing around her ankles, then receding. A wave crashed against the mouth of the cave, then filled it. The girl screamed, and I lunged for her, grabbed her arm, yanked her into the water, propelling us both out of the cave before a bigger wave crashed through. By sheer force of will, I dragged her, coughing and sputtering, up the rocky cliff to the top of the cave, where the waves had merely wetted the rocks. She sat on the rocks, shivering. Coughing. Out of breath.

I spun to her, taking her shoulder. Frantic. "The rabbit. The flower crown. It was you, wasn't it? Why did you bring them? Why?"

Another hard shiver. "Because the man told me to." An accent. Her voice had a distinctly clipped accent.

"Who? What man?"

"Michael. Now leave me be!"

Then she twisted away and ran, disappearing between the giant dark rocks. I clambered after her, but this time, she was gone. Gone. I stood, shaking, on the mossy rocks, legs braced as I scanned the horizon. There were no more signs of movement.

Peter came huffing up behind me. "Any luck?"

I shook my head. "Not many heroines get a happy ending."

"Has it come full circle yet? Your story, that is."

"Why should that matter?"

"Has it?"

I blinked. Shook my head.

"Then, Miss Temple, it isn't over."

27

"My sweet," said the fairy godmother, "remember well one thing. You have until midnight, and only midnight, to take advantage of my magic. At the last stroke of midnight, the coach will turn back into a pumpkin, the horses back into mice, and the coachman back into a horse. Do you understand?"

~CHARLES PERRAULT, "CENDRILLON" ("CINDERELLA")

I t was her face that haunted me, that girl from the shore. In the darkness of the old pump room, behind a curtain of filmstrips dripping with tinting chemicals, I saw her eyes every time I closed my own. Something about that waif had woven itself into my mind, and I wanted to return to her. Look for her on the shore. Shake the information out of her that I desperately needed . . . and then bundle her up and feed her every morsel of food she could hold. Assure her that she was not lost anymore.

Not every lost girl wished to be found, though.

I swished one strip of film in the tray of iron tinting, then clipped it to the line and swished another. Frame after frame painted with adhesive on the high points, dipped then hung.

The pieces simply didn't fit, and I mentally rearranged them, hoping for a solution. A connection to my own story, and an explanation for it all. But Peter's face kept returning to my mind, and questions about how he fit. About why he was so invested in the things that mattered to me. He'd been bent on warming up my heart again, he'd said.

"Everyone lies," my father had said once, in that confident way he had. It made him seem wise, the way he spoke, and this statement had proved true.

I held a marigold-tinted strip to the light, inspecting it for highlights and lowlights. Even tinting was a façade, coloring the scene in a specific mood. Creating an atmosphere. How was anyone to know what was real anymore?

I could still recall the exact moment I had realized the elusive nature of truth in the hands of humans. I had been bold and brilliant, searching for proof. Proof to clear an innocent man, and there was no reason on this earth I should have found it. But, after pleading with God, I had. Miraculously, I had found the supposedly stolen sapphire. I had rushed with it, in the final hours, to the courthouse. I had brandished it proudly, then slipped out to watch the trial . . . and crumbled in disbelief when he had looked down upon me from his magistrate's box, holding my gaze, and declared the man we both knew to be innocent . . . guilty.

It was a shattering like glass, this moment of understanding. I hadn't put words to it at the time, but a concept had flitted into my head at that exact moment that had never left me: *truth is relative.* It opened up to me the notion that truth might be bent and twisted to fit one's purposes, and in fact might become a tool. It was possible. Like a story massaged into a more congruent shape and coloring, stretching just beyond the bounds of reality.

Yet I hadn't ever been able to do it. The truth was far too precious and fragile a thing to be bent and warped that way. I never could mar the truth, so instead, I wrapped it in stories to protect and clarify it. I spun fiction . . . and let the truth shine out for itself.

I could often sense a fabrication after that moment—and there was a lie in the story before me. The girl by the shore, the woman in the shanty, the white rabbit and deer's flower crown, Peter Driscoll and his altruistic efforts. I just had to find the puzzle piece that didn't fit. Then the picture would make sense. All would be—

The door banged open.

"Smithy! I was just—"

"You need to leave."

"I'm almost finished with the tinting."

But the intensity on his normally distracted countenance, the absolute absence of color, stopped me from saying more. "The police have been here for hours. Questioning me, questioning Laura. Poking about. Everything is a disaster." He dropped the *Brighton Chronicle* on the messy desk, and there was my smiling face on the front, under the headline MOVING PICTURE ACTRESS MAKES OFF WITH PRICELESS SAPPHIRE. "The police have been here. I've shielded you, and now they think . . . they think I'm complicit."

I sighed, head in my hands. "People only believe this because they *watched* me steal it—on *film*. You cannot possibly think I've done this, Smithy."

His bullet-like dark eyes stayed on my face.

"You *do* think I took it."

"No one wants to come to the gardens." He shook his head. "Police are swarming, questioning guests . . . People don't want to see my films. I cannot sell tickets, and the constable has shut down my schedule for the week."

What he meant was, it didn't matter if I had taken the thing or not. The scandal was enough. My tongue went suddenly dry. I said nothing to defend myself—my shock was too great. "Very well. I'll keep out of sight until this blows over. I'll keep to the cottage and—"

"You've been sneaking it out, haven't you, Miss Temple? The sapphire. Wearing the thing about the gardens, claiming it as yours."

I blinked, stunned. He'd never noticed before. Not in many months, since I'd come to the garden. "Someone has said these things?"

"The dowager countess, who owns the Briarwood Teardrop. She has hired someone—"

"A private inquiry agent." The words came on a whisper. He'd told me he was hired to find the gem . . . but he made it seem we were on the same side. Now it felt distinctly as if we weren't.

"He has informed her of these things himself." His voice was low. Steady. "My work is suffering. My audience dwindling. And now . . . they're looking at me as a suspect. Me! After the years I've spent, building up my name. My work. My art. Miss Temple, you'll have to go."

"Oh Smithy, I'm—"

"Now."

Fear immobilized me. I couldn't quite fathom what was happening. How bad it truly was. A moment of silence, a split second for the wheels to turn and my head to accept his dismissal, and I gathered up my hat and gloves. I would go.

He pressed his fingertips into his forehead, closing his eyes. "Leave your costumes on the foot of the bed. Paste jewels. Everything that belongs here. Anything else you might have . . . borrowed."

My skin heated. Only then did I understand what *get out* actually meant. I saw spots. Bright ones. The swinging light bulb burning into my vision. The clutter in the room sharp and clear. My brain struggled to absorb the moment. "But, Smithy, I can fix—"

"You cannot."

"I'm sorry, it was—"

"Good day, Miss Temple." Then he turned his back on me, sorting through the newly tinted frames. The ones featuring my likeness, the ones tinted and neatly edited by me.

His hunched back was all he offered me now. All I'd see of him in parting. The sting was unexpected. Indescribably deep. I hurried out the door, leaving a glove behind. A hat probably. Fire pumping through my veins, I charged into the woods, up the path, and into Grasshopper Cottage.

Which was no longer my home.

I tumbled onto the bed, in the place where I was to leave nearly everything I'd considered mine. Face in the quilt, I lay there and shook. Shook like a track with a coming train. But I did not cry.

Regret. Sorrow. Stinging rejection peeled back layers to expose a rawness I thought I'd safely bound up for good. He hadn't broken any promises. Hadn't told any lies. Smithy had never agreed to become the object of my daughter-heart adoration, and he hadn't claimed to be a father figure to me. But he had, all the same.

I shook and rocked and frantically grabbed for a story to

wrap around my brain. A fairy tale. The most beautiful event that could ever possibly happen to me, that I might imagine it was actually occurring instead of this wretched reality. But I couldn't drum one up. Nothing felt beautiful and the world was all hard edges and washed-out colors.

The door opened and closed, then a gentle voice sounded. "Where will you go?" It was Mae.

I sat up, sucking in a breath, and tossed my loose hair over my shoulder with a bold grin. "Some other part that needs to be played, I suppose. Some other position. I never stay in one place too long anyway."

Those large, luminous eyes remained steadily on me. "You'll forget us that quickly? I fancied us friends."

My charade melted and I went to her, holding out my hands. "Of course we are." I took them in mine. "You've been all but a sister to me. But nothing lasts, you know. Nothing in this whole world. No matter how much we wish it."

She blinked. "It'll be terribly lonesome in the cottage."

My eyes grew warm. Moist. "Until Smithy finds another actress willing to work for peanuts and hide herself away in his pump room." I forced a bright smile. "Shouldn't take more than an hour, I'd imagine." I squeezed her hands and went to the wardrobe, sorting through borrowed scarves, costume gowns, and boxes of cheap paste jewelry and hats, searching for anything that was actually mine.

Which was almost nothing.

A few worn underthings, a milkmaid's frock and apron, and big, ugly boots heavy enough to leave a hole in the plaster walls. I grimaced and put them aside, choosing instead a simple skirt and shirtwaist I had made myself and a purple cloak that Gypsy Lee had given me.

It was good Mae had come after me, in the end. Much as I wished for no one to witness my humiliation, my foolish sweep of emotions, her being here prodded me into action. Kept me moving so I didn't slip into childish laments.

I was no better than the day I'd fled my father's house in tears at seventeen years of age.

"You'll go to that inquiry agent first, won't you?"

I laughed. Flimsy and brittle. "Lily Temple doesn't need a rescuer."

"I was only thinking he'd want to know what's become of you. What shall I tell him the next time he comes by?"

Reality settled cold and solid over me. He was done with me now. After every other case outing, he'd left a thank-you. This time, there had been none. And . . . he had betrayed me to the countess.

He was not coming back. Whatever he'd wanted with me, he was done.

"Tell him nothing, because he won't be around the gardens any longer."

"How can you be certain?"

"Just a hunch." I felt about the bottom of the wardrobe for any stray belonging that might have fallen. "He's here too often as it is. Can't have him forming an attachment, now can I?"

"Heaven forbid." She watched me with arms crossed over her chest. It was dim, but I knew her lips were pinched.

I rose and dropped my carpetbag on the floor with a huff. "Don't go looking at me that way, Mae. All men lie. They do what they must to achieve their ends, and I needn't help any along. I'd rather work toward truth."

She was silent for so long that I turned away and began tucking small items into the wilted carpetbag.

She sat on the edge of my cot. "If you really want the truth, you've got to start by letting go of what you know."

"What a strange idea."

"Tell me something you know, Lily Temple."

I couldn't stop seeing Smithy in my mind's eye now. Frizzy crown, crooked suit jacket, that blinking, half-startled stare with which he took in the world. The dear man who had belonged, in a way, to me. Had placed himself under my care, needed my help to launch his brilliance into the world. "I know that men will discard a person as easily as they drop a two of clubs in a round of cribbage. They'll lie when it makes more sense to do so than not. They'll do what they must to appease their conscience, but in the end they are wholly practical beings with a purpose, and they seldom show kindness unless it moves them toward their goal."

I shoved more and more things into the bag. "I also know that men are broken. They wear different suits, polish themselves to different degrees, but underneath they're all exactly as messy and selfish as the others. And I know that all it takes for a man to disappoint a body . . . is time."

"You do know a great many things." Mae gripped the edge of the bed, leaning forward, the shadows deepening the violet circles underscoring her lovely eyes. "Now tell me what is *true*, Lily Temple. Specifically of Mr. Driscoll."

A shift. A cool breeze. I thought with a sudden ache of those passionate brown eyes magnified by gold-framed spectacles. The pure heart that spilled itself upon a handsome face. Strength in hidden reserves and the gaze that saw everything—absolutely everything—and continued to shine with amusement at the world. At me, most especially.

"I'm going to make you do this. I refuse to let you completely ice over. The loss to this world would be too great."

But then the image faded.

I dove into my bureau drawer, scooping out its contents as regret threatened to unfurl inside. "It isn't as if one man truly is different than the others."

"Come now. Every person is unique."

I paused, rocked back on my heels. I blew out a long, slow breath as my head throbbed and thought of Peter. "I think maybe . . . Peter Driscoll is not *always* practical. He's no stranger to sacrifice, and he spends himself on other people. And he rarely does what I expect. He . . . he keeps coming back. Even when I don't think he will. When perhaps he shouldn't."

Her face shone in the dimmed lamplight. "And?"

"And he's rather clever. He knows things. Sees things." About me, for example. He was likely the only human who knew me entirely. The only one able to see what I didn't show and hear what I didn't say.

"A rare find, no?" She winked and bumped my shoulder. "One worth encouraging."

I dropped my gaze and fiddled with the clothes I packed. "I admit, he may be the one perfect man for me in the entire world. *If* I were to attach myself to anyone, which I won't." I shoved hair off my face, smoothed my skirt. Betrayal snaked through every relationship eventually, a dull poison, and the effects of it had simply grown too great. It had rotted anything resembling hope remaining in me. And he was, first and foremost, an inquiry agent—one who had approached me because of the sapphire. And he was still looking for it. "Well, it hardly matters now, does it? We've finished the case. I don't plan to work on any others. And now I'll be gone."

Her slender eyebrows arched.

I yanked open another drawer, rummaging through. "I've

a whole mess of trouble now, and no position. Why would I want to tangle myself up with some inquiry agent? It was an amusing story while it played out, but now it's finished." I dug deeper, dropping belongings half blind into my bag. Hopefully I was not making off with Mae's things. If I was, she said nothing of it.

Then at the bottom, my hand landed on something hard and smooth. A book. A rather old and weather-beaten one, though, from the feel of it. I fished it out and gasped.

Fantastical Tales and Fairy Stories
By G. A. Makepiece

I could scarcely breathe as memories, heady and warm, rushed over me. The way his face took on that distant, starry look when he told a tale. The warm seaside air blowing over my face as I listened. The feel of life taking shape as I illustrated the characters and stories he had animated with his words.

There was something so near perfect about those moments, about this book and its writer, that I hugged it. Little sense there was in embracing a book, but I wrapped my arms around it and squeezed tight all the memories, the characters, the beauty within.

A folded note lay inside the cover, but I dared not take it out now. I'd use it as a bridge, helping me to move from one place, one identity, to another. Never before had I been asked to leave. Never before had the leaving been so hard.

I stood, slapping the half-full carpetbag shut, and propelled myself toward the door, book under my arm. Yet there I lingered. I stood with my hand on the rough-hewn doorframe and looked over the face of one who was nigh on to a sister. "Do one thing for me."

Her smile was quick and sincere. "Anything for Lily Temple."

"It's about Bertie." I gripped the iron handle. "Take your own advice, will you?" With a quick smile, I slipped out the door.

I hurried toward the tennis courts, thinking to slip through the ivy-covered hole in the fence and be done with the place quietly, but instead I turned on the path and marched proudly toward the front gate. It was simply a position, and I was leaving it. People were sacked every day all across England. This was nothing special. Nothing at all.

My heart pounded as I approached those gates, and I plowed on with my head down, grip tight on that bag. I'd come out on top. I always did.

As Dahlia.

Jasmine.

No, Violet, perhaps.

Goodbye, Lily Temple. The world would roll on like the tide, folding you quickly into the vast ocean of the past.

But not yet. I paused beneath the fronds of a young willow and unfolded Peter's crumpled note, savoring his final words.

Once upon a time, there was a maiden. She needed rescuing, and the mighty knight set out to do just that. He slayed dragons before she was even aware they had approached her. He repaired a rotted bridge before she could cross it. He rushed headlong into the dangerous jungles to retrieve a gem she desired.

Yet, as it happened, through all of this rescuing, it was she who rescued him and pulled him up from the abyss into which he'd sunk. Her presence colored his life, animated his days, and drove him forward with a lighter heart. In the end, perhaps they rescued one another.

*Thank you, dearest girl, for the stories. Making them
with me. Telling more to me. Revealing your own.*

*Here's to your happily ever after. I'm determined to
get it for you.*

Tears bottled up behind my eyes. I marched harder, thinking quicker as I shoved the note away, forcing myself toward the practical. I needed lodging. Work. Coin. And some distance from Brighton. I'd make certain this story ended here, neat and clean. Which meant no more Peter Driscoll. He would linger with a sweetness, a tender memory. But that was all.

I paused at the gate to unlatch it, then looked back over my shoulder at the place I had never, in my truest heart, imagined leaving. My story was meant to come full circle here. But instead, it had simply . . . stopped. A penny dreadful whose author had run low on ink and rushed the story to an abrupt close.

With a deep sigh that fluttered the leaves climbing the gate, I moved quickly out onto the little walk along Somerhill Road and paced along the gate. But there I stopped, staring down at the ground.

Brightly colored petals, blowing about in the breeze. Their glossy surfaces glistened in the sunlight and my breath caught. Not just two or three, but a trail of them as if someone had poured them upon this walk. I blinked, looked out at the busy world, then back at the tranquil garden. I saw his face so clearly in my mind—his broad, lined smile of welcome. The glowing enthusiasm as he reached the part of the story where the gardener had spread the petals in the other world. Had tried to gently entice her back.

But I hadn't been the one to run away from the gardens. He

had. The gardener had. I turned back to look at its lush beauty once more.

Where are you?

I couldn't stay anymore. Not unless . . .

I paused. Froze. With sudden clarity, I knew with almost total certainty where the sapphire was. Who had taken it.

Was it too late? When tears gathered behind my eyes, I pushed forward, not allowing myself to linger. The new was before me, the past gone.

Yet . . . I rounded a corner and faced my past, wearing old brown tweed, a bowler, and a grim countenance. "Hello, luv." He stood, hands behind his back, looking down at me.

"What are you doing here?" I could dodge him. Sprint past him, dash into the crowded street. I wouldn't let him take me. I wouldn't.

"I don't think I need to answer that." He tipped his head to one side and smiled. "Time to go, luv."

I braced to run.

Then, "Men, take her in." He waved and four large men emerged from the hired barouche and encircled me. I darted, but they caught me easily. With bold steps, they shuffled me into the barouche and slammed the door. I didn't bother screaming, for the law was against me anyway. There was no one who would stop them. No one to rescue me.

I was finally headed back.

28

"My flower is ephemeral," the little prince said to himself, "and she has only four thorns to defend herself against the world. And I have left her on my planet, all alone!"

~ANTOINE DE SAINT-EXUPÉRY, *THE LITTLE PRINCE*

Well, then." Roderick Heath clutched the nag's reins as the mount stepped high through the marshy woods. "When are you planning to tell me why we're here?"

Peter grinned at him through the pointed ears of his overly tall Irish Draught. "Why does one attend a shooting party?"

"For anyone else, the answer would be obvious." A gun cracked through the air, and Roddy flinched. "I assume there's a remarkably good reason for dragging me along."

Bushes rustled out in the field. A flock of geese lifted off together, honking and flapping, a desperate ascent. Then the guns exploded in rapid bursts, pop after pop. A handful of birds fell from the formation into the small pond ahead.

"Hole up under a tree for a bit, won't you, Roddy? You needn't bother about bagging my game." Peter gave his mount's rump a pat and the animal sprang toward the action.

They charged into the lifting veil of smoke, into the chaos where a clump of mounted hunters shouted orders and the servant boys scrambled into the shallows, burlap slung over their shoulders. A few shouts and the others in their party moved farther out toward the marshes where the remaining ducks had gone, leaving the servants scrambling to bag the trappings.

Peter took note, as he had all day, of a particular hall boy, a lad of little more than twenty perhaps, with long, slicked hair and a neat way about him, who went by the name Clarence Yurt. *He* was Peter's reason. Spindly and quiet and rather nervous of disposition, the lad might be able to provide some much-needed answers.

Peter had no shortage of invitations to shooting weekends and house parties, being of the Driscoll family, yet he seldom attended. He had accepted this one because Clarence, who'd once been employed by Magistrate Fairchild, had quitted that household and taken up with this one, the Arthur Price household of Hayward's Heath. None of the servants who remained in Fairchild's employ made decent informants, still owing their allegiance to Fairchild himself, but one who'd peeled away from his employ . . . why, he was perfect.

Clarence, the lad in question, lunged for a duck, but a wiry groom pedaled through the water and, with one swift bump, sent poor Clarence stumbling and nabbed the bird from his grasp. A cry, then Clarence landed on all fours in the shallows of the pond, long hair flopping into the muddy water.

The groom guffawed, slapping backs as the other servants caught up.

Anger rolled through Peter. Jaw clenched, he urged his magnificent steed into the shallows, and the boys scattered toward their mounts, slinging bagged game over their shoulders and leaving poor Clarence with an empty sack.

"Come on there, lad." He leaned down, holding out a hand. "I'll take you back to the house."

"I cannot return empty-handed. They'll sack me for sure!"

With a sigh, Peter lifted his gun, took careful aim for several silent moments, then shot into the woods. A pheasant squawked and hit the dirt. "That'll do, I expect."

With a stunned, then grateful look, the boy schlepped through the muck and collected the bird, and returned to Peter's outstretched hand. Hesitating, the boy pulled himself up onto Driscoll's horse, shivering and dripping. "You're a rare sort, sir." Another shudder across his narrow shoulders.

"As are you, I believe." Peter angled his mount back the way they'd come and urged him onto the bank and back to the path. "In our entire time here, I've not heard a word of complaint from you. Not one. And you've worked harder than anyone."

"I know my place, sir." The boy dismounted and climbed onto the back of his own drooping nag.

They rode back through the sun-dappled woods in silence. When the horses reached the clearing, the lad finally voiced his gratitude. "Thank you for your kindness, sir. It's not many who show such mercy to a hall boy."

"Think nothing of it. You were, I believe, the one to clean the mud from my shoes, were you not? After my secret morning jaunt on the property that is not mine."

A shrug.

"That told me two things. One, you're a lad of good character. And two, you're used to keeping a man's secrets, which is the work of an experienced butler, or perhaps a decent head footman."

The narrow back before him stiffened. "I was a second footman once. I'm older than I look." He straightened.

"What you lack in girth you make up for in good sense and disposition. I've no doubt you made a fine second footman. You weren't sacked, I hope. Your master had the wrong of it, if you were."

"Oh no, sir. I left on me own. Mr. Price had hinted at a position when I came here with my master from town. Appreciated my hard work, he said, but hall boy was the only position open."

Peter looked the boy over, from thick, unruly hair to oversized boots. "Very good. Though it's no boon for you, I expect, giving up a life in town to serve in the country. Was it terribly difficult at the old house?"

He shrugged again. "He were a decent master."

"Yet you left a position as second footman to come play hall boy, a task normally given to a lad of thirteen or fourteen years, at most. He cannot have been *that* decent."

Clarence lowered his head and Peter allowed the silence to billow up between them. "He weren't a cruel man. But he had certain habits I could not abide. I left without a reference, so I took the position I could get."

"Sounds as though you made a wise decision, then."

His face relaxed. "Thank you, sir. I do hope so."

The house came into view, a pinkish-toned castle of sorts atop rolling fields and well-kept gardens. *What sort of fairy tale would Lily Temple tell about this place?* Peter couldn't help his mind wandering to her, even now.

"Do you know, I once left a place of employ—a barrister's office—because he wished me to dig up evidence that might make our very guilty client appear innocent."

Clarence blinked up at Peter. "You cannot dig up what don't exist."

"Of course not, and I told him as much. So he encouraged me to be *imaginative*."

"You mean, drum up something."

"Precisely. It's called falsified documents, and it's rather common in my profession. When I found out he was one of *those*, I sacked myself that very day."

"And did you regret it?"

"Not for a moment. The path I chose is not without its difficulties, and it has left me with a rather humble pocketbook, but my life is my own. One should always aim to err on the side of honesty, and of kindness. There's no substitute for either."

The elegant gelding shook his head, rattling his harness, then paused to lip at a tall tuft of grass before going on.

"I'm not quite as honorable as you, sir. I'm afraid I gave in a few times before I refused."

"Oh?" Peter's skin tingled, and he had to hold himself in check, waiting for the faucet to release another drop. "And what made you courageous that time?"

"It were one of our own. One of the servants. A good and faithful one who'd never done 'im wrong. The master wanted him put away for stealing, but he'd never steal. I couldn't ruin the man's life—he were but three and twenty years of age, with his whole life ahead of him."

"Rather disloyal of your master, treating his own servant that way."

"Well, he cared more for his family than his staff. The man planned to wed the master's own daughter, he did. T'weren't right, the two of 'em. Miss Rosella puttin' on airs and him groveling for her attention. Like a duck marrying a fish, just because they both live on the pond. But I couldn't conscience puttin' the man in prison. Or any of the others he wanted put away."

"Others? You mean to say, he makes a practice of this sort of thing? That he's a corrupt magistrate?" *Trading justices*, they were called. Magistrates who accepted clandestine bribes and gifts in exchange for a favorable ruling.

His head whipped around, countenance horrified, then miserable. "I didn't say it, sir. I didn't tell you he's a magistrate, or nothing. I didn't spill—"

"No, no, of course not." The stables came in view then. "I merely pieced things together. No harm in that."

The boy began breathing rapidly, a scared rabbit. He paled, and Peter wondered if he'd faint dead away off that nag.

Peter slowed his horse to look the boy in the eye, passion welling within him. "You're merely an honest lad, Clarence Yurt. And that's why you're here schlepping through mud after birds for tuppence rather than wearing livery and polishing footwear for a decent wage."

A pause, then Clarence began again. "An entire life it was for my master, locking up this one over that one, framing that other one, all because of who greased his palms." Clarence trembled. "He had all the politicians running to him, throwing jewels and pound notes his way . . . and none of us could say a word. Not anything. I've never been so frightened in all my life. I couldn't do it anymore."

"It isn't weakness that drove you away, Clarence Yurt, but integrity. You should be proud of the decision you made, the life you've endured these seven years, and you should only see blessing for your act of courage."

He gripped his nag's reins, staring at the animal with a frown. "Who are you, Mr. Driscoll? And how do you know all this?"

Peter stiffened. He'd forgotten himself—talking rather than listening. Clarence had not specified *when* he'd left the man's employ. And seven years was a very specific number for a stranger to know.

Peter mentally tossed around several responses, and finally settled on, "I am a truth seeker like you, Clarence. An inquiry agent. I'm merely trying to free those who are wrongfully punished and protect others who are about to suffer a similar fate." He looked the boy in the eye. "You will not see trouble for what you say, I vow it. But you may be able to save many lives and right the wrongs you witnessed."

Clarence angled his face down again, his overlarge nose standing out in profile.

"Is there anyone else who knows about what happened— what *truly* happened in that house?"

He shook his head slowly and urged his horse toward the mews. "Just the lad he had arrested—he'd found out far too much from Miss Rosella, my master's daughter, who the bloke was supposed to marry. Right mad she was about the arrest. Rather a spoiled thing, not used to being denied what she wanted."

"Where might I find her?"

"Northampton. Lady Forsythe's school for young ladies."

He threw the lad an approving grin. "Good work, Clarence. I'm glad to have found you. This talk has been more help than you know."

The boy kept his gaze averted. "You won't say anything? You won't . . ."

"No one will ever hear your name from me." Peter reined in and dismounted, and Clarence did likewise. "I'm quite practiced at maintaining privacy, and I haven't yet vexed one of my informants."

Clarence's face relaxed into a smile. "I do hope you manage to stop Fairchild. Too many innocent people . . ."

"I know. I'll do what I can." He handed his gelding's reins to Clarence. "Stable him for me, would you? I believe I'll make my apologies and depart for Northampton."

29

A conscience is that still small voice
that people won't listen to.

~CARLO COLLODI, *PINOCCHIO*

Roderick had different ideas on the matter. He rocked forward on his leather-shod toes, then back on his heels as he took in the latest update. Then he leaned against the hearth. "Get out of this, Pete. Now." He turned to face his master. "It's big. Too big."

"That's exactly why I must keep going. Don't you see? If I can prove his corruption, every single case he's touched will be reexamined. Makepiece will be released. Lily won't have to run any longer, and I won't even have to prove either of their innocence." Peter stretched, rolling his shoulders. After a day of riding and shooting, his body ached. But it thrummed with excitement too. The anticipation he felt when nearing the end of a puzzle.

He was getting close. He could feel it.

Yet . . . there would be no five hundred pounds from Fairchild. Roderick stopped, hands again smoothing his hair, face twitching with all the arguments eager for release. "He'll bury you, Pete. This is no longer some foolish error he made once in court. You know what he is, what he's doing, and if you expose him—"

"Then I'll be setting right years of injustice. And freeing the father of a young woman who desperately needs restoration." The more he thought about the case, awareness hardened in his chest. Magistrate Fairchild was corrupt. Had been for years. But he was brilliant and powerful and well-connected. And he'd gotten away with all this for a long time. Proving anything against him would be the trick.

Soon, they were on the train bound for Northampton, flying over rolling green hills in checkered patterns.

Peter released a sigh. "You might as well tell me what's on your mind, Roddy. You've been sour all day. I thought you wanted to leave."

Roderick fidgeted with his coat sleeve. "I don't know how to tell you this, but . . . well, I don't think she is innocent. Lily Temple. Every crooked magistrate tries his share of ordinary, guilty criminals, you know." Roderick leveled a solemn gaze at him, lower lip twitching and voice low. "She isn't worth it, Pete. She isn't. I know you have this excessive sense of loyalty to everything that takes a breath, but I'm begging you. Let this one go."

Peter only stared.

"You're starting to fall in love with her, and it's like quicksand. I know you."

Peter's heart pumped against his ribs. "Would that be so terrible, Roddy? Truly?" His heart had begun to defrost. He'd pictured his life with Sarah Swan for so long, but that image had disintegrated, and now there was Lily.

Lily.

Being around her was pure enchantment, and even thinking of her playful looks, her clever little quips, her bright and fascinating face, livened him. Infused his soul with color. What if he had that every day—in his home? In every aspect of his life? He shivered with delight.

"You are. You're in love. Have you gone *mad*?"

"Tell me, Roddy." He faced his man head-on. "Tell me *exactly* why you feel this way about her. What's at the root of all this?"

The valet stared down at his laced fingers lying in his lap. The whistle blew and feet pounded. China clinked from the dining car. Then the faithful valet lifted his gaze. "Because she's the very antithesis of everything you are, sir. Everything I've come to respect and admire most in you. Where you are genuine, she is a practiced fraud. You have roots, and she flits like a butterfly to whatever nectar seems sweetest. And mostly . . . where you are built of solid truth, Lily Temple is a spinner of stories. An actress. A thief. She has little use for the truth on which your character stands."

Roddy sighed, concern pulling his features down. "I know your mind, and it's telling you to reach out and pull her up. But believe me, it's much easier for a person standing on a chair to be pulled down by someone on the floor than for the reverse to happen. Marriage is seldom the rescue people think it will be."

Peter shook his head. Roddy's words rang with truth, and it jarred the spring-like bliss in his soul.

"She's a delight. She's unique and amusing and clever . . . everything a man like you could want. She's different than the women you're used to, as well. But she isn't what she seems. The deeper you dig, the more incongruities you're finding, aren't you? And I've done far more digging than you have."

"You have proof, I assume?"

"I can't give details yet until I've confirmed some things, but I've found evidence to suggest why Fairchild has been hunting her. Through every changing identity, one aspect has remained the same—she is a sleight-of-hand artist. A thief. Stealing what's beautiful for the pure sake of owning it for herself. Very high-value items from very important people." He shook his head. "Her view of right and wrong does not align with our legal system. And unjust treatment, to her mind, includes being held accountable for laws she deems foolish. Laws such as . . . rightful ownership. She is as different from you as different can be—and not in a good way."

A dull, iron-like weight pressed against his chest. "I see." He cleared his throat. "Well, then. I guess that's that." But doubt lingered. It was quite possible that each of those thefts had been a framing—as was, he'd decided, the sapphire's disappearance. Fairchild wanted her in the court system, where he was king and she his subject. Not because she was guilty, but because she'd found out something. She knew too much. Something that had to do with her father. That was the only answer that made sense.

Roddy's expression relaxed and he offered his master a single nod. "When it comes down to it, you're always wise, Pete. I'm glad I can count on that. Now can we go home?"

Peter shook his head. "I'm involved in this already, hired by two separate clients to find the truth. This is bigger than Lily Temple. There's more at stake. If her father truly is guilty, if *she* is guilty, they'll still face justice even if I bring down Fairchild. But those who are innocent . . . I cannot let this go."

Roddy only sighed and slumped down in his seat.

But their next destinations resulted in a series of disappointments. Miss Forsythe's institution in Northampton was apparently as secure as Newgate—no one in or out without express permission from the student's family. They'd happened upon the younger Fairchild daughter playing lawn croquet when they arrived, but after a brief exchange of words, a matron came rushing up and ended the conversation before they could even broach the matter they'd come to discuss. Rosella was not mentioned.

The Fairchild ladies had received only two guests during their time there, and one had been their aunt. Most gentlemen, the woman said with a sniff, knew better than to attempt it.

They stayed the night in a cramped little room, then traveled on to Newgate, where they were allowed audience with one Silas Caldwell, former stable boy for Fairchild, but they learned little save his intense bitterness toward Fairchild and his daughter Rosella, to whom he'd been betrothed. "I was a fool to love her. She's beautiful, wealthy . . . and I hate to think of how I fell all over her. I wrote her love songs. Poetry." He spit into the straw on the floor.

"What was her reaction to your imprisonment?"

He shrugged. "She pouted and flounced about, I'm sure, but years later, here I sit while she's off being preened and polished in some finishing school for young ladies. If only the outside of a person matched the soul . . . Rosella Fairchild and her father would look like dirt."

Then, in the morning they took themselves to St. Anne's, and Lily was gone. Really and truly gone. The quiet modiste named Mae confirmed it, assured him she was well. She'd left two days before, and no, there had been no man in brown tweed about when she left.

But Gypsy Lee had watched the entire conversation from over

Mae's shoulder. Her unblinking eyes never wavered from his face. A warning vibrated deep in Peter's brain at the intensity of her look. Yet she said nothing to him.

He tried to shake it away, but it echoed about in the quiet carriage. In the empty crunch of wheels in his lane. In the quiet of the great hall where Lily's liveliness, which had once lit up the space, was keenly missed.

He secreted himself away in the study, having avoided Iris Stanhope for the moment, and pored over his notes on Fairchild. He scanned the same lines over and over again, and his brain stalled out. With every idle wandering of his thoughts, Lily's image came to mind. He shoved it out over and over, until . . .

Protect her. Help her. Keep her.

Keep her? As in, keep her safe? But she was gone, and without a word to him.

She had been a sweetness in his life. The sweet Indian summer when one expected a cold snap. The song when one was used to stuffy silence. He saw her face so clearly, that bright-eyed, fairy-like smile. The flitting about in the gardens, and . . .

"She flits like a butterfly to whatever nectar seems sweetest."

A whoosh of air left his chest. Had it been an act? Was Roddy right?

Why are you calling me toward her, Lord? Why? Her, of all people!

He'd been honest and forthright all his life. He'd seldom acted in greed or haste. He'd been the protector of his family and lived with integrity. So now why . . . why would God instill in him this magnetic pull toward a woman like Lily Temple?

Why, Lord? Why?

He bowed his head and asked . . . and waited . . .

Nothing.

A knock sounded on the door, and it cracked open. "You've a caller, sir."

"Nothing more today, Frederick. I'm afraid my travels have me worn out."

The man hesitated. "If I may, sir, he's come a long way to see you. And he seems rather in a rush."

Peter frowned. "Very well then, send him in."

"Very good, sir."

With a sigh, Peter cracked open the large file of case records on his desk and thumbed through for Silas Caldwell's. He ran down the lines, scanning for familiar names among the witnesses, anything that looked off.

And he found it. Just not where he'd expected.

The crime Silas Caldwell stood accused of committing was theft. A rather costly necklace described as an elaborate setting with a large blue gem held by swirling gold vines.

No sooner had the door closed on the butler than it swept open again upon a stranger. A tall, anxious-looking man stood bowed in the doorway, hat in hand. His blue officer's uniform, complete with white sash and gold ropes across the chest, lent him an air of authority. He spoke with a gentle, rolling accent from someplace Peter could not identify. "I beg your pardon for the lack of warning on my part, kind sir." He bowed from the waist. "Are you Mr. Peter Driscoll?"

"I am." He rose and offered his hand, which the man shook.

"I am Captain Alexandre Velasco. I am told you have word about my daughter."

Mila. This was Mila's father.

With any luck, at least. The poor man's tortured eyes brimmed with hope.

"Yes. Yes, I hope I do. I shall take you out to meet her myself. We'll have to wait until the tide is low. We cannot reach where she is in high tide. Not safely, at least."

Another quick bow. "I understand. I shall eagerly await your word, then."

Peter looked over the newcomer. "You've come from Portugal? In mere days?"

His mustache quivered and his eyes moistened. "The moment I receive your kind telegram, I walk out of my house and straight to the docks. I have been traveling since. I have ship." He dropped his gaze, then lifted it again. "I lose everything. Well . . . perhaps. Until . . ." He pulled the folded telegram from the pocket of his uniform. "When a man is offered a small light in a pit of blackness, it becomes all he can see."

Peter allowed silence to blanket the moment with dignity as the visitor struggled to collect himself. Then he offered a steaming cup of tea. "You will stay here, of course, Captain. We should be ready to leave in a matter of hours."

The man nodded his thanks.

Peter sat, offering the man a warm smile. "Your English is quite good. Have you been to England before?"

"My wife, she was English. That is why they were traveling here, to visit her family."

Seven months. That's how long this man had lived with the belief that his wife and daughter had both perished. How long Mila had been stranded from her home. Had the woman in the shanty tried to send word? Tried to find the girl's family? He supposed they had no way of doing so. It would have been a needle in a haystack. Unless they *had* tried, and her true parents were not alive. The girl may have an entirely different story from this man, with no overlap.

"This girl . . . she hasn't been eager to talk to strangers. I haven't been able to speak with her very much."

A laugh burst out of him. "That is my Mila. She likes whom she likes, and there's no changing her mind."

"What I mean is, I cannot guarantee the girl we've found is Mila. I was hoping to confirm her identity through you before you traveled all this way."

He waved it away. "If it is not her, Mr. Peter Driscoll, you have still given me a few nights of blessed hope. And that is more than I've had in many, many months."

They talked comfortably for more than an hour, at which point Peter excused himself to freshen and change clothes. He explained that he'd been away from home and needed to attend to a few things.

He climbed the steps two at a time, anticipation speeding his every move. Then he leaned his back against the closed door and released a long sigh. Very soon they'd go back to the shore one more time. And he'd watch a reunion or utter devastation befall the man. At times, the worst grueling manual labor seemed an easier way to make one's living.

When he opened his eyes, Roddy was sliding in through the service door and delivered a pile of clean clothing and shined shoes. "Good day, sir." And just beyond . . . a note lay on his secretary. Swirling, feminine writing that he didn't know.

I know where it is. Come with me immediately, and I'll tell you everything you want to know. But you must come alone, and tell no one.

Roddy set the things down on the foot of his bed. "I say, Pete. Glad to be done with Miss Temple. I always did have a bad feeling about her, and my instincts may not be as keen as yours, but I'd say they're quite good."

Peter's gaze darted around, but there was no sign of anyone else still in his chambers. No sign, save the lightly fluttering curtains over an open window. It was her. It was from Lily Temple. She had been here, in his chambers. He walked to the window and shut it, staring out over the vast lawn as he did so. There was no sign of the familiar willowy figure.

He scanned the note again. A trap. It was a trap. She'd never before offered information on the sapphire, much less sought him out to give it. He moved to the window and looked out over the wakening estate. There, under the crab apple, something moved. Someone. "Roddy, I think . . . I think I shall go for a walk."

"Very good, sir. Clear your head before the trip. Shall I join you?"

"No, thank you, though. I'm overdue for a long, rambling walk. I shan't go far. Then we can see about this possible family reunion."

30

The witch shut her up in a tower in the midst of a wood, and
it had neither steps nor door, only a small window above.

~THE BROTHERS GRIMM, "RAPUNZEL"

When Draper's men had taken me, the first thing they'd done was yank the dark blinds down over the carriage windows. No one seeing in, no one seeing out. It had been dizzying, this sense of aimlessness. Of not knowing where I was. We turned so many times, curved and veered until I hadn't any idea what district we were even in.

I locked gazes with the brown tweed man from the gardens from beneath my cloak. "You cannot simply kidnap me. You've no proof of anything."

"We've danced around, years and years, you and I. You've no idea how long I've been on your trail. You think I'd pounce without absolute certainty? Without verifiable proof of who you are? Hide beneath that lovely purple cloak all you wish. I still see you."

I leaned, stiff and guarded, against the buttoned leather seat. "I'll escape."

"No, you won't. I've waited on this day for too long."

"What if I vow to lead you to the sapphire?"

He shook his head. "You don't know where it is any more than I do."

"How do you know?"

"Twenty-eight years in the Yard, luv. I can spot a lie. Besides, the sapphire isn't my case. You are."

"Very well. What about—"

"There isn't anything you can offer to persuade me, Miss Temple." He looked me over. "Say, what do you know about that Peter Driscoll man? He's an odd sort, turning up where he shouldn't. Is he involved in what happened?"

Tension pulled at me—a desire to say yes so that they'd drag him in too . . . and at least we'd be in it together. Could more easily escape between the two of us. But I admitted he was not. "He may well rescue me before you can take me back to London, though."

He laughed. "I have plans in place to make certain that doesn't happen. Seven years on this case, and *I* will be the one to bring you in. Not him."

I shot forward. "See here, I'm not an enemy you wish to have."

"I am taking you directly to Fairchild. As I've been tasked with doing. Whatever happens afterward . . . No threat will stop me from doing right."

Sickness washed over me. *God . . . what now?*

It struck me, the impossibility of this situation. How God was, really and truly, the only hope I had left.

I sat, arms folded, until the vehicle slowed and the four men sat at attention around me. They bundled me, in my long purple cloak, out of the carriage and up the walk to a gray stone townhouse packed in between several others on the dark street. This was a part of Brighton I'd not seen in a long time.

One of the four men was posted in the great front bay window to keep watch. The others led me up the narrow stairs into a plain room directly above the sentry with nothing but peeling wallpaper, a lamp, and a rickety table. Two of the remaining men stood guard just outside the room. Inside, the man Draper paused, arms crossed, watching me. "I admit, I never thought I'd see this day. I'd all but given up. Until . . . until the flickers." He heaved a chest-lifting sigh. "I do wish you well, Miss Temple. I've no plans to harm you. Tomorrow we depart for London and Fairchild himself."

"What you're doing is the worst harm you could do me." My body was so stiff I shook.

He gave a sad smile. "What I'm doing is what's needed and right. Even if it isn't what you desire." Then he shut the door and locked it with a scrape of metal, and their footfall sounded down the hall. Alone, frantic, I banged about the tiny space—the barred window, the locked door, the solid walls. A sense of claustrophobia squeezed me, such as I'd never felt before. No way out. No escape. I stumbled to the door and leaned against it, sliding down. I had nothing with which to pick the ancient lock. Not a hatpin nor hairpin . . .

I ran to the window and dug at the rotting sash desperately with my fingernails. The digging made the glass window pop open beyond the bars, but with iron over it, I was still trapped. I stood frozen at that window, shattering from hopelessness. I was trapped. Very trapped.

Three strained breaths. Wind blew on my hot face. A dance of flower petals just outside the window, raining down from a cherry tree. One petal, satin pink, lighted on the sill and I touched it.

Another breath. Then a slower one. A big, steady breath as I closed my eyes and a gentle weight crept over me. Thick peace blanketed me as if I were back in the garden, breathing in the flower-scented air, my bare feet on a carpet of soft grass, walled off from the rest of the world. Encased in my little Eden within the world.

Then that peace solidified into strength. Resolve. A comforting solidness rooted me to that rough wood floor, and I felt steady. There *would* be a way out. I knew not what it was, or even how I knew it, only that it would come. A feeling of certainty so deep came over me that I didn't know what to make of it . . . but I embraced it. Welcomed it. And it strengthened me.

What *was* that?

No sooner had I asked the question than I knew the answer, hearing it spoken in Peter Driscoll's gentle voice. *It's God.* My meager cry to him in the carriage, the bottomless desperation in my heart . . . then a solid strength. A fathomless peace. I'd felt it before. Had it come those other times when I'd cried out? Had I been waiting for a locked door to swing open, and missed what was sent instead?

I was not in the garden. But somehow . . . he had brought the garden to me.

I continued to breathe, slow and steady. Waiting. Listening. Now I *had* to leave this place—because I had questions for Peter.

The scrape of a key, and Draper returned with tea and toast in hand. "I won't have you starve, Miss Temple." He left it on the floor and exited again. Then, his voice sounded in the corridor. "She'll only be here a night. I vow it. We'll be leaving for London at first light. You won't be responsible for her."

"Good. Don't want any trouble on my hands."

"I'll personally guard her every moment. This one is a

sleight-of-hand artist. She's given the slip more times than I can count, and I'm taking no chances."

Yes. A sleight-of-hand artist. Misdirection. That was my secret strength. It was how I must escape.

I knelt at the keyhole, looking through, but the tiny hole was blocked by the end of the key, inserted from the outside. It was still in the lock. I fingered my long purple cloak, inspecting it. Forming an idea. My brain, when cleared of fizzling panic, worked well and fast. I quickly consumed the toast, downed the tea, and fingered the little saucer that had held my food.

"And you don't think she'll do it again now?"

"It is over now. She has been caught, placed under lock and key, and I have informed Fairchild. There's no more escaping. I plan to stand guard, as I said. All night, if necessary."

I huffed. All night? Striding to the window, I stuck my fingers between the bars and easily pushed the window out and looked down. No one—not a soul—on the walk. Dusk was falling rapidly and soon the world would be dark. I picked at the rotting window sash with my fingers, pulling off wood pulp . . . then one long, thick splinter broke off. I held it up—perfect.

"I suppose you'll want something to eat."

"It would be appreciated. It'll be a long night. Best get the prisoner something more as well."

"I'll see what the missus can pull from the larder."

"Fine," said Draper. "I'll be right here."

We'll see about that.

I leaned against the bars, listening to the host's footfall tromp down the stairs. As he went, I shoved my purple cloak out through the bars on the window and then the saucer, which fit nicely through the bars, dangling it as low as I could. Then I let the saucer drop, and it smashed on the ground. Then I dangled the cape's hood on my finger, fluttering it where the window should be, hoping the cape was long enough to be visible in the dimness. At least its hem.

Footsteps pounded as the guard on the lower floor likely ran to the window bay. "She's outside." The guard's voice boomed up the stairs to Draper. "Mister, she's escaped. Climbing down."

"Impossible." A scramble. "I'm coming. Don't let her out of your sight!"

I dropped the cloak into the bushes below, then ran to the door and shoved the hem of my skirt beneath it, out into the hallway. I leaned my cheek against the wood and jammed the long splinter into the keyhole hard. Fast.

Come on, key. Come on. Move!

I turned the wood splinter and shoved it in deeper. *Come on!* Finally, the key gave way, dropped from the keyhole, and plunked onto my skirt hem. I drew it toward me. But the key stuck against the door.

Too thick.

Footfall banged about. ". . . check the house. I'll go down the alley."

"She'll be harder to find without that bright cloak about her."

I felt about the floor. A knothole in the wood. I guided the key to it and yanked the fabric back. I dug at that little metal thing, pleading, wriggling it under the door until I pulled it out and held it.

With a quick exhale, I unlocked the door, closed it quietly behind me, and replaced the key in the lock. Someone huffed up the narrow stairs. I darted down the rear stairs and out the kitchen door . . . to freedom.

To an unknown future.

I sprinted, clinging to my skirt and barely daring to breathe. Up one street, down another, dodging the busy square. The overwhelming sense of rightness, that lovely peace, followed me about as if, no matter where I walked about Brighton, I was standing in the gardens, drawing my strength from it. Flooding with color.

And that kind, beloved gardener was with me.

I slowed on a quiet residential street before modest white brick homes and hailed a barouche. I gave him Peter Driscoll's address and sat back against the ripped leather seat, a smile on my lips and a giggle bubbling up.

It was *not* over. I wasn't going back. Yet another escape, I was still free with plenty more to my future. And my day of reckoning still lay somewhere down the road. I had only to decide who and what I would become next.

31

I have so great a desire to see my father, that I shall
fret to death, if you refuse me that satisfaction.

~CHARLES PERRAULT, *BEAUTY AND THE BEAST*

Something touched my shoulder. I snapped awake and
turned, my back sore against the bark of a sycamore
tree. And there above me was Peter Driscoll. Peter, with
his strong, clean-shaven face, his languid brown eyes upon me
once again.

"Peter. What are you doing here?"

"At my own estate?" He grinned.

"Oh." I grimaced and stretched. "Right."

"I'm tempted to ask the same question, but I'm rather afraid
of the answer."

My mind whirled to life and I straightened, recalling my
purpose. "Oh Peter, I've found it. I know where the sapphire
is. I should have known all along."

His wide eyes searched mine. "You know where it is?"

"I'm positive. Or nearly so."

He frowned. "Then why include me?"

I smiled and clutched the fairy-tale book he'd returned to me with a shrug. "I owe you."

He looked at me, then past me at the lane. "You've walked here."

"That's a crime, is it?"

"Lily, what's happened to you? Where are you staying?"

"Here and there. Mostly . . . here."

"At my house?"

"Well. Not *in* your house. And only until I could speak with you. It's very important."

"Where have you been since you've left the gardens, searching for the gem? No . . . you were caught. Scotland Yard caught up with you, and they took you."

My face heated. I frowned. "Now back to the gem."

"And you . . . you've escaped. You're on the run. They're still looking for you, aren't they? Are you all right? How did you manage it?"

"Peter, the sapphire." I grabbed his arms. "We can get it back, if we hurry. You must take me back to the caves. Then you can return it to the countess where it belongs."

"The caves? Who—Ah . . . yes. The one person in your vicinity that night who we neglected to consider as the thief."

"I should have known it was that girl. It wouldn't be Smith . . . or Draper. And besides, I learned long ago that a quick retort is a thin veil over guilt, and she had nothing but briars for words. She knew what she'd done, and so did that woman in the abandoned village. I'm hopeful she still has it. Come. Shall we fetch the bauble?"

He laid a hand on my arm. "There's another layer to this story."

He quickly laid out how he'd tracked the girl's story from the pieces I'd given him, and about the visitor who was waiting for him.

"The girl's father . . . in your house? He's *here*?"

"Mostly here." A new, deeper voice joined our duo. A man with dark hair and tanned skin strode around the tree with a pensive smile. "As much as one can be, after many sleepless nights."

I approached him, hand held out, breathless. "It *is* you. I believe I see the resemblance. How very lovely to meet you, Mr. . . ."

"Velasco. Captain Alexandre Velasco." He took my hand and bowed over it.

All I could think of was the lost little girl with her long dark hair, peering out at me from the gardens . . . now found. A welling up of tears stopped me from saying anything more. I blinked them back, and soon Peter was ushering us toward his carriage. We rode quickly, silently, to the coast. Awareness of what lay ahead had settled upon all of us, and everything that had happened in the past few days slipped into the background.

I spoke quietly. "Everything she said, that Gypsy Lee, it was all true, wasn't it?"

"It seems to have panned out." Peter smiled at me. "We'd never have connected the facts without her details. And the name."

I shook my head. "Perhaps there is a bit of magic in that woman."

"I suspect," Peter said, "her secret is similar to mine. She has no magic insight, just two good ears and a quiet mouth. What she learned about Mila . . . the girl probably told her herself. People talk to Gypsy Lee. She invites it with her very nature."

"How oddly alike you are." The words were out, half musing, before I could think better of it.

But Peter only smiled, as if I'd paid him a compliment.

We disembarked at the seashore and climbed together up the winding cliff face, the rocks that made rugged stair steps, until we reached the little village hidden in the inlet.

Peter pointed out the little shack. "She isn't always at home, but hopefully someone will be willing to tell us where to find her this time. Especially if we have you with us."

The man straightened and cleared his throat, brushing off his uniform. I knocked on the doorframe and heard no answer. I brushed back the cloth over the door, and the house was empty. Not just empty of people, but of belongings. Of any evidence that it had been lived in less than a week ago.

I turned back to the man, suddenly feeling as if we'd made the entire thing up. The girl, the odd happenings, the theft of the gem by someone that was not me. I stepped back to look at the house as a whole—yes, it was this house. This very house I entered and saw all those children.

Peter and I looked at each other. His face was drawn. Worried. "They must have gone." He waved us on, and together we tromped back the way we'd come. When we reached the high point on the path, I looked down over the shore glowing orange and pink, washed in sunset. No one strode below. Only shadows stretched over the empty patches of sand. But then I cast my gaze to the water . . . and caught my breath. There she was. Yes, this was her hour—the fading light of day, and she was out.

There, right at the water's edge, just outside the caves, still as an oak, with water lapping at her feet, was the mysterious girl. She was not stooping to collect shells this time, though. She was perched on a pile of driftwood, the remnants of a wreck.

"Captain." I pointed.

Was it? Was it his daughter? My insides twisted with excitement. Nerves. Can't-wait-to-turn-the-page anticipation.

He climbed toward me to look down, clinging to a boulder. That's when my heart truly began to misfire. In that silent moment when he braced one foot on a rock and looked down, studying the little lost girl. He stared forever, it seemed. Forever. Then he burst forward, scrambling down the nearly sheer rock face, clinging, tripping, jumping down to the shore. Down to his girl.

Peter climbed down after him, surely feeling the weight of responsibility over the whole matter. But me, I stayed exactly where I was, clinging to the rock, watching the sweetest of all stories unfold.

It's a remarkable moment, seeing a story come full circle, and they eventually do, it seemed. That's when you know they are complete. Romances end on a series of repeated notes from the beginning of the melody, terrified heroes face down the dragons that once defeated them.

Broken people return to the rocks that broke them . . . and find healing.

Peter Driscoll slowed, hanging back. Likely feeling the significance of this tale's closing scene as well. Those final moments, the way the circle closed, made a story what it was—tragedy, irony, or happily ever after.

This one, at last, would be a happy ending.

My pounding heart distracted me from noticing the details of this reunion, but I would never forget it. The experience was being imprinted on the reel of my memories as the captain drew nearer to her. Just before he reached her, she held up her hand, and there on her open palm . . . a glittering of bright blue.

A piece of the sky.

This. This is why she'd taken it. Whether she'd snatched it from my neck or it had fallen off at the bread table . . . she'd heard the stories. And she'd taken it for this—to transport her as it did in the fairy tale to another world. Her home.

And it had worked—in a way.

Her *home* had come to find her.

The captain stopped just behind her, watching. Then after a moment he touched her shoulder and she spun around, braids whipping the air as her hand came to her face . . . then shot out toward him, and she leaped into her father's arms. Leaped with all her might and clung to him and sobbed as if they were sinking again, and she alone was going to save him. She buried her face in his neck and wept.

Here, on the remnants of what must have been her shipwreck, with the sapphire in her hand, the shattered pieces of her life had been put back together.

32

Actually the best gift you could have given
her was a lifetime of adventures.

~LEWIS CARROLL, *ALICE'S ADVENTURES IN WONDERLAND*

Peter cleared his throat over and over, but the lump would not dislodge. He leaned back against the rocks, watching from a distance as reunification occurred, and healing surged through him as well. Perhaps the dowager countess was right—the sapphire somehow had a healing quality. For as many cracks and fissures life had built into his heart, this moment, with that gem merely in the vicinity, was deeply healing.

It was worth it, all this work. For outcomes like these, it was worth it. The hopelessness she must have felt. The utter loss. No one she had encountered—the woman in the shack, the locals about the village—would have had any idea how to help her. To return her home, or to locate her family. The situation must have felt so grim.

But now . . . sunshine. Rightness. A promising future. Restoration of something she'd lost.

Head bowed, Peter paced away from them, offering a measure of privacy. Thanking the Lord. A short walk to fetch Miss Temple—where *had* she gone?—and then he'd return for them. They'd stay the night at his estate, and he'd see them off when they were ready to go.

He shivered as he spotted movement near the caves and strode over to check for Lily. The air chilled considerably. But then, from the gaping mouth of a small cave . . . "Peter. Peter Driscoll."

Not Lily. Not even female.

Peter stopped. Listened. "Hello?"

Hiss and crash of waves.

"Peter. Can I trust you?"

He spun. Looked. Deep in the shadows, two eyes peered out at him. An indistinct form huddled in the dark. A man. "Josiah Fairchild must be stopped. And you . . . You can do it."

Something kept Peter from advancing. From entering the cave. "Who are you?"

A puff of laughter. "You should know. You've been to my house. Today, in fact."

"The shack. You live in the shack."

"Up until you found us. Now we must live somewhere else."

"You are the keeper of the children, aren't you? Where do they come from?"

"From the shipwrecks. There are men who plunder the wrecks for treasure, and I suppose I am one of those. Only I have a different view on what treasure is." A sigh. "The children are the first ones placed on the lifeboats, so they're often alone when they wash ashore. Both parents lost. I cannot let them die, and they've nowhere to go. So here they stay. With me and my daughter. She tends to them. I bring the food—and the stories."

The woman in the shack. That was his daughter. And the man . . . Peter squinted into the deep darkness. "Who are you, exactly? A name."

"You may call me Michael. The children do."

Peter sighed. "I know who you are. And you should tell Lily you're here."

"*No.*" The answer was quick and definitive. "It isn't safe."

"She has been looking for you, Mr. Makepiece. Madly. And it isn't as if she poses any threat to you. She loves you."

A pause. "I've seen her looking for me. That fairy tale on the screen, like a signal flare. And I've responded in kind, with my own signals. But that is all I can do for now."

The rabbit in his green jacket. The deer with the flower crown. All of it carried out by the little girl for whom he'd been caring.

"Where she is, Fairchild is sure to follow," he continued. "And Fairchild would see me dead for all I know about him. What you are beginning to find out too. Which is why you, Peter Driscoll, must bring him down. Show the world who he is."

"And how do I go about that? I cannot prove anything."

"Yes . . . you can. He keeps a log of every *token* he accepts. Every promise of favor. I've seen it. Find it, and use it well. And there are men who are wise to his corruption. They will help you in secret, if they can. How do you think I escaped prison?"

"A man on the inside."

"A guard escorted me out in the middle of the night, told me to vanish as if I'd never lived. He knew what Fairchild had done to me, and he said there had been others."

"But he was too afraid to come forward."

"Fairchild has a way of making people disappear. Like an illusionist."

Peter sighed, running fingers through his hair. "So what can I do?"

"You are a solicitor—you should know what comes next, where I do not. Talk to the people in that book. Look for others who know. Or suspect. Rally them to stand for the truth. You'll find the book in his desk, in the study. Now go, Peter Driscoll, and slay the dragon if you can. Then, take very good care of the maiden. She is a singular woman."

"Indeed. But won't you show yourself to her?"

He shook his head. "It isn't me she's looking for. Not really. The gardener in that fairy tale . . . it isn't me."

"Then who—?"

"You know. You know who she's truly searching for."

Peter inhaled and let it out. He did know. He'd told her as much himself. Lily Temple was the collector of stories, but at times she was too close to see them for what they were. What she truly wanted.

With a quick nod, Peter turned and strode over the sand, scanning the cliffs for Lily. She approached from behind, coming to stand beside him, her wide eyes full of the story they'd seen on the shore. The beauty of it. He embraced her, felt her melt onto his shoulder. He let her remain thus for a moment. Then, elated, he spun toward the cave . . . but it lay dark and empty.

Soon. Very soon.

33

"You're not the same as you were before," he said.
"You were much more . . . muchier . . .
you've lost your muchness."

~LEWIS CARROLL, *ALICE'S ADVENTURES IN WONDERLAND*

When the captain and his daughter approached, she tucked herself shyly into his side, burying herself under his arm. I knelt before the girl with a bright smile. "Mila. That is your name, isn't it? At last, we may truly speak." My heart swelled to see her slight smile.

Then she stepped forward, hand held out as her face shuttered again. "I took something of yours. I'm not sorry, because it helped me. Just like you said in the story."

The sapphire. Just like that, the brilliant gem with the flashing star in the center appeared on the girl's palm. I put one hand to my chest and took the stone from the girl, squeezing her hand for a moment. "Thank you for giving it back to me. That's more important than you taking it."

314

"I didn't *steal* it." Her face paled. "It fell. It fell in the grass and I picked it up . . . and then I . . . I borrowed it."

I smiled. "What matters is that you've returned it. I'm grateful for that. You've no idea how much. But I'm also glad that it was able to help you."

Her smile was, for the first time, quite brilliant.

Yes. Yes, there was something powerful about that stone.

When we drove home, my heart felt ready to burst. There they were just across from me, oblivious to the world. A pair, a remnant of a family. He brushed hair off her face with gentle fingers and I shivered. I'd forgotten what that was like, this featherlight touch from father to child. The kind that gave rather than took. That bestowed value and acceptance.

They climbed from the carriage first when we arrived at the Driscoll estate, and I hardly knew what to do with myself. The driver handed me down, and I smoothed my rumpled skirt.

Peter approached and took my hands. "Something has come up. I'm afraid I'll need your help once again, and since you've no position just now, you'll need pay. Will you do it?"

"Another tragic story?"

"I'm hoping this one has a brilliantly happy ending. And it's a large case, affecting many people. That is, if it all turns out right."

I eyed him. "You already have a plan, don't you? I can see it in your face."

"You're observant."

I lifted an eyebrow. "Well, aren't you going to tell me what it is?"

"Do you think that's wise?"

I balled my fists and stamped my foot. "Do you *ever* answer a question?"

"Haven't you—?"

"*Without* another question?"

He shrugged. "They're effective. It's my personal strategy for deflecting inquiry, I suppose. I do love to surprise."

"Very well then, I will help."

"Trust me that easily, do you?"

I shrugged. "I've just learned there's little point in arguing." I crossed my arms, then looked up at him with a sly smile. "I don't suppose you'll need a getaway driver, will you? I'd do that for no charge."

"I value my life."

"Ah, right. I haven't broken you out of prison yet." I sighed. "How about accommodations as my fee? I'm certain it'll be past a respectable hour by the time your plan is done."

"That I can do. We have guest chambers—"

"No." I stiffened, jaw tight for moment. "That is, no thank you. I would prefer to spend the night somewhere . . . unexpected. Somewhere unusual for me. For a lark, of course."

"Being followed, are you?"

I sighed, fingertips pressing into my forehead. "It's a long story."

"So I was right. Ah! I've just the place. Leave it to me, and come along. I'll drive you."

After seeing his guests settled, Peter did just that. Back in the carriage, we were away to some unknown location. Frankly, I didn't much care where I went at this point. Somewhere I could sweep up the tattered pieces of my heart and sob into a big, thick pillow once I was alone.

He watched me in the dark as we rolled back down the lane. "Are you well?"

"Quite well." I shoved sadness from my mind with practiced efficiency, sweeping into the needed role. But the scene from the shore replayed, surfacing and refusing to be pushed aside. The tenderness between father and daughter. The gentle affection. "Such a lovely story, isn't it?" I flashed him a bright smile, but then it washed over me in waves of undeniable longing—*I missed my papa*. I would never have him back. I knew that now. Even if I saw him again . . . there was no going back.

The carriage was quiet, and I felt the tears coming. Hot pricks that would not be contained. Twisting toward the window, I blinked, breathed deep and steady. A silent leaking of tears that seemed endless. How would I compose myself?

But he knew. Peter knew. The warm air was thick with mingled longing and sympathy, quiet compassion. His silence embraced me, comforted me, accepted what was happening with ease and skill common only among the best of men. "You'll have your turn, Miss Lily Temple."

I shivered, turning to shield my thoughts from him. "What ever do you mean?"

"The ending. The happy ones are always for other people, other daughters. Somewhere along the line you've convinced yourself of that. Just as you've come to see God. He's for other people, those fortunate few who have his ear, who live the right sort of life. God, and happy endings, healthy and righteous lives, are for the blessed few, and you, so you think, are not among them."

My lip trembled.

He leaned close and whispered to me a solemn vow. "You will have your own rightful ending, Lily Temple. And soon. You have only to hold on—just a little longer."

I turned toward him and sucked in my breath at the passion radiating on the face I'd once called bland. Every dimple and eyelash was alight with some unseen positive force. I thought perhaps he might light the entire East End if he was of a mind. "You can't know that."

"Oh, but I can. I do." He caressed my cheek. "You see, I've been working behind the scenes, and your story is about to take quite a turn. It's almost here, and it'll be everything you've ever wanted. You'll have your restoration, Miss Lucie Manette. I vow it."

Lucie.

Lucie?

Dread rolled and tumbled into a great ball as I looked up into his face. "Oh Peter. What have you done?"

34

"It is a ridiculous attachment," twittered the
other Swallows; "she has no money,
and far too many relations."

~OSCAR WILDE, *THE HAPPY PRINCE*

He told her. Peter unfolded the tale as flower petals opening, revealing the story that had been building, watching
her ever-changing face as he did so. He admitted what
he'd been doing almost since they'd met, despite Roddy's advice.
Questioning, gathering information, forging connections. All his
impressions of her, of events, that fed into his decision.

And what he'd done about it.

"Now all that's left is to bring to light what Fairchild has
been doing all these years, and so many will go free. So many
lives will be restored. Including the one you most care for." He
stopped just short of telling her about the man in the cave. It
had been a sacred moment, that little encounter, and he could
do naught but keep the man's secrets, as requested. Allow him
to stay hidden. For now.

It wouldn't be long.

She accepted his tale quietly, hands clasped in her lap, eyes shining with intensity. How much had she already known? Surprise never marred her features as he told her all the discoveries he'd made, the people he'd met, and what they'd said about the case. About Fairchild's corruption. Makepiece's disappearance after his trial. When he'd laid everything at her feet, all the effort and hope and risk, her bright, intelligent gaze found his. Never had she looked so vulnerable. "You truly think you can free him, then? And all the others? Set all this to right?"

"All I need is proof. And that, dear woman, is the case you agreed to take on." He took her hands, gathering her trembling fingers in his. "It's not just about Gordon Makepiece anymore, or about the sapphire, but every case Fairchild has mishandled. Every life he's ruined. He's a corrupt and wicked man, Lily. But I suspect you know that."

Her eyes glinted, lips pressed together. Then she parted them and ran her tongue over them.

"If I can prove even a few, I'm certain I can make a case and bring down the entire lot of his judgments. That'll reopen every case, and if it's anything like the trials of trading justices from Middlesex, many will be set free." He squeezed her hands, conferring strength onto her. "There is justice coming, Lily Temple, and I'm determined to bring it about. For all of them . . . but mostly, for you."

Her fingers trembled, but her voice held steady. "You've no idea what he's about. What sort of power he holds. Fairchild has nearly every duke and member of Parliament he's ever met in his pocket. Please, Peter. I'm begging you. Keep away from him. You'd very likely wind up in prison if he catches on, or worse. Vanish within the prison system."

"You'll break me out. Then you'll be driving my motor car. I did promise."

"Prison is one place my tricks won't penetrate. Not easily."

"I thought palaces were your only limitation."

She placed a hand on his arm. "I'm begging you, Peter. This is life or death."

"I'm not afraid."

She yanked back her hands. "Well, you should be. You're just now understanding the pieces of it, and I won't have you marching out into a battle you know so little about."

"Then tell me."

Terror flashed on her face. She gripped the seat with her left hand, steadied herself against the seat back with the right.

"What? What aren't you saying?"

A tigress. That's what she looked like—a young tigress. The sort of animal you could never predict—especially when cornered.

With a sigh, he turned to face forward but kept his peripheral gaze on her. They wound through the busy streets of Brighton until the muffled roar and hiss of water sounded on the distant rocks. "I'm taking you to the Walkers, by the way. I assume that's acceptable. They've been friends of my family's for years, and of course you know Adelaide."

When they approached the row of clean, white houses built in the Tudor style, the carriage slowed. After a moment of stillness, Peter turned to his companion. "Forgive me if I've overstepped, Miss Temple. I truly believed you were keen to see Gordon Makepiece cleared. For the truth to come out."

Her gaze snapped to his face, searched him with wide eyes. Evaluating, measuring, debating. The layers of her façade fell quickly away, revealing the raw center. Would that she were a book, so that he might understand as easily as words upon a page what he was seeing. "Can you do it without bringing Fairchild down?"

"Why?"

"Well . . . for one, he's dangerous, Peter. So very dangerous."

He took her hands and winked. "So am I." A smile. "All I want, Lily Temple, is to release the truth. Uncage it, and let it do what it will."

A cool breeze. A jerk of the carriage. A shuddering sigh, then she spoke. "Very well, then. You'll need my help."

"I was hoping to hear those very words."

"But this is the very last case for me." It was a whisper. "The very last."

"If you wish it."

She'd gone quite pale.

He frowned. "You'll be all right to go there, won't you? To see him in person? It won't bring on bad memories?"

"*Me?* See Fairchild?" She stared up at him with large, wild eyes. "I never agreed to that."

"You'll have to tell the officials what you know, and he will have to be there."

"Whatever for?" She was trembling.

"Because you have the truth, Lily. You know what truly happened. That's been clear to me since the beginning. My ability to defeat the enemy depends largely on you telling what you know."

"You don't think I've tried to tell them? I've gone to more officials than I can count! They don't listen."

"They'll listen this time. I'll make certain of it. I know the law, Lily, and I'm in your corner. They *will* hear you, as long as you tell exactly what happened."

"I've only an idea, in some cases, but I—"

"You do wish to free Gordon Makepiece, do you not? Whatever wrongs happened in the past, this is your chance to undo them. To repair what this man broke. Lily, your story is coming full circle. It's reaching its conclusion."

Those lovely slanted eyes lifted to him, a mix of emotion in their bewitching depths. "It's conclusion. Yes . . . the end. This is the end."

"Come, let me hand you down." He stepped onto the walk and held out a hand, helping her down. He leaned against the carriage, watching her face. Her bright, fearful face. "Lily, who exactly are y—"

She kissed him. Moved swiftly into his space, drew him boldly down by the lapels, and pressed her lips into his with an eager, feminine sweetness, caressing his cheek with one hand while the night around them held its breath. Affording them this private moment, letting them linger, undisturbed. Then she moved back a mere inch, observing his face. It had been brief—a stolen moment of privacy in the shadow of the towering elms—but enough to know that her lips were invitingly warm. Expressive. A fluttering of dragonfly wings touching down for an impulsive moment, then lifting away.

Yet leaving radiant warmth where they touched.

When she stepped fully back, he fought to think again. To reason. But he found he couldn't even speak yet. Fingers to his lips, he merely raised his eyebrows and looked at her in question.

Her smile was quick. "That is *my* method of deflecting questions."

He cleared his throat. Made an odd noise. "Quite effective."

At the moment, his brain still operated worse than a badly built motorcar engine with a rusty crank. "Well, then. Let's . . . let's have a knock."

Have a knock. Had he truly just said that?

He watched her profile as they climbed the steps together. The tip of her head, the guarded look . . . she was hiding something from him. Many things, perhaps.

Why, God? Why her? Before he'd met her, he'd finally come around, his heart and head catching up to what his lips had been saying for years. Being alone was good. He'd be all right. It was his choice to remain thus.

But a glimmer of hope had still existed, the little thing that refused to be tamped down, that secret longing to find a remarkable woman with whom to share his life. One with certain characteristics, though—topmost of which was trustworthiness. Steadiness.

He spent his life drilling deep into the minds of people, and catching lies. He didn't wish to do the same at home, with his wife. No, he couldn't bear it. Couldn't bear to link arms with a woman who stood for everything he did not. His entire job, his larger role on this earth, was uncovering truth. Hers . . . masking it.

His tastes were simple. Why couldn't God have brought him that sort of woman? A kind, devoted clergyman's daughter or shop owner's sister would have been perfect. All he'd ever wanted. This . . . this made no sense. *Of all the women in the world . . . why one I cannot trust?*

They rang the little electric bell and waited. She flashed him a smile and his heart thumped. Oh, how she played with his senses. With his mind. It was almost cruel, how dearly he wished to take her and kiss her playful smile. To embrace all that energy and color and life.

Yet Roddy's stern face interrupted his flight of fancy. The wrestling match intensified. No, he couldn't do it. Couldn't. Love her, yes. Enjoy her, of course. But could he *trust* Lily Temple?

No. The notion swept over him with rapid calm. *So why, God? Why have you embedded her in my heart?*

He closed his eyes, anguish twisting inside. Then the notion settled on him, thick and comfortable.

I didn't ask you to trust her.

I asked you to trust me.

A rush of remorse, then of freedom, swept through his soul.

He remembered the man in the cave. The words he'd spoken concerning her. She was searching desperately for the gardener. For her father. But as the man had pointed out, it was not the earthly one her heart truly sought. Her search was bigger, more significant, than that. She was longing for God with every fiber of her being, even if she didn't know it, and that meant God was searching for her. Drawing her to himself. Calling out in a way that she was compelled to answer. And Peter's heart lightened to the point of delight.

She was precious to God. She was in his grasp—or very nearly. And he had urged Peter toward her.

Peter looked upon her afresh, with a reckless, unbridled affection, taking in her face. Her bright eyes and piquant features. That little rosebud of a mouth that might say any number of surprising things. This . . . yes, this is what God intended to happen.

There was no one else like her. Not the entire world over. When she smiled, that private little smile meant only for him, it loosed something in him.

He opened his mouth to voice his thoughts, but the look on

her face when she turned to him stopped him cold. He frowned. She was pale. Drawn. "You'll be all right, then?"

A solemn smile.

"What? What is it?"

"I'm not certain I can do this. Fairchild, I mean. Not certain I can go through with this."

"It's the right thing, Lily. The noble one."

"I didn't say it wasn't the right thing. I'm just not certain I'm able to do it."

He reached out and fingered a strand of her loose hair between two fingers. Soft. Impossibly soft. "Very well. You can let me know tomorrow."

"And . . . I'm not Lucie Manette, Peter."

"Well, you're not *exactly* her, of course—"

"No, I mean . . . you have the wrong character. It's not Lucie's story I was telling you."

His gaze bore into hers, trying to understand. His steady confidence shifted underfoot.

"It was . . . well, I can't . . ."

He took her by the shoulders. He was trembling a little. "I always listen, Lily. So, speak. I'll hear it, whatever you have to say."

A rainbow of emotions flitted over her face—fear, anger, hope, and . . . something else. Dread?

But then the door opened, and polite requests were required.

35

To live will be an awfully big adventure.

~J. M. BARRIE, *PETER PAN*

A t times when your story pounds a rhythm in your ears, overtaking your senses, spinning out of control, the only cure for it is to fill your head with another story.

Which I accepted with open hands from Adelaide Walker that night.

When she led me to her well-appointed sitting room, inviting me to sit with her, she told me what had happened to her in France. After years of tutoring, she spoke French quite well, and she'd been able to appeal to her captors. To beg them for mercy.

And they'd fallen under the heady spell of her love story. One particular nurse, at least, had.

She'd spent time with her love for three sweet days, and he'd told her everything that had happened to him. About how the entire regiment save three or four men had been slaughtered that day in the Boer region. And when officials had later reached the battlegrounds, they assumed the entire lot had perished.

About how he'd later switched identification papers with one of the other survivors trapped in the French hospital so that the soldier might escape and Pelletier might remain in enemy territory without the added risk of being a high-ranking captain. How he'd made the man promise he'd post his final letter to Adelaide in return, and how he'd never dreamed he'd see her again.

Until the man posing as Pelletier had escaped and arrived near-dead on British shores. Thus the investigation had begun, ultimately leading to France and the real captain.

It had been a miracle, they'd both agreed, them being brought together for three precious days, and then she'd been by the captain's side as he'd drawn his final breaths, holding his hand and speaking love over him. A sacred encounter, she called it.

Her father had come in one week's time to fetch her back to England, laying out a large sum of money and a great deal of threats to the hospital guards, and Adelaide had grieved in his arms the entire journey back.

Now she was here . . . alone, but safe, having lived through some of the worst grief imaginable.

She smiled through my bumbled apology for the tragic end of her story. "We shouldn't have taken you there. Shouldn't have let you witness . . . shouldn't have *left* you there! Heaven sakes, we've done everything wrong by you." I shook my head. "We never should have interfered. I'm afraid we've made a mess of things."

Her eyes sparkled as she smiled at me, emotion glistening on her features. "Do you know how long I've loved Captain Pelletier, Miss Temple?"

I blew out a breath as my heart twisted. "Plenty long, I'm certain."

"Sixteen years. I've loved him since I was a girl, climbing over the garden wall and running to explore the creek with him." Tears coursed down her cheeks as if they had ready-made paths. "Sixteen years I'd waited. It was my *dream* to marry him, and after quite a long wait . . . I was able to do it." She extended her left hand in the soft glow of lamplight, showing off her plain gold band with a glowing countenance. "But only because of your blessed 'interference,' as you call it. We were married in the hospital, the day after you left."

"Rather a short marriage, I'm afraid." Warm tears budded in my own eyes. "Oh, I'm so sorry, Adelaide. What sort of love story have we left you with?"

She gave a short laugh. "The kind that leaves me a married woman, legally bearing the name of my love forever." She placed a hand on her belly. "And able to offer that name to our child. Trust me, Miss Temple. All of that interference . . . you've no idea how it has changed things for us. I was very nearly ruined. In name and in heart."

"And still he died." I sniffed.

"It was a tragedy, yes—many times over. But now with *hope* woven in." The tears poured in earnest, even as she smiled, and I could not help but think of Annfrieda and her well of tears. "Thanks to that soldier and thanks to your meddling."

I took her hand, squeezing it. "You're a far better woman than most, Adelaide Walker Pelletier. I wouldn't have been able to face such heartache the way you did."

"Yes, but look at what I'd have missed if I hadn't." She twisted the gold band on her finger, a tender smile upon her face. "You can't fight the ending of your story just because you're afraid of the pain."

What was it about her? Slight of frame, quiet of voice, there was a resolute strength about Adelaide Walker that had brought her this far. That had carried her through fire, grieving but still steady. It matched what I saw in Peter—that settled, deep-seated peace nothing could rattle. Looking at her face, I was hungry for this peace. Hungry for what I'd had only a taste of in that little locked room.

For years, I'd been running and restless. Running away, yes. But also running toward something that seemed elusive and impossible. That garden experience. The safety, the devotion and intimacy . . . the sheer beauty.

How that echoed things Peter had said. Maybe he was right, and that garden held more significance than I realized. Perhaps it *was* my Eden. All I knew was that a great, yawning desire had stretched wide in me, and that little taste had only opened it wider.

She left me in the sitting room to retire early, saying the coming child wore her out every day, even though he was not yet born. I gladly sent her on and sat in the candlelit quiet, staring straight ahead. Letting my thoughts spin. I stood and walked to the shelves of books, running my fingertips along the spines. Hoping to spot one in particular.

"You, lovely storyteller, are missing out on the greatest narrative in history." Then I saw what I sought, there on a little round table by an overstuffed chair. A great leather-bound volume sat beside a slender vase holding bright, yellow flowers, with a few scattered petals fallen on its lovely cover.

Little breadcrumbs on the path, beckoning me. Inviting. A taste of the gardens.

I picked it up and, intimidated by its sheer weight and volume, decided to treat it as I would any other book I was meeting for the first time. I would read the beginning and the end, and see if the story resonated with me. Hesitation still simmered in my heart.

It began of course with the story of creation, just as I'd remembered it. Darkness and light, oceans and stars, animals and plants. But then . . . a garden. A lavish, thriving, full-of-life garden where humans communed deeply with the Gardener. I read for two and a half chapters, drinking it in, picturing the lush Eden, then flipped to the end. And to my surprise God, being a rather masterful storyteller, had brought the massive volume full circle. In the beginning . . . a garden. Beautiful, rich, and intimate. But humanity had to leave it.

Then in the end, another garden came to life on the page, even more lovely. Intimate and rich. Boundless. One that was still to come. Reading its description resonated with every cell of my body.

I pulled out the sapphire, now hidden neatly within the folds of my sash, and held it up to the lamplight. How I wished it could bring me back to the garden and I could drink in the richness of what was. Of what I'd felt there as a child. But perhaps . . . there was a new garden. A restored, even better one to which I could look forward. And that warmth, that intimacy, would return.

Just as it was meant to be.

I replaced the gem and allowed the maid to show me to my guest chamber. I dreamed of a wondrous garden that night . . . and a smiling gardener with an aged face wreathed in welcome. I sat and talked with the gardener as I had once to an in-the-flesh man, telling him everything. Hesitantly at first, and then words tumbled out, raw and true and passionate until my shoulders relaxed and my heart felt freer.

I woke in the morning with the refreshing sense that I'd spent the night sleeping heavily under the stars.

This. This is how they did it—that Mr. Driscoll and Adelaide

Pelletier. They could walk over life's burning coals and come out with strength and confidence on their faces. Because they had spent time in the garden, drinking in life from their source.

They had met the Gardener.

◆

Peter came for me midmorning, asked me how I was, and I merely grabbed his arm. "Come. We must do this right now, this very minute. Before I lose my nerve. Or come to my senses." This was right. I had fought it for many years, but it was the only way back to the garden for more than a mere visit.

"You'll speak with him? Speak with Fairchild?"

"Of course not. I'm going to help you sneak into his house and find proof."

"And do what with it? Go to the police with stolen evidence? Lily, this is too big to handle the wrong way."

"It *is* big, which is exactly why we need to do it my way. Trust me, Mr. Driscoll. There's no justice where thieves are involved. Only outsmarting them. We're going to take the train into London and see what we can find at his house." I put a hand on his arm. "I want the truth to come out. It has been hidden for too long, and this is the way to do it. Now, then. Are you in, or must I do this alone?"

36

No, no! The adventures first, explanations
take such a dreadful time.

~LEWIS CARROLL, *ALICE'S ADVENTURES IN WONDERLAND*

Sneaking into the white terraced stucco on Eaton Place went more smoothly than I'd anticipated. Would that the rest of our escapade had gone as well.

The fashionable Belgravia Square had been largely asleep as we'd slipped between the homes and located the right one. We had entered through the cellar, skirted the lively servant's hall echoing with voices, and come to stand in a long, shiny entryway cloaked in shadows.

A house. Just a house, like any other. That was my mantra as we stood before those grand stairs, listening to the echoing laughter from the servant's hall. Stone and wood and fabric over furniture was all it was, really.

"What if he's in residence?"

"He isn't." I ran my hand along the white bannister, thinking of the stories this place told of its residents. "Thursdays are club nights. He won't be back until two at least. Perhaps not until morning. The staff will have the night off too." Streetlights shone through the brightly colored stained-glass windows, throwing patches of color along the polished floor and the blue-and-white provincial furniture. It was a light and airy house, full of wood painted light cream with gold edging. Its master was equally light and airy, in a way, living without the heavy burden of work and strife known to most men.

Hadn't he been born a working-class lad? Yet here he lived among gold and glass, tall windows in the French style, and cherubs smiling down from a hand-painted ceiling.

Peter stood in awe of the place. "Just look at this vase. It must be worth more than my entire stable of horses. And this piece. What opulence the man has accumulated for himself." He touched the gilded edge of a looking glass. "How many innocent people had to suffer so this could hang in his hall?"

Sickness roiled through me. "Please focus, Mr. Driscoll."

"Right, of course. We need to find the study. There's a record book there that should have proof of everything. Although I still don't know how it'll do us any good, stealing it as we are."

"This way." I tugged his arm and we slipped around the grand staircase, deeper into the shadows.

He hesitated. "You seem to know the way quite well. Almost as if you'd been here before. And his schedule—you know that too."

"It's to your benefit, isn't it?" This wasn't the time for explanations. Or doubts.

Still, his brow creased with worry. "You've done this before. Broken into Fairchild's home."

Footsteps.

I stared at him in the darkness, willing him to understand.

Willing him to see and grasp this part of me as he knew every other. I dared not say it aloud just now—or much of anything, for that matter.

"Hello? Is someone there?" A female voice echoed through the halls. A servant?

Silence fell, with a background of pinging clocks here and there. A soft buzzing from electric lights on the wall behind us.

I pointed to his shoes. My satin slippers were blessedly silent, but his worn leather soles creaked with every step. He slid them off with a nod, then turned and stepped—onto something. Squeals and hissing, then a creature shot around the room, banging and clawing, knocking over an umbrella holder with a crash.

Cat.

"Mouse?" called the female voice again. "Oh, Mousey . . . Here, kitty! Is that you?"

Mousey? I cringed. Who on earth saddled a cat with that sort of name?

The footsteps neared. A woman huffed with the exertion of each hurried step.

"Come on." I grabbed his arm, yanked him off his feet. We darted over slick tile, slid over polished hardwood, around another bend and directly to the study door. I grasped it—

Locked. I spun to face Peter, muscles tense, and tightened my shoulders in a shrug.

"Hello?" A man's voice this time, echoing down the hall. "Is someone about? Master Fairchild?" Shoes clicked on polished wood. "Mrs. Payne, what is it? Have you heard someone too?"

We were at the end of a hall. A dead end.

Their voices lowered, murmurs muffled.

I shoved Peter stumbling back down the hall, toward the

335

clicking shoes that had started up again, then veered left. I pointed up an angled back stairway and together we climbed. Frantic. Breathless. "There's one other way into the study. Remember the vines at the hospital?"

He shot me a panicked look.

We took the stairs two at a time. "Don't look that way. You'll only have to go *down* them this time."

Crunch.

Pain lanced up my leg as my foot rolled under me, dropping me to the steps. I fell into the wall, biting back a whimper, and Peter caught me. I'd heard bones popping and breaking, it seemed. I blew out a breath and clutched the ankle as shards of pain shot up the length of it. Just sprained, most likely, but painfully so.

Rotten foot, turning on me that way.

"Shall we go back?" He leaned me against his chest, caressing my hair, my back. "We can, you know."

"Of course not. We'll be caught. And Peter, when a man ends up in prison, innocent or guilty, he's in Fairchild's grasp. Remember that. He is king of that lair."

He stilled. "Surely an innocent man can be exonerated."

"Sometimes, but that takes time. Until then, anything can happen. We *must not* be seen. Not even a chance."

"Then we won't be." He pushed me to standing and supported my weight up the remaining stairs. My heart pounded as I limped into a narrow upper hall at the top. The boards squeaked with every move.

Halfway down, French-style folding doors opened into a gallery that ran in a balconied circle overlooking the study. Peter helped me into the quiet room and I closed the doors behind us, pausing to listen for footsteps.

None sounded.

Grasping the oiled railing, I eyed the large boat of a walnut desk below us, the neat piles of papers covering its surface. A ladder, built into the bookshelves, lay temptingly just out of reach. I eyed my companion. "Exactly how adventurous are you feeling?"

"I don't think I knew the meaning of the word before you."

"You'll have to climb down. Can you manage it?" I pointed into the wood-paneled abyss below. "Everything you need is in that desk—you only have a few minutes, by the sound of it. The servants seem a good sort. They won't let a suspicious noise go untended."

A grim nod, then he climbed—that tall, elegant man—onto the slick railing in his stockinged feet, hanging on to the wooden trim above.

I bit back a smile. "A bit like a monkey."

He cocked his head to the side and grinned.

"Just leap out a little and grab the ladder."

He shook his head. "I don't think I can make it." Instead he grabbed the thick column, wrapping himself around it. "Could do with a tail about now." Clinging to the thing, he slid down, inching over every spindly notch and groove, until he had neared the study floor. Then he aimed for the rug, leaped, and tumbled onto it.

I lifted my hands in silent applause. "Now, to the desk. The desk."

I could hardly see around the giant chandelier that hung between me and Peter. A dangling crystal affair strung up by no less than five ornamental chains. Peter yanked open one drawer, then another, feeling about the bottom of each. As if he knew what he was looking for, and where to find it.

Finally I heard his whispered cry of victory. He dug out a book and leaned back to show me. With a salute, he paged through, absorbing who knows what filling the pages. He frowned, flipped faster.

"What? What is it?"

Shoes scuffed up the back staircase. Coming my way. I waved at Peter, but he continued poring over that ridiculous book, his face animating with each turned page. I waved harder, nearly falling over the bannister. Rotten chandelier blocked everything I did.

Nothing was going well.

"Look at this, Lily. It's incredible, the sheer number of—"

"They're coming!"

Footfall, creaking up the stairs. Onto the landing. Down the hall toward me.

I eyed that drop. The ladder against the shelves. I could do this. I scrambled to stand on the bannister, curling my throbbing ankle into my other leg. I hadn't time to inch down the column as Peter had.

The doors rattled behind me. I braced, focused on the ladder, then leaped.

And missed.

With a cry, I grabbed the air. Caught hold of brass and dangling glass pieces. Scrambled for a better grip on the gaudy chandelier just as the doors below me banged open.

"What is the meaning of this intrusion?" There he sat, in all his glory—Josiah Fairchild, bearded, suited, and red with anger in his wheeled chair. Peter froze and I swung from the clinking, rocking chandelier. A crack above me, and the chandelier jerked. Plaster rained on my head. The man looked up and locked gazes with me, and his mouth fell open. "What . . . in . . . heaven's . . ."

I clung with trembling arms, blew hair off my face, and offered a wavering smile. "Hello, Papa."

And then I fell.

37

You must learn to be strong in the dark as well as in
the day, else you will always be only half brave.

~GEORGE MACDONALD, *THE DAY BOY AND THE NIGHT GIRL*

crashed with a thud onto the rug below—which was far too
thin, I found out. Jolts of pain at every angle. I lifted my
head, parted my hair like a curtain, and looked from Peter,
shocked and rigid Peter, to my father in his wheeled chair. My
heart was in my throat. Josiah Fairchild was a man full of many
words. They crowded every silence, every waking moment. But
in that instant, he was dangerously silent.

As I blinked through my hair, Papa rose to his full majesty
in that chair, and towered over that room as if from a throne
with a growl. "What manner of reprobate is *this*?"

"We've intruded." Peter stepped forward. "I beg your pardon, sir, but—"

"YOU have intruded. Upon my home. My private study. My
daughter." He grabbed the wheels and yanked, jerking the chair
around. "What do you *dare* claim is the reason for this?"

I limped over to stand between them. "You wouldn't dare arrest Peter. He is my guest, and this is my father's house. He's stolen nothing, damaged nothing, broken not one single law." I stepped back, forcing Peter to do so as well, so as not to have his feet stepped on. "He's not done one thing against you, and—"

"You're right." His face curled into a snarl. "It is *much more* than one thing. Weston! Carlisle! *Now!*"

I shoved Peter toward the back wall. "Run!" We stumbled and fell against the windows. Fumbling with the sash, I flipped the latch, threw the window up, and hurled myself into Peter. We fell out onto the lawn. Footsteps pounded down the corridor—servants. Butler, footman, driver. I scrambled up and grabbed the sash, pulling it down. I rolled into the grass, cringing at the further abuse to my body.

It was worth it, though. Worth it.

"Peter!"

He grabbed my hand and we ran, eyes wide in the dim garden, praying we didn't snag a tree root. Run into a wall.

More lights flashed on outside the big old house, voices and scuffling footfall sounding outside. We ran and flattened ourselves against some shadowed brick wall. Catching our breath. Was it Fairchild's wall? Or the next house? I should know this neighborhood. This property. I'd spent so many years finding stories among these flowers and shrubs. And one night years ago, I'd fled it in much the same manner.

I could feel it this time—feel my story's circle returning to the beginning, preparing to close. So many echoes of that night that I couldn't forget. My pounding heart. The tightness of fear. The chill of betrayal and aloneness. The memory of my father's face.

"I know where she'll go," a voice was saying. Then the deep voice lowered. I took a step toward it, straining. Then another.

". . . call up to Newgate . . . morning . . ."

Newgate. Prison. But what was the rest? What were they planning? Hands out before me, I eased a few steps back toward the house. Toward the voices.

But they ceased. The lights went out.

And the world was inky dark. Distant lights dotting the hill were all I could see. The sudden realization that Peter had left his shoes behind flashed through my mind.

"There! I heard something!" said one of the voices.

My breath came in panicked gasps.

Then the dogs came. Barking, snarling. Papa had used them to keep intruders at bay. Was I an intruder?

A threat. I was a threat. And so was Peter. Wait . . .

Peter! I swung around. Felt nothingness.

Cold, metallic awareness. He'd gone. I was alone. I was once again the swindler's daughter, and he had fled.

I twirled about, called out in a desperate yell-whisper. *"Peter!"*

"Shh!" He pulled me back against him. "I'm *right here*." Back into the steadiness of his chest. He was there. He'd been no more than two inches behind me in the pitch black. I turned, and there he was, solid and real, and . . . still there. Silent, but *still there.*

Tears wet my eyelashes.

"Rosella."

I shivered as Peter spoke my name with wonder. My true name.

"I should have known." His fingers found the outline of my jaw, my collarbone. "*Daisy* Fink, *Flora* Cross, *Marigold* Fontaine, *Astrid* Carmichael, *Thorndike* Clay, *Lily* Temple . . . *Rosella*. A rose by any other name would still be a rose."

"Yes. Yes, I am Rosella."

"Rosella was meant to be at a finishing school. I tried to visit you there."

"And you were likely told you couldn't see me." I shook my head. "Father had to save face when I left. Protect his reputation, and maybe mine too. He pays them to pretend I am there. But my sister—did you see her?" I nearly held my breath.

"Lenora, I believe. She was . . ."

"Well? Was she well?"

"Feisty."

I exhaled a laugh of relief. "Much the same, then." I straightened. "Father did what he thought he must to protect her. And me."

"He paid them to lie. And you happen to have quite a long record—your other identities do, at least. That was his doing too, wasn't it? I'd wager you never stole a thing."

"No." I swallowed. "Nothing." He knew a great deal now. Too much, actually. But my father didn't know that, of course. Which could mean only one thing. I fell against him. Trembled into his chest. "Peter."

"What is it?" His hold tightened. Fingers smoothing my hair.

"Peter . . . You must get away. And I must disappear now. I cannot tell you where. You must keep to yourself, and never let on what you know about my father. Not one word, and never ever speak of me to anyone. We must cut all ties." Why was this so hard? Why? "This is goodbye, Peter. I cannot see you again, and this is the end of Lily Temple. It's the only way to keep you safe."

I felt his chest bounce with . . . something. *Laughter?*

I pushed back, blinking away the wetness. "Is goodbye normally *amusing* to you?" I wanted to stamp my foot. Kick a tree.

He moved close and I could see his smile—one eye crinkled nearly into nothing. "No, only that you think I won't find you."

Hope feathered around my pounding heart. Then regret. Dread. "He can have you arrested whenever it suits him, for whatever reason he dreams up. And he will, if he realizes you know even a little bit of the truth concerning him. He'll tangle you up in the legal system so terribly that—"

"I'm a solicitor. Legal matters are my specialty. And besides, I've broken no laws, as you said. He has no grounds to arrest me."

"He doesn't fight fairly. Remember, he is the most elaborate storyteller ever. When he wants a person in prison, he doesn't need a legal reason, or even a true one. And once you're there, he . . . he can do anything he wants with you. He won't spare your life. You cannot—*must not*—find me. Peter, he's done this before. With Silas Caldwell, the boy I loved once. I meant to marry him, and Papa couldn't tolerate the idea. Especially when he realized all Silas knew about him. Too much." I shook my head. "Silas told me things about my father, but I didn't believe him. Not for a long time."

"Because he was your father and you loved him."

"I prayed I'd find that necklace." Tears warmed my skin. "That I could find the proof I needed and free Silas. And miraculously, I did. I found it at the very last possible moment. I ran with it to the courthouse and gave it to my father just before the trial. Then I stood in the back of the courtroom and he looked right at me." Tears began streaming. "Stared at me as he found Silas guilty and sentenced him. Looked me right in the eyes, *knowing* what he was doing."

"So Silas was right about him."

"I never thought my father would actually go through with it, sentence him and leave him in prison, but he did. Without hesitation." Tears leaked in earnest. I didn't stop them. "He'd had Silas framed with that necklace. That beautiful, terrible sapphire. I dug it out of his desk drawer that night and took it with me so I'd always remember who he was. So I'd never be fooled again. And so I'd have proof if I ever had the chance to use it one day.

"What he did was wretched. With you, it'll be even worse. You're infinitely more of a threat than his servants. And justice *does not win*. He doesn't let it. Consider me dead, Peter Driscoll. Vanishing is the kindest gift I can offer you. The most merciful."

"Do what you must. But remember, Daisy, Flora, Marigold, Lily, Rosella . . ." He swept one finger down my cheek. Kissed my head. *"I know you."*

A tremble. I buried my face in his chest again, indulged in his affection. In the safety of his embrace as his palms anchored me to him with gentle pressure. "I won't make it easy on you, Peter."

"Good."

"In fact, I know how to make it quite impossible. You *will not find me*. I vow it."

He twisted loose strands of hair, then brushed them off my face. "I accept your challenge, my dear flower. Change your story, your clothing, your name . . . but you're still you, and I'll find you." Then he drew up my chin and kissed me most ardently, a seal and a promise.

One that would doom him if he dared keep it.

Without another goodbye, I tore myself away for the last time and ran.

38

It is so silly of people to fancy that old age means crook-
edness and witheredness and feebleness and sticks and
spectacles and rheumatism and forgetfulness! It is so silly!
Old age has nothing whatever to do with all that.

~GEORGE MACDONALD, *THE PRINCESS AND THE GOBLIN*

I used to believe all stories came to a nice, neat close. A circle
that completed, if given enough time. Now, it seems more
of a shadowed path through the woods, wandering this way
and that . . . until some unseen destination is reached. Or maybe
several destinations at various points along the way. That's how
mine had turned out, after all these years.

I rocked in my creaky rocking chair, thinking how Lily Temple's story had come full circle, thanks to George Albert Smith
the filmmaker. That's how it happened in fictional tales, and
Lily had been pure fiction. Soon after he'd sacked me, he'd
killed me off for the sake of his shows. Not literally, of course,
because . . . Well. Here I am.

But he drummed up a story and fed it to a hungry press,

offering it up as an explanation for the end of her flicker. One final installment showed, and I heard the people of Brighton filled the garden to bursting for it.

He must have been ecstatic.

And yet, much later in a distant seaside village, as yet undiscovered by the holiday-goers from town, here I sat. The view from my creaky old rocker was much the same as it had been during all the important seasons of my life—the ocean. Just as I had a lifetime ago at St. Anne's Well Gardens, I could close my eyes and hear the water, no matter where I was. It was the same sea, but different rocks it hit.

I paused the rapid jabbing of my needle and leaned back, breathing in deeply of the moist air. I didn't tell stories anymore—at least, not in front of people. Even now, after all this time, I couldn't bear to be found out. Not that anyone would even remember me.

I still told tales, I suppose, with the garments I crafted. I had an eye for it, I had discovered, and I loved to shape reality—or people's perception of it, anyway—as I'd always done. Only it was the gowns I made that told the tales now, on the stage of the town streets. All while dust settled about me and the world passed by the ancient woman who'd become a fixture on her porch.

I relaxed my hands and let them fall to the silk spread over my lap, and thought of Peter. I used to think of Papa in quiet moments, and all my conflicted feelings about him . . . but now it was Peter. Always Peter. My heart was full of him, even now.

I know you too, Peter Driscoll.

I grimaced, shifting an inch to the right and puffed out a breath as I settled in again, relaxing into the luxurious daydream. This was my talent now—reliving the past. Living out, in my head, what might have been. It was a way to hurdle the barriers and live the life I'd have chosen if I could. A way to experience the future that had been stolen from me. Much like escaping into a book.

It was not terrible, this life of mine. But neither was it grand. It was simply . . . peaceful.

I had dipped into the pages of the Bible with all this spare time and marked it up with yellow. God had, it seemed, dropped breadcrumbs, just like my flower petals, along the way. Little traces of Eden, of what once was, to draw me on. To what, I did not yet know. From creation to re-creation, humanity struggled through their existence outside the garden, longing for a great many things and achieving few of them.

I saw myself in that.

Then on Monday, May the sixth, the slap of thick papers at my feet jarred me. I startled with a grunt, one of the privileges of being an old woman. No one ever minded what you did. Nor what sounds you made. I stirred, blinked about the too-bright day to look for Sammy, the little lad who delivered the rags.

But it wasn't Sammy standing before me, blocking the sun. It was a tall, sophisticated, rather angry-looking man with a cockeyed grin. "Found you."

My heart flattened hard, and I thought of Peter. But of course, it wasn't him. I straightened in my chair. "I beg your pardon, lad. Have we met?"

He lifted one eyebrow and shoved the rag toward me with his toe. "In case you're wondering what you've done to him." Then he spun with a crunch of gravel and strode away.

I scooped up that paper faster than I'd ever tucked into a dinner and inhaled the words on every page, eyes lighting on one headline, then another.

It was on the bottom of the second page, right-hand side. I read the article twice, then shot out of my chair and threw aside the unfinished garment . . . and the old-lady pretense that had hidden me these six months past.

Laying hold of a bicycle leaning against the post, I hopped on, skirts dragging the ground, and rode with all my might. Up the dusty road, whipping past the children who always avoided me, the young couples who ignored me, and watched them stop in shock and stare at the old woman pedaling like mad. I threw back my head to laugh and the gray mop wig flew off, rolling through the dust behind me.

No matter. It was time to reenter my other story. The real one. The circle was forcing itself closed after all, and I wouldn't let it happen this way. Not this way.

The lines on the day-old newspaper ran through my mind as I pedaled.

LONDON SOLICITOR ARRESTED.

Peter Driscoll had been charged with the murder of Brighton and Hove flickers actress Lily Temple in the process of stealing the Briarwood Teardrop. He was being held on both counts, awaiting inquisition in London.

My father. He had done this, playing off Smithy's little publicity stunt. He'd taken the murder of a nonexistent woman . . . and pinned it on Peter, the man who knew his secrets.

I was circling back again. Back to the beginning, where a man I loved was being falsely accused of something . . . all because of me. Because of what he knew of my father. Papa was an exacting magistrate and a clever con man. He wouldn't let a servant or a solicitor end his reign. He had let Peter go initially—of course he had, for our escape had been too easy—but he was building a case. Forming his deception to make it perfectly airtight and unexpected. No, he would never let Peter or even his own daughter bring him down. And he had a great many tools to keep that from happening.

Well, I had a few of my own.

At the station, I threw down the bicycle and leaped up onto the platform beside the rumbling train. A puff of steam rolled across the feet of hurrying passengers, and I dashed through them, searching for one particular face. "Roddy! Roderick Heath!" What was he thinking, throwing down the news and running off?

I ran after him, yelling his name. Six months it had been since I'd seen him, but still he wore his irritation for me like a lady wore a veil to go into a seedier part of town.

I ran to him, boots thunking on the platform. "Roddy, tell me. How did this happen?"

He grimaced, reached inside his suit jacket, and pulled out a clipping. "He called in a favor to the Dowager Countess of Wiltshire, who happens to own the Brighton periodicals. He had this printed. Promised her he'd get her sapphire back if she did."

The sapphire. I still hadn't been able to part with it. I had meant to . . . but how to get it to Peter or even to its owner without giving myself away? Without endangering him?

Seems he'd managed that quite nicely on his own. As was his habit.

I unfolded the clipping and read what Peter had asked Lady Claire to print. It was a veiled threat—a clever little soliloquy that mentioned several of the names in the logbook, taunting my father with the fact that he'd seen it, that he knew enough to ruin him, but not divulging any secrets to the average reader. Only my father would understand the meaning, the implied threat that he needed to make things right and give himself up. Or he'd be ruined.

I sighed, palm to my forehead. Of all the boneheaded moves . . .

But also brilliant. There was no justice where thieves were concerned . . . and Peter Driscoll had managed to outsmart him.

Almost. "So he had this printed, and my father saw it."

"Then it was Fairchild's move, and he had Peter framed. Because of you."

My father, in turn, must have released Silas Caldwell to fulfill Peter's request. Because the position of gem thief was now open . . . for Peter. Irony only my father would mastermind.

My story was coming full circle. I could feel it. The past echoed louder and clearer as I neared the climax.

Only this time, I was going to win. Or die trying.

Going through the proper channels and all their processes only gave him the chance to do away with Peter, and it'd be too late. No, justice would not be had. Not quickly enough, anyway.

So that left outsmarting him myself.

I faced Roddy. "Where is he now?"

"Prison. Didn't you hear me?"

"Yes, which one?"

He grimaced. "The holding cell at that derelict country estate. Wiltshire something."

Yes, I knew it. I could be there by morning. And I'd go, armed with a plan.

It was unlikely I'd succeed, but even knowing that, I grabbed the handle and swung aboard that train and returned to face my story. I journeyed toward my Peter, toward his prison in the Brighton countryside, and stood in the rain before that abandoned old mansion, dressed as myself—as Rosella Fairchild—and forced myself to do the hard thing this time. For Peter.

And that is how I came to sit in that dilapidated parlor one rainy day, drinking my orange tea, waiting to meet with the guards, Constable Willis, and a friend of the king's, to tell a most important story.

39

Both felt sad, they knew not why; but it seemed as if
they were to be parted from one another for ever.

~ BROTHERS GRIMM, "JORINDA AND JORINDEL"

I felt the weight of my tale as I surfaced in the reality of the Wiltshire Manor's parlor again. The one where Peter awaited my last-ditch effort. A sudden weakness swept through me as I realized how utterly impossible this was, freeing him with a mere story. Succeeding in this ridiculous plan.

But I lifted a teacup to my smiling lips and let my tale rest for a beat in the wake of their stunned silence. They had listened, I'll give them that. For all their hesitation, every slack-jawed face was angled my way, every gaze upon my face, with not a hint of wandering attention.

A clock bonged deep within the house, and the men startled, one jumping a little.

"You were Evrémonde, weren't you?" It was the dukeish-looking gent who sat forward, offering this. He was the cleverest of the bunch. I could tell.

Carrington, that's who he was. Yes! The Baron of Carrington.

"What are you talking about?" spat poor Mutton, the prison guard. "This is utter—"

"The Dickens character. If she isn't Lucie Manette, then she must be Charles Darnay of the Evrémonde line, the titled heir who renounced his greedy family and ran away to live in poverty."

I smiled. "Brilliantly done, sir. I had to, of course. It was unconscionable, staying there under his roof, eating his food, knowing how it had all come to be. Knowing who he actually was and what he had done."

Mutton shook his head. "You had a lifetime before then to leave, if you were going to. Fishy story, says I."

I straightened. "Sometimes you can be so close to a story you're living that you can't see what it's truly about. I stood in the back of that courtroom, after having rushed in with the proof at the last moment, and watched my father convict Silas Caldwell of a theft he knew he couldn't have committed. And in that moment, so many things made sense that I hadn't seen before.

"But it wasn't until I visited my former fiancé in Newgate that I saw my story for what it was." I took a deep breath and relived the memory of that dank prison corridor. The horror of it, the sight of Silas in that cell.

"'The wretchedly spoiled daughter of a dirty crook'—that's what he called me, and he was right. I was practically drowning in the material wealth of ill-gotten gain. I had been for years. I despised my story, so I decided to do precisely what a dear gardener named Gordon Makepiece had done for me as a child, whenever a tragic ending set me off—I rewrote the ending into one I liked better. I cast off my life as decidedly as Silas Caldwell had cast me off, so I could be someone new. Someone of my choosing rather than the one into which I was born."

"So, Makepiece." One man straightened, frowning at me. "He was framed too?"

"I was foolish enough to ask for his help. To tell him everything. He found out even more on his own, and my father found out—he always does. That's when I ran away. Yet . . . the truest part of me still wished to set things right. To remove the harm I'd caused Silas and then Mr. Makepiece. And perhaps to prove to Silas, but mostly to myself, that I was different than he thought. And decidedly different from my father. And with God's assistance . . . here we are." I shrugged, and again felt the heaviness in the room as my story lingered, enchantment prolonged.

Mutton shot to his feet. "What a cartload of—"

"That'll be all, Mr. Mutton." The heavily mustached constable silenced his employee with an upheld palm. "So what you're claiming, young lady, is that not only has a respected magistrate *framed* this Peter Driscoll for both murder and thievery, despite several witnesses verifying the crime, and has done so on countless other occasions, but also that you are, in fact, Rosella Fairchild, the magistrate's daughter . . . and also Lily Temple the *deceased* actress?"

"Yes. Well, not deceased. Clearly." I fiddled with the rim of my cup.

Dying rainfall splattered against the windows for several moments. It was tapering off. This is how a criminal must feel, waiting for a judge's verdict. Waiting to hear his or her fate laid out by another.

Constable Willis and the Baron of Carrington exchanged

looks. "We will certainly take your story under advisement," said the constable.

"You will release him, won't you? Considering the nature of this matter."

The baron sighed. "I'm afraid we cannot do that quite yet. We must confer with the reigning authori—"

"Surely you see what that will mean for Mr. Driscoll. Any delay and he will be swept away. *Killed.* But release him before he's taken to Newgate, and our story will come full circle. I will have righted my father's wrong." I blinked away tears. "Please . . . don't let this story close in a tragedy."

"I understand your concerns, but there must be some sort of verification of your . . . *story* . . . before we can proceed. Rest assured, miss, we will look into the matter."

I rose. "*Before* Peter leaves this place, I hope."

They exchanged looks.

"Fairchild is on his way. Due in as soon as the road's clear."

They all turned together to look out the long windows. Clouds lingered, but the ground was drying up.

Here. He was coming here.

"I'm sorry, miss." The baron shook his head. "For the moment anyway, our hands are tied."

Wheels crunched up the drive. He was here. About to come through that door and see me. I rose. "Very well, then. It seems my encounters with the British legal system continue to reap anything but justice. Should you choose to champion the truth one day, I shall offer my public testimony to anyone who will listen, but I will not remain here and be tangled in more of my father's deceptions."

I clutched my purse strings. Breathed long, shaky breaths. Steadied myself. Then, I did the only thing left to me—I turned and walked out of the room. "Good day, gentleman." Down the corridor and out the back door, onto the puddled walk around the back of the house, and slipped around the lane as the carriage lumbered up.

And I begged God for mercy on Peter.

40

Lies, my dear boy, can easily be recognized.

~CARLO COLLODI, *PINOCCHIO*

The storm had left a damp eeriness in its wake, and six men huddled around a fireplace to ward off its chill. The roads were clearing, and the prison carriage had arrived. The men could be heard disembarking outside.

Charles Robert Carrington, Baron of Carrington, stared out the window where he'd watched the peculiar woman who'd told the story move across the lane and disappear. She had her hooks in him, he had to admit. Or rather, her story did. He meant to shake it off, but something prevented him. It was rather pleasant, having one's head swimming in a well-told tale. It nearly made him want to talk Fairchild into releasing Peter, but he wasn't certain yet that he could, or that he should. Or if he believed her completely. He hadn't enough information. "If only she'd stayed an hour more."

"So she could what, tell us even more stories?" Mutton sneered as he spoke. "You'll not get the truth out of that one."

"I'd have pried the truth from her . . . or tripped her up in a lie."

"She nearly had me believing her," said a man called Harry Winston, shaking his head. "I don't suppose any of you have actually met Lily Temple, have you? Might confirm what she looks like?"

They all shook their heads. "She did resemble the woman in the flickers, but it's impossible to tell for sure."

"It weren't her," growled Mutton. "The woman is dead, and there are witnesses. Plenty of 'em."

"I suppose she has nothing to lose by attempting this." Carrington rocked back on his heels. "But then again, she could be anyone. Truly, anyone. All we know for certain is that she is a magnificent storyteller."

The door banged open and boots stomped at the entrance. The transport guards were here for the prisoners. They clattered up the large stone steps.

"However, some parts of her story were quite true." Carrington fiddled with his teacup. "In fact, I believe I know how the sapphire originally went missing from the dowager countess. Which would verify part of her story, at least."

All heads swiveled his direction, eyes blinking. Waiting.

But then there was yelling, and the men turned their attention to the stair. Four of them peeled away to help.

It was the necklace that had sealed it for him, that cursed Briarwood Teardrop. Years ago, nearly a decade now, his clerk had passed a request across his desk from one Stewart Mansfield, Earl of Wiltshire, regarding the impending legal troubles of his son, Earnest Mansfield. The same Mansfields who legally owned the Briarwood.

If Carrington recalled the details correctly, Mansfield had

secured a position at London Bank and Trust for his son, and there had been rumors of embezzled funds during his brief tenure there. The elder Mansfield wished to inquire at Carrington's law offices as to his options in relieving his son of the consequences of such actions. His clerk had turned it down for him, knowing Carrington was tied up in court for at least a month, but the name triggered the memory. Especially the hints about the legendary blue stone becoming available, under the right circumstances. Now those hints made perfect sense to him.

Especially after hearing the late earl's widow, the dowager countess, was the one searching for it now. The man evidently hadn't told his wife how it had vanished, and perhaps he'd even shut down the investigation himself.

Yes. Yes, he was quite certain he had the details correct.

Would it be a jump to assume that Mansfield had then approached Magistrate Fairchild about favoring his son in the verdict? And offered the gem as payment? His wife would have reported the gem stolen, and the rest of the story would have played out exactly as Lily Temple had suggested.

"What say you, Carrington? Is it true?"

He shrugged. "There's truth to her story, but how much? That, I cannot say. We don't even know for certain who she actually is."

Thump. Thump.

The sound came closer, down the hall. A shuffling, then the chief of London's police stood in the doorway.

"Sir. We didn't expect you to come in person."

"Of course I came." His craggy face creased deeper. "The magistrate has a personal stake in this batch of prisoners. He'd have come himself if not for these confounded roads back here."

Carrington's spine stiffened. Hairs bristled. "He won't be

359

presiding over these cases at all. It would be a conflict of interest, sir, if he is personally involved."

His frown deepened and released. "You can be sure he'll be watching carefully over the proceedings, then."

Carrington hesitated. Considering.

Behind him, the prisoners were led out to the waiting transport in leg irons. There were seven of them, all local men from Brighton and Hove. Including one Peter Driscoll. They all kept their gaze to the floor as they shuffled out between their guards, except one—a lean man in spectacles with a quiet, watchful look about him. He turned and stared directly at Carrington, meeting his gaze.

That would be him. A rather serious-looking bloke whose face shone with innocence. Carrington's heart pounded, his sense of justice rising quickly to the surface as the men continued outside to the waiting transport.

Carrington cleared his throat. Turned to the chief of police, summoning the right words. But at that moment, the prisoners just outside caught his eye. The one he supposed was Peter Driscoll, the one wearing spectacles, gave a backward glance. Bit out some words to the guard. Then he spat on the man and jerked forward.

Blinking, Carrington reeled in his conflicted emotions and snapped them shut. Her story may have truth in it—a great deal of it—but a lie was like cyanide. The smallest drop would poison an entire glass of otherwise pure water. No, he couldn't trust anything Lily Temple had told them. Not without more information.

And Carrington would personally see to the matter. He'd make certain Fairchild was not involved in Driscoll's trial, and he'd investigate her claims. It would be at least a week before the inquisition, and that would be enough time for him to track down a few leads. Surely Fairchild would not do anything serious in that time.

In the meantime, Peter Driscoll would have to wait in Newgate for truth to release him . . . if, in fact, he was innocent.

41

Get thee away quickly, and at sunset I will be
waiting for thee at the door of the garden.

~OSCAR WILDE, "THE STAR-CHILD"

Y ou look relaxed." Roderick Heath grimaced at me across
the carriage, stating this as a fault.

I sighed, feeling lightweight as air. Shaking. "I suppose I am." How could one explain the feeling of releasing
one's entire story after hiding it for so long? It was a cool dip
in the pond on a sticky summer day. Fresh water to loosen and
wash away years of accumulated grime. "It felt good, even if
nothing else works out the way it's supposed to."

"You don't have Peter with you."

My heart fell. "I do not."

"When you asked me to be your getaway driver, I had hoped
to be taking you *both* away in this carriage."

"Indeed. I did too." I leaned back against the buttoned
leather carriage seat and let the sea breeze cool my warm face,
hairs tickling my skin. "That would have been far easier."

Roddy hated me. I could feel it rolling off him in waves.

"You'd better sit up and tell me your whole plan. And it better be more than batting your eyelashes and begging the guards to release him. Because evidently *that* has failed."

I gave a light laugh. "I told them a story. *The* story."

"You . . . you . . . *what*? A story. That's your plan, a *story*?"

I sighed, brushing stray hairs off my forehead and leaning back. "Why must adults trivialize fiction so?"

"Because it's *a story.*"

"Children instinctively know its worth, but then they grow up and view stories as a mere indulgence, relegated to those elusive 'spare moments' that rarely come, and it's a shame. A shame! The value of stories cannot be measured. Except this one."

He glared, arms crossed. "Speak faster."

"The value of storytelling in this case is threefold." I held up a finger. "First, a story is the perfect way to wrap up important truths so they aren't lost in delivery. You see, I've approached one of those men before. A baron, I believe, and a barrister. I recognized his crest on the carriage outside as we left."

"Baron Carrington?"

"Yes, that one. I wrote a letter to him, and to a few others, and told him what my father was doing. What he had done with Silas Caldwell." I sighed. "Despite what that man says about me, I did everything—*everything*—to have him released."

"So. The letter."

"The baron likely skimmed and discarded my statement of the facts without a thought. Perhaps it didn't even get past his clerk. But wrap it up in a story . . ."

"How do you know he believed anything you said this time?"

"A storyteller always knows when she's enchanted her audience. When she's enticed them to cross the line from disbelief into her story world."

He huffed. "So that's your grand plan? Hope that someone in there believed your story enough to release him? Because let me tell you, Fairchild's men were not far behind us, and he's likely snagged his prisoners by now. What's more, the man is a *baron*, for heaven's sake, titled nobility, which means he'll be even more of a rule follower than Peter. His reputation is at stake, with nothing to gain by fighting for Peter. Don't you see how utterly *useless* this is? How much time we've wasted?"

"No, that aspect of the story was more for the others—all the innocent people my father already has in prison. Telling the truth is meant to change things for them. Now that these men know, or at least suspect, they'll open up all his cases and sort things out, set free the innocent ones."

"Except Peter. He'll be dead by then."

"Ah, but the story was for Peter too." I held up two fingers. "The second benefit of fiction is that Peter, if all went as planned, heard our entire story through my perspective. From our rather unusual meeting to . . . well, all of it. I was able to accomplish something I could not do in person—convey to him how I felt. How . . . how deeply I love him." Affection welled up in my breast.

He stared at me, as if demanding proof.

"I gave him the sapphire. Slipped it into his coin purse after I used it for a little prop today, and he should now have it in his possession."

Roddy was unmoved. "A lot of good it does him now."

"Ah, but there's more." I pressed my lips together in a grin. "There was a third benefit, remember? You see, I paid a visit to Samuel Draper before I came to this prison today, and I told him about my father. Everything."

His voice was softer. "He didn't arrest you, at least. Evidently."

"Of course not. I've broken no laws. For years, I've been a missing person case for him. I had not yet reached the age of majority when I left home and my father reported me missing. Set the Yard on it. And nothing thrilled Draper more than the prospect of locating the elusive daughter of a high-profile magistrate and returning her home. But when I paid him that visit, I convinced him there was a much bigger case for him, and I showed him my father's logbook. Thankfully, I had the foresight to lift it before Peter and I escaped the study. Did I tell you we broke in?"

This time, he actually cracked a small smile. "You got *Peter* to—"

"I promised Draper to leave it in the gardens for him, so that he may have all the proof he needs to bring down the biggest criminal of his entire career. He'd be promoted. Rewarded. Applauded beyond his wildest dreams in a story that will be nothing less than sensational. It's all he ever wanted when he was tracking me down, but this is even larger. Even more shocking to the world, and he could have the whole case and all the rewards that went along with it. But only after he did one small favor for me."

"I can't wait to hear what that is."

I smiled. "Mr. Heath, take me to the gardens, if you would." There, where Peter and I had met, our story would come full circle. One way or the other. A few moments more, and I would see what sort it would be. A tragedy . . . or a romance.

42

A man is as free as he chooses to make
himself, never an atom freer.

~GEORGE MACDONALD, *LILITH*

The story wove around Peter's worn-out senses like a field of glowworms. Ordinary words . . . but strung together with so much meaning. He sensed the trueness of every sentiment, every picture painted with her softly spoken words. She might change her name, change her position . . . but her affection for him was solid. Sincere and true. That fact was woven through every line of her story.

He breathed it in with aching hopelessness, leaning his face against the bars. Every once in a while her soft voice had faded in the distance, but his mind filled in the pieces of their story. She was attempting to wield it like a crowbar to pry open the bars of his prison . . . but it would be in vain. He knew that. These men, enthralled as they seemed to be by her story, judging by the silence in that room, would not be convinced to break the law on his behalf. They would not. He'd been around this sort enough to know that much.

He heaved a sigh as she reached the part about arriving at his house after her harrowing escape—which she had blithely glossed over at the time. She was like magic, this woman. A true sleight-of-hand artist. But this time . . . this time . . .

He shook his head. Her gentle storyteller voice had ceased, her footsteps echoed down the corridor, then the front door opened and shut.

"Sit back."

The harsh whisper jolted him. It was near. Peter pushed back off the bars and there stood Samuel Draper, the man of shadows . . . holding a key. With a glance behind him, Draper inserted the key and turned it slowly, cupping his hand over it to muffle noises.

Then, finger to his lips, he nudged the cell door open and slipped inside. "Time to go, Driscoll."

"What's the meaning of—"

"No time. They'll be coming for you any minute."

"How did you—"

"With this." He held up a key. One that had been well-guarded, rattling around on Mr. Mutton's chatelaine until now. "Had a deuce of a time finding the right hall, I'll tell you."

"What are you doing in here?"

He paused from unbuttoning his shirt. "Let's just say . . . playing the part of Sydney Carton."

He blinked. Sydney Carton, from the Dickens tale. The look-alike. The escape.

"'Ere, put these on, gov'ner. Time to get you out of here."

Peter accepted the items. "And you?"

He waved it off. "They won't hurt a hair on my head. Fairchild will come to look over the prisoners and see his own man waiting for him . . ."

"They'll let you go?"

"Long as I don't let on what I know."

Peter scrambled to put on the items. They weren't exactly look-alikes, Draper and him, but near enough. To a stranger, they might pass as similar. Height and build and coloring, at least.

"I'm giving you a head start. Now you'd better take it. I'll need those, gov." He pointed at Peter's spectacles, which Peter gladly surrendered.

"One more thing." He urged Peter out and shoved a small leather pouch into his hands. His coin purse, which had been taken upon his arrest. "You'll need this back."

Peter gave a grim nod and ducked out. He paused, a hand on the man's shoulder. "Thank you, Draper. Thank you." Hurrying down the corridor, he paused and listened to Lily begging for his release. Pleading with the men.

He held his breath. Hesitated.

But they refused. As he knew they would.

Head down, he wove up one corridor and down another, searching for an exit. Stumbling instead upon caved-in rooms and broken-down staircases. How would he ever escape? Most doors and windows had been secured. Only one would be open—the front door.

At last, breath caught in his chest, he saw sunlight streaming through the great hall. The front door stood ajar. It was too easy. Too simple. As if she'd paved the way for him, just as easily as she picked a lock or freed herself from a locked room. But that was impossible. She didn't even know what Draper was doing.

He inched toward it, toe-heel, toe-heel, rolling each footstep silently. Then he reached out his hand for the sunshine and a voice arrested him. A man blocked his way.

"Constable Willis."

"Well, there. What are you doing?"

43

And the child smiled on the Giant, and said to him,
"You let me play once in your garden, to-day you shall
come with me to my garden, which is Paradise."

~OSCAR WILDE, *THE SELFISH GIANT*

I stood shaking in my sparkling silver and blue gown, ostrich feathers tied into my hair—a guest this time, no longer a resident of the gardens. Other girls scrambled to lay out cheeses and fried oysters. Music played and the night swept on in a schedule I did not even know.

The garden was crowded tonight. Much more than usual. I remained in the back, keeping to myself. I wasn't here for work or to tell stories on the stage. I wasn't even here to soak in the gardens and delight in them.

I was here for Peter.

But he hadn't come. He was not lingering at the glass house, in the cave, or at the cottage. Not on the wooded path or at the pump house. The glowworms lit up a lonely field, with no one standing on the knoll to watch them.

After a desperate search, I had run back down the well-lit path, past the monkey house and the glass film set, and now I stood on the hill above the crowds as the bioscope show whirred to life and the audience applauded.

Smith was replaying the fairy tale of the gem. This particular bioscope show drew a magnificent crowd each time, I suppose, what with the news sensation of its leading actress. That final installment just after my "death" must not have been enough—he would milk that drummed-up drama for all it was worth, then do it all again.

I lowered myself to the grass, perching on a tree root as the images flickered across the screen. It was the saddest installment playing tonight, of course. But I deeply loved this one. I hugged my knees to myself as Bertie, dressed as the gardener, observed the fairy with solemn eyes through the looking glass. I sat fascinated as he stepped through it himself and scattered handfuls of petals, those magical maize-colored pieces that glimmered with traces of the garden. I smiled when I, as the fairy, paused and picked up that petal on the screen. My fingers glowed with color where they touched it.

It was different, experiencing this particular installment as part of the audience. I hadn't even noticed the gardener while filming it, but now he filled my vision. That tender face, the heartbreak streaked across every feature. The affection as he touched the looking glass that held the fairy he'd so lovingly nurtured into being. His head tipped to one side while she, played by me, danced and talked and laughed in the other world. Forgetting the gardens, forgetting him. He was important to her, but only a piece of her world. A small fragment.

Yet his attention never strayed from her. How he watched her with such longing. Such affection. Then he scattered even more brightly colored petals in the bleak world, a reminder to the fairy of the world she'd forgotten about. An invitation to return. Little breadcrumbs back to where she belonged.

Breadcrumbs. Small remembrances. Little nudges and co-incidences.

And like moving from a sepia-toned to a full-color world, I saw with sudden clarity the real story playing out. The one Gordon Makepiece had always meant for me to see. Though I wasn't looking for him, crying out to him, I sensed God again on that hill. Felt him. The sweeping awareness of a magnificent presence I could not see . . . but could not deny. Just as I had in that locked room, and earlier in these very gardens. He was speaking to me in my own language—fairy tales. Leaving me breadcrumbs, enticing me back to the garden.

Then the gardener strode through the blooming flowers, seated himself on a large rock, chin in hands, and waited. Waited for her to finish with the distractions . . . and to come draw life from the gardens again.

As she finally slipped through the looking glass, from gray man-made chaos to a richly colorful enchanted garden, it struck me then which of the two on-screen worlds was the real one. The true one. I nearly wept as the gardener's face wreathed in smiles at her approach.

Then she sat beside him, that bland, sepia-colored fairy looking as wilted as a plucked rose. She sat, basking in his presence, and I watched in wonder as her face—my face—flooded with color. With life and richness. Like a hungry flower drawing up water, the fairy came to life the longer she sat there, until she glowed.

But it wasn't the garden that had transformed her. It was him. The gardener who adored her more than she realized and awaited the moments they could sit together. And the garden was, as it had been for Gordon Makepiece and me, merely that place of connection.

Yes, the garden. Where everything was the way it was meant to be. Where the gardener dwelled. I covered my face and listened to the clacking of the bioscope machine as the story came to a close and the film tail whipped against the metal reels. Another petal this was, this film being shown tonight. A little breadcrumb dropped at the right moment, in the right path, that I might turn from my distraction and find my way back. That I might once again desire my true home and go there, and saturate myself with it.

"*You're drawn here,*" Peter had said. "*Like the fairy who has not yet realized it's her source of life.*"

Oh Peter. Peter Driscoll. What wisdom he had. And how God used the man, even now, to bring clarity to my mind. My heart. He was yet another flower petal dropped in my path.

The audience rose and began talking, but I was lost in my own thoughts. I shut my eyes and basked in that presence. I sank into an honest conversation. One that left out the rest of the world for just a moment. It was a father-daughter moment that filled the deepest reaches of my heart, where I never thought I'd feel life again.

Then I lifted my head up and through misty eyes noticed a familiar figure in the distance. I blinked. Not Peter, but incredibly familiar. His gait, his posturing . . . I rose and stepped closer. Was I mistaken? Was I seeing this man aright? It was impossible!

A dwarf hat that curled at the top and shoes that curled at the toes. A wide belt over an ill-fitting suit. A puff of white hair and beard, hat set at a slight angle, like his smile. His sense of humor. A few guests had dressed as the characters, so he didn't stand out terribly much.

Except to me.

Which is precisely as he wished. It was a secret hint—the white rabbit, the flower crown . . . now the dwarf.

I moved closer, through the throngs, and stopped to watch him from a distance. His merry eyes twinkled, and he watched everyone, ready to burst forth with tales and fantastical spins on reality. It was *him*. The gardener. The storyteller, the tender of roses and of lost children. The father to whoever had need of him. It had been years, but I knew his face. Yes, it was him.

Gordon Makepiece had returned to the gardens.

Hand to my chest, I watched him, rooted to the spot with utter shock. How easily he spoke to everyone, especially the children, and I watched their faces light with every word from his mouth. Every expressive flick of his fingers. I knew what they were feeling, because for so many years, for most of my childhood, I had felt it too.

I had come under his spell as my spirits lifted, the line between reality and imagination pleasantly blurred. Life was naturally hard, but the man was ever full of beautiful stories that softened the edges. That encouraged listeners to grasp not the fantastical but the heady, important truth wrapped up in it. A common bug dressed up in lights. Ordinary flower petals dropped as breadcrumbs in a colorless world.

For a moment, our eyes met. I knew the exact second he spotted me, and it gave him pause. He stilled. Lifted his eyebrows. Then, a smile—slow and warm, spreading over his face. The twinkle in his expression had magnified into a glow. Into gladness. I didn't dare go to him—there would be time for that later, when it was safe—but I touched my fingertips to my lips and blew him a kiss.

Thank you, dear friend. Thank you for the stories.

With a great grin, his hand flew up into the air and he caught my kiss, planting it directly over his heart and holding it there. Then he bowed low and vanished into the crowds.

And in that moment, everything I'd done, all I'd risked, the coming betrayal of my own father, was suddenly worth it. I had dreaded this, but things were finally being set right. And I was stepping from a sepia-toned world into the life-filled garden.

With a great sigh, one that released the past to make room for the future, I turned and slipped toward the fringes, toward the edging hedgerow out of sight of the other guests, once again scanning for Peter. My Peter.

I couldn't help but think of him that way.

Whatever had befallen him, he wasn't able to come back for me. That didn't mean he hadn't escaped, did it? That he wasn't safe somewhere? He'd have found the gem by now, if he'd looked in his coin purse at all. He couldn't help but see the sparkle of the star sapphire that had so captured England's attention. I'd left the imitation with the police . . . but the real one with the only man as true as the gem itself. He would deliver it where it belonged.

Unless Draper had seen it first and taken it. Unless Draper had not held up his end of the bargain at all.

Whatever had become of Peter Driscoll, whatever his fate, he had not made his way back to the gardens, so this was to be the end of our story. It would come full circle with me here alone, setting things right.

It was time.

I removed Papa's little black book from my bag, tucking it

into the hedgerow for Samuel Draper to find. It was the final piece of my journey. The end of what I had hoped for . . . and was never to have. Papa had been lost to me years ago, but now it would be certain. Permanent. He would never forgive me, and I couldn't trust him. Turning back toward the crowds, blinking away tears, I scanned for the roofline of that stately hotel where we'd always stayed when we came to the seashore together. Where he even now might be.

I'm sorry, Papa.

This would have to be a sufficient goodbye. It was all I'd get.

I turned away from my father, away from childish hopes, expecting a surge of pain, but instead a great, unexplainable comfort engulfed me. A presence and an embrace even larger than Gordon Makepiece's, muffling the ache of loss. Of the broken world. Of fear and uncertainty.

And I *knew* that embrace. I'd felt it before, but like Peter standing beside me in the pitch black, I hadn't seen it for what it was. Hadn't always realized it was there. It had just . . . been. Swelling up to surround me when the nettles of the world threatened. When the cliffs came too near. I would not have my father back, and perhaps what I'd always hoped for in him hadn't even existed. But that desire would not go unmet.

"Lily, can't you feel it?" Peter's words, echoing back to me from the cliffs of France. *"Can't you feel him calling out to you from every story that wraps itself around your heart? The hero on a quest, the hardship, the crisis and rescue . . . they awaken what is buried within. . . . What you've lost sight of, but never lost. Because it's yours."*

God has placed eternity in the heart of man.

In the heart of me.

Then it was time to go. Any longer, and someone might recognize me.

It was an intense anxiousness, feeling a story closing. Nothing would ever be the same again. Nothing. I blinked. Tears stung.

I hadn't any notion of what I should do next. Of what my life should be now, or how to know what had ever become of Peter Driscoll. The music began at the bandstand, sweeping me up in its pull. I plucked a rose, one last yellow rose so I could carry its colorful petals into whatever came next. I swayed with the music, letting the atmosphere of the gardens affect me even as I prepared to leave.

As I rounded the path toward the woods, the wind eddied and blew a handful of red petals about my feet. There was a vague trail of them, winding along the fringes of the hedges and out toward the quiet gardens.

Curious.

I looked back toward the now-distant crowds, scanning for a little dwarf, the merry face of Gordon Makepiece. The night held all the flavor of him. Colorful dancers spun in pairs, laughing and talking.

But then, a tap on my shoulder. I turned, yet there was no one behind me. I frowned, then strong arms spun me around from behind, and warm breath was in my ear. "Get me away from here." And we were spinning, spinning into the red poppy fields, stirring up a flurry of color to match the music, leaving a trail of velvety petals behind us.

Tall and lean with a wide hat, terribly thick glasses, and the most horrid bushy mustache any man had ever had the misfortune to wear . . . he swept me up in the frame of his arms, guiding me toward the wooded path. Toward the shadows. How strange he looked, how utterly ridiculous. But with that wide grin, the one eye crinkled in amusement, the strong, masculine face, he was still most thoroughly, most delightfully . . . "Peter!"

"Shhh." He kept his gaze down, hat shadowing his face, but he threw me a wink and twirled faster.

And I was caught up in it. Swept away like a gentle cyclone. I threw back my head to laugh, heartily laugh out all the tension, the wondering, the prayers. Peter. My Peter.

On the path we slowed our steps, and the petals floated like scarlet snowfall about us—the Gardener, showering us with his created beauty. One-two-three, one-two-three. One. Two. Three.

His eyes. His smile. It was all the same beneath that disguise, and it felt almost silly, believing that could hide him. All that quiet passion. The steady kindness.

"You're late. Where have you been?"

"I had a certain gem to return to a countess. Do you know, she believes it will heal her grandson?"

"Did it?"

A sigh. "Perhaps. She wouldn't allow me to stay. Besides, I had an appointment to keep at the gardens. Something about returning to the beginning . . ."

I flushed. "You took quite a risk, meeting me out in the open this way. I should never have suggested it. He's come back to Hove, you know. My father."

A shrug. A wink. "Where's your sense of adventure?"

I laughed and reached up to his face. Touched the familiar nose and cheeks, the chin. "You're here. You're *here*."

He beamed down at me, those steady brown eyes sweeping me with affection. Then sobering. "I'm sorry I couldn't give you the reunion I promised with him."

I rested my palms flat against his chest. "It ended the way it should, Peter. And . . ." I smiled at the powerful glow still residing inside. The presence surrounding me. "There have been . . . other reunions. Other fathers."

His smile was radiant. Knowing.

He always knew, though. Knew everything. Knew me. He drew close and rested his forehead against mine. His breath cooled my face.

"It seems you weren't able to find me after all, were you? I did warn you."

"Ah, but I did!" His grin was contagious. "Are you not standing here before me?" He spun me away and pulled me close again.

"Only because I came out of hiding."

"I see. And what might have caused that to happen?"

I gasped. Pulled back. "You didn't! Is *that* why you pulled that stunt with the papers?"

"Well, I also wanted justice and truth and everything else . . . but I knew that notice in the paper would draw you out. That you'd come running and try to rescue me."

"Didn't you realize how risky that was? How utterly foolish? What if I hadn't seen it? Hadn't been able to free you?"

He released me, smiling into my face. "But you did." He bent down, kissing the top of my head, smoothing fingers through my hair. "I'm not through having adventures with you, Lily Temple. May I still call you that? Or . . . Rosella. My dear Rosella. I hope you'll consider a low-order solicitor. Will you?"

I pulled him down by his coat, tugged off the mustache with an irrepressible smile, and kissed him. It was an eager, grateful, delicious kiss and I lingered in it. Delighted in it. Let it go on as long as he wished, and melted into his embrace. How he held me close. Then I moved back, touching his lips with my finger. "Don't ever do that again."

"Kiss you?"

"Risk your life."

He laughed and kissed my forehead. But made no promises. "I am free, though, aren't I? All is well. Fairchild has been outsmarted."

"Don't be thanking yourself for that, Peter Driscoll. It was I who broke you out of prison."

He raised one eyebrow. "I believe it was Samuel Draper. He broke me out while you were busy trying to convince the guards of my innocence."

"But was I?" I gave a coy smile. "You underestimate me, Peter Driscoll. And that Samuel Draper—why, I can't imagine he's even read the Dickens novel. He isn't clever enough to carry out such a prison escape."

"You! You put him up to it."

"I thought surely the very literary method of escape would tip my hand. Sydney Carton?" I laughed. "Yes sir, it was I who filched the key off of Mutton. I who left it out in the open and I who got Mutton momentarily off into the hallway so Draper could come fetch the key—along with your change purse, by the by. And it was I who approached Draper with the offer in the first place, and designed this entire madcap plan. All he had to do was follow my instructions and unlock a simple door. And then of course, while he went to release you . . . it was I who provided a most elaborate distraction." I twirled and bobbed a quick curtsy. Then I straightened and drew near to Peter again, a wry smile on my lips. "A story is never simply a story—it always serves several purposes, if it is a worthwhile one. So you see . . . I do believe, Peter Driscoll, that *I* broke you out of prison."

He blinked at me.

"That's right. Me, and my story. The ultimate sleight of hand. Which means . . ."

He huffed out a breath, jaw shifting right. "Oh, very well then."

◆

I clung to the wheel and shoved that pedal to the floor, hurtling that poor Stanley Steamer on the ride of its life. "Whoooo!" Dirt flying, wheels spinning, wind socking us in the face, we *flew* down that open road. Not even Roddy's getaway had been this good. Never before had I been so alive. Or flown so *fast*.

It was a thrill, charging past everything. A blur of color. Of life. "Hold on to your hat, Peter Driscoll. Lily Temple does not slow down."

The poor man white-knuckled the dash, blond hair blown straight back along with his scarf. He shouted something above the growling engine. I stared at his lips, trying to make it out.

"What?" I yelled back.

He clamped his hat to his head with one hand, pointing ahead with the other. "I said, *cow*!"

And there it was. A great, hulking brown mass in the road around the curve. I screamed, gripping the wheel, and jammed at every pedal-like object at my feet. The car skidded, twirled, and spun to a stop. Mere yards from the cow. Fool thing only mooed and continued munching grass, staring at us as if we'd gone mad.

Peter flopped back in his seat, hands over his face. "Maybe I should drive the rest of the way."

"Nonsense. I got us stopped, didn't I? Have I ever told you

the story of the runaway stallions, and the girl who saved the carriage by giving them their heads?"

"Enough. Enough with the stories. Haven't they gotten you into enough trouble lately?"

A smile flickered. "Hardly."

I maneuvered the vehicle back onto the road and experimented with the pedals. The levers. I was a child on holiday. A horse without a harness. Trouble, indeed.

"But what about—?"

I leaned over and kissed him again, enjoying the feel of him melting at my touch. "I will never give up telling stories, Peter Driscoll. You'd best accept it now as my one flaw."

Yet it was strange, the more stories I told, the more life made sense. The more fiction wove through my heart, the clearer the truth became. Because there was a great deal of truth in fiction—the sort too important to just be spoken outright.

What heroism looked like.

What it meant to love authentically.

And more than anything, who the rescuer of our souls was. That was the truest story. The largest. The one we try to express in the tales we spin. Or rather, it has been trying to express itself, in every longing. Every truth. Every make-believe tale. It is part of our natures, our every story, and he wishes it this way. Because he waits for us in the garden. Longs for us to see the petals, to understand . . . and to draw near.

He has eternity written on our hearts, and in every story we tell.

AUTHOR NOTE
ON THE HISTORICAL RESEARCH

I often create imaginary settings based on existing ones, but this time, the setting was quite real. The real history of St. Anne's Well Gardens kept adding to the novel and bringing pieces of it to life—which was wonderfully fun!

The legend of the well is real, as are all the elements—Grasshopper Cottage, the tennis courts, the pump house, Gypsy Lee and her caravan, and even George Smith's glass film set. George Smith himself is a real historical person as well, and his brilliant manipulation of filmstrips was the beginning of modern-day cinematography. All the cutting and splicing, the hand-coloring of frames, were taken from the pages of his life and work. He and his wife, actress Laura Bayley, rented the well gardens for several years and hosted shows, exhibits, balloon launches . . . and of course, moving picture bioscope shows.

He was a sleight-of-hand artist before meeting the Lumière brothers and taking up moving pictures, and he brought that talent to film. He could make it look as though a woman blew up her stove and flew up the chimney. As if he had removed his head and put it on the table. He made a woman disappear and reappear. His creativity blew me away, the more I studied the man. We don't even know, when we sit down to watch a movie, how greatly this man influenced everything we now enjoy.

Gypsy Lee told fortunes in the garden for years, and her caravan wheels actually had grass growing up around them, it had been there so long. Her predictions concerning the king and the lonely woman who soon met her husband . . . were true.

Lily Temple and the sapphire were entirely fictional, as were most of the other characters. But they became real as I set them in the very real gardens and let them animate the story. I have used lines from existing fairy tales to place at the beginning of each chapter and tried to give a sense of old-style fairy tales in the entire story. From the Brothers Grimm to Hans Christian Andersen and even Oscar Wilde, these stories fascinated and delighted me. I hope you see a flavor of them in this book.

More than that, I hope you read this combination of real settings and fictional people, this slightly whimsical fairy tale of a story, and you see threads of truth woven in. A few colorful petals in a broken world. If you do, it's because God graciously tucked them in there for you.

Is there *anyone* at Hurstwell
VIVIENNE MOURDANT
CAN TRUST?

Turn the page for a sneak peek at this haunting
tale from Joanna Davidson Politano.

1

I carry a deep sadness of the heart which
must now and then break out in sound.

~FRANTZ LIZST

I was playing a piece by Berlioz the night my father died, the
second movement of *Symphonie Fantastique* with arpeggios
smooth as a horse's gallop. Footsteps stopped and a figure hovered in the doorway, and I knew what was coming before our
maid even spoke the jarring words. "He's gone, Miss Vivienne."

"I see." I did not smile, for that would have been wicked, but
I did relax, more than I had allowed myself to in many years.

Her steady footsteps crossed the carpeted room past where
I sat, and she threw open the drapes on every long window—
drapes that had remained drawn for years to keep my father's
headaches, and his resulting temper, at bay.

It was dark outside, still very early morning, but so many
hours had passed in the waiting. The maid turned, those wise
old eyes cast my direction. "Night is passing, and day is soon
to come for you, Miss Vivienne."

We shared a solemn smile. Then she gave a brief curtsy and
left me.

A breezy emptiness infilled my soul at the sudden silence, a sense of unfettered spring air blowing through hollow places. Gone were Father's company and his uncanny business sense, but so were the sting of fresh lashes across my fingers as I practiced, that voice bellowing through the halls, the silent fight always knotted up in my belly with nowhere to go. Suddenly, it had all gone slack. It was over, and I was alone in the world.

I grieved the man, but I couldn't say I was unhappy. I looked over the vast spread of pianofortes that awaited restoration laid out before me with a new sense of ownership, of delight. It was *my* repair shop now, and darkness would have no place here anymore. *God, you are the master of this house now. The master of me. No one else shall ever be.* I felt his heady presence with the coming dawn and I welcomed it.

After several deep breaths to acknowledge the passing of a soul, I lifted my fingers to the ivories in the flickering candlelight and began the piece again from the beginning. The song was the perfect end to our tumultuous years together, powerful dissonance brimming with deeply textured tones that climbed to a rich climax as the dawn crested, colorful light brimming through the room, then simply stopped at the obvious point of conclusion, and the room was empty. Quiet and peaceful in morning's rosy glow.

Within the hour, familiar footsteps—masculine ones—sounded somewhere in the foyer, and my breath caught. I kept my fingertips poised on the ivories, feeling the oddness of Richard's presence in this house. Things were shifting already.

I continued playing as his footfall entered the room and crossed to me. He stopped at the pianoforte and sat beside me, the bench creaking under his weight. The slight bump of

Richard's shoulder as he slid close was all that passed between us, but it was plenty. I paused, for I suddenly couldn't remember what came next in the piece.

Oh, how Father would hate this.

I almost began to play again, but Richard's arm came around me, solid but cautious. I felt every inch of its gentle weight. We'd known each other all my life, and this was the first time he'd ever dared. I looked up into his face, and he smiled down at me—a solemn, affectionate look that expressed every word he didn't need to say. The regret for my loss, the relief at my freedom, the uncertain hope of what was to come between us.

I played on for several minutes, and he listened without a word, as he always did. The song came to a gentle conclusion and I sat motionless, fingers still perched on the keys. The enormity of his masculine presence nearly undid my calm. What would happen now? Father was gone. There was nothing stopping Richard from . . . well, anything. I could feel his keen scrutiny on me. Deciding.

I looked up at him, and he leaned nearer, those familiar crescent-shaped eyes and clean-shaven chin, and laid his forehead on mine.

I ran my tongue over my lips that had gone dry and met his gaze. "So, now what?"

His hand lifted to my cheek and stroked it. "Everything's different now, isn't it?" A gentle smile. "What will you do with your life?"

I closed my eyes. "Oh, I have a few ideas."

His finger came down the side of my face and teased my lips. "Anything that includes me?"

"Perhaps." I looked up. "How are you at handling horses? I've been meaning to hire a driver."

His look was amused and sympathetic all at once. Oh, how I adored this man. "Better than handling certain redheads."

I smacked his arm, and somehow it relieved the night's tension. Filled the cracks with a bit of joy.

"I bet I can guess your plans." He leaned back. "After your mourning period, you'll go out and continue to perform, maybe even better than before, and with a newfound joy that no one will truly understand. You'll appear in concert hall after concert hall all over the Continent and amaze your audiences . . . then come home to a quiet house and live the simple, uncomplicated life you were always meant to have. One you fully deserve."

I gave a polite smile but said nothing to contradict him. I'd known for years what I'd do with myself when I finally possessed freedom, but I dared not shock Richard with it. Not yet. I'd at least let him kiss me first.

"You'll have your pianoforte shop, perhaps a few students, and your friends. Modest and simple and delightfully musical, a life of high quality is what fits you best."

Few people actually knew me, as it turned out. I was a Chopin nocturne—surprising, complex, and impossible to master.

Many tried. I'm happy to report that they had all failed.

Well, nearly.

ACKNOWLEDGMENTS

This story took nearly two years and many, many creative people to fully unfold. I started writing it when my third baby was born, and I credit him, sleeping on my chest as a newborn, with the delight I had in the writing process. Thank you, little buddy, for joining me on my writing adventures. Even if you slept through them.

The biggest debt of gratitude goes to my Creator, the ultimate creative. When I hunted and searched for him in the lines of this story, tried to shoehorn him in, he gently lifted my hands off the keyboard and asked me to trust. To spend time in the garden. When I finally did, he unfolded what this story was actually about. Showed me what he was up to. Thank you, Father, for coming alongside me in every project. Thank you for being too big for us to pin down in mere words.

Jennifer K and Susan T, you ladies have my deepest gratitude. You jumped right in and waded with me through the mess of a rough draft, helping me bring order to the chaos. Thank you for letting me talk out the story, brainstorm, ask questions, and go down so many rabbit holes with you. (Thank you, Jennifer, for reading it so many times!) I cannot imagine what this book would have been without your wonderful insights, your hearts, and your enthusiasm along the way. I am deeply grateful for you both—your help, and mostly, your friendship.

To my local cheerleaders, Rachel and Angie. Once again you have cheered me through the writing process, keeping me grounded and encouraged at the same time. Your enthusiasm for my stories has meant so much to me in the years we've known each other.

And Dad, I can't tell you how much I enjoy talking "story" with you and shooting storylines and ideas back and forth. It's been a few years since we talked this story over, but several big elements of this story—including the necklace Lily wears—I owe to you. Thank you for always being up for a chat, and for listening to me prattle on. You've given me some true breakthroughs! But mostly, thank you for walking through the writing process with me.

Allen Arnold, story ranger extraordinaire, I greatly appreciate your humor and wisdom, your direction and bold ideas. It's such a pleasure to be able to tap into your creativity and talk out a rough draft with you. I appreciate the help you've always so graciously offered, and all you've taught me about writing. Your help is invaluable and just wonderful.

Vince. I cannot express how deeply I love you, and how much I appreciate the way you've partnered with me, lifted me up, and kept me grounded. It touches my heart more deeply than you know when you pour so much into *my* dreams, *my* writing. Sometimes it feels like "our" dream instead of mine . . . even if the last thing you'd ever dreamed of doing was writing a book. Every writing break you've given me, every flustered evening you've calmed, all the understanding you've offered on rough days . . . they all build into and deepen my love for you. I am so blessed by you.

Joanna Davidson Politano is the award-winning author of *Lady Jayne Disappears*, *A Rumored Fortune*, *Finding Lady Enderly*, *The Love Note*, *A Midnight Dance*, and *The Lost Melody*. She loves tales that capture the colorful, exquisite details in ordinary lives and is eager to hear anyone's story. She lives with her husband and their children in a house in the woods near Lake Michigan. You can find her online at www.JDPStories.com.

A FORGOTTEN LETTER.
A SECRET LOVE.
A VAST ESTATE.

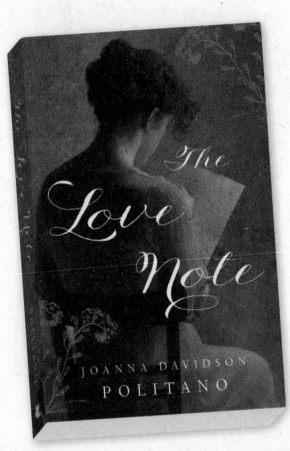

Can one determined woman put the pieces together?

RAINA'S DREAMS ARE ALL ABOUT TO COME TRUE.

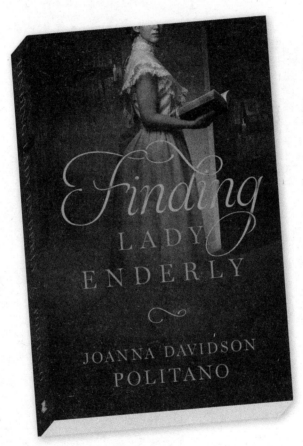

But some dreams
turn out to be nightmares.

ℝ Revell
a division of Baker Publishing Group
RevellBooks.com

Available wherever books and ebooks are sold.

Two homes hold secrets in these standalone novels

from **JOANNA DAVIDSON POLITANO**

A Rumored Fortune

JOANNA DAVIDSON
POLITANO

LADY JAYNE
DISAPPEARS

JOANNA DAVIDSON
~POLITANO~

— MEET —
JOANNA

JDPStories.com